Praise for
Mother Doesn't

"Deeply moving and profoundly suspenseful, *When Your Mother Doesn't* is the unforgettable story of two sisters navigating their way through loss and grief in search of love, and what it means to be a family. A very fine novel from an engaging voice."
—Carla Buckley, author of *The Deepest Secret*

"I devoured *When Your Mother Doesn't* in greedy gulps, fully steeped in this gripping story of three broken women who understand each other so little, yet are bonded by so much. Beautifully written and unflinching, this book is a gem."
—Kristina Riggle, author of *Real Life & Liars*

"A heart wrenching and poignant story about mothers and daughters and the secrets they keep. With a plot that twists and turns, Kelly masterfully weaves a compelling narrative which explores how abandonment and sacrifice play out against a backdrop of adversity. Told through multiple perspectives, the novel addresses the complex ways in which women are forced to protect themselves and their daughters. An interesting and provocative read that will have you guessing until the very end."
—Tamar Ossowski, author of *Left*

"Slowly peeling back the layers of a complicated set of relation-ships, Jill Kelly takes the reader on a journey of discovery with her compelling and artful new novel. This is a book full of secrets, loss, and moments of beauty. It will linger with you long after you've closed the final page."

—Alice Kuipers, author of *Life on the Refrigerator Door*

"A vibrant voice, powerful and poignant. Jill Kelly weaves a compelling tale that will stay with you long after the final page."

—Colleen Faulkner, author of *As Close As Sisters* and *Just Like Other Daughters*

WHEN YOUR MOTHER DOESN'T

Also by Jill Kelly

Fog of Dead Souls
(a thriller)

*Candy Girl: How I Gave Up Sugar and Created a Sweeter Life
Between Meals*

Sober Truths: The Making of an Honest Woman
(a memoir)

Broken Boys
(a thriller)

Sober Play: Using Creativity for a More Joyful Recovery

The Color of Longing
(an unconventional romance)

WHEN YOUR MOTHER DOESN'T

A Novel

Jill Kelly

Skyhorse Publishing

Skyhorse Publishing books may be purchased in bulk at special discounts
for sales promotion, corporate gifts, fund-raising, or educational
purposes. Special editions can also be created to specifications. For
details, contact the Special Sales Department, Skyhorse Publishing,
307 West 36th Street, 11th Floor, New York, NY 10018 or info@
skyhorsepublishing.com.

Skyhorse® and Skyhorse Publishing® are registered trademarks of
Skyhorse Publishing, Inc.®, a Delaware corporation.

Visit our website at www.skyhorsepublishing.com.

10 9 8 7 6 5 4 3 2

Library of Congress Cataloging-in-Publication Data is available on file.

Cover design by Georgia Morrissey
Cover photo credit iStock

Print ISBN: 978-1-5107-2584-3
Ebook ISBN: 978-1-63450-001-2

Printed in the United States of America

For all the daughters who have raised themselves.

The Reunion

Part I

"Are you headed east?"

The woman stood a respectful distance from her. Frankie finished washing her hands and looked up into the mirror. The woman behind her was easily sixty. Although her face was carefully made up and her ash blonde hair was cut in a short bob that framed her face nicely, it was the look of someone hanging on at the edge of something—something she didn't want to know.

The woman was rigidly thin and smartly dressed. The Columbia Sportswear jacket, linen trousers with a deep crease, fashionable pumps—all in a rich shade of camel—all shouted money. Women who looked like this made Frankie feel frumpy with her loose clothing and extra pounds, and tonight she'd definitely dressed for comfort: soft black cotton slacks and a tunic of red and black. Her own dark hair needed brushing. She'd washed it before she set out and let it dry on its own. The side with all the wave was a tangle.

"I said, are you headed east?" The woman's eyes looked right at Frankie but they were too dark to read in the mirror.

Frankie turned toward her, her hands dripping. She didn't want to say yes or no. She didn't want the woman to know she was traveling alone, and she didn't want company. She needed solitude and space to think about what was waiting for her in Kellogg.

"I'm not asking for a ride," the woman said. "I've got my own car." She held up a computerized key as proof, the kind of key to something big and expensive.

Frankie's jaw and shoulders loosened their grip a little and she nodded to the woman. "Yes, I'm headed east."

"Montana?"

"Idaho, actually."

"Could we talk a minute?"

Frankie felt a surge of irritation. She'd been on the road for nearly two hours, and she was already weary. She'd stopped at the rest area outside the Dalles, hoping there'd be a coffee stand, but the welcome station was closed. It was 8:30 and the end-of-August dark was coming on. But she didn't want to be rude, and what difference would a few minutes make anyway? She could be kind to this woman. Maybe it would soften her heart toward Lola.

The woman followed Frankie out of the rest room and they stood next to the big map display. She took a small flask out of her Coach bag and took a swig. The fumes reached Frankie and a familiar irritation flashed through her. She pushed it down. A minute passed, maybe more, and the woman said nothing, just fidgeted with her handbag.

Finally, Frankie said, "What is it, ma'am?"

There was no response. Frankie turned away to leave, and the woman gripped her arm, then pulled her hand back.

"Please," she said. "Please."

Frankie turned back toward her.

"I'm not a bad person," said the woman. "I just can't do it." She didn't look at Frankie as she said this. Instead she looked at her hands, hands of loose skin and summers in the sun that were much older than her face. "I just can't do it."

"I don't know what you're talking about. I don't know how . . ." Frankie sighed. "How can I help you?"

"Thank you, dear," the woman said, and she touched Frankie's arm again. Then she reached into her bag and took out a blue velvet pouch and a manila envelope and handed them to Frankie. "Wait here. And thanks." She paused and looked as if she were going to say something more but she didn't. Instead she stepped off the curb and hurried across the wide parking lot to a late-model Volvo, the only other car in sight.

Frankie looked down at what the woman had handed her. The pouch was full, a bit heavy. It felt stuffed with paper and in the bottom something hard, round and hard. The thin manila envelope was blank on both sides and sealed with clear tape. She pushed her curiosity aside and looked across the pavement. The car was a nondescript color, beige or tan, and fading even more into the gathering gloom.

The woman stood next to the Volvo talking to a boy, who yawned and rubbed his eyes. She handed him a dark gym bag that looked as big as he was. Then she took him by the shoulders, turned him toward Frankie, and gave him a push. He moved slowly, and Frankie watched him struggling with the bag. Then she realized the woman wasn't by her car any longer, and she saw the headlights come on.

Frankie hesitated for just a moment, unsure. Then she could see what was happening and she started across the parking lot, yelling, "Hey! Wait! What are you doing?" She ran past the boy but the woman had already pulled away and was speeding up. Frankie watched the taillights fade as the woman drove onto the freeway. And then she was alone in the parking lot with the boy.

The dark was full on now and the lights from the rest stop shone down on the boy's dark hair. His face was in shadow but she could feel him watching her as she crossed the pavement. He had set the bag down and had stepped through the straps so no one could snatch it away. As she moved closer, he sat down on the bag.

She walked up slowly and sat down on the curb a little distance away from him. "I'm Frankie," she said, holding out her hand.

After a moment, he held out his and she shook it. It was small, soft, no real grip. He hasn't learned how to do that yet, she thought. "What's your name?"

"Teroy."

"Nice to meet you, Leroy."

"It's Teroy," the boy said, spitting out the T.

"Sorry, Teroy. I'll bet that happens to you a lot." Frankie had to will herself to stay in this conversation. Her mind wanted to dart off in a dozen directions, most of them impossibly complicated.

"Yeah, that's okay." He stared at his shoes. Frankie looked at them, too. They were new. Nikes.

Frankie glanced at the rest of him. He was a thin, wiry boy but with a trace of baby still in the cheeks and jaw. He had dark eyes, long lashes. Something about the eyes reminded her of the older woman, but maybe she was just hoping. His brown hair, straight and silky, was cut well. His clothes were new and the right size, but somehow they didn't fit him. Frankie wondered if the Volvo woman had picked these out for him, if he'd had no choice about that either. The skin on his face and hands looked brown in the odd light from above, but whether from summer tan or heritage, she couldn't tell.

"What's your last name?" she asked.

"Thompson," he said, the voice still low and almost muffled.

"Is that your mom's name, too?"

He shook his head.

"Your dad's then?"

The kid just looked at her and she couldn't read his face. She nodded at him.

"How old are you?"

"Nine."

Frankie looked around. Behind her, past the restrooms, were a couple of trucks parked sideways but there were no cab lights. She didn't want to wake a sleeping trucker.

She waited another moment, looked over at the boy, and said, "It's getting cool, Teroy. Do you think we could get in my car? It'll be a little warmer there."

A look she couldn't read crossed his face and some of the horrors that happened to kids these days swirled through her mind.

"Hey," she said as lightly as she could. "I don't have a bag to sit on and my butt's getting sore. My car's got comfy seats."

The boy grinned at that, just a little, and then shrugged his shoulders and stood up in that effortless way kids do.

Frankie stood, too, though with more effort, and they walked over to her old Civic. She unlocked the passenger side and the boy pulled on the seat to get in the back.

"Don't you want to sit by me?"

He shook his head.

"Okay," she said and released the seat catch. The boy muscled the bag in first and climbed in after it.

Frankie went around to the other side and got in behind the wheel. Then she remembered the pouch and the envelope and she went back to where they'd been sitting and retrieved them off the pavement.

Back in the car, she turned as best she could to look at the boy behind her. "Can I ask you something?"

He nodded.

"Who was that woman? The one you came here with."

"Mrs. Louise." The boy's voice was even softer than it had been before.

"Is she related to you?"

The boy shrugged.

"Yes? No?" Frankie tried not to sound impatient.

He shrugged again. "I don't know."

"Okay. Were you living with Mrs. Louise?"

He nodded.

"Did you live with her a long time?"

He shrugged.

"Is she your grandmother?"

He shook his head.

Frankie decided to see what would happen if she waited. So she waited and continued to look at the boy. Finally, he said, "She said she wasn't related to me. That she wasn't related to anybody like me."

"Honey, do you know where your parents are? Your mom or your dad?"

He shook his head.

"Who took you to be with Mrs. Louise?"

"My mom."

"How long ago?"

She saw his chest heave and then a flash of something in his eyes—in an adult, it would have been bitterness. "A lot of nights," he said finally.

"Okay, Teroy. Just one more question. What did Mrs. Louise say to you when you got out of the car?"

The boy's face brightened just a little. "That you're a friend of my mom's and that you will take me to her."

Frankie nodded and turned back to the wheel. "Why don't you get some sleep now," she said over her shoulder and she started the car.

By the time they got on the road, it was a bit past nine and when she looked back, the boy had fallen asleep anchored to his bag. For the first half hour, Frankie let the anger and bewilderment wash over her. She had only unkind thoughts for Mrs. Louise, for the boy's mother, for his father. How do you just dump a kid on a stranger? She could have been some molester, some sex trafficker, some child slaver. She could have refused to take him and left him at the truck stop, at the mercy of someone else.

She realized she hadn't asked the boy if he were hungry or thirsty or even if he needed to go to the bathroom. For a brief moment, she turned the anger on herself. She'd only thought to ask questions, to solve the problem. She'd seen the kid as a problem, just as she'd seen the woman as a problem, as an obstacle in her way. Not as someone who was suffering. How could the kid not be suffering? She might not know much about kids but she knew about abandonment, Frankie did. She knew about suffering. She told herself that was why she'd put the kid in the car, and that was why she wasn't stopping at a police station to turn him over to someone else.

The car clock turned 10:00 and she felt a deep pain in her chest. She wanted to call George, call Dimitri, but even if that were possible, and it wasn't, none of them would get the irony of this. A child thrust upon her as she went east to confront her most intimate model of bad parenting. She could call Callie but advice was not something they had ever shared.

She crossed the Columbia at Biggs and headed east along the river, then north. She was ready to stop about 10:30 but the motel signs in the small towns, already few and far between, all said NO, and so they didn't stop until Pasco, where a bored clerk at the Holiday Inn took her credit card and gave her a key without even the usual hint of corporate politeness.

She'd locked the boy in the car. He was still sleeping when she came back so she got her bag and computer out of the trunk and took them to the room, all the while unsure that her choices were the right ones, all the while worried someone would snatch him away. But he was there when she went back, sleepy and docile, and he stood by the car as she pulled his bag out. It didn't weigh all that much and a great sadness washed over her. Then she put her arm around him and they went up to the room.

While he was in the bathroom, she wondered again if she should feed him but he said no when he came out, and he put the bag next to him on the bed nearest the windows, crawled under the bedspread fully clothed, and was soon fast asleep again.

She waited a few minutes, sitting there on the edge of the other bed, watching him sleep. Then she gently pulled his trainers off, tucked his feet back under the bedspread, and went down the hall for a soda and a bag of cheese curls from the vending machine. Once back in the room, she sat down at the small round table in the corner and pulled the velvet pouch and the manila envelope out of her purse.

She ate the cheese curls slowly, pulling one from the bag at a time and chewing thoughtfully. She took small sips of the soda and put the bottle back down between each sip. She'd learned to soothe herself this way when the anxiety ran high. Curiosity and fear were doing a tug-of-war in her chest. She wanted to know and she didn't want to know what was expected, for that's the way it felt. Expectation. Responsibility. Things that always seemed to land on her.

Then the cheese curls were gone and there were only a couple of sips of soda left. She thought about going back to the vending machine but she let the urge pass, then dredged up her courage and picked up the velvet pouch. The blue cords had been tightly knotted and she worked them free. From the mouth of the pouch, she pulled out a thick wad of money folded in half. On the outside was a hefty layer of old, worn bills, an assortment of fifties, twenties, and tens. It looked like someone's savings. In the middle of that were crisp new thousand-dollar bills, ten of them. She counted them all and it came to $14,682. A jumble of questions played around in her mind but they told her nothing.

She picked up the pouch again and up-ended it. Wrapped in dingy pink tissue paper was a heavy gold locket about the size of a silver dollar. She opened it. On the left side was a snapshot of a teenager with her arms around a shaggy mutt. The girl was mugging for the camera, and she looked happy. Frankie looked for a resemblance to the boy but nothing was evident. On the other side of the locket was a grainy black-and-white cutout from a magazine of a young Kevin Bacon.

She picked up the manila envelope. It felt wrong to tear it open, and so she got her manicure scissors and carefully slit the tape. Inside was a folded sheet of yellow legal-pad paper with HENRY LEE printed in a neat hand and an address in Victor, Montana. Under the address was a number written like a social security number: three digits, two digits, four digits.

She put the papers back in the manila envelope. She wanted a walk in the fresh air to clear her head. But she didn't know the town, she didn't know the neighborhood, and she didn't want to leave the boy alone in case he woke up and needed her. So she used the toilet, brushed her teeth, climbed into the other bed. She was already exhausted from the trip, and it had barely started. She realized she was exhausted from the thought of the days ahead that she hadn't lived through yet.

Frankie woke with a start. Next to her on the bed against her flank was Teroy, curled into as small a space as possible. In one hand, he held a Transformers action figure. In the other, a handgun.

Her heart pounded in her chest and in her ears. Frankie took a deep breath, reached over, and very gently took the gun from Teroy's hand. He shifted in his sleep, mumbled something she couldn't get, then curled in on himself again.

Outside the night was coming to a close.

The gun was not a revolver, but one with a clip of bullets. Frankie had never held a gun before and she wasn't sure how to get the clip out of it or if the safety was on. She got up and set the gun down on the table and turned on her computer. Before long, she found a site that could tell her what to do. Then she buried the clip in her suitcase and put the gun in her big computer bag.

His duffel was still on the other bed. It gaped open. She hadn't wanted to go through Teroy's bag. Everybody deserves privacy. But now she knew she had to. She pulled it between her and the boy so she could keep an eye on him and then she carefully pulled out the contents. Six pairs of neatly folded white underpants. Six neatly folded t-shirts in red, blue, and green. Two pairs of jeans. Six pairs of athletic socks. A red-and-blue striped sweater. A navy fleece jacket. The clothes were all new, stiff from no wear. A well-thumbed *Ultimate Spiderman* graphic novel. A clear plastic toiletries kit with toothpaste, electric toothbrush, floss, shampoo, and two bottles of Flintstone vitamins. There was a cloth wallet with fifty dollars in it and a picture of the girl from the locket, though she was older, maybe mid-teens. Again she was clowning for the camera but this time it looked forced. In the duffel there was also a small stuffed dog, old, very worn. Not a toy from Teroy's childhood. Maybe the girl's? And a notebook with a ballpoint pen in the spiral. It contained an assortment of drawings: airplanes, cars, trucks, something that resembled the Transformers toy clutched in the boy's hand. On the front his name was printed: T. ROY THOMPSON. Now she knew how to spell his name. Somehow that made him more real to her.

There were no more weapons.

She put everything carefully back in the bag. She wasn't going to pretend to T. Roy that she hadn't looked but she wanted to treat his things with respect. She put the bag back in the center of the empty bed.

The clock read 5:54. No going back to bed now. She made tea water in the coffeemaker in the bathroom and sat down again at her computer. There was an email from Callie. The subject line read "WTF?" She passed that by and opened a couple of messages from editing clients. Projects if she wanted them. She didn't, but she needed them. Work had been slow the last month and if she didn't work, she didn't make money. So she said yes and tried to figure out a deadline that would work and how she could do the work from the road.

At last, she turned to her sister's email. Callie had only been in Kellogg a day and in that time, she'd become fifteen again.

Where the fuck are you? I need you to get here now. Time has not mellowed the bitch. She's impossible.

Frankie deleted the message without replying. Time enough to deal with Callie—and with Lola. She went to take a shower. The boy was still asleep when she came out, so she made more tea and sat in the armchair, meditated, and thought about nothing at all.

The toilet flushing woke her. The bathroom door was closed and Frankie saw that the duffel was open. Then she heard the sound of the electric toothbrush. A bit of relief washed over her although she couldn't have explained why.

"Good morning," she said when he came out.

He nodded at her.

"I'm a morning person. How about you? Are you rarin' to go in the morning or does it take a while?"

"Takes a while," he said.

"Got it. Are you hungry? Let's go downstairs and see what they have."

He nodded again and picked up the Transformers toy.

An hour later, they'd packed and checked out. It was just past ten and they had another two hundred miles to drive. Frankie asked the desk clerk about a toy store, and they stopped and she bought a doodling book for T. Roy and some comic books. She would probably have given him anything he wanted, but he wouldn't choose so she guessed at what might appeal to him.

Once in the car, she hoped he would settle in. Secretly, she hoped he would sleep again. He was so much easier while he slept. Of course, she knew that was unrealistic. And she knew some of it was because she wanted to sleep again herself. Sleep was preferable to the day that lay ahead.

They followed the I-90 signs out of town and were soon on the road. The traffic was light with occasional caravans of semis. Again, T. Roy had wanted to sit in the back and he spread out the new books.

"Do you get carsick reading?" she asked him.

He shook his head.

"Okay, well, if you need anything, let me know." She could see his eyes in the rearview mirror.

He nodded this time, then bit his lip. "Are we going to find my mom today?"

"Not today, T. Roy. Problem is we don't know exactly where she is. It's going to take some sleuthing to find her. Do you know what *sleuthing* is?"

He shook his head again.

"Well, you know what a detective is, right?" She held his eyes in the rearview mirror. "Well, sleuthing is what they do. They gather clues and pieces of information and then solve the puzzle. I'm going to need you to be my assistant detective, okay?" She saw a glimmer of interest in his eyes.

"Okay," he said.

They were quiet then for a few miles and she put her mind on the road ahead. Then he spoke again. "Where are we going now?"

"We're going to see my mom. I haven't seen her in a long time, and she's sick."

The boy was quiet a long moment and then he said, "Did she leave you when you were little?"

Frankie looked into his eyes in the mirror. "Yes," she said. "Not as little as you but yes, she left me."

"How old were you when she went away?"

"Sixteen."

FRANKIE

Fall 1984

Frankie sat at the kitchen table. She had four pages of Latin homework to translate and the fight from her mother's bedroom was all she could focus on, that same old battle. It was Sunday night and the start of Lola's weekend and she was going out. The nights she didn't work, she always went out. But Callie wasn't allowed out with school the next day.

"You can't make me stay home!" Callie was shouting now. "You're not even really my mother." She stomped down the hall and into the kitchen. She wore a fuzzy pink sweater, a short black skirt, and patterned stockings. Her red hair was carefully curled, her face made up like a department store cosmetics clerk. It was all perfect and excessive. *Callie, the teenage hooker*, thought Frankie, then felt bad for her unkindness. Callie flounced into the chair across from Frankie.

Frankie loved that word, *flounced*, but she'd never say it to her sister, who was already ashamed of Frankie's love of books and her nerdy friends. She went back to her Latin, hoping the fight would soon blow over.

A few minutes later, Lola came into the kitchen. Frankie saw that her mother was dressed much like Callie, although her thick blond hair was pinned up, her skirt was a little longer, and her boots had high heels.

Lola didn't look at the girls. Instead she went to the refrigerator, got a fresh pack of cigarettes from the carton in the vegetable bin, and took the vodka from the freezer. She poured herself a tall drink and put the vodka back. She moved slowly, deliberately, and Frankie's gut clenched. This was what happened before a showdown. Frankie kept her eyes on the paper in front of her, but the words blurred in the tension.

Lola brought the cigarettes, the drink, her lighter, and an ashtray to the table and sat down at the end. She removed the cellophane from the pack, thumped it four times on the table, then opened it and took one out. She lit the cigarette and carefully positioned the four objects in front of her.

When Frankie looked up, her mother and her sister were staring at each other. Callie scowled but Lola had that indifferent, inscrutable expression on her face. Frankie tried to distract herself by thinking of the Latin origin of the word *inscrutable* but it didn't work.

"You can't make me stay home," Callie said again, although some of the fire was gone from her voice.

"You're right," said Lola. "I can't."

Callie looked at Lola with surprise.

Lola drank from the glass. "You're old enough to get in trouble, Callie, if that's what you want. Old enough to fuck some guy."

The girls looked at each other. Their mother never used *fuck* in front of them.

Lola sucked on the cigarette, blew the smoke out slowly, and spoke again. "Actually, you're old enough to get pregnant. Old enough to have an abortion. Old enough to have a kid. Do I think that's a good idea? No, I don't. But hey." She seemed to ponder the drink in her hand. Then she said, "You're fourteen, Callie, and your hormones are running wild and you want to follow them wherever they lead. Chances are they are not going to lead you to some nice boy who will love you forever although you may think so. And even if they do, you probably won't want him." She took a hit off the cigarette. "Are you interested in bad boys?"

"What?" Callie said slowly.

"Just what I said. Is it a bad boy you're going out to meet tonight?"

Callie shrugged. "I guess."

Lola nodded. "So what do you want, Callie?"

"What do you mean?"

"Just what I said," she repeated. "What do you want?"

"I want to go out tonight and I want to come back when I want to."

Lola seemed to think about that for a few seconds. Then she nodded. "Okay."

"You mean it?" said Callie.

"Sure. What else do you want?"

"What are you doing, Mom?" Frankie said. This was all going fast, going wrong.

"Stay out of this, Frankie. This isn't about you," said Lola. "I'm waiting for an answer, Callie. I'd like to get this settled." There wasn't any anger in her mother's voice, just a cool, objective tone that made Frankie feel sick.

"I want to go out any night I feel like it and come home when I want."

Again Lola seemed to think about it. "Okay. What else?"

"I want to do my homework when I feel like it."

"Deal."

"I want my own phone in my room."

"That's fine but you have to pay for it. What else?"

"I want more allowance."

"No," said Lola. "You want more money, you get a job. Just like you'll pay for the phone."

The doorbell rang. Lola got up. As she passed Callie, she pressed her hand on the girl's shoulder and said, "Stay put. It's my turn to say what I want—and what I don't want. I'll be right back."

They heard a low murmur of voices and then the front door closed and Lola came back and sat down.

"You'll get a C average until you graduate. It may not seem that I think school is important but I do. But if you don't get a C average, then you drop out and work." Lola looked at Callie and waited.

"Okay," Callie said.

"Are you on birth control?"

Callie hesitated, then shook her head.

"I don't work tomorrow," said Lola, "so after school we'll go to Planned Parenthood and get you set up."

"I have cheerleading tomorrow."

"No. Tomorrow you don't. Tomorrow you'll be home by 3:30 and we'll go. Do you want to go, too, Frankie?"

Frankie shook her head.

Lola shrugged. "Suit yourself." She looked at Callie. "Do you know why I said yes to all these things?"

"No," said Callie.

"Because this is not a prison and I am not the warden. Some parents are wardens and I'm not one of them. And I don't want to fight about this with you anymore. What I am is smart enough to know that I can't stop you from doing what you're going to do. Nobody could stop me."

Callie grinned at her but Lola shook her head. "This isn't a game. Life gets serious really quick when you get old enough to have sex. Men can hurt you. They can break your jaw or your arm as well as your heart. You need to always have a way out. That's why drugs are such a bad idea. Drugs make getting out impossible. Stay away from drugs. And don't get pregnant. When you're pregnant, there's no way out, no way at all. I know. I've been there. You hear me?"

Callie nodded, the grin gone from her face.

The doorbell rang again and Lola got up. She touched Callie's shoulder again and they listened to her heels clicking down the hallway and then the door closing behind her.

Callie looked at Frankie, her eyes gleeful, and went out to the hall where the phone was. Frankie heard her sister say, "It's cool. Come get me." And then the house was empty and Frankie set her heavy heart on the table next to her Latin book and went back to her studies.

Spring 1985

The house was quiet when she came home, the only sign of her mother the perfume and cigarette smoke that always trailed after her. Frankie put her books in the bedroom she and Callie shared, made two slices of peanut butter toast, and turned on *General Hospital*. She was relieved to see that she had only missed the first scene, the recap of the latest scandal that had rained down on the residents of Port Charles. Five days a week, this was her ritual.

The phone rang but she let it go. It would be some man for Lola or one of Callie's cheerleader friends. Only Roxie called Frankie and each day they talked at 4:05, right after *GH* so they could compare notes. When the commercials came on, Frankie got up and left the room. She didn't want to know any more about diapers or kids' cereal than she already did. So she made more toast or looked through the mail or checked the fridge and the cupboards to see what she could make for dinner.

There were usually leftovers from Lola's dinner shifts at the Hilton if she remembered to bring something home. Then they had steak Diane or pork chops with stuffing or some salmon or chicken dish with strange-tasting sauces. And baked potatoes. Sometimes Lola brought home a dozen baked potatoes at a time, and Frankie had become a master at toppings. Baked beans, chili, frozen vegetables, and sour cream. And apples on the side. Always sliced apples. Frankie worried about their health. She was afraid they'd get scurvy or rickets or cancer, things she'd read about in the encyclopedia at the library. So she made sure they bought orange juice and apples, even when there was little else.

Tonight there was little else. She found a pound of hamburger in the freezer. She set it in a bowl and set that bowl in a bigger bowl of water, like she'd learned at the farm. There were two cans of vegetable soup. Callie would be delighted. Camp stew was one of her favorites. Frankie heard the *GH* theme song come on and she went back to the living room for the final scenes and to wait for Roxie to call.

At five, the doorbell rang. Frankie was scraping the thawed meat off the frozen chunk and putting it in the big frying pan. She felt a surge of annoyance. Callie and her keys. Shaking her head, she went to the door. But it wasn't her sister.

The man had been looking out at the street and now he turned back to look at her. He didn't say anything, just looked at her. She didn't feel afraid; she just felt examined, so she examined him back. Tall. Thick gray hair. Gray eyes. He looked old but he wore jeans and a t-shirt and a leather jacket. Not old-man clothes. And there was something else, something comfortable that she recognized.

"Frances," he said.

She nodded, still wary but not afraid.

He smiled and there it was again, that something comfortable. "I'm John Blalock."

The name meant nothing to her.

He tried again. "I lived with you at Eiderdown and at Calliope before that. With you and your mom and Dewey and Snow."

At the mention of Dewey, something passed through her but she said nothing.

"I'm Callie's father," he said finally. And he smiled again. "Can I come in?"

She hesitated, then shook her head. "I don't remember you. And we don't let strangers into the house."

"Fair enough," he said. "Could we sit here on the porch and talk for a minute?"

"Okay," she said. "Just a minute." She closed the door on him, grabbed her jacket, and turned off the stove. All the while she was thinking that Roxie would never believe any of this. It was just like something on *GH*.

They sat together on the cold concrete steps of the little porch. He had been living in Alaska, he said, working on fishing boats in the summer. He told her some of his adventures and it sounded exciting and exotic to Frankie.

"What do you do in the winter? Isn't there snow all the time?"

"There is. But I go to college."

"Aren't you too old for college?"

He laughed and the sound of it opened a little window in her. "No, anybody can go to college. But I guess I am a lot older than most of the students. How old do I look to you?"

Frankie thought for a moment. "Fifty?"

"Wow! Do I look that old?"

She nodded, felt embarrassed.

"I'm your mom's age."

She felt even more embarrassed. "I'm sorry . . . I don't . . ."

"Hey, no problem. Gray hair, right? Tough Alaska skin." He rubbed his hand across his leathered jaw. He was quiet a moment and then he said, "Does Callie live here with you?"

"Yes, of course. She's my sister."

"Does she ever talk about me?"

He looked very sad and Frankie felt sorry for him. She wanted to lie and say yes to make him feel better, but she couldn't. "Not really," she said.

"She's forgotten me."

"I guess."

"Will she be home soon?"

"I don't know. She has things after school."

He nodded, then looked at his watch. "I've got to go. I have an appointment downtown. When is your mom here? I want to come by and see her."

"She works different hours different days. Can she call you?"

He thought for a moment and then took out a piece of paper and a pencil from his jacket pocket and wrote a number down. "She can leave me a message here." He stood up. "It's good to see you, Frances. You've turned out fine."

Frankie blushed, then said, "Frankie. Nobody calls me Frances anymore."

"Frankie, then. See you later, Frankie." And he went down the steps and got in a Jeep that she noticed for the first time. She went inside to phone Roxie.

Frankie was reading in bed when she heard her mother come in. It was just past midnight. From the quiet, she assumed Lola was alone. Callie slept the sleep of the dead in the twin bed up against the far wall, her head buried under the pillow.

Frankie went down the hall to the kitchen. Her mother was putting food away in the refrigerator. There was a lot of it and Frankie was glad. The tip jar was out too and on the table was a thick stack of bills and a big scattering of coins. It had been a good night and her mother would be in a good mood.

"Hey there," said Lola. "What are you doing up? Isn't there school tomorrow?"

"Yeah, there is."

"Is something wrong? Do you need some warm milk or cocoa or something?" Lola pulled out the gallon of vodka from the freezer and filled a tall glass half-full. Then she sat down at the table, lit a cigarette, and started separating the bills.

Frankie stood in the doorway a moment, then sat down, too. She'd been excited all evening. Excited to tell Roxie about the man's visit. Roxie had squealed in delight at the drama. Excited about keeping the news from Callie, who she decided shouldn't know until Lola did. Excited about what this all might mean. But now all that excitement had suddenly leaked away, and she felt afraid of her mother and her closed face and her indifference to just about everything.

"What's up, Frankie?" The bills were in neat stacks of ones and fives, and she had moved on to the coins.

"A man came to the door this afternoon. He said he had been at Eiderdown with us. He knew you and Dewey and Snow. And he said he was John Blalock and that he was Callie's dad."

Lola looked up. Frankie couldn't read the expression on her mother's face, but she knew it wasn't happiness or excitement or even curiosity.

"What did he look like?"

"Tall, gray hair. He looked old, Mom, though he said he was the same age as you."

"Did you let him in?"

"No. You told us not to. We talked out on the porch."

Lola nodded and stubbed out the cigarette. "What else did he say?"

"That he'd been living in Alaska, working on fishing boats and going to college."

Her mother gave a small *humph* sound that Frankie knew only too well meant disgust and disappointment.

"Who is he, Mom?"

Lola said nothing for a moment. She took a big sip of the vodka, then twisted the glass this way and that on the Formica table.

"He was Cassie's husband."

Frankie felt a small, old longing rise up in her chest at the name. She didn't remember much of Cassie, although there was a red-haired woman with a sweet voice that came sometimes in her dreams. And because it made Lola so sad, there were no photos and they never talked about Cassie to each other so the memories had grown dimmer and dimmer.

"Is he Callie's dad?"

"Yes."

"Is he my dad, too?"

"No."

"Why didn't he move with us to the Landing?"

"You'll have to ask him that." Lola finished the vodka and lit another cigarette. "What did he want?"

"He wants to see you. And I guess he wants to see Callie. He left this phone number for you, said you could leave a message for him there." She handed her mother the paper. Lola put it on the table without looking at it.

"What's going to happen? Is Callie going to leave us and go with her dad?"

"No, don't be silly." Lola shook her head but her expression remained indecipherable. "I'll take care of this. Nothing for you to be concerned about. Did you say anything to Callie about this?"

"No."

"Smart girl. Go on up to bed now. And Frankie?"

She stopped and turned in the doorway.

"You know how you go weird? Don't go all weird about this."

Frankie nodded and went up to bed. But she didn't close the bedroom door, and a few minutes later, she heard her mother come out to the hall to the phone. Frankie left her bed and crept to the door, staying out of sight.

"I'm looking for John Blalock," she heard her mother say.

And then, "I'm fine, John." Her mother sounded weary, disgusted, familiar. "What do you want?"

And then, "That's not a good idea."

Then a silence. Then, "It's been nine years. She's forgotten you."

And then, "Yes, she's forgotten Cassie, too."

Then another silence. "You left us. I saved your daughter. Twice, actually. She needed you. Frances needed you. I needed you. But you couldn't be bothered. So we made our own way without you."

Frankie listened to the anger and ice in her mother's voice. It made her sad. For her. For them.

Another silence, a briefer one. Then, "Go back to Alaska, John. Leave my daughters alone."

And then, "No, she's my daughter now, and that's your doing."

And finally, "You want to do something for Callie? Send us money from Alaska. You obviously know the address. Goodbye, John."

She heard her mother hang up and go back into the kitchen. Then she heard the freezer door open and close. Frankie went to bed and she knew she couldn't tell Callie any of this. She couldn't talk about it with Lola, and Dewey and Snow had moved their family to Montana. She lay awake a long time with a longing in her chest for something she couldn't remember.

March 1986

"Who do you know named Blalock in Juneau?" Callie came into the living room and put her books down on the sofa.

Frankie was watching *GH*. "What are you doing home? It's Friday. Don't you have a game tonight?"

"Yes, but it's away and for some weird reason, the buses aren't going and we have to drive there on our own, so Hank is coming to get me at six. Who's this letter from?" She handed Frankie the envelope, who glanced at it and laid it on the coffee table.

"A friend of Mom's." As soon as Frankie said it, she regretted it.

"So why is it addressed to you?"

"I don't know."

"Maybe she knows where Mom is. Open it. Let's see."

"No, I'll open it later. I'm busy." She gestured toward the TV.

"Oh, come on. Open it." Callie moved toward the table, but Frankie picked it up and put it in her pocket.

"Frankiiiiiie!"

Frankie shook her head. "Do you need something to eat before the game? Can I fix you something?"

"No. I'm going to go take a shower." Her sister headed out of the room and said over her shoulder, "And I'm not going to forget about that letter."

Lola had left them just after school started in the fall. Frankie had come home to a note on the kitchen table and four hundred dollars in cash. *I'll be travelling for a while*, said the note. *Take good care of your sister. Lola.*

Her mother's makeup was gone from the bathroom. Her curling iron. About half of her clothes. No cigarettes in the fridge, no vodka in the freezer.

Callie waited three days and then moved into Lola's room.

At first Frankie found it strange to sleep alone in a room. There had always been someone there in the night. And she had grown used to reading until Callie came in and was safe. Now she gave that up and worried herself to sleep. On October 1, she called the landlord to say her mother was traveling on business and the rent would be late, but Mr. Maharis told her he had received a check from Lola. Then every couple of weeks, an envelope arrived with two hundred dollars and no return address. Frankie had called Lola's boss at the Hilton and asked for a job and now she waitressed Saturday lunch and dinner and Sunday lunch. So they had money for the phone and the electric bill and food. Frankie made Callie earn her own money for cheerleading and clothes and makeup and the phone in her room. Callie was pissed but seemed to have enough. Frankie had no idea where it came from, as Callie didn't have a job that she knew about, but she couldn't worry about that, too.

When a month went by and they had no word from Lola, Frankie wrote to Dewey. He called in the evening three days later. Frankie relaxed into the sound of his familiar voice, his gentle listening that had made her mother's moods bearable when she was a child. She told him how they were managing and what she was doing to make it work. She didn't tell him about the nights Callie didn't come home or the arguments they had when she wanted some boy to stay over. It was one thing Frankie held firm—the house was hers.

"I miss you, Dewey. And Snow and Bliss and Tim. I wish we still lived on the farm."

"We miss you, too, Frankie. We want you to come and stay with us, you and Callie. I'll send you bus fare. You two can go to school here. I know it would be hard to leave your friends but we'd be here for you. We'd be a family again." He paused a moment. "Did you know we wanted you all to come to Montana with us?"

"No. Lola didn't tell us." She tried to keep the resentment from her voice.

"Well, we did. And we want you to come now."

Frankie paused. "I don't know. I don't think Callie will do it."

"Well, you talk it over with her. I'll send the bus fare just the same. Are you still at the same address?"

"Yes. I miss you," she said again.

"We love you, Frankie. Come live with us." He hung up and she burst into tears.

She talked to Callie the next day and the day after that and the day after that, but her sister was adamant. "Stop talking about this, Frankie. I'm not going. Dewey's not going to let me live the way I want. I just know it. I'm happy here. I like school and cheerleading and I love my friends and I love Hank and I don't want to move. And what about when Mom comes back? If we move, how will she find us? Did you think about that?"

Of course she had. She'd worked it all out. But she saw that the dream of moving to Montana, of being a family again with

Dewey and Snow, was just that—a dream. And it wasn't going to happen. She couldn't leave Callie. So when the money for the bus came, she sent it back, saying they couldn't come, they couldn't leave school, they would wait for Lola. And Dewey sent the money back and said use it for whatever they needed. Each month after that they received a little something from him, sometimes with a note from Snow or a funny card, and on those days she didn't feel so alone.

Now Lola had been gone six months and they had their routines. Frankie was focused on finishing her senior year and waiting to see if she would go to college. Mrs. Shepard, her Latin teacher, and Mr. Schecter, her guidance counselor, had helped her apply for scholarships since she had the grades and the test scores to get a full ride. At the same time, no one at school knew the girls were on their own. She and Callie covered for each other, making excuses for Lola's absence at school appointments, saying she traveled for work. The sisters were determined to stay out of the child welfare system. They'd learned that on the farm. No matter what happens, you don't put a kid into the system.

Callie came into the living room, her hair wet from the shower. She was drinking a chocolate Slimfast and she sat down in the rocker and rocked and sipped. Frankie no longer argued with her about what she ate. Lola had been right; Callie was going to do what she was going to do. Frankie could only take care of herself.

"You read that letter yet?"

Frankie shook her head.

"Why not?"

"Because I'm watching *GH*—as you can see. I like to do one thing at a time."

"You're so weird, Frankie. You know that?"

"So you tell me."

Callie gave that *humph* that she'd learned from Lola. "I won't be back until tomorrow."

Frankie could feel Callie looking at her, waiting for her response, maybe hoping to pick a fight. And suddenly she was tired of protecting Callie from everything and getting no respect or thanks for it. She took the envelope out of her pocket and handed it to her sister.

Truth was she had already opened the card, had picked up the check and the wedding photograph that fell onto the carpet, had recognized the faces, had read the words. There weren't that many: *Dear Frankie and Callie. Lola and I were married at Christmas. We hope you'll come and visit this summer. Here is our wedding gift to you. Your father, John.* And Lola's scrawl at the bottom: *Happy New Year! Lola.*

Now Callie read the words, looked at the picture. "What is this? Some kind of joke?" For just a second, she looked like she had as a kid when someone was playing a trick on her. Her face was open, vulnerable.

Frankie felt sad for her. "I don't think so," she said.

"Who is this guy and why does he sign it 'your father'?"

"Because he is, Callie. He's your father."

"You mean like the sperm guy?"

"Yes."

"I thought I didn't have a father."

"Everybody has a father, Callie."

"I know that. But why don't I know him?"

"I don't know."

"But you do know something." Callie was angry. "You better tell me what you know and right now, Frankie."

Frankie didn't want to do this now. She wanted to finish *GH* and the big event that always happened just before the end of the show on Friday and then talk to Roxie about it and about the letter. She didn't want to deal with Callie, but it was too late for that. The cat was not only out of the bag, but running wild through the house, as Snow had told her once.

Callie stopped rocking. "How do you know he's my father?"

"I just know, okay?"

"No, it's not okay. And what's he doing with Lola?"

"I don't know," said Frankie. "I thought she didn't trust him."

"Well, clearly, she trusts him enough to marry him." Mascara and tears were running down Callie's cheeks. "This is fucked up, Frankie! I'm so mad, I could spit."

Frankie didn't know what to say so she said nothing and Callie cried a little more and then sniffled and blew her nose with a loud honk. The doorbell rang. She blew her nose again and the doorbell rang a second time. The girls burst out laughing. "Hank," they said in the same breath.

"You look like a raccoon, Callie."

"Thanks for the vote of confidence."

"Go clean up and I'll let Hank in. We can talk about this tomorrow."

"I don't want to talk about it again," said Callie and an ugly look crossed her face. "She's got somebody else now, somebody that should belong to me. She doesn't need us and I don't need her. She isn't my mother anyway. I'm through with her." She tore the card and photo into tiny pieces before Frankie could stop her.

"I'm through with both of them. And you'd better be through with them, too." She stomped out and disappeared down the hall.

Frankie thought about warning Hank. He was a gentle guy and how he handled Callie's moods, she didn't know. But it all seemed too complicated to explain, and so she said nothing. That was her way.

Spring 1990

When Frankie unlocked the door, the two boys were right there to greet her, their tails in the air. Maurie chirped and purred loudly. Dwindle held back as always. She dumped her purse and the graduation program onto the desk, put the zip-bag of food she'd pilfered from the tea table into the fridge, and then sat down on the daybed to pet them. They crowded around, wandering on and off her lap, Dwindle bumping his head into her hand, into her chin when she leaned toward him, Maurie plopping down next to her, his front paws on her thigh.

It had been a good day. The sun had come out after weeks of rain. The speaker, a former state poet laureate, had been inspiring, making them laugh, making them hopeful. She had met her friends' families, their boyfriends from home. There had been a lot of teasing and picture-taking. It was a real celebration. And when she walked across the stage to get her diploma, her friends had cheered and hooted and made her blush. But then it was over. And although Tildie's parents invited her to dinner, she said no, said she had other plans, and she'd headed home on the bus.

She'd moved to the little apartment in John's Landing in the spring of her first year. After Callie took off. After Lola stopped paying the rent. She'd gone to meet the landlord of the house in Southeast, Mr. Maharis, and asked him to help her find something smaller, something midway between campus and downtown now that her mother and sister had moved away. He didn't ask any questions, just took her to see several places he had near the campus, then got his sons to help her move.

She got by. Her social work scholarship paid her tuition. Mr. Schecter had helped her get that and the Rotary scholarship, which gave her some book money. She also had a work-study stipend and she still worked weekends and vacations and summers at the Hilton, where the pay was small but the tips often huge and she got fed and took food home.

She'd been mostly relieved when her sister left. Callie had not stopped being angry with Lola and John Blalock, whom she refused to acknowledge as her father, and she took out that anger on Frankie. She demanded her half of the money that had come with the wedding card, even though Frankie said they needed it for bills. In the end, to stop the nagging and badgering, Frankie wrote her a check for it. She found out later from Hank that Callie had spent it on cocaine. Callie slept late, she stopped doing any of the chores they had divided between them, she stayed out all night more and more. But mostly she turned mean. She criticized everything about her sister—her clothes, her hair, her delight in *GH*, her friend Roxie.

And then one day in February, Frankie came home from class and found Callie in a fury. She stood in the doorway and watched her sister throw clothes into a large backpack that she hadn't seen before. Callie looked up at her but went on packing.

"What's happened?" Frankie said finally. She could see what Callie was doing and she didn't know how to stop it.

"I'm out of here, that's what's happening. I've had it with this place and its petty minds."

"Where are you going? Do you have a plan?"

"No, I don't have a plan. Geez, Frankie, not everybody has to have a plan. I have dreams. And those dreams aren't going to happen in this dump." She went on putting jeans and t-shirts in the backpack.

"You're only sixteen. Are you sure you want to be on your own?"

"Stop trying to be my mother, Frankie. Besides, Lola went out on her own when she was my age."

"Well, she was actually seventeen."

"Big difference." She went into the bathroom and came back juggling her makeup kit and hairbrush and curling iron and hair dryer.

Frankie looked at her watch. She'd recently gotten a Friday night shift at the Hilton and she needed to change and get the bus. Then she said, "Do you have any money?"

Callie tried to stuff the hair dryer in the bag and then threw it and the curling iron on the bed in disgust. "Why? Do you want to give me some?" She looked over at Frankie.

Frankie said nothing. She wanted to cry, she wanted to beg her sister to stay. She wanted Lola to come back and take care of things. She wanted Dewey to fix it. She wanted something she had no name for. And so she pushed it all down and said, "Is somebody taking you?"

Callie opened her mouth and then closed it again. She zipped up the backpack and hefted it on to her shoulder. Frankie went to her room then and took the plastic bag from her secret place and counted out twenty five-dollar bills and put them in a small burlap bag that had come with pencils in it. She found Callie at the front door and handed her the money.

"Don't just disappear, Callie. Please. Call me or write me. I love you. That won't stop."

For just a minute, Frankie saw the Callie from their early days and she thought maybe her sister might hug her, but a horn honked and Callie turned and went out and closed the door behind her. There was nothing for Frankie to do but put on her uniform and go to work.

Later that night, she had come home to find Hank on the porch. And he told her how Callie had been dropped from cheerleading weeks before because she came to practice drunk and how she broke up with him for no reason and when he pushed her about it, Callie told him she'd been sleeping with his dad and they were going to run away together. Now his dad was gone and his mother had locked herself in her room and Hank didn't know what to do. Frankie listened and let him sleep on the couch until late the next morning when she had to go and work the lunch shift.

Soon after that, she moved to the apartment and her world became the college and studies and work. Roxie had moved to Ashland for school and was out of her daily life. When asked about her family, Frankie said they lived out of state and couldn't afford to visit her and people never asked again.

Now Dwindle and Maurie had gone to sleep in her lap, and she didn't care that it was her one good dress and they'd get cat hair on it. She petted them and loved on them and kept away from the ache in her heart that had been there all through graduation with no one of her own to celebrate with her.

She'd sent out three announcements. One to Roxie, who had sent her one back. One to Dewey and Snow, who had sent a card and a check of congratulations. And one to the address in Juneau that had been on the wedding gift check, but there was no reply. She had no way to reach Callie. There had been no word from her, and Hank's dad had come back alone from Seattle a few weeks after they left. If she was still there, Frankie didn't know where.

She looked at the clock. Just past five. There was a long evening ahead. She was sorry she hadn't planned to work tonight. She needed the money. While she had a paid internship with Child Protective Services coming up, it didn't start until September and somehow she had to cover her expenses for the summer. She'd have to look for another part-time job. Maybe Mr. Maharis needed someone in his rental business. The thought made her weary.

She picked the cats up gently and set them down and went to take a shower. Then she put on her pajamas and fixed herself a cup of tea and a plate of the hors-d'oeuvres and cookies from the commencement reception and settled down with an Anne Tyler novel that had just come in at the library. She was about fifteen pages in when the doorbell rang.

"Mr. Schecter."

"Hi, Frankie. Congratulations!" He handed her the yellow roses and daisies in his hand. "I wasn't sure I'd find you home. Thought you might be out celebrating with friends. Hey, are you sick?"

"No, why?"

He pointed to her pajamas.

"No," she said. "I just like to hang out in them."

"Cool! Can I come in? I just wanted to give you the flowers and congratulate you in person."

"Sure, I guess." And she stood aside to let him in.

She hadn't seen him in a couple of years, although he'd called once in a while to see how she was. He looked different somehow, and she realized she'd always seen him in a suit and tie. Tonight he wore jeans and a sport shirt and running shoes. He looked much younger somehow, like a regular guy. He wasn't handsome exactly, more nice-looking.

"Can I get you a cup of tea, Mr. Schecter? Or a diet soda? Or orange juice. That's all I have." Frankie felt nervous. Surprises weren't much of a good thing.

"Diet soda would be fine. Just in the can."

She got a cola out of the fridge and brought it to him. He had taken a place on the daybed and she was amazed to see Dwindle settle into his lap.

"He never does that," she said.

"Cats like me," he said. "I have three myself."

"Wow! I didn't know that." For a few minutes, they talked cat names and ages and cat antics and he made her laugh and Frankie relaxed a little bit.

Then there was a lull in the conversation and the nervousness crept back in and she wondered what he was doing there. He didn't seem to notice, just went on drinking from the can and petting Dwindle. He looked up at her and smiled. It was lopsided, his smile, and it made him look a little goofy. The kids in school had made fun of that as they did everything else, but it wasn't mean. They all liked Mr. Schecter.

He was looking at her and she felt embarrassed. She said she needed more tea and left him there with the cats.

"Are you excited about your internship?" He had followed her out into the tiny galley kitchen. He seemed to fill up the whole space, and she was excited and afraid and something new was moving in her body at having him there.

"I guess," she said. "It doesn't seem very real yet, and it's not much money." Then she blushed. "I didn't mean to say that. I'm so grateful you got me that opportunity. And maybe it'll turn into a regular job." She took her tea and squeezed past him.

"What are you going to do for the summer?" He sat down on the daybed again.

"Go on waitressing. Look for another part-time job. Do you suppose there's anything at school for somebody like me?"

He shook his head. "I doubt it. Everything pretty much shuts down except for summer school. How about the college? Can you get something there?"

"No, not once you graduate, but I'll find something."

"I'm sure you will." He looked at her and gave her that lopsided smile. "So, the reason I came over is, well, I'd like to take you to dinner to celebrate your graduation." He paused. "But I don't want to take you to dinner as Mr. Schecter, your old guidance counselor. I want it to be a date."

She couldn't quite take this in. She knew she was supposed to say something cute and flirty back. That's what the girls on *GH* all did. But she couldn't find any of those responses that she and Roxie had practiced for just such an occasion.

"What do you say, Frankie? Want to get dressed and go to dinner with me?" He smiled again.

And suddenly the lopsided smile looked cute and sexy, and she blushed and went to put her good dress back on.

Summer 1994

Frankie was trying to listen to Tawanda. She really was. For thirty minutes she'd taken careful notes on the intake form. The names and ages of Tawanda's four children. Where they were now. Where their fathers were (prison, Tacoma, who knows? who knows?). How long since she'd had an address. How her parents were worthless. How men were worthless.

Frankie didn't need to write down the last two. She'd been doing intakes for the past four months and the last two were a given. Each time she wanted to tell the woman who sat across from her that she knew how she felt. That she didn't know her own father, that she only knew his name from the birth certificate, Jimmy McPhee. That she didn't know where he was. Had never met him. That her mother had abandoned her. That the men in her life had been worthless as well. But of course, she didn't say any of this. Her six months at CPS had taught her the strict boundaries between client and counselor. Her two years here at the Flora T. Simonson Shelter for Women and Children had reinforced them.

She looked at the clock on her desk: 4:45. There were two questions left on the form and she'd have to ride hard on Tawanda's meandering mind if she was going to leave on time. There was no paid overtime and she was tired. It had been a long day. It had been a long week. She focused on the notes, wishing there was another chocolate bar in her drawer.

"Prostitution, shop-lifting," said Tawanda. She started to badmouth the police, but Frankie moved right on to the next question.

"My grandmother. Ida Washington. 1923 SE Pine."

Why did all black women seem to have grandmothers and white women didn't? Frankie didn't. Lola had never talked about her family. And what about the McPhees? Was there a grandmother there she could have known all these years?

"Thank you, Tawanda. That's been a big help. I appreciate your honesty." Frankie recited the closing formula as she closed the file and stood. The young, pregnant woman pushed herself out of the chair and went down the hallway into the residence end of the old building.

Frankie locked up the file, grabbed her jacket and her bags, and hurried out. 5:10. If she hustled, she could make the 5:25 on Glisan.

The bus was only half-full so she got a window seat. She thought about Tawanda, who was twenty-two, a year younger than she was. Four kids already and another on the way. She'd heard the women at Flora T. talk about their babies with a love and devotion that seemed to disappear when the kids got older. Is that when Lola had loved her, when she was a helpless baby? She didn't let herself go down that road very long. Thinking about Lola always brought up a mix of longing and bitterness that made her feel sorry for herself and she hated that, hated feeling lonely and scared.

The bus moved on up Glisan past the big houses of Laurelhurst and the hospital, and she closed her eyes as she always did when it went past Mike's Bar and Grill at Sixtieth. That had been their place. She hadn't been there in two years. She hadn't seen Jeff Schecter in longer than that.

"Hey, guess who got married last weekend?" Roxie had said one evening as their daily phone conversation wound down.

"Who?"

"Heidi Hillman."

"That's not surprising, I guess." Heidi had been one of the pretty girls in their class. Long blond hair, blue eyes, homecoming princess, stylish clothes. She and Frankie had had only one class together, chemistry junior year, and Frankie had tutored her for a couple of weeks before the final exam. Heidi had been grateful and friendly, but it was the kind of friendly that led nowhere.

"Well, yeah, but it's who she married that's the surprise. Want to guess?"

"No," said Frankie.

"Mr. Schecter. Isn't that a hoot?"

The air left Frankie's body in one dizzying exhale. The room went dark, her mind went blank. She laid her head on the table to keep from falling over. The phone rang and she let it go. Then it rang again and she picked it up.

"Frankie? What happened? Why did you hang up?"

"Sorry. Something was burning on the stove and I dropped the phone and it must have clicked off."

"I thought you weren't going to eat at night anymore."

"I'm not. I was fixing something for tomorrow's lunch. Look, I've got to go. I've got a big mess here."

She had never told Roxie about her relationship with Jeff Schechter. She had never told anyone. About those first awkward dates, about his kindness and sweetness as he taught her about sex. Within two weeks of her graduation, they were together every minute they could be. They had jobs during the day and each other at night. And that went on all the warm days of that summer and into the first cool days of fall.

He encouraged her to lose weight, to get different clothes, a different haircut. They laughed about how they were playing out *Pygmalion*, and he called her "my fair lady," but she didn't mind for he adored her and she let him and then she adored him back.

And then there was less time together as school started and he had parent conferences at night. Frankie began to live for the weekends, for late Friday night when Jeff would come over and make love to her and they'd have waffles and sometimes champagne in bed the next morning and then stay in bed all day or get up early and go hiking up the Gorge or to the beach and they'd find a secluded spot and make love again. And her need for him grew and grew and she thought it was love.

And then Halloween approached and Jeff had to chaperone the dances on Friday nights and go to the football games and the wrestling matches. He said she'd be bored and he'd come later and sometimes he did and sometimes he didn't. She didn't understand what she had done wrong to make him pull away. What had happened to the way he felt about her all summer?

She bought a bottle of vodka, kept it in the freezer. It had always put Lola in a better mood, but it made her sick, not relieved. So she turned to what still worked: chocolate, and ice cream, and grilled cheese sandwiches. The weight started coming back on, all those pounds she'd worked so hard to lose at Jeff's urging, and she felt guilty and ashamed of her body and the only relief seemed to be to eat more.

Their relationship dragged on another month. There were no weekends, no days in bed. He came on Sunday nights for a few hours, sometimes on Wednesdays. She didn't ask why he gave her so little of his time. She was afraid he would say it was over, that there was someone else. And she didn't see how she could live if he did that. But then one Sunday night, he said just that and it was over and she didn't die, not exactly. But she moved through the first weeks in a kind of gray sludge of wretchedness that she didn't know came with a broken heart.

Frankie felt a hand on her arm. "Isn't this your stop, Frankie?" Beatrice was pointing at the corner ahead. She always got on the stop after Frankie did and Frankie had gotten in the habit of saving a seat for her.

"Yes, thanks," Frankie said, pulling the stop cord. "I was lost in memories."

"Hope they were good ones," the older woman said.

"Not really." Frankie gathered up her bags and stepped out in the aisle.

Bea put her hand on Frankie's arm again as she went by. "You take care now," she said. And the kindness in the woman's eyes brought tears to her own. She nodded and hurried off the bus.

It was another four blocks to the little house on the edge of the Montevilla neighborhood. Dwindle and Maurie came rushing up at the sound of her key in the lock. She set the mail down by the phone, petted them and fed them, and headed straight for the shower to wash off the office. Clean, free of memories for the moment, she put on sweats and a t-shirt and took her lean entrée and diet soda out to the small back patio and lost herself in *Beach Music*. She was a big Pat Conroy fan.

She heard the phone ring. Roxie, probably. She would call her back after the warmth left the yard. An hour later, she went inside. There were two messages. Roxie checking in. Then Mr. Maharis, her landlord and boss for her second job, with a question about an account that couldn't wait until she came to work on Saturday. She didn't feel like talking, not after the day she'd had, so she picked up the mail and took it into the living room and sat on the sofa. The cats followed.

There wasn't much. A balance due from her dentist. The alumni magazine from her college. She turned to the personal news in the back. Weddings. Lots of them. Grad school. Law school. It made her weary.

The last item was a thick manila envelope with what felt like a magazine inside. Frankie didn't remember ordering a magazine. There was no return address, and a dozen stamps had been used instead of a postage label.

She opened it. It was a copy of *Cosmopolitan*. She was even more perplexed. This was definitely not a magazine she would buy. Sticking out of the top, midway through the pages, was a piece of paper, Plaza Hotel stationary. She pulled it out and read, *My first big break! Many more to come! New York is great! C.* Underneath was a phone number.

She sat there. Not moving, not thinking. There'd been nothing from Callie all these years. No calls, no letters, no cards. She'd wondered if her sister was dead from drugs or drink. She went carefully through the magazine, not sure what she was looking for. And then there she was, Callie all grown up. In the photo, she was seated on a sofa next to an astonishingly handsome man in a tuxedo. She wore a white fur jacket over a clingy silvery dress short enough to show off her long legs and the silver strap stilettos she was wearing. Her lips were red, her eyes outlined in silver. Her body was turned toward the man, she had her hand on his shoulder, but she looked straight at the camera, straight at Frankie with a look of defiance that Frankie knew only too well. It was Callie all right.

Frankie read through the text on the page but it told her nothing. All fashion fairytale and purchasing particulars. She read through the note again but she didn't need to. She'd memorized it the first time through. She put the open magazine on the coffee table. This was good news, wasn't it? Callie was okay, she was doing well, she was alive. So why did Frankie feel as though someone had slapped her, had broken her heart again?

Dwindle climbed into her lap but instead of comfort, it seemed too much and she picked him up and put him on the floor. Anger surged through her and she got up and went outside. The night was coming on, clear and blue. The winter, too. The air had that crispness of the turn.

Why was Callie connecting now? Showing off? Wanting to make her jealous? The handsome man, the fancy clothes . . . even though she knew that none of it belonged to Callie. It was borrowed, all for show. Still . . . She'd heard a news report that fashion magazines were a cause of anorexia. Not in her case. She looked down at her clothes, at the body she carried around that was so different from Callie's. Twenty extra pounds, maybe thirty. She didn't own a scale, didn't want to know, in most ways didn't care. But the picture had made her feel bad just the same. She wasn't thin, she wasn't beautiful, her life wasn't glamorous. She wondered if Callie's life was glamorous, like the picture. She suspected it probably wasn't. But all the same.

She knew her anger wasn't about that. It was about neglect. About a sister abandoning a sister. About mothers abandoning daughters. About having no family. Everybody was supposed to get one of those, right? Why didn't she get one? She finally grew cold in the autumn air, in her body and in her heart. She went in to call Mr. Maharis and see if she could solve his problem since she couldn't solve her own.

It took three days for her to get up the courage to call the number on Callie's note. The phone rang four times, then beeping, and a mechanical voice. "The number you are calling is no longer in service."

Summer 1999

Frankie woke when the pager went off. She looked at the clock. Just after midnight. She thought about waking George but decided against it. It would ring again if it were an emergency.

It was a warm night and they'd left the curtains open onto the backyard for the breeze. She threw off the sheet and pulled down the ivory silk nightgown sticking to her damp skin. It had been a gift, like all the other expensive things she had, and George liked for her to wear it. Although she preferred cotton, she didn't mind. It was an easy enough way to please him.

She heard the back door thunk. Dwindle. She got up and went out to the kitchen to let him in. She gave the old boy a pet and put down some fresh food. She poured herself some grapefruit juice and went out and stood on the patio. After a bit, she heard the door behind her but didn't turn.

"It's a lovely night," he said, coming up behind her and putting his arms around her. "And a lovely woman." He pulled her long brown hair back and kissed her neck. His mustache tickled her skin and she gave a laugh and he laughed, too. She could feel the heat of his body through the thin fabric of her nightgown.

"The pager . . ." she said and he said, "Shhhh," and turned her then and kissed her mouth. She kissed him back but, as always, she felt no urgency, no passion, just affection.

He had already showered. He smelled of her citrus soap and she wondered if his wife wondered about that. Not that he might shower late at night—there was a full bath at the office and George and his sons both used the shower often before going home—but it had a manly soap, Irish Spring or another of those heavily scented deodorant soaps. The bathroom reeked of it and so did they when they came out clean. She'd asked him once if he wanted her to get another soap for him at her house. But he'd said no, and Frankie didn't ask again.

"Are you coming in Saturday?" he said, pulling away and straightening his clothes.

"Do you need me?"

"I always need you." He winked at her and kissed her again. "There are contracts piling up. Marla doesn't do a very good job. Maybe you could work with her, see if you can figure out why she's so slow." He turned to go back into the house.

"We both know why she's so slow," she said, following him through the screen door.

"Yeah, I know. But Michael just loves her and she needs the work." He went into the living room and came back with his jacket on. "How do I look?"

"Perfect," she said. "Not a hair out of place."

He ran a hand over his mostly bald head and grinned. "Bye, Frankie. See you Saturday."

"Bye, babe." She couldn't call him George. She'd known him as Mr. Maharis for too many years to do that. But she couldn't call him Mr. Maharis when he'd just gotten out of her bed. She walked him to the door, watched him walk down the street a ways and then get into the Lincoln. Then she closed the door and had the house back to herself.

She felt restless, vaguely unhappy, as she always did when he left. She pulled the red satin sheets off the bed, put on the new yellow cotton ones she'd ordered from Company Store. She took a shower, dressed in cotton pajamas, fixed some eggs and a toaster waffle. She began to slow down. She wasn't sleepy but she needed to go back to bed. If she didn't, she'd struggle all the next day at Flora T.

Dwindle followed her into the bedroom. He'd become more needy after Maurie died. He stayed away when George was there although he let the man pet him, but when she was alone, he took up position on the second pillow as if he were the real partner.

She lay awake a long while; 2:00 rolled by on the digital clock. She wished Roxie were up. She'd call her and hear that familiar voice. She missed her. Roxie didn't live all that far away, in Kelso, fifty miles up I–5 where her husband was a librarian for the city and she stayed at home with their two boys. But they only saw each other once a month for a few hours when the family came to town to run errands and visit Roxie's folks.

Roxie knew about George. She'd teased Frankie about living a *GH* life with a married lover who was her boss. "You might as well be living in Port Charles," she'd laughed. There wasn't any judgment in her words, and maybe even a little envy, though Frankie knew that Roxie loved Alex and her kids to pieces. But it didn't feel all that *GH* to Frankie. Well, maybe it had a little at first.

She'd gone to work in the rental company office the July after graduation. She'd started out answering the phones and then slowly learned most of the business—the rental agreements, credit checks, accounting for first and last deposits, arranging plumbers and painters and yard crew. She'd worked full-time for three months and then part-time during her internship with CPS, until the counselor opening at Flora T. came up and she moved into a full-time job there. But her salary at the agency wasn't great, and in exchange for her Saturdays and an occasional Sunday, Mr. Maharis let her live rent-free instead of a paycheck. When he gave her a raise a year later, it wasn't more money but a move from the studio in John's Landing to the little house in Montevilla. And when he bought a new car for his older son, Michael, shortly after that, he sold her the old car, a '90 Camry, for fifty dollars.

He was the closest thing to a dad, to a parent, she'd had since Dewey. She didn't believe Lola had ever really been a parent. More like a foster mom doing it for money or a neighbor who takes in a stray child because nobody else will. But Mr. Maharis seemed to genuinely care about her and she felt both gratitude and affection.

Then one Saturday night, they worked late. Everyone else went home about four but Frankie had a stack of rental agreements to process and Mr. Maharis stayed in his office doing whatever it was he did in there. About eight, a kid brought in two big bags that smelled like food from Nicolas's on Grand, and Mr. Maharis had bustled out and taken the bags into his office. He came out about ten minutes later and invited her in to dinner.

The little round conference table was spread with the red checkered cloth they used for the employee anniversary celebrations. A bottle of retsina stood on the table with several bottles of beer. There were two places set and candles burning.

It was unmistakably romantic and Frankie felt uneasy. "Hey," she said. "What are we celebrating?"

"I closed the deal on a pair of houses in Northwest. They will be excellent rentals." He held one of the chairs out for her.

"Gee, that's great." She didn't know what else to say. That didn't seem like a big enough event for all this effort, but she didn't see how she could say no, and the food smelled delicious.

It *was* delicious, and they ate a lot. Frankie agreed to a glass of beer although she didn't much like the taste, but with the grape leaves and two spicy lamb dishes, it tasted good. Mr. Maharis talked about the rentals and then about how he had gotten into the business when his dad died though he had wanted to be a policeman. His family had moved to Portland from New Jersey when he was nine. He had enlisted during the Vietnam war, but he was older than most recruits and he got officer training and then ended up pushing papers in Hawaii.

"Were you disappointed?" Frankie asked. All she knew of Vietnam was that it had been a terrible ordeal for Dewey and the other men on the farm, or so Lola had said. Broken them or turned them mean and violent. Mr. Maharis didn't seem either.

"At the time, I was," he said. "I was stupid and raring to go. Now I see how lucky I was. Got out of the war with my pride and my body intact." He smiled at her. "How about your dad? Did he go?"

"I don't know," said Frankie, and the old shame about family welled up in her. "I never knew my dad. But I grew up around some guys who went. They had lost buddies over there and didn't talk about it much."

She never told people about the farms. She'd told Roxie when they first met and Roxie had cautioned her to keep it to herself.

"People will think you're a hippie freak. You don't want that," she'd said.

Mr. Maharis nodded. He held up the beer, offering her more, but Frankie shook her head. "You don't drink much, do you?"

"No," she said. "It doesn't agree with me."

"That's good," he said. "It's good to know what agrees with you." He smiled again and then reached over and touched her hand. "Do I agree with you?"

Frankie wondered if she should pretend to be surprised, play dumb and coy, like the bimbos on *GH*, or just say what she thought. Why didn't anybody ever teach you these things? "What are you asking, Mr. Maharis?" she said finally, hoping her voice sounded kind.

He gave a low chuckle. "I'm in love with you, Frankie. I've been in love with you for years. But I . . . I was afraid to tell you." He looked down at the table but he didn't move his hand. "It all seemed, well, impossible. I'm your boss. I'm old enough to be your father. I'm married. All those things make it wrong, I know. But I love you and I want us to be . . ." He hesitated and then looked in her eyes, "I want us to be lovers."

He looked relieved and suddenly Frankie wanted to laugh. For she felt relieved too. She had been afraid that he wanted to marry her. That he was going to divorce his wife. This, this other arrangement was much more appealing and that surprised her. She wasn't in love with him and didn't feel particularly attracted to him. She didn't know how that was going to work. But she did like him. She liked him a lot. He was a kind, gentle man, like Dewey in that way, and he had something Jeff Schecter never had—a sense of humor. And she was tired of being alone.

The bar scene didn't work for her. She didn't like drinking, didn't like how stupid people got when they drank. And the mean ones? No thanks. She'd seen plenty of that in her life already. Roxie had met Alex through online dating and she'd urged Frankie to give it a try. And she had. But the men were all looking for something that she wasn't. Slim, blonde, beautiful. It didn't matter how nerdy or fat or unattractive they were themselves, they all expected perfection. She couldn't give it to them and even if she could have, she didn't want them either. So she stayed home and worked and saved money and dreamed of another life in some other universe.

"What do you say, Frankie? Could you love me, too?" Mr. Maharis sat waiting across from her at the little table in the office she'd been in hundreds of times.

She felt shy all of a sudden. "Yes," she said finally. "Yes, I could."

So they'd moved into their affair. Mr. Maharis came Tuesdays and Thursdays. Those nights, he was there waiting for her when she came back from Flora T. He always brought food and cooked for her. He left the refrigerator full of groceries. He paid attention to what she liked, Fujis, not Braeburns, organic 1% milk, only Tillamook cheeses. She taught him to play canasta and Yahtzee and Boggle, games they'd played at the Landing. They listened to music and he taught her to dance and to love early rock and roll. He was a gentle lover, kind and passionate, and while she didn't return the desire, she gradually came into her body in a different way. And they settled into what they had together.

She is following Lola through the woods. "Hurry," her mother keeps saying. "Hurry up!" And soon she is more than running; she is flying. They go past cabins with loud music and shouting, they go past a dark house with a tractor on the front porch, and all the time she can't catch up with her mother.

The phone woke her at six, Dwindle purring away next to her. She shook off the dream and went out to the kitchen to the phone.

"Frankie, did I wake you?"

It took her a moment to recognize the voice. "Dewey?" she said. "Hi, how are you?"

"Fine," he said. "Fine. How about you?"

"I'm good, too."

She had been to Montana once to visit Dewey and Snow and their kids, after her freshman year of college. Dewey had sent her a bus ticket. It was a long trip and she'd hated the bus and being by herself. But the four of them lived in a large cabin Dewey had built on ten acres a long ways out from Missoula. It was woods and streams and beautiful. There was a big garden and chores and it was like being back on the farm, only just with people she loved. She was sorry to go home after two weeks and she remembered it as paradise. But she had never been back.

"Any word from your vagabond sister?"

"No."

"And your mother?"

"As if," she said.

"Hmmm. Well, the reason I'm calling, other than to hear your lovely voice, is that Bliss has decided to go to nursing school in Portland and we need to find her an apartment. And I remembered you worked for somebody for a while who rents places."

"I still work for him," said Frankie.

"I thought you worked with children."

"I do. I work for the agency during the week, but I work for Mr. Maharis on Saturdays."

"Whoa! When do you have fun?"

"I don't really do fun, Dewey. I'm not that kind of person."

"Oh, come on. Everybody's that kind of person, Frankie."

"Not me." This question always embarrassed her. She was happiest working, busy. Roxie had accused her of being a workaholic, but Frankie knew it wasn't that simple. When she wasn't working, she felt adrift, untethered, anxious. But when she was working, she felt connected, a part of something. And there was peace in that. She changed the subject. "When is Bliss coming?"

"At the beginning of the summer. Her program starts early in June."

"That's good. We have a lot of rentals then. Will she have a car?"

"No."

"Okay. I know just where to look."

They talked then of Snow, who was teaching third grade, and of Tim, who was finishing up at the University of Idaho. And then she heard the alarm go off in the bedroom and she needed to get ready for work and they said their goodbyes and hung up.

She made some coffee and breakfast, put a lunch together, got dressed, and headed off to the bus stop on Glisan. A block from her house, a car pulled up alongside her and parked. Dimitri got out and spoke her name. He looked like George standing there, the same build, the same stance. His hair was still dark and thick, though, and his eyes were an astonishing green. He wasn't handsome in the same way that George wasn't handsome, but he had the same easy way about him. The other son, Michael, had never had much use for Frankie. He was tall and thin like George's wife, Ruth, and there was a sparseness, a tightness about him. He treated her like an employee, not like a person. But she and Dimitri got along well.

From the look in Dimitri's eyes, she could see that there was bad news, and she was glad that it was he who had come to tell her whatever there was to tell.

Summer 2000

In August, nine months after George died, Dewey talked her into coming to visit Montana for two weeks. In the end, Bliss had gone to Bellingham in northern Washington for nursing school and Frankie hadn't seen Dewey and Snow the way she'd hoped to. Tim was building his own cabin on the land. He and his girlfriend, Jenny, were expecting a baby, and there was a great sense of excitement and something else Frankie couldn't put her finger on.

She mentioned it to Dewey one late afternoon as they sat on the porch of the main cabin drinking lemonade. This was her favorite time of day, for she had Dewey to herself, and they talked and rocked and sometimes just sat in silence.

"I think I know what you're sensing," Dewey said, stroking his beard in that movie-mountain-man way he had. "I was really happy when Tim said he wanted to build here and bring Jenny into the family. It's a sense of continuity. Not just the baby but the second cabin. For it will outlast us and be a mark of our being here. All those years ago on the farms, I think that is what all of us were most hoping for. To leave some evidence of our being here. Does that make sense?"

Frankie nodded and tears streamed down her face.

"What is it, little lamb?" Dewey said.

She shook her head, put her glass on the floor, and wiped the tears away with both hands. But they didn't stop, so he scooted his rocker over closer and put his big hand over hers and let her cry. She had told him one afternoon about George and he had listened without judgment and acknowledged her sorrow. And it had done her more good than the half-dozen sessions she had had with the EAP counselor.

Finally the tears slowed and he handed her a big blue cotton kerchief. She blew her nose and wiped her eyes. "I don't have that," she said. "Continuity. I don't feel I'm part of something the way you all are. There's just me and now without George I'm more alone than ever. I feel cursed." She looked over at him. "You must find me pretty pathetic."

He laughed, that low chuckle she remembered from her childhood. "No, Frankie. You're not pathetic at all. You've been dealt some pretty difficult cards. Or maybe you've chosen a difficult path. Either way this isn't an easy life you've got."

"What do you mean 'chosen'?"

"Some of us believe that we choose our circumstances. We choose our parents, we choose how we look, we choose our challenges in order to learn whatever our souls have come here to learn."

Frankie frowned. "Do you believe that?"

"I believe it for me," he said. "When I came back from 'Nam, I had to make sense of what had happened or go crazy. I could be a victim of all that horror, or I could learn from it and have it change my life for the better. So I decided to believe that I chose to go there."

"I thought you got drafted."

"Oh, I did. But I decided to believe that before I was born, I chose war as part of my life path so I could understand myself—and other men—in that way."

Frankie frowned again and he smiled at her. "Believing I chose that experience empowered me to make other choices. Like moving to the farm. Where I met Snow and we had Bliss and Tim. Where I met you and Callie and Lola."

"You could have made that choice anyway."

"I don't think so. After 'Nam, I craved peace. There's no other way for me to describe the longing I had for green and quiet and open space. And peace." He leaned back in the rocker and finished the last of his lemonade. "You probably think these are the rantings of an old fart."

She shook her head. "I never heard any of this before." She looked out across the big garden into the woods and the mountains behind it. "So do you think I chose all of this . . . this loneliness, this emptiness?"

"No. No, honey. But you could think about what having chosen Lola and Callie to be in your life might be teaching you that you can use. Maybe that's already helped you in your work. Maybe it made you more loving with George. I don't know."

"Uh oh, sounds like Mr. Philosophy has come to call." Bliss stood behind her dad. Bliss looked like Snow, the same curly brown hair, the same dark eyes, the same curvy figure. "Whatever he's said, Frankie, take it with a grain of salt." The daughter put her hands on Dewey's shoulders and kissed his cheek. "Dinner's ready—and it's something special."

The something special was a chocolate-blackberry birthday cake with candles for Frankie. They all sang to her and there were presents and cards and she so wanted this to be her family. But it wasn't. For a short time, George had been her family and now he was gone, too.

The stroke had not taken him. Instead he had lingered in and out of a coma for nearly three months. Finally pneumonia had let him go. Dimitri asked her not to visit him, to let Ruth and the family have this time, and she had agreed although she went once in the middle of the night. But the old man in the bed was not the man she knew and loved and she didn't go back. Then George was moved home and there was nothing more for her. Dimitri asked her not to go to the funeral and she agreed to that, too. She had thought her house would be unbearable without George but it wasn't. The reminders were gentle, sentimental. It was the rental office that she couldn't do anymore, and so she told Dimitri she was going to concentrate on her job at Flora T. and she made do with the money from that.

She still missed George terribly sometimes. Not the sex. That had been nice but nothing special. No, it was having someone to care about, someone who cared about her. A sense of belonging with someone. Now she had no one. Or maybe that wasn't true. On a whim, or maybe not, she decided not to drive straight back to Portland.

Frankie parked her car at the Vancouver airport. She could have driven to the address but she didn't want the stress of finding it, and a cab back to the airport would make a good excuse if she needed to escape quickly. She was anxious and weary from the drive.

There was rain in Vancouver and that was fine with her. The city looked reassuringly like home. Green mountains. A small but respectable number of skyscrapers in the city center.

They drove the freeway for a while, then through neighborhoods that became poorer with each turn. The driver asked her for the address again: 1517 Frances Street. She thought about telling him about the name coincidence but didn't want to get him chatting.

They pulled up in front of a two-story home in what was clearly a development—houses and yards all from the same design. The house needed painting, probably needed a lot of things, and the lawn of moss and crab grass was in need of a haircut. But there was a park directly across the street with tall evergreens that softened the bareness of the neighborhood.

"You want me to wait?" The driver looked back at her.

Frankie hadn't thought about that. All she'd imagined was driving from the airport to the place where he lived and telling him who she was. "Can I buy an hour of your time?" she said in reply.

He nodded and she handed him fifty dollars American. "Come back at three. I'll either be here or in the park."

"You got it."

Still she hesitated. She could just go back to the airport, get something to eat, maybe a hotel for the night or head on down to Bellingham. She felt sick now with anticipation. Then she took a deep breath, gathered up her purse, and got out of the cab. The rain had stopped and there were patches of blue in the gray. It was cool but no cooler than Portland. She zipped up her rain jacket and made her way up the walk to the front door.

She heard the doorbell ring somewhere in the house, heard a dog bark in response, but no one came to the door. She tried again, and this time, a kid of eighteen or nineteen opened the door, a Jack Russell terrier squirming in his arms. "Hey, man," he said, "why didn't you just come in? I was in the bathroom." He stopped when he saw that she wasn't whoever he had been expecting.

He smiled but shook his head. "We don't have any money, so whatever you're selling or collecting for, we're a dead end." He smiled again and started to close the door.

"Wait," Frankie said. "I'm looking for Jimmy McPhee. Does he live here?"

The boy stopped and turned back to her, opening the door again. "I'm Jimmy McPhee," he said.

Frankie shook her head. "No, the man I'm looking for is at least fifty, maybe older. An American."

The boy looked her up and down, but it was suspicious now. "What do you want with him? Do you work for the US government?" he asked.

Frankie shook her head again. "No, I don't work for anybody. Is he here? Does he live here? It's something personal."

The boy put the dog down, and he barked once and ran out into the front yard. The boy moved past Frankie and whistled him back.

"Look," he said. "Why don't you come in? Maybe my dad can help you. I'll call him at work."

She stepped into the living room. The sofa and chairs were worn and mismatched, but the room was neat and she felt a little more at ease. She perched on the edge of the sofa and the dog came to sniff her while the boy disappeared down the hall.

In a moment, he was back, phone in hand. "My dad wants to know your name."

"Frances," she said, "Frances Ashby."

The boy repeated the information, listened a few seconds, then closed the phone, his face full of curiosity now. "My dad said to ask you to wait. He's on his way."

Frankie nodded and took off her coat and sat back on the sofa.

"Do you want a beer or a cup of tea?"

"Tea would be great." Frankie got up and followed him to the kitchen. Again, it was shabby and neat, the walls in need of paint but the counters wiped clean, the dishes neatly stacked in a dish tray. She expected things to look foreign, look Canadian somehow, but this could have been any American kitchen.

"So you know my dad?" Jimmy said. He put two cups of water into the microwave and hit the minute button three times.

"What did he say when you said my name?"

"Nothing. He was just silent. And then he asked that you wait." He looked at her, the curiosity still there in his eyes. "Did you know him in the States?"

"I think so." Frankie didn't know what else to say or she couldn't say them out loud. *I think he's my dad. I think you're my brother. I think you're my family.* "How old are you, Jimmy?"

"Actually, it's Jamey. My dad is Jimmy and my mom calls me Jamey. Some of my friends call me Jimmy but at home it's too confusing."

"Does your mom live here?"

He shook his head. "They're divorced. Are your parents still together?"

"No," Frankie said. "I never knew my dad. And I haven't seen my mom in a long time."

"Wow, that's tough," said the boy.

Frankie shrugged. "It is what it is."

The microwave dinged and he pulled out the cups, put tea bags in them, and handed one to Frankie. He put sugar on the counter and got milk out of the fridge, but Frankie shook her head and went over to the little kitchen table and sat down. He doctored his own but he didn't sit down. Instead he leaned against the counter. Frankie realized he was as nervous as she was.

"Where do you live?"

"Portland," she said, and for the next ten minutes they compared Northwest cities and the rain and the green and how lucky they were to live where they did. Then she heard the front door open and her heart beat very fast. He came into the kitchen and whatever instant soul recognition she had been hoping for didn't happen. She didn't know this man. What's more, she saw right away that he didn't look like her.

He stood in the doorway a long moment and looked at her and his face opened into a beautiful smile. "Frances," he said. "Wow, Baby Frances all grown up."

He was slender, an inch or so shorter than his son. He was ruddy and fair, his thinning hair blond, his eyes a pale blue. He wasn't handsome but he looked boyish still, and his face was friendly.

They watched each other for a moment. Then he said, "You don't remember me, do you?"

She shook her head.

"Not surprising. You were only two when I left." He came and stood next to his son. "I lived on a hippie farm, Jamey, back in the sixties, before I moved up here."

"But not at Eiderdown," said Frankie.

"No, it was called Calliope and it was in Washington, near Olympia. Anyway, I knew Frances's mother there. I was her . . . I was her boyfriend." He looked at Frankie. "Boy, did I love your mother! She was so beautiful and so wild. I guess that's the word for it. Wild. Those were some days." He got silent, maybe thinking of those days. Then he said, "How is your mom? Wild as ever? And Cassie and John? Do you still know them?"

Frankie hesitated and then said, "Cassie died when I was six at Eiderdown. In California. In a car crash." It felt odd to speak of Cassie again.

A look of sorrow crossed the man's face. "I'm so sorry to hear that. She was a wonderful person. Everyone loved Cassie. You and your mom must have been heartbroken, Frances. She was like a sister to Lola and a mother to you."

Then he seemed to shake off the sorrow. "How about you, Frances? Where do you live? What do you do?"

"She lives in Portland, Dad. She works with kids from lousy homes."

Frankie had forgotten the boy was there, so intent was she on Jimmy. She wondered if she should ask her questions with the boy in the room, but she didn't know how to get him to leave. She glanced at the clock. Forty minutes had gone by and the cab driver would be here soon.

Then Jimmy opened a door to what she needed to know. "How did you find me, Frances?"

"Well, when my mom left, she left behind a box of papers. And your name was on a couple of them. Letters and . . . and my birth certificate." Frankie watched his face as she pitched these last two words at him.

But it was the boy who picked up on it first. "Birth certificate? Dad?" He turned to Jimmy, surprise and confusion racing across his face.

Jimmy put his hand on the boy's arm. "It's not what you think." His voice was quiet. "Either of you." He shook his head and gently pulled the boy toward the table. "Sit down, son." And they joined Frankie at the small wooden table.

"I'm not your birth father, Frances, although I wish I'd been. Your mom was six months pregnant when she and Cassie and I moved to Calliope. I was there when you were born and I tried to be your dad and your mom's . . . your mom's husband as much as she would let me. I wanted you both to come up here with me. I didn't want to leave you or your mom but I had to leave. I loved you both so much. But your mom wouldn't come with me. She . . . she didn't love me like that. And I couldn't stay . . . the war . . . the draft, you know."

"I don't remember you," said Frankie. A great sadness was washing over her. Here was someone else who had left her.

"You were too little to remember. I wrote to her for a year. I sent pictures. But she never wrote back."

"I didn't find any pictures," said Frankie.

"Your mom wasn't the sentimental type."

"No," said Frankie, "no, she wasn't."

"But the birth certificate, Dad." Jamey's voice broke in. "Why are you on the birth certificate?"

"Because I asked to be. I was so in love with your mom and I believed she could learn to love me too and then we'd be a family, you and me and Lola. It didn't matter to me that our genes weren't the same. And Lola said okay. She wasn't going to put Tony's name on there. She didn't want him to have any claim on you."

"Tony?" said Frankie. Her heart beat faster.

"Your father, your real father, was a guy named Tony. He was your mother's boyfriend in San Francisco. We lived together in a big flat."

"And Tony lived there, too?" Frankie said.

Jimmy shook his head. "No, it was your mom and Cassie and me and a couple of other guys, Jackson and Charles, no, that's not it. Clark maybe. But Tony didn't live there."

The doorbell rang.

"Jamey, would you go get that?" Jimmy tipped his head in the direction of the sound. The boy hesitated, then got up from the table and went into the front room.

"That's probably my cab," said Frankie.

"Please. Stay a while, Frances."

She shook her head. "I can't. I . . . you . . ."

"I'm not what you want me to be." Jimmy looked disappointed and sad, too.

"No," she said. Then after a minute. "What was his last name?"

"Whose?"

"My father's."

"Honey, I don't remember. Maybe I never knew. He wasn't my friend. He was Lola's. Well, I'm not sure he was really a friend to her either. Anyway, you'll have to ask Lola." He paused a few seconds. "You look like him though. You always did."

"Why didn't Tony move to Calliope with you? Why did he leave us?"

Jimmy looked at her. "It's all pretty complicated. And to be honest, it's not my place to tell you. But far as I know, Tony doesn't know you exist."

The boy came back. "It is your cab," he said to Frankie.

She stood and Jamey held out her jacket. She wondered if he was being polite or if he was eager for her to be gone.

"I wish you wouldn't go," Jimmy said again, standing up, too. "I loved you a lot in those days."

But not enough to stay, she thought. "I appreciate all you've told me, Mr. McPhee. And I need to go." She went on through to the living room.

"At least can I have your address and phone number?" Jimmy followed her to the door. "Maybe I could get in touch with Lola through you."

Frankie turned to look at him. "I haven't seen Lola in thirteen years. She left us when I was still in high school. I have no idea where she is." She waited for the shock value of what she'd said to cross his face, but instead he just nodded and put his hand on her arm. It seemed a gesture of affection, of reconciliation, until he said, "Who was 'us'?" and she felt it as a restraint.

"What?"

"You said 'us.' Did Lola get married?"

"No. She left me and Callie, my sister."

"You have a sister? Could she be my daughter? How old is she?"

She loosened his grip on her arm and opened the door. It was raining again. "She's not your daughter, Mr. McPhee. She's nobody's kid, just like me."

Spring 2005

"The phone rang while you were in the shower." Dimitri was dressed to go. He handed her a cup of coffee and then pressed his lips to hers. He kissed just like his father, and Frankie wondered if that was genetic. Then she wondered about the funny things she wondered about.

"I'll check the message," she said. She put the coffee down on the table and wrapped her arms around her lover and kissed him back. They held each other for a long moment. Then he pulled away, an apology in his eyes.

"Rosanna and the kids are back tonight so I won't see you until Thursday. Unless you want to come in and push some contracts around." He grinned. It was a joke between them. He wanted her there in the office, so he could see more of her.

She shook her head. "I've got my own projects to do, thank you very much. Want to bring a movie for Friday? Sure you don't want some breakfast?"

"Yes and no, no time." He held her tight, kissed her again, and headed out through the kitchen door. Two half-grown cats streaked in and made a beeline for the food bowls.

"I'll call you," he said from the deck. She heard his car start, the sound diminishing as he backed out of the driveway. She felt sad, sad and empty when he left, as she had with George. Did all women feel this way or just those in love with married men?

She busied herself for a moment with Jake and Ruby, littermates from the Humane Society the summer before. After old Dwindle died, she tried going without a cat for several months but it was too lonely.

Dimitri had shown up at her door on a Thursday evening eighteen months to the day of George's death. He, too, brought food from Nicolas's restaurant but he didn't proposition her. They talked and had dinner. It was only after he left with a brief hug that Frankie wondered if they'd just had a first date. The next Thursday he was back. She made dinner this time and again it was nothing serious, two friends having a meal together. They talked about their jobs and their dreams.

Dimitri wanted to leave the business to his brother and become a travel writer. "But I think it's too late for that. What with Rosanna and the kids . . ."

"Maybe it's not too late. What does Rosanna say? Would she travel with you?" Until this point, they had not talked about his family and where it fit into whatever was starting up between them. But Frankie wasn't going to pretend he wasn't married.

Dimitri laughed. It wasn't a bitter laugh but there was no humor in it. "Not likely."

"You haven't told her what you want."

"No. In our family, no one does what they want. Well, maybe with the exception of my dad." He looked at her and then looked away.

She nodded. In his quiet way, George had done what he wanted. He had kept his young man's vow to stay married to his wife and support his family. There had never been any mention of divorce in the years he had been with Frankie. At the same time, she knew she had been some kind of fantasy-come-true for George, some dream of romance and affection and even intrigue that wasn't there in his marriage, maybe not in any marriage.

"What about your dreams, Frankie? Do you want more than this?"

"Yes, of course, but I don't know what that is." How could she explain that "living your dream" seemed the most hurtful thing that someone could do? She didn't know if Lola and Callie had left in search of their dreams but left they had. How could you just take off and leave a loving person behind? She admired Dimitri for his unwillingness to leave his wife and kids. She had admired that in George.

"Well, if you had a dream, what would it be?" He smiled at her in encouragement.

"I'd have a cabin on some land in Montana where some friends live. And I'd live there all summer with five cats and my lover."

"And kids?"

"Sure, as long as they weren't mine."

"No biological clock ticking?"

She shook her head. "I'd be a lousy mother. I know it. I've seen all the hurt that can happen when you're a lousy mother—or father. I wouldn't wish that on anybody."

"I don't think that's true, Frankie. That you'd be a lousy mother. I've seen you with my kids."

"For five minutes. It isn't about being friendly for five minutes. It's about being . . ." She stopped, looked at him, and got up and went into the kitchen with her dishes. "I don't know what it's about," she said, coming back into the room. "That's why I won't do it. I only know what it isn't, not what it is." She sat down again. "That probably doesn't make much sense."

He smiled at her. "Not much. And it doesn't matter." He leaned forward and kissed her very softly, then leaned back again.

A long moment of silence followed and Frankie knew the choice was hers. Just as it had been with George. Except that she knew already that it wasn't as it had been with George. She had liked George. He was kind to her, very kind, and she had come to be very fond of him. But there was already something happening in her body and in her heart when she was around Dimitri. A tension, a need. She hadn't experienced this since that summer with Jeff Schecter. It made her wary. But it also made her say yes.

She had been afraid an affair with Dimitri would be too similar to what she had had with George, but it wasn't. He came by for lunch often and they spent Wednesday and Friday afternoons together. Rosanna and the kids were gone for the weekend about once a month to a family house at the coast. Dimitri always worked Saturdays and was on call for emergencies every other Sunday, so there was a weekend to look forward to each month.

She and Dimitri understood each other. He, too, had family anger, family hurt. Michael was his mother's favorite, Dimitri, the unwanted second child years later who didn't measure up. To please his father, Dimitri had joined the business right out of college. To please his mother, he had married a girl from Portland's Greek community. "It was crazy, Frankie. I just couldn't seem to stand up for myself."

"No, you did it for others. That's different," she said. "Did you love Rosanna?"

"Yeah, I guess. But to tell the truth, I was already in love with you. I fell in love with you that day we moved you to the studio over by John's Landing. But you didn't seem to notice me, and I told myself you were just a kid and I was, well, too shy to ask you out." He stroked her hair. "Then you came to work for us and I could see how my father felt about you and then it was too late. My mom was going on and on about Rosanna and how perfect that would be. Grandkids who were Greek on both sides. And I liked Rosie well enough and I couldn't have you and I went through with it." He smiled at her and began to sing, "Oh, it's sad to belong to someone else when the right one comes along."

"England Dan and John Ford Coley," Frankie said. "I love that album and you're a terrible singer."

"I know," he said. "My kids tell me that all the time."

Frankie tucked away his words. *I fell in love with you. The right one.* And bit by bit, she let herself love and be loved again.

Frankie found a fresh stack of case files in her inbox when she got to the agency and she worked on them straight through lunch. Dimitri called at 2:30. He did that most days when the front-desk girl in his office went across the street to Starbucks. He always found something to talk about, something he'd seen on his drive to work or read on the Internet. She loved him for that, that he paid attention to what was going on around him. And what was going on with her.

The phone rang again two minutes later. She laughed as she picked up the phone. "What'd you forget to tell me?"

"Frankie?" It was a woman's voice.

"This is Frankie."

"Hey, it's me. Callie."

She wanted to say "Callie who"—to stall for time, to give herself a chance to think. She hated the phone for that very reason. There was no time to prepare. No time to make sure the walls were in place around her heart.

"Frankie, are you there?"

"I'm here, Callie." She hadn't spoken her sister's name in years, not even to herself.

"Look, I'm sorry I haven't called in a while. Life gets, well, like, overwhelming and I just always seem to have so much going on. But I think about you. Doesn't that count for something? Aren't you happy to hear from me now?"

Frankie felt dizzy. In the early years, she'd imagined this phone call. How they'd get close again, tell each other about their lives, laugh about Lola and what a terrible mother she'd been. She'd imagined it all light and breezy. But now she felt angry, angry and sick.

"It's been fourteen years since I've heard from you."

"No, it hasn't."

There, there was the voice she recognized. Defensive and about to manipulate. It was Callie after all.

"I sent you magazines and pictures. And called you once from Vegas. And then I've called several times from New York."

"Callie, we haven't talked since you left here."

"Well, I didn't leave a message. But I called and you weren't home."

Part of her wanted to hang up, wanted to hurt Callie, wanted to shout *What about me? What about me?* Instead she said nothing, just waited. Her sister waited, too, then spoke.

"Frankie?"

"I'm here." She sighed. "Why did you call, Callie?"

"Well, I'm getting married and I want you to come."

Frankie said nothing. She didn't know what to say. "Frankie, are you there?"

"Yes . . . yes, I'm here."

"Great. We're having a big wedding and I want you to be my maid of honor. We'll send you a ticket for the airfare and put you up in a great hotel and you send me your measurements and I'll get the dress made and it'll be very cool, I promise. Say yes, Frankie, please say yes."

"When is it, the wedding?"

"June, of course. June 16. Can you get off work? Wow, I guess I don't even know what you do."

"I can ask," Frankie lied. "I'll get back to you."

"Oh, great! I'm so glad you'll come. It'll be terrific, I promise you." And Callie rattled off her phone number and email for Frankie and then it was, "I've got to go. See you soon." No *I love you. I miss you. How are you? What's your life like?*

Instead there was Frankie, left holding the phone.

Summer 2005

The room was crowded and noisy. Ten to a table, at least twenty tables, maybe more. The men wore black suits, the women black dresses. Even the bridesmaids wore black silk dresses. It looked more like a funeral than a wedding. But it was what Callie had wanted and Frankie could see why. There were only two spots of color in the room: the red roses on every table and Callie in her long, red silk dress.

Frankie was not surprised that her sister had become a beauty. An elegant haircut, flawless makeup, a way of walking and standing that took great practice and then looked effortless. Heads, both male and female, turned to look at her when Callie walked down the street. She didn't return their looks, but Frankie knew she was pleased.

Callie's polish and perfection made Frankie nervous and unhappy. She had starved off twelve pounds before the trip east, but twenty extra were still sticking to her frame. She felt huge next to her model-thin sister. And frumpy. Her casual clothes and comfortable shoes that were so right for Portland were all wrong for this world. She ended up wearing the same thing every day she was in Baltimore: the one decent pair of black slacks she owned and the long black tunic—her go-to-meetings-with-clients outfit. Now she was stuffed into a black silk sheath that made her feel like a sausage. She had sent her measurements to Callie as requested, but Callie had assumed she'd made a mistake and asked the seamstress to make the dress smaller. She clearly remembered Frankie from thirty-five pounds ago.

What was surprising was Scott, the fiancé. After the handsome guy in the magazine, a square-jawed man-boy with startling blue eyes, long lashes, and carefully tousled hair, Frankie assumed he'd be a model too. Scott was a different story. He was a decade older, short, stocky, balding. He wasn't ugly. He had wonderful eyes and a lovely smile with expensively perfect teeth. But he wasn't someone Callie would look at twice and Frankie wondered what the attraction was. She didn't wonder about his attraction to her sister. But Callie could have anybody and probably had. What was Scott offering that was so irresistible?

Frankie wanted to ask Callie this and a hundred other questions, but they were never alone together. Scott and Callie had a house in New Jersey but Scott's family all lived in Maryland, so they'd chosen Baltimore for the wedding and rented most of a floor of a fancy hotel for the guests. For a reason that now seemed foolish, Frankie had assumed she and Callie would share a room. She had both yearned for that and dreaded it. But her fears were all for nothing. She had a room to herself. In the end, she was relieved. It was someplace to escape to, someplace to feel like herself. There were several meals with the family, a fancy luncheon for the bridesmaids, who all seemed to know each other. Frankie had expected Callie's friends to be models, too, but they weren't. They were the wives of Scott's friends and business partners. These women were pretty enough but not glamorous like Callie. Frankie wondered if that was on purpose. That would be so like her sister.

Frankie sat alone at the head table. The best man, Frankie's escort at the church, had gone to sit with his wife. The newlyweds were out on the floor, dancing to a terrible rendition of the pop song "Lady in Red." For an accountant, Scott was a terrific dancer and it was fun to watch them. She wondered what kind of dancer Dimitri was. They never went out but they had never danced in the living room or out on the patio either. She'd ask him.

She hadn't talked to him since she'd left. The three-hour time difference meant their schedules wouldn't mesh for the morning coffee break call and she would never call him at home. Not for the first time, she wished they were a normal couple, a married couple, and that he had come with her to her sister's wedding.

She had not told Callie about Dimitri. She wasn't ashamed to be having an affair and she knew Callie wouldn't care about that. But in their one heart-to-heart conversation, Callie had laughed in the wrong places. Laughed when she told her about Jeff Schechter, laughed when she told her about Mr. Maharis. Frankie had laughed, too, made fun of her own naïveté, but it had cost her a great deal to do that. She didn't need her sister to be impressed, but she wanted to be understood, and Callie didn't understand any better at thirty-two than she had at sixteen.

A waiter came by and she ordered a gin and tonic. She seldom drank but she needed something to calm the nervous sickness in her gut and she hoped that would do it. She felt conspicuous alone in the front of the room but didn't know what else to do except go to her room and that she couldn't do. Not yet. There were the toasts to get through, the cutting of the cake. Helping Callie change for the get-away and taking care of the dress and then the bouquet ordeal.

The drink helped and she ordered another. The best man came and asked her to dance and that was okay. And the band got livelier and each of the ushers danced with her in turn. It gave her something to do and then the food came and the head table filled up again. One of Scott's partners, well on in his cups, told off-color jokes and everyone laughed and nobody noticed Frankie and she was glad.

The food was delicious. She was hungry from dancing and from nervousness. She was also a little tipsy from the alcohol and knew the food would settle that down. Her sister, of course, ate next to nothing. Callie pushed the food around, ate a couple of bites of the prime rib, a carrot, maybe two, a sip of red wine. She smiled a great deal, leaned into Scott so he could kiss her, seemed to bask in the beam of his happiness. But Frankie could feel there was something off, something else going on in her sister.

As the meal came to an end, Callie whispered something to Scott, who nodded, and she stood. "Want to come, Sis?" she said.

Frankie got up, a bit confused. It wasn't time to do the dress thing. They still had to cut the cake. But she followed Callie out of the room, down the hall, and into the elevator.

As soon as the doors closed, Callie took off her shoes and handed them to Frankie. "I knew these were a bad idea," she said. She had shown the strappy red pumps to Frankie with great pride. They were Jimmy Choo's, she'd said, and rattled off what they'd cost. An astonishing sum of money for a pair of shoes.

"Do you have another pair that will work?"

"Oh, I'll have to put them back on. I can't not wear them. But I don't have to wear them at this minute." The door opened and she led Frankie down the hall. The hotel room was a disaster:

cyclone, hurricane, tsunami. Dirty dishes on a tray, full ashtrays, newspapers, clothes, towels. That hadn't changed since high school either.

Frankie cleared off a chair and put the shoes on the floor. Callie rummaged in her purse, which lay on the dresser, and then went into the bathroom. She didn't close the door. In a moment or so, she called out to her sister, "Want some?"

Frankie got up and went to the door of the bathroom. Callie stood in front of the counter, a small mirror in front of her with two lines of white powder. "What is that?" said Frankie, although she already knew.

"Cocaine." Callie looked at her like she was from outer space. "Geez, Frankie, you're such a hick. You want some or not?"

Frankie shook her head and Callie shrugged and put the two lines up her nose with a rolled dollar bill. Frankie didn't try to stop her. The drug wasn't going to put any distance between them. That distance was already there, had always been there. This trip hadn't changed that. They weren't sisters. They had come together by accident. They were an accidental family. And Callie was an accident waiting to happen. Hell, maybe she was, too.

"Get me a drink from the mini-bar, will you?" Callie was now touching up her makeup.

Frankie opened the little refrigerator. It was half-empty. "There's coke, beer, and scotch," she called.

"No vodka?"

Frankie rummaged in the bottles. "No."

"Shit. Okay, scotch then. Is there any club soda?"

Frankie found a can of soda water and two airplane bottles of scotch and took them to the bathroom.

"Fix us each one, will you? There should be ice in the bucket. If not, the machine's at the end of the hall." Callie turned back to the mirror. And then as if to make it sound less like an order, she said, "And we'll have a toast to my future," and she gave a strange laugh.

There were a few cubes in the bucket, and Frankie poured the scotch in the two glasses and then filled them with soda.

Callie came out of the bathroom. She took a sip of the drink Frankie handed her, then got two more bottles of scotch from the refrigerator, poured them into an empty glass and topped them off with a little soda. She left the drink Frankie had made next to the empty bottles.

She perched on the chair Frankie had cleared so Frankie sat on the edge of the unmade bed across from her. They raised their glasses in silence and Callie drank off half of hers.

Frankie broke the silence. "I hope you and Scott will be very happy. I know that sounds lame, but I do want you to be happy. I want us all to be happy."

Callie gave her a look she couldn't read. "Are you happy?"

"Yes. My life is good. I like my job. I have good friends."

Callie gave that same strange laugh. "You have pretty low expectations."

Frankie swallowed the hurt. "Maybe," she said.

"Definitely," said Callie.

"I don't find high expectations useful."

"I find life unbearable without them," said Callie.

"What expectations do you and Scott have?"

"Scott? I think he has everything he wants now. He has me. And all this." And she waved her arm in a wide sweep to take in the room. A few seconds went by as the two women surveyed the mess in the room and then they both burst out laughing. For a moment, they were helpless and the tears rolled down their faces.

"Shit, shit, shit," said Callie, when she could catch her breath. "Now I'll have to redo my makeup." She got up and went into the bathroom.

"Shouldn't we go back down?" Frankie called to her.

"Nah, let them wait. They're not going to leave before I come back. No one would disrespect Scott that way, believe me."

Frankie looked at the drink in her hand. She didn't want it. She dumped it into a dirty glass on the food tray and picked up the can of club soda. Then she stood in the doorway and watched Callie line her eyes with a steady, practiced hand. Now was the moment to ask, maybe the last moment. Frankie screwed up all her courage and said, "Do you ever hear from Mom?"

Callie looked at her in the mirror. "No. You?"

Frankie shook her head. "I guess it's because Alaska's the end of the world."

"Alaska? She left there ages ago. That thing with my dad, it didn't last long."

"Where is she now?"

Callie shrugged. "I had an address in Idaho. That's where I sent the invitation but I never heard from her." She looked at her sister in the mirror again. "Don't stress over it, Frankie. She's a witch. And I don't mean the New Age kind."

Frankie nodded but the hurt rose up in her just the same. "Do you ever wish it had been different?"

"What?"

"Our childhood."

"I don't ever think about the past."

"Never?"

Callie shook her head and blotted her lipstick. "Nope, it's a big fat waste of time. You can't undo what you've done and you can't do what you didn't. Why bother?"

Frankie didn't know what to say to that. She thought of the past so often, wished for something else to have happened. "Aren't there things you wanted that you didn't get?"

Callie looked at her in the mirror. A few seconds went by and something crossed her eyes that Frankie couldn't read. Then she shrugged. "Sure, but then I just decided I wanted something else instead. It's much easier that way."

She gave herself a final appraisal in the mirror. "Okay, let's go. As that French model said, it's time to let them eat cake."

Spring 2007

Frankie took her coffee into the second bedroom, which had become her office. After Baltimore, she had not gone back to Flora T. The sadness of the children, the apathy of the mothers, the rage of the fathers, she couldn't face it anymore. She had wanted to do good, to save people all her life. She wouldn't have called it that, this impulse to serve. It just seemed like interesting work, a good way to earn a living and do something for others.

After George died, after Jimmy McPhee wasn't the father she was looking for, she had thrown herself into the work harder than ever. She'd volunteered for a bigger caseload, written grants, created new programs, all trying to get parents to love their children and take better care of them. And a few did. A few mothers got jobs, were admitted into transition programs to take college classes, were reunited with their kids. But for every one she helped, three more came into the system. The women came in battered, addicted, traumatized. The kids came in silent or sullen or hysterical. And her efforts seemed paltry and her exhaustion pathological.

Then Roxie told her of a company looking for a freelance editor and she passed their editing test and got hired on. Now she had steady work and a steady income and a fifteen-step commute from one room to the next. Her old friends from Flora T. thought she was crazy to work at home. Where was she going to meet a man? But she liked the solitude, she liked the work, she liked the freedom. She didn't tell them it was the ideal life for her relationship with Dimitri. Life went on calm and good for another year. And then that ended, too.

Michael Maharis came by late one afternoon in early spring. She had a shock seeing him there at the door, a jolt of fear for Dimitri's life, but he quickly reassured her that his brother was fine, not to worry. He'd come instead on a different errand.

"My mother would like to see you," he said. "She wants to thank you for all your loyalty to the family."

A wave of uneasiness washed over her, but Michael was smiling, friendlier than she'd ever seen him. "Okay," she said. "When should I come?"

"Oh, I can drive you over now. She's having one of her good days. Could you do that? I'll bring you right back."

"Sure, I guess. Let me save my documents and just change my clothes." She put on her new pair of dress trousers and a long tunic, both in chocolate brown. She pulled her hair back and put on simple earrings. She wanted to look serious, mature as befit the occasion.

Michael drove a gangster car, a black SUV with tinted windows. He was taller than his father and his brother, but thinner, less substantial somehow. Frankie assumed the big car was compensation for that.

Once in the car, Michael's friendliness seemed to evaporate. So they rode in silence. It had been many years since Frankie had been to Ruth's house. That's what they all called it, Ruth's house. When she'd first worked in the rental office, all those years ago, she'd taken papers to the house twice for George's signature. There she had met his wife. The first time she had been offered coffee but had said no. From the dismissive look on Ruth Maharis's face, Frankie realized she'd made some kind of social gaffe. But there seemed no way to repair it. Then once she and George became lovers, she never went to the house again. She had never wanted to.

The house was in Laurelhurst, a neighborhood of old wealth, a few blocks from the Greek Orthodox church. Michael parked in the driveway. Frankie didn't wait for him to open the door for her, afraid he wouldn't and she'd look foolish. Dimitri liked to do it. He usually hugged her when she got out. She smiled at the thought.

Michael said nothing, just went down the driveway to a door at the side of the house and waited for her to catch up. The door opened into the kitchen, an old 1940s kitchen, small and heavy with appliances. At the sink stood an older black woman in a black uniform trimmed with white collar and white apron, and Frankie felt as if she'd entered a time warp.

"Mr. Michael," said the woman as she turned toward them.

Michael didn't acknowledge the woman, just moved on through a swinging door into the dining room and then into the living room. Frankie nodded at the woman and followed him to the arch between the two rooms. In the living room, Ruth Maharis stood waiting, thin and elegant. She wore a dark gray silk dress, nylons, stylish pumps. She, too, had dressed for the occasion or maybe she always wore good clothes, Frankie thought. Some women of that generation did. Older than George, she was in her mid-seventies now.

The living room was more elegant than before. The old comfortable overstuffed furniture she remembered had been replaced by leather and chrome that did not suit the old house or the old woman. In one of the low leather chairs sat Rosanna, Dimitri's wife. Michael went to stand behind his sister-in-law. The uneasiness returned.

"Miss Ashby, thank you for coming." Ruth Maharis had a surprisingly sweet, melodic voice. It was a startling contrast to her angular body. Maybe George had loved that voice.

She remained standing, and Frankie had no choice but to do the same.

"I won't waste your time with social niceties." The sweet voice had an edge now. "I don't propose to know why you have sought to destroy my family, why you seduced my husband, and now my son. Frankly, I don't know how you have done it. You're certainly no beauty, you have no money, you have no charm."

"Mother . . ." Michael's voice held caution.

The older woman took a deep breath. Frankie felt sick at the insults, dread at what was coming. She wanted to look away, change the channel, turn the set off. Instead she felt locked into the gaze of George's wife.

"You're right, Michael. Thank you," Ruth Maharis started again. "I . . . we want you out of our lives. I want you to break it off with my son. I want this family to have nothing more to do with you. If that takes money, Michael will arrange it with you."

"It isn't about money." Frankie spoke for the first time. "It's never been about money."

"That's too bad," the older woman said. "That would be a lot simpler."

"I love Dimitri. I loved George."

"That's also too bad. And it's beside the point." She paused, looked at her son. "Dimitri will not see you again. If he does, I will disown him. And he will not see his children again. We are all agreed on that."

Frankie looked at Rosanna. She was small and pretty, light brown hair pulled up in an elaborate French roll that had gone out of fashion twenty years earlier. Her eyes were pale, her Barbie features sculpted. She glanced up at Frankie, nodded, then looked down at her hands.

"And Dimitri?" Frankie said. "Has he agreed?" She looked back at the mother.

"He has."

The knife went in deep. Frankie felt the wound in her heart, in her throat, her body awash with fire and ice. She found the courage to go numb.

"Michael will take you home now. Goodbye, Miss Ashby. I hope to never see you again." And the woman turned and left the room and went up the stairs.

Frankie watched the woman's feet climb and disappear through the banister poles. Then somehow she got through the kitchen to the back door. The maid threw her a look of sympathy. She got into the SUV and Michael drove her the two miles to her house. When they got out, he went to the back of the car and pulled out a duffel bag and followed her up to the front door.

"For Dimitri's things," he said.

Frankie looked at him. There was something in his face she couldn't read. It wasn't sympathy and it wasn't anger. She wanted to figure it out. It felt important to know. She willed herself to stay numb, went into the bedroom, emptied the drawer where her lover kept fresh clothes. She put his electric toothbrush and his shaving stuff in the duffel. The book he had been reading. The mug he always used for coffee. Maybe he would get it, get the message, get the memory. Maybe not.

Michael followed her from room to room, the Gestapo of the heart. And she turned to Michael and saw that he wore a look of victory.

"You wanted me, too, didn't you?" Frankie said.

She saw him stiffen, a brief look of being caught out. Then his face went hard and cold. He gave a bitter laugh. "Dream on."

She handed him the duffel.

"Do you want money?" he said.

She said nothing, just looked at him.

"Suit yourself," he said. And then he was gone and Frankie was left alone with her grief.

She waited for a letter from Dimitri, a phone call, something, but there was none. She wrote to him each night, long letters of what she had done during the day, of what she was feeling, but she didn't send them. She wouldn't jeopardize his life any more than she already had. She didn't blame him. He loved his kids and she had always known he would choose them over her if it came to that. And it had.

A month after the meeting at Ruth's house, she got a letter from the Maharis Company. It contained a yellow post-it note in Dimitri's hand and the deed to the house. The note read, *The least I can do. D.*, and a name and phone number. They belonged to a lawyer who could help her with the transfer of ownership. His fees had been paid. And when the transactions were over, she was cut loose from the two men who had truly loved her, adrift and alone.

Late Winter 2009

The shower water had run cold but Frankie went on standing there, thinking of Dimitri. She still missed him, still thought of him most days. She got out of the shower and stood in front of the mirror as she toweled off the wet. She was gaining weight, she could see it. Too much sitting at the computer for work, too much ice cream keeping her company in the lonely evenings. She knew she would never be thin like her sister but she didn't want to be fat either. She would start walking the next day. She sighed, put on some clothes, and went into her office to finish a project for a new client.

The phone rang at four. "Hey, Roxie. What's shakin'?" she said.

"Are you still friends with Roxie?" It was a woman's voice, cigarette-deep, cigarette-raspy. Unmistakable. Even after more than two decades.

Frankie sat still as a statue. She stopped breathing, stopped thinking. And then as she started to feel again, when the shock of it loosened its grip, anxiety rose up out of her gut, filled her throat with wet cement.

"Frankie?"

She swallowed the cement down. "Mom."

"You still friends with Roxie? How is she?"

"She's good. Married. Kids."

"That's good. I always liked her."

"No, you didn't."

"Well, no. But you did. So I'm glad you're still friends."

Frankie didn't respond. She had had this conversation too in her head so many times and now she had nothing to say. She heard a match, the intake of smoke. It broke something free in her. "What do you want, Lola?"

"Why? Can't I just call my daughter and see how she is?"

Frankie paused a few seconds, her anger spreading. "If you were a real mother, yes, of course, you could. But we both know, let me rephrase that, the three of us know that you aren't a real mother."

Lola gave a low laugh. "Good for you, Frankie! No holds barred. I taught you well."

There was a bit of silence and Frankie wondered if her mother were in town or coming through town. Would she say yes to seeing her? She needed time to think about this. And then she didn't, for Lola said, "Do you have Dewey's number? I've lost it."

Not Dewey. Lola couldn't have Dewey. Dewey belonged to her. And then the spite fizzled even though she didn't want it to. And she told her mother to hold on and she went to get her address book and gave Lola the number.

"Thanks." There was another brief silence.

"Don't you want to know how I am?" Frankie asked. She couldn't help herself.

"I'm sure you're fine," her mother said. "You were always fine. If you'd needed me, I wouldn't have left." And she was gone.

Summer 2009

Frankie read through the last pages of the manuscript. It had been a complicated piece to edit, long and poorly written, and she was weary of the words. She checked off her list of things to watch for and then sent it off, attaching her invoice in a separate email. Then she disconnected the data stick and went to put it in her purse. The laptop was in the car, her bag as well. She moved to the kitchen and put down dinner for Jake and Ruby. She felt a sense of urgency to leave. It was coming on six and she didn't want to cross paths with Tom, who was coming to housesit.

The doorbell rang. Frankie sighed. Not quite fast enough.

He stood on the porch, backpack and laptop at his feet. He smiled at her although the smile was tentative. "I wasn't sure you'd still be here." His voice was low, soft like he was. He was a little taller than she, bookish glasses over his large gray eyes, so owl-like she'd wanted to laugh when she met him.

"I'm just on my way. Any questions? I've left instructions about the cats and about watering the garden." She left the door open for him and moved toward the kitchen. She hated that it was so awkward.

"I brought my computer," he said. "I didn't know if you were taking yours."

"I am."

"Well, good then." He stood in the kitchen doorway.

"I haven't left you much food, I'm afraid."

"No problem," he said. "How you've been, Frankie?"

"Okay," she said, giving the spotless counter another wipe. "Busy with work. You?"

"Same. Read anything new lately?"

"No, I don't read much when I work. Too many words." Frankie knew he was as nervous as she was but she couldn't help him. She put the sponge in the holder. She felt Ruby's paws on her thigh and she picked the Maine coon up and cuddled her. "Well, I'd better get on the road. I want to get as far as I can before dark." She met his eyes for the first time.

He nodded. "Have a safe trip. I'll take good care of things here. And hey, I hope your mom's okay."

She nodded back, gave Ruby a squeeze, put her down on the floor. Then she picked up her purse from the table and went out through the back door. The August heat hung on from the day but it was a relief from the tension of the kitchen. She got in the car and headed out of the neighborhood and toward the freeway, setting aside her guilt about Tom.

She had met him through Roxie. He'd studied library science with Roxie's husband, and her best friend felt their mutual interest in books would bond them. Tom turned out to be a kind and gentle man who knew how to listen, and Frankie wanted to feel something for him, she really did. They had coffee, went to a lunch a few times, then a dinner date and a movie, the normal progression. He had wanted to hold her hand a few times, had given her a hug one day after lunch. She had let him. It seemed safe enough. But she knew what was coming. Of course she knew.

She let him stay one night. He was a kind, benign lover and she kept hoping that something would spark, some feeling would arise in her for him, but it didn't. She tried again with him, then a third time. And that third morning when he kissed her goodbye, she said, "This isn't working for me. I don't feel what you want me to. I'm sorry." And he looked sad and offered to go slower, give her more time, but she shook her head and wished him well.

Then came this trip she didn't want and she couldn't find a cat-sitter she trusted. So she'd swallowed her guilt and phoned Tom, who liked her cats and was easy and gracious about coming to stay for however long she was gone. She knew she was taking advantage of him, maybe sending mixed signals, but she needed someone and she thought she could trust him.

She pulled onto I-84 at Sixteenth Street. There was still post-work traffic and the stop-and-go kept her focused on the road until she reached the 205 turnoff where most of the traffic got off to go north and she didn't, heading east instead. She wondered if she should just turn back. She didn't want to do this. She shouldn't have to do this. But she had promised.

She'd gotten the email from Callie first. While Frankie emailed her sister regularly, Callie seldom wrote back and never revealed anything personal. Frankie didn't even know that her sister had moved to Pittsburgh. Now Callie was planning to drive out to the West Coast. She was leaving right away. Could she stay with Frankie for a day or two on her way to California?

Sure, Frankie replied. *I thought you said you'd never come back to Portland.*

The response came right back. *Well, I'm not coming back there! I just want to visit. I'm headed to L.A. Going back to work.*

Frankie started to ask about Scott in all this and then let it go. It wasn't her business. *Okay,* she wrote. *Let me know when you will arrive.*

Then Dewey had called, not more than fifteen minutes later. He was calling about Lola.

"What's wrong with her?" Frankie said.

"Something with her heart, I guess. She's not feeling well. Had some tests. I can't get away with school starting so soon. I was hoping you would go and visit her."

"You know she's not going to let me help her."

"That well may be. But you will have done what you can. It's about you, Frankie, not about Lola. It's about what you choose." Dewey seemed to be leaning more and more on this philosophy stuff. Sometimes he was right, sometimes he was just annoying.

She shook her head at the phone. "I can't, Dewey. Don't ask me." Dread rolled in a slow wave through her chest.

He said nothing for a moment and the dread got stronger. "It would be good to forgive her, Frankie. Not for her, but for you."

She listened to Dewey's voice, its baritone sweetness, its magical calm. He made it sound so easy. But it wasn't and she said so.

"No, I won't pretend it is," Dewey said. "But going to see her, finding out who she is now, that would be a step." He paused. "Despite what you think, Frankie, she loves you."

"It isn't about what I think. It's about the evidence. I don't have any evidence of that."

"Of course you do. She could have given you up, put you into the system, but she didn't."

Frankie had never thought of that, even in all those years of working with mothers who chose their addiction over their kids, handing their kids over to the state so they could run wild with their lovers or hole up with some other junky.

"There are lots of other ways your life could have gone," Dewey went on. "It's not been all that terrible, has it?"

Compared to what? she wanted to say. Instead she took a deep breath and said, "Yes and no."

"Fair enough," Dewey said. "Fair enough." He paused a second and then said, "You could come on to Montana afterward, you know. See us for a few days. Help us send off Tim and Jenny. They're packing up to move to Denver for the internship Tim got. You wouldn't have to be with her long." He paused again. "Can I count on you to go?"

"Yes," Frankie said, feeling the blanket of obligation settle on her shoulders. "I'll go." But when she hung up, she had a better idea. She called Callie, told her of Dewey's request, asked her if she'd go to Lola's and check up on her.

"You've got to be kidding," said Callie. "That's not part of my plan."

"Why? When do you need to be in L.A.?"

"Well, I don't have a date to arrive, if that's what you mean."

"Exactly, you could come through Idaho on your way to Portland. It's not that much out of your way."

"But Dewey asked you to do this. It's your favor for him, not mine."

Frankie sighed. "What if I meet you there? What if we do this together?" she said.

"I don't know, Frankie. I don't want to see her."

"Well, I don't either. But it would be a lot easier if you were there. Please, Callie."

"Okay, but I won't promise to stay long."

"Me either. Just a day or two to figure out what's going on."
They talked logistics for a moment, then made a plan.

Now Frankie was headed up the Columbia Gorge on her way
to Idaho. It was a beautiful evening. The day started to cool, and
she rolled down her windows and let the air from the river wash
all thoughts of Callie and Lola out of her mind. The Gorge was
always a beautiful drive, no matter the weather or season, and she
was drawn into its beauty. The miles rolled by and as the dusk
settled in, she pulled into a rest stop just west of the Dalles to
stretch her legs.

The Reunion
Part II

Just past noon, on the outskirts of Spokane, Frankie took an exit announcing a Subway, a Burger King, and a Taco Bell. Surely, T. Roy would eat something at one of them. They settled on burgers and shakes and spent the meal talking about the Transformers toy that seemed attached to T. Roy's left hand. He showed her some of its many features and she was relieved to see him animated. While the boy was in the bathroom, she called Callie.

"Where are you, Frankie? Do you know what a dump this town is? No wonder she ran away. There is absolutely nothing to do in this place. I struggled to even find the liquor store. You'd better be on your way because I'm not sticking around here. I'm going crazy with her shit. And it's so quiet here I could scream."

Frankie let her sister rant and ramble for another minute. Then she broke in. "Okay, Callie, I get it. I get it. I'm in Spokane, just stopped for some lunch. We'll be there in about an hour, I'd guess. Can you give me some directions to the house?"

"Who's 'we'?"

"What?"

"You said 'we.'"

"Directions, Callie? If you want me to get there, I need to know where to go."

T. Roy had come back to the table and Frankie smiled at him. She wrote the directions down on the back of her Burger King receipt.

"An hour, Callie. Maybe a little more." And she closed the phone and asked the boy if he wanted ice cream.

Frankie had imagined her mother living in a little house near the center of town. Lola had grown up, she'd told them, in a little house with a treeless yard and rooms stuffed with big dusty furniture. And somehow Frankie had thought her mother would live there, in that house, that that had been the point for Lola of coming home. Instead Callie's directions had taken them through the six blocks of town and past Silver Mountain Lodge and out a short ways to Three Pines Park, a senior community of manufactured homes. They circled past a deserted swimming pool guarded by the namesake pine trees and into a maze of short streets and cul-de-sacs. Each of the homes had a carport with an Astroturf floor, and a big window box of plastic flowers.

"This is it," Frankie said to T. Roy. "Wow, what a color!" Number 365 was a double-wide and a startling shade of blue.

"It looks like a swimming pool," the boy said.

"It sure does," said Frankie. Frankie wondered if Lola had had it painted that color or bought it that way. Lola had always liked being noticed.

"Is that your mom's car?" T. Roy's eyes were wide.

"No, I think that's my sister's car."

The narrow driveway held two cars, an ancient black Buick convertible and a red Mazda Miata. Frankie parked a couple of houses down. She didn't want to be there yet.

T. Roy unbuckled his seatbelt behind her and slid over toward the passenger door.

"Let's wait a minute, okay?" Frankie said.

"Aren't you excited to see your mom?"

"It's been a long time. And I don't . . . we didn't. It's pretty complicated." She looked at him in the rearview mirror. "You probably wouldn't understand."

"I'm smarter than you think," the boy said.

"I'm sorry. I didn't mean to insult you. I think you're very smart. . . . Actually, I'm pretty scared." Frankie felt a sinking feeling. She'd been here less than five minutes and she was already trying to placate somebody. But it *was* complicated. To Roxie and other people she met, she'd made light of the distance she kept between her mother and her sister and herself. She'd pushed all of that down, way down, and even a couple of kindly therapists had been unable to unearth it. Now it threatened to spill out her throat. "Do you know about meditation?" She looked in the mirror again.

T. Roy shook his head.

"It's pretty simple. You sit still, close your eyes, and breathe. And you watch yourself breathe. It would help me to do that for a few minutes. Okay?"

He shrugged but closed his eyes. Frankie unclenched her hands from the wheel and closed hers. She let the waves of panic tighten her throat and grip her heart and sicken her stomach and the breathing helped and she came back into herself.

A loud rapping on the window next to her cheek made them both jump. She turned and looked directly into Callie's fury. Frankie popped the door locks and forced her sister to back up as she opened the door. She said nothing to her, just went around and moved the passenger seat forward so T. Roy could get out.

"Callie, this is T. Roy. T. Roy, this is my sister, Callie. Whatever happens, she isn't mad at you." And she took the boy by the hand and headed off down the street.

"Where the hell are you going?" Callie had to run to catch up with them.

"Watch your language, Callie. T. Roy doesn't need to hear that kind of talk. We've been driving for hours and we want to stretch our legs, don't we, T. Roy?"

"I guess," said the boy.

The trio walked in silence for a block although Frankie could have sworn she heard her sister's thoughts sputtering and sparking. She looked good, Callie did, photo-shoot good. Her hair was short but expertly styled, a shade of chestnut that really looked good on her. Her makeup was perfect as always. She wore tight jeans, a t-shirt of soft gold, and an embroidered denim vest. And high-heeled sandals that probably cost more than Frankie made in a month. She looked fabulous and Frankie felt fat and dowdy.

"How long has it been, Callie, since the wedding? Five years?"

"Four." Her sister looked over her shoulder. "What about Mom?"

"It's been twenty-eight years. A few more minutes won't matter," said Frankie. "I thought we might try to sort some things out. You could give me a report and all that before we go in."

"Okay, if that's what you want," said Callie. There was a sudden friendliness in her voice.

Her sister still had the two personalities, Frankie saw: the hot-headed tramp and the open child. *Or maybe she's just that way with me,* she thought. "Tell me about her," she said aloud.

"She has some kind of heart problem."

No kidding, thought Frankie.

"And her liver's not good. She doesn't talk about pain. Things just don't work very well and she gets tired quick. Who's the kid?"

"Later," said Frankie. "That's it? She gets tired?"

"And nauseated some of the time. She's lost some weight. She doesn't eat much. Just smokes and drinks endless quantities of vodka."

"She has a heart condition and smokes and she has a liver condition and drinks?"

Callie shrugged. "You know Mom."

"Yeah, I guess."

They had reached the little community hall and the boy pulled away from them to check things out. Frankie leaned against the chain-link fence that enclosed the pool.

"It doesn't sound too bad. Why have you been so miserable here?"

Callie looked at her sister. "She still has the viper's tongue."

Frankie shook her head and closed her eyes for a few seconds. All the years disappeared, and the full weight of her mother's scorn lay on her chest—the sarcasm, the belittling. No one crossed Lola without scars. She dragged herself back to the surface. "How much does she need?"

"I've got no idea what she lives on. I've had my hands full just staying out of her way," her sister said.

"You were coming here to find out what she needed." Frankie heard the bitchiness in her own voice.

"I know, I know. But it isn't that simple."

"Have you come up with any kind of plan?"

"I don't even have a plan for myself."

Frankie looked at her sister. She didn't know how to read what was going on. She had never known. She pulled back and kept her voice even. "Well, we need to figure out something. I'm staying only a couple of days. I have to deliver the boy to his family in Montana." That idea formed as she spoke it.

"Well, you're the planner. I'm the go-with-the-flow sister, remember?"

Frankie again felt the weight of the past on her. Then she nodded and moved toward the gate in the fence and called to the boy. "All right," she said to her sister. "I'll make the plan, I'll sort out the finances. But three days is all I'm promising. And we're not staying at the house with you. Not if she's smoking. I won't expose the boy to that." She looked at her sister.

Callie shrugged.

"How are you?" Frankie said. "How is Scott? When did you move to Pittsburgh? That seems an odd choice. Don't you all think that anything that isn't New York is the pits? No pun intended."

Callie looked away from her sister and over at T. Roy, who was half-climbing up the fence. "Scott and I are done."

"Oh," said Frankie. She looked at Callie but her face was unreadable. "Do you want to talk about it?"

"No, I don't."

"Okay." They stood silent a moment then, watching the boy, who'd found a stick and was running it along the fence.

"Who is he?"

"Who?" Frankie said.

"The kid. That kid right there."

"Just somebody I agreed to give a ride to."

"You and strays," Callie shook her head. "What a sucker you are!"

Now who's got the viper's tongue, Frankie wanted to say but she didn't. She felt sad and discouraged. She realized she had hoped for something different to happen but it was already the same. She took a deep breath and said, "Let's go. No sense putting this off any longer," and she headed down the street with her arm around the boy. She didn't look to see if Callie was following.

T. Roy raced ahead when he saw Frankie's Civic down the street. In a moment, he was back.

"Hey," he said. "Somebody stole your sports car." He was jumping up and down with the news.

"What the hell?" Callie took off with him although she was hobbled by the sandals. By the time Frankie caught up with them, Callie was coming out of the house. "That bitch. She got my keys and took my car."

"Mom?"

"Hell yes, Mom! Who else?"

"Obviously she shouldn't drive," said Frankie.

"Hell no, she shouldn't drive. She doesn't have the energy for it and she could conk out at any time. She feels faint sometimes, she has these spells. I don't care if the bitch kills herself but what if she kills somebody else? Or worse, wrecks my car."

"Okay, I get it. Watch the language. Where would she go?"

"Where would she go?" Callie looked at her sister. "That hasn't changed. Some place with vodka and men."

Frankie couldn't yet muster the urgency to chase after her mother. She looked at Callie a long moment and sighed. "She's got what, twenty, twenty-five minutes on us? Let's let her get where she's going and then we'll go and look for the car. Your car is easy to spot and it's not like the town is very big." She turned to the boy, who stood a little ways from them. "Let's go inside. I need the bathroom and maybe T. Roy does, too. Any milk and cookies in there, Callie?"

The boy grinned.

The moment she stepped in the door, Frankie regretted it. A pall hung in the air—old smoke, old cooking, and old stuff. The bathroom was clean—Callie had always been fastidious about that. But everywhere else was a shambles. Beds unmade in the rooms she passed, clothes on the floor, on the chairs, thrown wherever they'd been discarded. A full ashtray sat on a stack of *People* magazines. Next to it a half-dozen coffee cups, the milk scummed over.

She picked up a raggedy afghan that lay in a heap near the couch, folded it, and laid it across the back, then straightened the cushions.

"Still a neatnick, I see." Callie's voice held that ancient criticism.

"Yeah, I still like things tidy. How about you, T. Roy? Are you a tidy person or a messy person?"

The boy shrugged. He sat at the kitchen counter eating from a bag of chocolate chip cookies. The counter was littered with pop cans and beer cans, another ashtray, a heap of unopened mail, a plate with the remains of fried eggs and toast.

"Jesus, Callie," Frankie said. "You don't just give him the bag. Even I know that." She took the bag from the counter, got a small plate, put four cookies on it, and placed it in front of him after clearing a space. Then she opened the fridge, took out a half-gallon of milk, sniffed it, and poured him a glass.

She held up an empty can. "Recycling?"

"How would I know?" said Callie.

"Of course you wouldn't." Frankie sighed. She ran a sink full of hot, soapy water and filled it with dirty dishes. She drained the cans and put them into a paper bag. She found a big mixing bowl and put the mail in it for later. It felt good to do something after the inactivity of the long trip. But mostly she didn't want to talk to her sister, she didn't want to have to find their mother, and she didn't want all the old stuff to start up again.

Once Frankie had cleaned off the counter and scrubbed it down, Callie came over and sat next to T. Roy. "How did you meet Frankie?" she asked the boy.

T. Roy looked from one sister to the other. "Mrs. Louise gave me to her."

Callie frowned.

"We met in the Dalles," said Frankie. "It's a town on the way."

"I know what the Dalles is," said her sister. "I haven't forgotten everything."

Frankie shrugged. "T. Roy needed a ride and I needed company. That's the story."

"I'll bet," said Callie.

"Look," said Frankie, turning from the sink with a sponge in her hand. "My life is complicated. Your life is complicated. Let's just stay out of each other's business, okay? We'll sort out things for Mom, and you can go on to L.A. and T. Roy and I will move on as well."

Callie shrugged.

Frankie waited.

"Okay," said Callie. "It's none of my business."

"You're right," Frankie said. "It isn't." She wiped down the stove top.

There was quiet for several moments. Callie stood next to the boy, watching him eat the cookies. He took his time, small bites and sips of the milk. She fiddled with the stack of bracelets on her wrist, a jumble of gold, copper, and silver wire.

"You don't smoke anymore," Frankie said.

"No. Not since the wedding. Scott didn't like it and I never smoked all that much."

"Hasn't it been hard being around her smoking?"

"Actually, no. Well, sometimes. But she stinks of it. It's enough to turn anybody off." She fiddled with the bracelets again.

Frankie gave the stove top a last wipe and put the sponge in the sink. "You had enough, cowboy?" she said to T. Roy.

He nodded, drank down the last of the milk, and got down off the stool. Then he picked up the cookie plate and glass and came around and put them in the sink. Frankie and Callie looked at each other. Frankie smiled and Callie shook her head.

"Do you have any idea where she is?"

Callie shook her head again. "I've only been here two days. I know where the liquor store is and the grocery store. But we haven't gone out. Not as if we would. That's why I've been going so crazy."

"We could call the police."

"No." Callie's tone was so abrupt that Frankie looked at her. The trace of something hard and real sparked in her sister's eyes.

"We don't need the police," Callie said in a softer tone. "You said it. My car will be easy to spot. We can just drive around and check out the tavern parking lots."

"What about her neighbors?" said Frankie. "Any of them drinking buddies?"

"Hell if I know. Haven't met a one."

"I'll go ask." And Frankie picked up her bag and headed out the sliding door to the little porch. T. Roy was right behind her.

Neither next-door neighbor answered her knock, but across the street, Frankie saw curtains moving and she headed through a maze of gnomes, sleeping Mexicans, and black midget jockeys to another sliding glass door just like her mother's.

The man who came to the door must have been eighty. He was thin and frail, wispy, Frankie thought. But his eyes were sharp, dark points in his face. And his voice was amazingly rich and deep. "Can I help you, young lady? And young gentleman?" He smiled at T. Roy, who got shy and hung behind Frankie.

"I'm Frances Ashby," she said. "Your neighbor across the street, Lola, is my mother. She's taken off without telling us where she was going and we're worried. Her health isn't good. Do you know where she might have gone?"

"Lola's girl, huh? You want to come in?" He shuffled his way back from the door to let them enter.

But Frankie stayed outside. "No, thank you, sir. We're getting pretty worried. Any ideas? Any places she liked to go or that you went with her?"

"We never went out although I asked." His smile was almost shy and he suddenly looked decades younger. "But I'd see her car sometimes at the Jug, down on Silver Mountain Road."

"Thanks, you've been a big help." She took T. Roy by the hand and retraced their steps through the yard kitsch.

Callie was sitting on the couch when they got back. She'd taken off her sandals and was reading a magazine.

"Oh no, you don't," Frankie said.

"I'm not going to look for her."

"Oh yes, you are. I am not going into some tavern alone looking for a woman I haven't seen in decades to try to drag her home. I can't even be sure I'll recognize her."

"Oh, you will. Believe me, you will. She's still Lola."

T. Roy had gone back to the counter and was playing with the Transformers toy.

"Look, we're either in this together or the boy and I will move on."

"Oh, all right." Callie got up from the couch.

"Thank you. The quicker we get her settled and things sorted out, the quicker we can both leave."

The Jug was exactly that: a tall round brown building shaped like a jug. The building was ancient, paint flaking, the letters on the hand-painted sign fading into nothingness. But it was doing a lively business in the middle of the afternoon. The parking lot was full of shabby pickups and old sedans and a few newer SUVs. Around toward the back, out of sight of the street, was Callie's Miata. They parked next to it.

"Let's get this over with," said Callie.

"No," said Frankie. "You go get her. I'm not leaving T. Roy alone in the car in a tavern parking lot. I won't do that."

"But I . . ."

"Just go, Callie. Do what you need to do. We'll be here."

"Oh, fine! I'm getting all the dirty work in this deal." Callie slammed the door and they listened to her sandals crunch in the gravel.

Frankie turned the key and rolled down the windows. It was already getting hot and stuffy in the car. She breathed in the quiet. Her sister gave off something hard this time, something dark, something more than just East Coast edginess. She wondered what had happened between her and Scott. She'd only met him at the wedding, but she'd liked him.

"Why don't you like your mom?" T. Roy's voice startled her. She'd forgotten he was behind her.

"It's complicated."

"That's what all grownups say when they don't want to tell me something."

She shifted in her seat so she could see him. "Well, it *is* complicated. My mom wasn't a good mom. She wasn't around a lot and we had to take care of ourselves. Well, I had to take care of Callie. My mom wasn't a warm, hugging mom. Or somebody I could talk to about my . . . about being sad or when I was afraid. And I wanted her to be."

T. Roy's eyes were serious, solemn even, and he nodded. "Did your mom hit you?" he asked.

"No," said Frankie. "She never hurt me on the outside, just on the inside. Do you understand what I'm talking about?"

He frowned, then shook his head.

"That's okay. See, it is complicated." She stretched her arm out and patted his shoulder. "Did your mom hit you?"

T. Roy bit his lip and looked out the window.

"No need to say anything," Frankie said. "Some things are private, right?"

He gave a tiny nod and she felt a deep stab of pain for them both.

They were quiet then and a moment later they could hear crunching in the gravel and Callie appeared. Alone. She leaned into the window. "She won't come. She's drinking and playing cards with two old guys. They'll drive her home."

Frankie shook her head and sighed.

"What?" said Callie. "Frankie, she's . . . she's impossible. You go in and talk to her."

"No. Did you get your keys at least?"

Callie held them up.

"Okay. You go home or do whatever you want and we'll go find a motel and get settled. We'll come back over after dinner."

"I . . ." Callie looked at Frankie.

She nodded. "Okay. Just follow us and we'll all have some dinner and then go back to Mom's."

Callie smiled in relief and got in her car.

In Kellogg, there were two motel choices: the Guesthouse Inn & Suites and the Silver Mountain Lodge. No Motel 6, No Day's Inn, no Holiday Inn Express. The Guesthouse was really the only option, although she groaned when the clerk told her the room rate. "We do have a pool and a fitness center," the girl said brightly. "Your son will like that."

"And there's no place else in town?"

"There are two motels in Wallace," she said. "Would you like me to call and see if they have a room?"

"How far is that?"

"About twelve miles."

"No, we'll take a room here. We'd like to be on the top floor, facing away from the street, and not near the elevator." Frankie put her credit card on the counter and filled out the registration form. She took the keys, then turned back. "Is there someplace we can buy a swimsuit for the boy?"

"There's a shop over at the lodge. They're on sale 'cause it's end of season. I got this great two-piece just last Saturday. It's yellow . . ." She stopped. "I'm sure you'll find something there."

So Frankie sent T. Roy and Callie off for a suit and she took their bags up to the third-floor room. It was quiet there and when she opened the drapes, the picture window looked out onto the hills in the distance.

She made a cup of tea, got a large chocolate bar out of the stash in her suitcase, and pulled a chair in front of the window. Her mind was racing with her need to work and make some money, her desire to get things over with her mom, and sorting out what to do with the boy. She yearned for the simple life she had left behind of cats and work and only herself to worry about.

She finished the chocolate, then wrapped her hands around the warm cup and settled them on her lap. She closed her eyes and let her mind go to the breath, to a mantra of safety. "All is well. I am well. All things are well."

She had about thirty minutes of peace before Callie and the boy came back. T. Roy was excited about going swimming and went into the bathroom to change.

"What do I owe you for the suit?" she asked her sister.

"It's on me. He's sweet, kind of like having a little brother."

"Not exactly," said Frankie.

"Tell me about him."

"No, look, there's nothing to tell. I'm doing his grandmother a favor and giving him a ride to Montana. That's all."

"Bullshit, Frankie. I always know when you're lying."

Frankie looked at her sister. "Okay. Let's take him down to the pool and we can sit and I'll tell you the story."

"Oh good," Callie said. "I love a good story."

So while T. Roy swam and played with two little girls who were in the pool—sometimes calling over to Frankie with "Watch me! Watch me!"—she told Callie about Mrs. Louise and the rest stop and the photos and the address in Montana. She didn't tell her about the money or the gun in T. Roy's bag.

"You know this is all preposterous, don't you?" said Callie. "How are you going to find his mother with a couple of photos and an address?"

"What's your advice then? Give him to the police? Put him in the system?"

"No, no, of course not. We can't do that."

"That's right. We didn't let anybody do that to us. And it's not going to happen to T. Roy."

"You could just keep him, raise him yourself."

"He's not a puppy, Callie. He's a boy and he wants his mother."

They were quiet a moment and watched him play with the little girls.

"Did you and Scott ever talk about having kids?" Frankie asked her sister.

"Only when we decided to get married. I told him I wasn't doing that, not for him, not for anybody."

"Why not?"

"It's a full-time job. Even I can see that. I don't want to spend my life doing that." She looked at Frankie. "Our folks had the right idea. Let somebody else raise your kids."

Frankie waited for Callie to ask her about her own desire for a child but she didn't and then the moment passed. "Do you ever miss the farms?" she said.

Callie shrugged. "I have some good memories, especially of the Landing. Remember going to the beach with Charlie? I liked Charlie. I liked having other kids to play with. I liked running wild. Guess I got started early, huh?" She smiled. "What about you? Fond memories?"

Frankie shook her head. "Not so much of the Landing. I loved Eiderdown. I loved living with Dewey and Snow. And Cassie." She looked over at her sister, wondering if the name would upset her, but Callie just nodded. "I liked having a big family."

"It was certainly an antidote to Lola."

"That it was." She looked at her watch and sighed. "We've got to talk about money."

"I'm sorry I haven't been through Mom's papers."

"That's okay. We can do that tonight or tomorrow. But what if there isn't any? Can you and Scott give her any? Send something every month?"

"I told you there isn't any Scott anymore." Callie kept her eyes on the kids in the pool.

"Oh, yes, sorry. You sure you don't want to talk about it?"

Her sister shook her head. She looked grim.

"Is he giving you a settlement? Do you get the house?"

"No." She looked away from Frankie and over at the kids in the pool. "I have some money of my own. I'm going to find some-place to work and start over."

"But I thought you and Scott were pretty comfortable. You had that big house and those cars and well, we ate out a lot when I was there and you guys seemed to live pretty well."

"We did, but well, the money is just gone and the house and everything. He made a bad investment. That's why we moved to Pittsburgh. To start over. But it didn't work." She looked at Frankie. "So I don't have enough for Mom, too."

Frankie sat and thought a moment. "The problem is I don't either. I get enough work to support myself and save a little for the future or an emergency but not enough to support her as well. Even if I wanted to."

"You mean you don't want to?"

Frankie looked at her sister. "Do you?"

A while later, Frankie went down to a pizza place a block from the motel and picked up dinner, leaving Callie to get T. Roy showered. When she got back, Callie was watching TV and T. Roy was asleep on the bed.

"Did he shower?"

"Yes, but he didn't want to get dressed. He wanted his pajamas."

"No big deal. What he needs comes first."

They ate the food, both of them complaining and compar-ing it to Portland and New York and pizzas they had known and loved. They laughed for the first time together and that felt good.

Frankie was tempted to ask again about Scott and maybe talk about her own disasters with men, but she didn't know how and so she let the moment pass.

When she'd had all the TV noise and Callie's company she could stand, she started cleaning up. "It doesn't look like we're going over there tonight. Why don't you head on back and we'll come over right after breakfast."

"I'd rather stay here with you." Callie suddenly looked fourteen again.

Frankie smiled at her. "Yeah, I know but I have to work and you'll be bored here. You can't watch TV and there'll be nothing for you to do. At her place, you can watch TV or, even better, go through her papers. See if you can find bank statements, tax receipts, her mortgage, anything that can give us a clue about what she lives on."

"I don't like it there. I could sleep with T. Roy or on this little couch. And I'll bet you have a book I could read. You always have books. I'll be quiet. You won't even know I'm here."

Frankie tried to find that hard place in her heart that would help her hold her ground, but she couldn't. "Okay," she said and she rummaged in her suitcase and handed her sister three paperbacks. Then she went down to the lobby, found a quiet corner, and worked until midnight.

CALLIE

Fall 1987

The new espresso place was two blocks from the hotel. It was crowded but then a window table opened up and Callie took it. She was early and she watched the couples reading the Sunday *Seattle Times*, munching their scones and sipping their fancy drinks. None of them were her age or even in their twenties. These were old couples in their forties.

Bill had wanted her to be a couple with him like that. Their first Sunday in town, they had come here and ordered cappuccinos and blueberry muffins and he had bought a paper and wanted to sit and read the sports section. The sports section! She'd hung on for twenty minutes, read the comics, tried to do the Jumble. Then she'd left him there and gone back to the hotel and turned on the TV. She hadn't run away with him to Seattle to do old people stuff.

The boy came in then, a scrawny guy in a Huskies hoodie and jeans. He didn't look for her, just got in line. He waited patiently for his turn, a guy just waking up, scratching his scraggly beard, adjusting his jeans.

"Share your table?" he said.

She went along. "Sure, have a seat."

He tore the bag of pastries open and pushed them toward her. "Want one?"

She looked at them, then at him. Then she nodded and tore the maple bar in half and ate hungrily.

"Those are my favorites, too," he said.

She stopped mid-bite and looked at him.

"I didn't mean anything," he said. "I was just saying. Eat whatever you want." She nodded and finished the maple bar, licking the frosting from her fingers. She watched him to see if this had any effect—it had a big effect on Bill—but this guy wasn't looking at her.

A few minutes went by. He sipped his drink. Callie got up and went over to the water jug on the counter and poured herself a glass. When she got back to the table, he was reading the paper. She felt a surge of impatience. She didn't have all day.

"How about we do this?" she said.

"We're already doing it. Sit back down." His voice was low, and its steadiness surprised her. He handed her the thick ad section. "In a couple of minutes, put what you have for me inside the paper and pass it over. I'll do the same." He sipped at his coffee and went on looking at the paper.

She nodded and sat down. Under the table, Callie pulled the bills from her pocket and slipped them into the ads. Then she folded the pages and handed them to him, and he handed her the front section. She didn't feel anything different in it. She wondered if he was going to rip her off, but then she opened the paper casually and saw the envelope and all of a sudden it was fine. She felt like a spy or something. She felt like they were pulling something off. She smiled and he took it as a smile for him and he smiled back. She counted out 120 seconds and then she put the paper with the new birth certificate in her backpack and headed back to the hotel.

Bill had hung around her neck for three weeks. He wasn't a bad guy. Old, a bit paunchy no matter how many sit-ups he did every morning. She didn't mind old, and he had money, he liked sex, he would do what she wanted. He was much better in bed than his son had been and he knew how to show her a good time. Nice restaurants, a good hotel, new clothes. It was the talk about marriage that depressed her. About divorcing his wife, about them settling down in one of the high rises they were building in the Pearl or maybe a house out in Tigard.

"But I don't want to live in Portland. I don't ever want to go back there," Callie had said. She stood in front of the bathroom mirror, lining her eyes with a soft brown to make the blue stand out. Her long red hair fell down her back.

"But baby, that's where my business is. That's where all this money comes from."

"I don't care. I'm not going back to Portland. You can if you want to."

"Don't you want to be with me?"

"Not in Portland. That's a hick town, a dump. I'm moving on, not back. How about Alaska? Couldn't you do your work in Alaska? Or maybe New York?"

He shook his head. He was standing at the window looking down at the street. "You don't understand what it takes to get a business going."

She looked at him in the mirror. "Of course I don't. I'm a kid. But I'm not going back to Portland. I'm done there."

He looked at her then and she smiled her best smile, the cute, charming one, and he smiled back and said, "We'll figure something out."

But he didn't. And then the phone calls started or maybe they'd been going on the whole time. The wife would call in the early morning or late in the evening, and Callie left the room, went into the bathroom and turned on the water or went down to the ice machine on the next floor, but she heard enough to know that Bill had not told his wife that he was leaving her, heard enough to know that she was expecting him to come home from this "business" trip, heard enough to know that Bill was playing them both. And she said nothing, glad that it wouldn't go on much longer and she'd really be free.

And then they were lying in bed together, sex just over, and he said, "I'm going back. Today. My wife isn't doing well without me. And Hank . . ."

Callie was already out of bed, pulling on her clothes. She turned on her best livid. "You think Hank is going to welcome you back? Not the Hank I know." She waited a beat and then turned to see the effect.

Bill looked stricken.

She eased her face into sympathetic. "But I guess it's worth a try. But I'm not going back. I told you that."

"But I'll feel terrible leaving you here. I . . ."

"You did promise you'd take care of me, Bill. That's why I left with you." She turned on sad.

"I know I did. And in Portland . . ."

"Bill, I'm not going to Portland. How many times do I have to tell you?"

"Okay, I get it. Let me see what I can do."

"Okay," she said, smiling at him. "I know you'll figure out something. I'll go get coffee. Blueberry muffin? Orange juice?"

He nodded. She kissed him on her way out.

She was gone a good while. She walked down to the water and then wandered through Pike Market. When she got back to the hotel, he was gone and so were his things. He'd left an envelope of cash and a note. "The hotel is paid through the end of the month. Use room service. And this should get you started. I love you, Callie. I always will. Your sweetheart, Bill." Nine hundred dollars and a nice place to stay for two weeks. Not a bad start.

She met Jimmy a week after she got the birth certificate. She'd been hanging out with some street kids who prowled Pike Market, selling drugs, shoplifting, what they called "scrounging." Several of the boys wanted to hook up with her but she held back. She was careful not to carry much of the money on her and she told no one about the hotel room. She didn't trust them and she hadn't decided what she was going to do next.

Jimmy was sitting in a booth in a coffee bar at the market with two of the girls from the scroungers, and they were laughing and flirting with him. The only place to sit was next to him so he slid over. "I'm Jimmy," he said, holding out his hand and smiling at her in a way that said he saw her. He wasn't good-looking. His nose had been broken and sat a little crooked on his face. A thin pale scar ran across one cheek. His brown hair was thin and long, very long, pulled back into a ponytail. But his cheek bones and eyes looked Native American to her. She shook his hand and there was something in the grip, in the warmth, that made her relax.

Jimmy was full of funny stories. He managed a band that worked the cruise ships up and down the West Coast. The guys in the band were in their thirties, like Jimmy, and not very original—he chuckled when he said this—so they made their living playing golden oldies for the seniors who took the cruises. They got free room and board and decent pay, and it was a steady gig. "Two of the guys are really into sex, I mean big time," he said, "and there's plenty of that on board, too. All those lonely widows and unsatisfied housewives."

"What about you, Jimmy?" It was the first time Callie had spoken. "Are you into those lonely widows too?"

"Nope," he said. "I have a sweetheart here in Seattle and I am faithful to her."

"Aaaah," the other girls said in chorus.

Suckers, thought Callie. She hadn't met a man yet who wasn't interested in a cheerleader skirt and knee-highs. She eased out of the booth then.

"Going so soon?" Jimmy said, smiling that same I-see-you smile at her.

"Things to do." Callie smiled back. She liked him. There was something easy and familiar about him.

"See you around then," he said and turned back to the others.

Two days later he was there alone. It was as though he were waiting for her. They drank coffee, ate doughnuts. She spun him a story about an abusive stepdad, a smothering mother in Northern California. About hitchhiking north to find something better. A good job, maybe a chance to do some modeling or acting. She made it all up on the spot, watching his reactions.

"I admire your ambition," he said. "Modeling, acting, those are hard roads to travel. But you've got the looks for it." He offered her a cigarette, lit hers and his. He didn't laugh when she coughed up smoke, left the rest of it in the ashtray. He just smiled at her. "Is there much of that happening here in Seattle?"

"I don't know. I haven't been here all that long. Eventually I want to go to New York but I'd rather go with some connections and some money. So I figured I'd put some money together here first."

"That sounds pretty smart. Do you have a decent place to stay?"

A red flag went off. "Why?" she said.

"Oh, I'm gone a lot and I need somebody to watch out for my sweetheart. The last guy neglected her. Really pissed me off. And I was thinking you could stay there. While I'm gone. There's plenty of room and you could even stay there when I'm in town, but I wouldn't want you to be uncomfortable."

Callie was perplexed. She couldn't read him. He wasn't coming on to her. He seemed straight enough but he was almost too straightforward. Most guys weren't. She nodded. "I've got a place for another few days. Until the end of the month actually. So yeah, I might be interested. Would there be rent? I'm not working yet."

"No, if you watched out for my girl, that would be fine. Would you like to meet her?"

"Sure, I guess." She still felt cautious.

So they took off, walking north out of the commercial area around the Market and up into a more residential section. Jimmy chatted about his next cruise. He'd be gone nearly six months, south through the Panama Canal and into the Mediterranean.

"Wow! I thought you just went back and forth to Alaska."

"In the summer we do. That's our main gig and why we mostly live here. But in the winter, we take these longer cruises 'cause the money is so much better. With nothing to spend it on, we're socking it away."

"That's my goal, too," she said.

They soon came to an old Victorian with a view of the harbor. It sat up on its lot, two dozen steps to the front porch. At one time it had been purple and orange and yellow but all that had weather-faded now to gray. The lawn was mostly weeds.

"Home sweet home," Jimmy said.

"Do you own this?"

"I wish. Even in such shitty shape, the old girl is worth a fortune. No, I rent the downstairs." He unlocked the ornate wood door and gave a little bow. "Welcome to my castle, little girl."

Callie lived in the sparsely furnished rooms of the castle all that winter and spring. Jimmy's sweetheart was an African Gray parrot named Trudie. Every time she came into the room, it gave an appreciative whistle that made her laugh, and it would call out two phrases from time to time—"Hey there, matey!" and "Goddamn!"

Shortly after Jimmy left on the big cruise, she got a job as a cocktail waitress in a hotel bar near the Market. Her world became the castle and the job and the kids at the Market, who didn't understand why she bothered to work. She soon gave up trying to explain her dreams. She began to believe she was older than them, twenty-two like the new birth certificate said.

There was also extra money to be made on the job. The men who stayed alone at the hotel flirted with her, left room cards with their tips. She'd known men paid for sex but she'd had no idea so many of them would. She was tempted from the get-go. She wanted to go to New York with $10,000. She still had some of the money Bill had left her, but it was going to take a lot of $5 tips to get that much. Yet something in her held back. It wasn't anything romantic that made her hesitate. She didn't believe in love and she was unsentimental about her body. She was grateful she had a good one and planned to use it to full advantage. And that was what made her hold back. What was the full advantage?

One night, two of the customers were rowdy and grabby, insisting she party with them in their room. The bartender Steve came to her rescue and eventually the men quieted down and left.

Steve was a handsome guy in his early fifties, thick reddish hair, cowboy jaw. After closing, he poured them both coffee and sat her down at the bar. Callie liked Steve but she didn't like advice and she was pretty sure that was what was coming. She sat on the edge of the stool.

Steve laughed. "This isn't what you think it is, Callie. I'm not going to fire you."

She looked at him. "I didn't think you were going to fire me. I think you are going to give me advice."

She was surprised to see him blush. "That obvious, huh? I just want to be sure you know what you're doing. I want you to be smart. There are a lot of mean men. I know. I've been with my share. Until I met Lyle, of course." Lyle was Steve's boyfriend. He showed up at the end of the shift each night and walked home with Steve.

"Well, I'm not going to be sleeping with gay men."

"Gay men don't have any lock on meanness. And many, many more men are bisexual than you think. Or maybe they're just sexual, looking for it anywhere they can." He took a sip of his coffee and poured a little more bourbon into it. He pushed the bottle her way but she shook her head.

He didn't say anything more for a moment and she grew impatient. "So how do I be smart?" she said at last.

"Go with the quiet ones. The gentle ones. You know who they are. They come in alone. They're more polite than charming. They're shy. Introverts. Do you know any introverts?"

She nodded. "My sister, Frankie. She'd rather read than go to a party. A real stick."

"Exactly. Those are the guys you want to flirt with. They will be generous because they will be grateful. You'll be a fantasy come true rather than just another roll in the hay."

"Any other advice, old wise one?"

"Don't sell yourself cheap. Figure out what you're willing to do and what you want for it. Like a menu. And don't do anything you don't want to do, no matter how much money is in it."

"Teaching the pup the ropes?" Lyle had come up behind them. He walked around the bar and poured himself a diet coke. "Telling her about the plague?"

"Lyle, we don't know that."

"Tell her anyway."

"What plague?" Callie didn't like the sound of this.

"Callie, honey, there are a lot of STDs. Do you know what those are?"

"Of course."

"Well, there's a pretty bad one circulating. Mostly among gays. But bisexual men are going to be passing it to women. Just don't go with anybody who won't wear a condom."

"And that includes blow jobs," said Lyle. "And kissing."

"Okay, okay, I get it," said Callie. "I'll be careful."

And she was. Slowly the money piled up and, during the days, she went around to Seattle's few modeling and acting agencies and she got good photos taken and lost enough weight to get a few department store gigs and a little photo work in ads for Metro Transit. At five-foot-nine, she wasn't really tall enough to model, but her wasp waist, full breasts, and long curly red hair were distinctive, and she traded on all that everywhere she went.

Summer 1988

Callie woke up to the sunlight streaming into the room from the half-open curtains. She had thought there'd be portholes, but there were windows just like in a regular room. It took her a moment to figure out where she was. This room had a glass door out onto the sea, so it wasn't Jimmy's cabin on Deck 1 or her own windowless room on Deck 5. She rolled back away from the light and the man was there, asleep on the other half of the bed. He lay on his back, his jaws clenched and grinding. His left arm was flung out against the wall as if he were holding it up. The light caught the silver hairs on his chest, and for a brief moment, he looked more interesting than he was.

Callie moved away from him and got up. There was cold water in the ice bucket and she drank it down. Pot didn't have much effect on her but it made her awfully thirsty. There was still bourbon and a little vodka and she poured herself a glass of those, too. Then she pulled her clothes on—the little pleated skirt, the sweater two sizes too small—and went out onto the veranda with the drink. The breeze was brisk and cool, the ocean sparkling in the early morning summer. She stood a moment watching the land go past in the distance, a house from time to time. Nothing much, nothing interesting. Lots of evergreen trees. Just like Portland, just like Seattle. *What made it Alaska?* she wondered.

She went back into the cabin as quietly as she could. The old man went on sleeping. He'd left the cash on her purse. She counted it out, $400, and she put $250 in her bra and the rest in the front pocket of the silver chain bag. She took the pack of cigarettes from the table as well and then slipped out into the hallway, deserted around four a.m., and made her way downstairs.

Her cabin wasn't nearly as nice. Twin beds pushed together, barely enough room to walk around. Curtains on the wall to give the illusion of a window. But it was quiet and blissfully dark and she spent a good part of each day sleeping. She showered, then pulled on real clothes—jeans, a t-shirt. She thought about packing everything up. Then she wouldn't have to come back to the ship if they wanted her to stay. Then again, it might be easier to just take her backpack. She could always talk them into getting her new clothes.

She checked the clock: 5:10. She could go up to the Lido and get coffee and something to eat. She had time to kill. They weren't letting people off the ship until 8:30. And in the Lido, she was bound to see Jimmy and she could give him his share of the money. She wanted that to be square between them before she left.

In early May, Jimmy had come home for a couple of weeks. And she asked him for the favor she'd been thinking about. "Any way you could smuggle me aboard on a trip to Alaska this summer?"

He looked up at her. "Whatever for? Cruises aren't all they're cracked up to be. You feeling the need to go on a trip?"

"Not exactly but you make it sound like fun. And I've got a friend who lives in Juneau and I'd like to visit her."

"Hmmm. I might be able to swing it. We haven't had a hair and makeup girl for the band in a long time. But you'd have to come for the whole summer, not just one cruise."

Callie shook her head. "I only want to go once. I don't want to quit the bar. I like working there. Besides, who would look after Trudie? No, I just want to go once. Like on vacation. Is it expensive? Maybe you could get me a discount?"

"It's pretty expensive, even for the cheapest rooms. But we do get a family discount. Let me talk to my boss."

Jimmy made it happen. In early August, there was a cancellation on an inside room and the band put their comps together for her because Jimmy asked them to, so it didn't cost her anything except taxes. So here she sat in the Lido on Deck 9 in the early July morning. In the time it had taken her to shower, the ship had arrived in Juneau. She could see the city center, if you could call it that, ahead of her. She hadn't known what to expect, but she had expected more than this—more than a few brick buildings, a few shops, a few taverns. Not a high-rise in sight. She took her coffee and wandered to the other side of the ship. On the other bank, there were sparse houses, something that might have been a sawmill, some warehouse buildings. No doubt about it: this was a dump. She would have to revise her plans.

"Daydreaming of making your fortune? I'm afraid the era of horny miners is long gone."

She turned and smiled at Jimmy. "It's not much of a town."

"No, though actually most of the people are really friendly. Or they pretend to be anyway. They need the money we bring them." He sat down at the table with his coffee.

"You're up incredibly early," she said.

"Nope. Haven't been to bed yet. Poker."

"Did you do well?"

"Most excellent. And I lined you up a couple more dates, if you want them."

Callie felt a surge of annoyance. Not with Jimmy. He was only doing what she had asked him to. The pimping had been her idea. She was closing in on the ten grand for New York and why not do some vacationing seniors? More gratitude, more money. Win, win. No, the disappointment was in her plan to stay in Juneau. She shook it off. "Sure, who and when?"

He handed her a slip of paper. She glanced at it, put it in her little bag, and then handed him his share from the night before.

He pocketed it without looking at it. "Shall I get us some breakfast?" he said.

"Sure, why not?"

Callie was one of the first off the boat. It was going to be a beautiful day, the air cool and clean. She had left her backpack behind. No point in taking it; she couldn't live here. She pulled out the little map of the town that had come with the ship's Juneau brochure, but she didn't see the street she needed. She wandered over to the row of buses awaiting the passengers doing excursions. A handsome kid smiled at her.

"Going on the rainforest hike?" he said with a big smile.

"No, I'm looking for this address."

He took the old envelope. "Yeah, I know where this is."

"Can I get a cab there? Or maybe you could drop me off." She pulled out coy.

He smiled at her. "You don't need a ride. See that big brick building?" He pointed up the hill. "Take the street in front of it up three blocks, then turn right. That's the street. Just keep climbing. It's maybe two blocks or so further on up."

She chatted him up for a few minutes. It was good to see someone her own age. But she knew she was just putting off what she needed to do and she needed to go early just in case. In case of what she wasn't sure, but she needed to go early.

She climbed the steep hill. The shops were all below in the flat part of town. Convenient for the aging tourists. Up here there were law offices, a lot of them. She passed a real estate office, a dentist, then turned the corner and climbed up into a sort of residential area. She had always imagined they lived in a log cabin, but the address turned out to be a shabby green four-plex and the apartment number was up an outer staircase that was none too solid.

She knocked on the door and waited. She could hear a radio inside, the drone of a male voice giving the news or a traffic report or the weather. She knocked again.

Then the door opened. Dark hair going gray, thinning on top, a mustache with streaks of dark. A lined face. Taller than she had imagined, maybe six feet. Thin except for the paunch. Like any one of her johns, she thought.

He was talking over his shoulder. And when he turned to look at her, his eyes went wide and he dropped the coffee cup in his hand. It didn't break but coffee splashed over his legs and he jumped back. They both looked down at the mess and then at each other. "Holy shit," he said finally.

"Who is it?" a woman called from deep in the apartment. Now Callie was surprised, too, for it wasn't Lola's voice. A wave of disappointment swept over her and she realized that that was really who she had come to see.

The man stared at her. She stared back. Finally, he said, "You look so much like her. Like when I first met her. You're thinner, taller, but so much the same. I can't get over it."

"Who is it?" the woman's voice approached, a tinge of impatience riding on it.

"It's my daughter," John Blalock said.

Callie stayed two hours. Blalock called his work and said he'd be late. The woman, Margo, left for her own job after ten minutes of wary curiosity. Then it was just the two of them and neither one knew what to do. Callie had a list of questions in her head, but now they seemed meaningless so she told him about living in Los Angeles, studying pre-med. Her black boyfriend who played college ball and hoped to make it to the Lakers. Only the cruise ship part of it was true, and then only sort of. A friend had gotten her a ticket. He was with the entertainment crew. She'd come on a lark, remembered he lived here.

"I can't get over how much you look like her," he said again.

Callie shrugged.

"You don't remember her, do you?"

"No. I've seen some pictures of you and her and Lola, but it doesn't mean anything. I only remember Lola and Frankie and the Landing."

"She was a wonderful person."

Callie looked at him. "I got Lola instead."

Guilt, shame, pain crossed his face and she was glad.

"I was a wreck after the accident, Callie. I was no good for anything."

"So you say. But you could have pulled yourself together, seen a shrink, I don't know. You just . . . you just left me with her."

The pain stayed in his eyes and she watched it, encouraged it.

He got up and went into the kitchen with his cup. She heard the cupboard open, the sound of a lid off, then on, and he came back. A faint odor of whiskey wafted up from the cup when he set it on the scarred coffee table.

"I'll have some of that, too," she said, standing up.

They looked at each other. He tilted his head and just like that she knew who he was. "First cupboard next to the stove."

She went into the kitchen, went through the same motions, but it was only coffee she poured in her cup. When she came back in, she didn't sit again, rather leaned against the kitchen doorway.

"Where's Lola?" It was time to put the other elephant on the coffee table.

He said nothing, just looked at his coffee, then at her.

"She was here, right? You married her, right?" Callie felt close to tears and it surprised her.

He shrugged.

"Right?"

"Yeah," he said finally. "She was here. We got married."

"And? Where is she?"

More pain crossed his face. "I don't know. She got restless. Eight months, give or take. That was all there was. She got restless. I loved her and it didn't matter."

Callie's tears had evaporated. They had been replaced by a deep sense of relief. It wasn't her fault that Lola had left her and Frankie, for Lola had left him, too. Lola was a leaver. Callie was also glad. Glad that this man who had abandoned her had been abandoned as well. And she was glad that he was weak, weak and pitiful. That way she didn't have to love him.

Fall 1993

The Village loft was crowded, the party in full swing by the time Jonathan got off the damn cell phone and they got out of the car. Forty minutes Callie had sat there while he blathered on. His phone calls were never interesting. They were always about money and people she didn't know. Now she'd be too late to make a big entrance, the whole point in coming, to have the right person see her walk, see her carry the dress in her original way. And it was a great dress. Tight in the right places, full in the right places. Just the shade of red to set off her long hair and her pale, pale skin. She looked like a million bucks. But then so did everyone else.

Now the room was so crowded that no one would see. Dozens of people huddled together with drinks and that fake laughter they'd all perfected. Jonathan immediately saw someone he knew, asked her for a scotch, as if she was the waitress. She shook her head, then shrugged and made her way to the bar. She ordered a double scotch and a club soda for herself, but when she turned back with the drinks, he'd been swallowed up by the crowd.

As she scanned the room, Callie's eyes caught those of a drop-dead gorgeous boy about her age. He was watching her, she knew it. She smiled, not too coy, just cute enough, and then scanned the room again. No sign of Jonathan. Her eyes came back to the boy.

He was still watching, an odd little smile playing on his perfect lips. *Bemused*, that was the word for it, she thought, a word she'd learned from the *New Yorker*. He was bemused and beautiful. The requisite cheekbones, a straight slim nose, a good jaw, those lips, all in perfect proportion. His eyes were dark, smudged across the arched bone above by dark brows. Silky blond hair, too long for business, too short for an actor. He wore the loose charcoal silk jacket and slim trousers like a second skin. *One of us*, she thought, moving in his direction.

"Want a scotch?" She held out the glass. "My date has disappeared into the throng." Another *New Yorker* word.

He shook his head and smiled again. "No, but I can find someone who does so you don't have to hold the glass." He took it from her, stepped over to a cluster of women, and returned without it.

"Dare," he said, putting his hand out to her.

She looked at him for a moment, then took the hand, and said, "Truth."

He laughed. It was an odd laugh, musical and almost girlish. Then he said, "Let's try it another way." He pointed to himself and said, "Dare." Then he pointed to her.

Now she laughed. "Callie. Your name is Dare? Really?"

He shrugged. "It's Darryl. But it was too gay for St. Louis. Hell, it's too gay for New York."

"And you're not gay."

He tilted his head. "I can be if you want."

"What?"

"Lots of New York women want only gay friends."

"Well, I don't. Do you model?"

He nodded. "Gay strike number 2. I wanted to be an actor but I am who I am. I just couldn't be somebody else, even for money."

She laughed again, longer this time.

"What's so funny?" he said.

"I just never heard it described quite like that. And I'm somebody else for money all the time."

He smiled and she was charmed even more. "Been in anything I'd have seen?" he said.

"What? No, nothing you'd have seen. How about you? Been in anything lately?"

"I shot a *Vogue* spread about a month back. Looks like they might use one or two."

"Wow! I'd kill to be in *Vogue*."

"Let's hope it doesn't come to that." He grinned at her.

It took her a second to get it. Then she grinned back and something in her opened up and they were connected. Just like that. She moved a little closer to him, shifted her angle so that they were side by side to see how that felt. From this vantage point they watched the crowd, no more need to talk.

"Callie." Jonathan stood before them. He was a short, stout man, more fifty than forty. Thinning gray hair, clean shaven. The tailored suit was impeccable, but for all that there was something rumpled about him. Or maybe it was something unhealthy. "What happened to that scotch?"

"Hello, Jonathan. I got several of them but kept giving them away. I couldn't find you in this throng."

He looked at her, then tapped his watch. "We're late. The car is waiting."

She looked at him, then at Dare, who tilted his head again and lifted his brows. She leaned in and kissed him on the cheek

and then followed the older man into the press of people and out
to the town car. It was well on into the early hours of the morning, but the streets were full of people. Light spilled from cafés
and restaurants, voices rang out against the cobblestones, taxis
slithered by on the wet streets. So different from sleepy Seattle
and even sleepier Portland.

The November cold hit them as they left the building but
Callie didn't shiver. She'd learned two things in her first months
in Manhattan. First, never wear a coat at night if you can help it.
No one will see the dress or, more importantly, you in it. Second,
a tab of speed is a marvelous thing. It could keep her awake all
night, it made food unappealing, and she never felt the cold.

Jonathan was sulking. He had turned away from her and was
looking out the window. She liked him least like this. The anger
she could deflect, the desires she could manage. But when he
pouted, an impenetrable wall came up and there was no room for
her and she needed there to be. She leaned lightly against him, to
let him know she was there, but she didn't talk. That wasn't how
to do it.

They drove uptown. She felt a vague hope that he would
change his mind, just want to get a hotel room, but they pulled up
in front of the tall apartment building a few blocks from Central
Park and the driver ushered them out.

"Come back at six," Jonathan said to the driver, and Callie
flipped the inner switch that would let it all happen.

Jonathan handed the invitation card and fifty bucks to the
doorman, who let them in and turned the penthouse key in the
elevator. Callie used the gleam of the chrome walls to freshen her
lipstick and blusher. Her curls had grown wild with the damp of
the night air but they would have to do.

The elevator opened into a foyer of marble floors and purple tulips. *Impeccable*. It was another of her favorite new words.

They followed the laughter and jazz saxophone into a wide living room of white leather furniture and an astonishing view of the city. Five old guys, six beautiful young women. *The way the world works*, thought Callie. Two of the men she recognized from the time before. One was Richard. She didn't know any of the women, wondered if they knew what lay ahead.

The speed was making her jangly so she had a vodka tonic, then another. The men talked money, sports, cars as though the women didn't exist. In ones and twos, the women wandered off to the bathrooms. Their eyes were different when they came back. Coke, maybe something stronger even. Callie didn't do any of that. She stuck to the speed, an occasional drink, or something to help her sleep.

When the clock rang three, the bowl went around. Some ritual from the seventies, Jonathan had explained. Only instead of car keys, they used credit cards. Callie made a wish, picked a card. G. Elson. Someone she didn't know. Good. She'd had Richard once but never wanted that again. There was a deep ugly meanness in him. The kind of man that Steve, the bartender, had warned her about.

She went first, wanting to get it over with and not wanting to be part of a threesome. "Mr. Elson," she called out, and a fat man with a waistcoat and goatee looked like he'd won an Academy Award. He beamed at the others and followed her into the bedroom to the right of the fireplace.

"You're very beautiful," he said as he unzipped her dress.

"And you're very . . ." she searched for a word that would work, "distinguished."

He beamed again.

She sat on the bed and held out her hand. He reached out his but it was empty and she pulled hers back.

"Ah," he said, and took out an envelope from his jacket.

She smiled, took the envelope, and put it under her dress, which she had thrown across the wing-backed chair in the corner.

"Now," she said, "what would you like?"

Very ordinary things, it turned out. Very ordinary things. By four, he was sound asleep and she took a shower, got dressed, and went out into the living room. It was empty, only a thin blanket of cigar smoke and perfume to show for the night. In the dining room, a feast was set out. Fresh fruit, warm bagels, scrambled eggs and bacon in chafing dishes. She wanted to tell somebody that she knew where *chafing* came from, that it had nothing to do with skin rubbing skin but was from *chauffer*, the French word for warming. She was working her way through old copies of *Reader's Digest*, learning new words all the time. But there was no one around, not a sound in the place. She pulled strawberries and pineapple from the bowl with her fingers, ate scrambled eggs with the serving spoon, let herself have one piece of bacon.

The elevator opened at the press of her finger and she rode down in silence. There was a cab waiting at the entrance and the night doorman refused her tip with a smile.

The apartment was quiet, her roommates asleep. She put on pajamas, striped cotton. They'd been a gift from Steve and Lyle at the going-away party at the castle. The cloth had worn thin, but she was loathe to replace them. She hated the sentimental. That was Frankie's thing. Still, the kindness of that time was something she didn't want to let go of.

She made coffee and sat at the kitchen table with her date book. G. Elson had been very generous. Three thousand. The penthouse parties always got her two. Maybe he was rolling in it. Not hers to question. He had included a card with a phone number in blue ink. *Private line*, it said. Geoffrey. She hadn't known his first name until then. She toyed with the card for a moment, then slipped it into the pocket in the back of the organizer. Jonathan's interest in her was waning. It might soon be time to move on, and a generous man with ordinary desires would be a good step.

She looked at the day ahead. Her movement class wasn't until two. Then yoga. Then a manicure. Somewhere in there she had to return last night's dress and then go across town to pick up tonight's. Thank god for hungry designers. They were saving her a fortune.

At 6:15, she turned off the little lamp and sat in the dark for a moment. Thinking about the little house in Portland. Getting up for school. Frankie. Lola. Longing washed over her. Not for the place or even the two women. She'd pushed that away long before. No, the longing was for someone else to . . . to do what? She couldn't find the idea, the word. She sat a moment longer but then heard one of the roommates in the bathroom, so she slipped down the hall to her room and went to bed.

She met the handsome Dare again at a shoot for a Men's Wearhouse brochure. Callie had gotten a last-minute call to show up. They wanted a few "action" scenes with pretty girls just in case, and the Wearhouse art director had asked for a "good-looker with long red hair."

"That's you," said Angela, her agent. "The money's good. It's eight hundred for the day, two days guaranteed. You need to show up at four tomorrow morning. Will that work?"

"Sure. Will we shoot late?"

"Not past three."

Angela didn't ask why and Callie appreciated that about her. G. was taking her to dinner and then "out and about." That's what he'd said. "Out and about." Two weeks after they'd met, she had called the private number on the card he'd given her. Jonathan's firm was folding, it turned out, and there was no money for her. She was relieved to leave the one and take up with the other.

The shoot was in a loft in the Garment District. She rode up the freight elevator with three big guys and two white sofas wrapped in plastic. At one end of the enormous space, the windows were being hung with a cityscape mural that had twinkling lights in it. A buffet table was being set up with crystal and silver serving dishes.

In a corner at the other end were makeup chairs and tables. She went over and introduced herself to the hair girl and the makeup girl first thing. She'd learned early on that getting in good with them was critical. She hadn't worked with either of these women before, but she'd come with her hair wet as requested and that earned a few points.

She stripped down behind a screen and pulled on her terry robe. When she came back to the chair, the hair girl, Trini, was talking to a thin, sharp-faced guy who was showing her styles he liked. He reminded Callie of an animal. A weasel or a ferret. Callie approached with a warm smile. She guessed he was Malcolm, the art director. And so he was.

"Very nice hair," he said, keeping her hand too long in his. "Mind taking off your robe so we can see what we're working with." It wasn't a request.

Callie smiled again and dropped her robe without any suggestiveness. She was all business no matter what he had on his mind. He took his time looking her over, asked her to turn around, spent too much time focused on her bra. "Beautiful," he said, then pointed out a style in the hair book. "Let's go with that one," and he walked away.

Callie looked at Trini, who shook her head and muttered, "Dick wad," and they both laughed.

Callie spent the next two hours in the chair getting extravagant curls put in her long hair and a silver glamour on her face. Trini and Suzanne, the makeup girl, were friendly but talked mostly to each other and that was fine with Callie. Early mornings weren't her best time. Malcolm came back as she was finishing up. He wanted some minor adjustments made to the hair. When he'd walked away, Trini said, "I love a meddler" and they laughed again.

Trini was just finishing up with her when Callie saw Dare in the mirror. He was behind her a ways talking with Malcolm and three other men, all models. She hadn't forgotten him. Not the way he looked, not the way he had been with her. As though he liked her for who she was, not what she looked like. Jimmy had been that way with her. Steve and Lyle, too. But so far in New York, it was all about looks and what you were willing to do with them.

She didn't think Dare had seen her, but as she was waiting for the wardrobe man to decide what she'd wear, he was suddenly right there beside her. "Miss Callie," he said. He leaned in slightly so their arms touched. It was the nicest sort of acknowledgment and her heart eased open for him.

"Mister Dare. How come I haven't seen you around?"

"I've been jet-setting. Winter in Rio, Greece, all the fashionable fashion ports of call." He struck a silly pose with a hat from the accessories cart.

"Working?" Callie said.

"Oh, of course, my dear. I may have Park Avenue taste but I have no Park Avenue money."

"Ah, that old dilemma." Callie, too, put on a hat and they clowned around until the wardrobe man lost patience and asked her to settle down. Dare went off to Trini's chair and Callie tried on the clothes for fit. The dresses were pretty simple, pretty ordinary. It was a men's fashion shoot after all, and the women and their outfits were ornamentation to show off the suits and jackets and a line of tuxedos.

Callie looked forward to talking with Dare but it didn't work out that way. Just before the shoot started, Malcolm's assistant rang a gong and Malcolm asked for silence. He led them through a ten-minute meditation and then said he needed all of their focused energy on the set so there would be no talking except at breaks. He went on and on about it, about the Zen nature of posing, of being "in the moment of the photo." He seemed impervious to the rolling eyes of the models, the silent snickers of the crew. Callie wasn't impressed one way or the other. Every shoot director had some tic or mania. That was just part of the job. But as the day progressed, she had to admit that it was restful, the silence on the set. Usually there was a lot of chaos and chatter, the sounds of dozens of people at work. This time people kept their voices low, their attention on the task. She didn't know if Malcolm got better pictures this way but she felt less hyper.

She and Dare had several sessions together. Party scenes. He wore three different suits, she two different dresses. Malcolm seemed to like them together and she took that as some kind of sign. Fate maybe. And Dare was friendly with her, his smile open and inviting, but it wasn't a come-on that she could read. It was just as well, she thought. There was no room in her life for a man without money.

Fall 1994

The cab was hot and smelly inside. It was a warm night for early October and traffic had been stalled for ten minutes. She was only six blocks from the Plaza but her shoes were impossible for that kind of a trek, and she needed to make a more elegant entrance than just walking up to the door. G. would forgive her for being late. That was never a problem. She could make an entrance and that was good for both of them. People would see her, admire her. Then they'd admire him.

Tonight, she wore a gray linen suit, the skirt slightly pleated and short enough to show off her legs but long enough to be tasteful, the jacket pinched in at the waist. No blouse, in fact nothing underneath. G. liked costumes, liked role-play. Tonight she was going to be the seductive secretary who suggests they get a room. These games were fun for both of them although she'd had trouble finding a designer who'd loan her suits and daywear. The big borrowing game was in evening dresses. And while she had the money to buy one suit, one wasn't what she needed. She needed access to dozens, to a whole wardrobe, as she saw G. three nights a week.

Trini had suggested she approach Malcolm at Men's Wearhouse, that maybe he had a connection. "There's always a connection," she'd told Callie the next time they worked together. And indeed there was. Malcolm was delighted to get her call. He suggested they meet for a long lunch at 36, a see-and-be-seen place down near the Twin Towers. She knew the code, knew what "long lunch" meant. She'd have to see if it was worth it.

Malcolm spent the first hour of lunch describing his greatest fashion photo hits to this audience of one. It took all of Callie's acting skills to pretend to be interested. But halfway into the meeting, he ordered his third double martini and she knew she had him. Turned out there was a contract designer, Moses Shay, that the Wearhouse used regularly. Shay had a women's line and women designers. Malcolm gave her the guy's card.

"Can you call him now? Put in a word for me. I could go around and see him tomorrow." Callie had moved to a chair next to him at the table when she came back from powdering her nose. Now she lightly stroked the inside of his thigh. "Sure," he said and pulled out his phone.

Callie took a long time pushing her Cobb salad around and by the time they left 36 and found a nearby hotel, Malcolm had had a half-dozen drinks. The sex was quick and limp, and Callie left him snoring after an hour. She was tempted to go through his wallet, take a few bills. She certainly deserved payment for her performance. But that didn't fit in with her code. Men could give her money. That was all right with her. But she wouldn't steal it, she wouldn't justify that. And Malcolm was the kind of guy who'd have her arrested. She could smell it on him.

Finally the traffic got moving, the doorman at the Plaza was prompt and courteous, and she was shown to G.'s table without delay.

"Good evening, Miss Ashby," G. said, standing for her arrival.

"Good evening, Mr. Elson." She stepped straight into the secretary game.

They talked of his work over dinner and she pretended to take notes, all the while sending him flirtatious looks that were both subtle and clear. G. was a banker, work that connected him somehow to the International Monetary Fund. Callie had tried to read what she could find. She didn't want to be a beautiful airhead. She wanted to be beautiful and smart. But she couldn't make any sense of the IMF or what he did there.

At the end of dinner, his plate of halibut wiped clean, her salad barely touched, the waiter brought a spectacular dessert of meringue and fresh berries. "Congratulations, Miss Ashby," he said, dropping a fresh napkin in her lap.

"What's all this?" she said, looking at G. He was beaming at her. She didn't like surprises. They never turned out well.

"Well, Miss Ashby, tonight is an anniversary of sorts. It's been just a year since you came to work for us. And I thought we should celebrate." He tucked his dessert spoon into the mound of raspberries and cream.

She relaxed a little, took a tiny bite. "It's lovely, Mr. Elson. Thank you for remembering."

"Oh, that isn't all." He put down his spoon and placed a small silver box next to her plate.

She looked at it, trying to keep her expression fond and playful. She'd been dreading such a turn. Jonathan, and Marcus before him, had been old hands at the mistress game. That's why she'd chosen them. Simple rules. A clean financial arrangement. Desire the only name of the game. But G. was a different sort of man. He was fifty and rich and powerful but he had no wife, no kids, only an angora cat named Tallulah. And not so deep within him was a fat fourteen-year-old that nobody had liked.

"What's all this, Mr. Elson?" Callie said again. "I can't accept a gift from my employer." *Stay in the game*, she thought. *Stay in the game.*

"Just open it, Callie." He went on beaming.

Inside the box was not the ring she'd been dreading, but a set of keys. She looked at them, smiled, and looked at him. "What are they for?" She knew they couldn't be keys to his apartment, not the one he shared on Central Park West with his mother, whom she had not met and never would.

"Let's finish the dessert and I'll show you." She could see the excitement in his eyes and she grew more curious, curious and hopeful.

She sat back and watched him move the spoon to the dessert and to his mouth and back again. In the last year, he'd put on twenty pounds and, if she cared about him, she'd urge him to slow down, find a gym, make other choices. But she didn't. He wasn't her husband, he wasn't her worry.

After dinner, they went out into the night and he gave the taxi driver an address she didn't recognize. She didn't ask any more questions, just settled herself against him and watched the city go by. They headed downtown. For some odd reason, she thought of Lola, wondered if she'd like New York. They circled past the towers and drove by 36, where she'd had lunch with Malcolm. It had become a Thai place. Then they turned onto a quiet side street off Bleeker and pulled up in front of a narrow brick building wedged between two bigger lofts, both in the midst of renovation. G. paid the driver and they got out. He unlocked the front door and they walked up two flights of stairs. There was no doorman, no reception, but the stairs were carpeted and clean, the walls free of graffiti tags and obscenities.

On the third floor, there were two doors. He unlocked #5 and held it open for her. There was a tiny entryway with a coat closet and then the space widened into two surprisingly large rooms that looked out to the street with floor-to-ceiling windows, remodeling that must have cost a fortune. On the left was the living room and kitchen, on the right, a bedroom and bathroom. The lamps were on, the light a soft glow. The furnishings were modern and elegant. The walls painted lovely colors: mango, eggplant, lily. The bed was made up, fresh flowers everywhere.

"Do you like it?" His voice was more tentative than she'd heard it since that first night at the credit-card game.

"It's amazing," she said. "Just amazing. Is it ours?"

That was the right question. He put his arms around her and kissed her. "It is. We have a three-year lease. I'm so glad you like it. I wasn't sure about the furnishings, wasn't sure exactly what you'd like. You can change anything you don't like, of course. Just call the designer, but I know you're busy with all your modeling classes and your work and I just wanted to take care of everything."

"You've done an amazing job, Mr. Elson. I'm proud to be your secretary. Let me show you how proud." She unbuttoned the jacket to her suit and moved his hands to her breasts.

Fall 1998

It was 3:30 in the morning and even for a New Yorker, the din was unbelievable. This was another art director's extravaganza, a photo shoot in the casino at the MGM Grand. The Vegas gawkers and the slot machine addicts contributed to the noise.

Callie was standing at the roulette table. The flamingly gay photographer stood across from them perched on a ladder contraption that he swore gave him special angles. He was trying to include the very handsome croupier in the shots. Callie stopped worrying about how feasible that was and went back to the blank place she'd learned to inhabit behind her face until it was time to go "live" again.

"Do the lights seem hotter than usual?" Dare took her hand below the table. He had lovely hands, smooth palms, long slender fingers.

"Yes, I thought it was just me." She was relieved to hear him say that. She'd taken an extra half-tab of speed at midnight to make it through the night and now sweat was trickling down her ribs.

"How's my face?"

"Handsome as ever."

"Let me rephrase that, silly. How's my makeup?"

"Still okay. Mine?"

"The upper lip is looking a little damp."

"Ah, Dare, you say the sweetest things."

He dropped her hand and waved at the art director. "Harvey, we're melting over here."

Harvey told the photographer to get it going and in thirty-five minutes he had the shots he wanted. She and Dare moved together through the casino to the changing room. The makeup girl changed her eye shadow and lipstick to match the pale green satin dress and did damage control with the sweat. Callie's thick hair was swept up with a sparkly clip and a few tendrils spilled down the back of her neck. Harvey had wanted her to lighten it, strawberry blonde was what he was after, but she refused. The red hair was her signature. After a fuss, he agreed.

The four-hour shoot became six, then eight. The casino was balking at roping off the area a second time. The posing became harder and harder. Callie could see her own fatigue mirrored in Dare's face, where a gray shadow darkened his jaw and his throat. Finally at nine, Harvey let them go. They stripped out of the finery in the change room, shrugged on hotel bathrobes, got their faces off, then made their way past the glazed eyes of the gamblers to the elevators. When they got to Dare's floor, he took her hand and pulled her along with him. "Come snuggle with me," he said.

"I'm too tired to be good for much," Callie said, disappointment rising up. This wasn't how she had pictured their getting together. A chance encounter at a party, a gallery opening where she had been recognized and whispered about, a Broadway play date, then supper out somewhere chic and costly, then home in a long taxi ride pressed together before falling into bed at her place.

Of everybody she knew in New York, Dare was her favorite and she knew they were meant to be together. She'd known it the night they met, eons ago when she was still with Jonathan. Here was somebody she was sure she could love.

"You don't need to be good for anything. I just want you to hold my hand." He smiled at her.

His room was just like hers, only tidy. His clothes were neatly hung in the closet, shirts on one side, pressed silk slacks on the other. No sign of a suitcase. On the little table by the window, an open notebook with a Mont Blanc pen beside it, a florist's vase of pale pink tulips. On the bedside table a short stack of paperback books. It looked like he lived there. She was glad they hadn't gone to her room.

The mini-bar held only bottled water. She took one and downed a Xanax while he was in the bathroom. When he came out, the robe was gone. He wore black boxers and he was, well, breath-taking. Callie had never seen such a beautiful man. He was long and just the right amount of lean. His skin was smooth and the most amazing warm color, not brown, not gold, just gorgeous. He smiled at her but it wasn't seductive. It was exhausted.

She moved past him into the bathroom, used his toothbrush, washed some of the sweat and hot lights off. She wanted a shower, a long soak in the tub, but she also wanted Dare and so she pushed aside her need to be perfect and went out to the bedroom. He was sitting on the bed, watching TV, the sound done low. He smiled at her again, the same fatigue in his eyes. "Want a tee?" he said.

It took a few seconds to figure out what he meant. "Sure," she said, and he pointed to the dresser where a black t-shirt lay neatly folded. Lauren on the label. Of course. She felt suddenly shy, something that never happened to her. She took the shirt and went into the bathroom and put it on.

This time when she came out, the curtains were pulled, the room dark except for the glow of the TV screen. She climbed into the other side of the bed next to him. He leaned over and kissed her cheek and handed her an eye mask. "I like the TV on," he said. "I hope that's okay." He put on his mask and lay down flat on his back, his hand on top of the covers. She lay down next to him, not touching him.

"Hand, please."

She turned on her side toward him and put her hand in his. He raised it to his lips. "Thank you," he murmured and sighed with contentment. In less than a minute, he was asleep.

Disappointment washed over her. Frustration. Confusion. How could he not want her? He wasn't gay. She knew that. He cared about her. She cared about him. He was a healthy young man. She was a beautiful young woman. Why wasn't this happening? Maybe he was just tired. She couldn't fault him for that. But how he could be too tired for sex? Men were never too tired for sex with her.

She wasn't tired. The Xanax was taking the edge off the jangles from the speed, but it wasn't going to put her to sleep. She'd had enough all-night shoots to know she wouldn't sleep until late afternoon.

She lay there a while. G. moved across her mind. They'd had quite a lovely eighteen months together in the apartment. Most days he would come and have lunch with her there or in the neighborhood. His office was just a few blocks away. They got together the same three nights a week, dining out, going to shows and parties. He seemed to understand her need to be seen. His sexual needs remained ordinary. She would have indulged him in some of the things she charged extra for, but he never asked and she never suggested them.

The apartment had come with one condition: monogamy. She didn't mind and she figured she could always work around it. So for a while, her life seemed settled. Plus he paid her account at Dean and DeLuca, gave her an American Express card with an astronomical limit. One of her modeling friends encouraged her to stockpile cash from the card. "Think of it as your rainy day fund," she said. Instead, Callie built up a good wardrobe of time-less suits and black dresses and shoes that would be in style forever.

Then it had ended. G. had come to dinner that Wednesday as always. She'd helped him off with his coat, brushing the snow from the thick gray wool. Scarf and gloves onto the little table by the door. Coat upon the hook, next to her own great coat of black cashmere, his birthday present to her. He settled into the Queen Anne chair with its soft red velvet and she knelt down and slipped off his Italian loafers and then brought him a scotch, three fingers and one ice cube, like always.

He smiled at her when she handed him the drink, but it wasn't the usual I'm-glad-to-see-you smile or the I'm-relieved-the-day-is-over smile. It was a sad, I've-got-bad-news smile. Jonathan had worn the same smile when he couldn't afford her anymore. With Jonathan, she had been relieved—he liked kinky games too much—but she had grown fond of G. And one man and steady support had its advantages. It had made her career so much easier.

"What is it, G.? What's happened?" She sat down on the ottoman and put her hand on his knee.

"I'm getting married, Callie." He looked stricken.

There was a brief rush of fear, of irritation. She didn't love him, didn't want to marry him. But she didn't want things to change. She wasn't ready for it to end. She took a deep breath and smiled her most tender smile. "Isn't that supposed to be a good thing?"

He got up and moved to the big window and looked down onto the street. "I don't know. I don't love her. But my mother wants a grandchild. She wants two. And she wants them now. She's seventy-three and she wants them now."

And just like that, Callie knew who the bride would be. Blonde. Born rich. Born thin. Sharp features. Thirty-five or so. She had seen her with G. twice. Once outside his office. Once in a restaurant near their apartment. She had assumed the woman was a colleague. There had been nothing romantic about their energy together. But it was her. Of course, it was her. One of his own kind.

"Does this change what we have?" She was pleased with how calm she sounded, how reasonable. "Can we still be friends?" She left the ottoman and went to the window and placed a hand gently on his back. "I would like that," she said.

"I can't do that, Callie." He turned to her and put his arms around her. "It's not in me to be unfaithful. I have been faithful to you all this time. I know lots of men don't care about that but it's important to me. My integrity. My word. And I've proposed to Alicia and been accepted and so things have changed." He smiled that same sad smile. "We both knew this wouldn't last forever. I will miss you. You can't know how much I will miss you."

She clung to him, pretended to be there with him in this big moment in their relationship, but her mind was spinning out into the future. Money. The apartment. Paying for her classes. Her hair, her clothes. Where was that all going to come from? She began to cry softly.

"Don't be sad, darling," he said. "You have made one man happy for a very good while." He took out the pale blue linen handkerchief he always carried and wiped her tears. He kissed her forehead gently. For the first time, she felt like his daughter, not his lover.

He went back to the red velvet chair and slipped on his shoes. Then he took a long white envelope from his breast pocket and laid it on the end table. "Don't open it now. Wait till I've gone."

She helped him on with his coat, handed him his hat and gloves. She felt like a hatcheck girl in a fancy club, the envelope her tip.

She had not seen him again, except in the papers. The announcement of the engagement on the society page. The wedding picture on the same page three months later. It was not the woman she had guessed. It was a girl about her age, a plump, plain-faced girl in a sweater set and pearls in the first photo and poured into a Vera Wang gown in the second.

G. had been generous though. The envelope contained fifteen thousand-dollar bills and the lease on the apartment, signed over to her for the next thirty-six months, rent and all taxes paid. The American Express card worked another month, then it didn't. But when his daughter was born, she sent him a nice note and he paid the rent for another year. Good ol' G.

Callie opened her eyes to the room at the hotel. She had drifted off but the speed was too strong to let her really go under. Dare went on sleeping soundly. He hadn't moved a muscle. Corpse pose. His grip on her hand had loosened though and she slipped out of bed, put on her robe, and went up to her own room. Clothes everywhere, papers, dirty dishes from room service and half-smoked cigarettes. She preferred Dare's room with its neatness, its order. She tossed dirty underwear onto the closet floor, stuffed the papers in the trash, put the dishes outside. But it still didn't have the calm of Dare's room. She felt edgy and uneasy.

She looked out across the city, then down to the pool. The sun was high and heat radiated from the window despite the chill in the room. This was an ugly place. Ugly people. Ugly vibe. She went to take a shower.

It felt odd to dress for summer. New York was into the crisp cool of fall. Cute jackets and tight pants and ankle boots. But it had to be ninety degrees outside, so she put on a short black denim skirt and a t-shirt in a shade of green that did well for her and small emerald earrings, another gift from G. She took a long moment deciding on shoes, then slipped into high-heeled sandals with subtle green and black stripes.

She went first to the dining room but it was crowded and noisy. The clothes on the tourists were as loud as the voices. So she went deeper into the casino to a bar far enough off to one side that the perpetual ka-ching of the slot machines was muted. The hostess took her order for iced tea and left a menu.

A quick glance told her there wasn't much model food on the menu. Club sandwiches with all that bread, burgers and fries with all that fat. Even the salads were full of things she wouldn't eat in a million years. She was down a couple pounds though so she ordered two scrambled eggs with ham and a fruit cup. When the food came, she ate slowly, putting her fork down between bites, the way she'd been taught in the agency class. It showed a dis-interest in food that was part of the life. Callie felt grateful that she had never really been interested in food. Some of the other models she knew craved stuff—bread and pasta and chocolate. They kept their weight only by purging, an idea Callie found dis-gusting. And while the speed did help keep her weight right, she also didn't care all that much about what she ate or how it tasted.

The waitress came by to check on her. "Those three men want to buy you a drink," she said, setting the tea pitcher on the table and gesturing with her hand into the dark of the bar.

Callie knew who she was talking about without turning to look. She'd noticed the men when she came in. She'd noticed everyone. Two guys at the bar with an empty stool separating them. Four well-worn women with umbrella drinks in a booth just down from hers. And three guys in their early forties at a table in the center of the bar. They were finishing breakfast and drinking beer. The only prospects.

She smiled at the waitress. "Tell them I'll be happy to have a drink with one of them, but only one. And it has to be the shy guy." She looked over at the table and gave a wave of her hand. Two guys grinned and one guy blushed. "The guy who's losing his hair."

The waitress chuckled and filled her glass with tea. Callie went back to picking out the pineapple and grapes from her meal. She heard a whoop of laughter and then the man stood there beside her. She turned her head and met his eyes. They were amazing eyes. Gray-green-gold with long dark lashes. Great eyes. But they were the only beautiful thing about him. His skin was scarred from acne, his dark hair soon to be a thing of the past. His nose was a little too big, his lips a little too thin. But when he smiled, it was a shy smile and she liked something about it.

"May I buy you a drink?"

She made him wait another moment, just looked at him in appraisal, and then gave him her sexy smile, the one she'd practiced until the twinkle in her eyes was just right. "Sure."

He sat down across from her and the waitress came right over. She stood next to Callie, who asked for a glass of white wine with a club soda back. He ordered a double scotch.

She waited for him to speak but he sat there, looking up at her and then down at the table.

"Was it a bet?" she said. "Which one of you could buy me a drink?"

"No," he said. "Well, yes, I guess. We all wanted to meet you. You're an amazing-looking woman. We figured you were an actress or a model. I mean, nobody looks that great in real life."

"Is that a compliment?" She put on her teasing tone.

He blushed. "Uh, yes, of course. I think you're spectacular."

The drinks came and she poured a tiny amount of the wine into her club soda.

"You didn't really want a drink, did you?"

"I don't drink much ever. But I'm glad you wanted to sit with me while I finish my lunch." She took a cigarette from the pack in her purse and waited for him to light it for her.

He blushed. "I don't have a lighter. I don't smoke."

"No problem," she said and she put the cigarette back in the pack.

He suddenly looked more at ease. "Are you a model or just that gorgeous?"

"I do fashion modeling."

"I knew it. Are you from L.A.?"

She shook her head. "New York."

"No kidding. I'm from Baltimore. Or I was. Now I live in New Jersey."

"I could tell by the accent," she lied.

And he told her of growing up near Memorial Stadium, of playing high school ball, of going to Baltimore City College in accounting. Another grateful guy, just like Steve and Lyle had told her. But he didn't talk just about himself. He asked questions about her, too, and so she told him about growing up in Montana on a ranch and her parents' divorce and moving with her dad to Juneau and then coming to New York on a dance scholarship that hadn't worked out.

The two guys he'd been sitting with came by and gave him the thumbs up, but he ignored them and she did, too, as if what they were talking about was the most important thing in the world. And all the time that she talked and listened, she was trying to decide whether to take him on for the afternoon and how much money might be in it or to go up alone and get some sleep.

There was a familiar lull in the conversation. The question would come next. One direction or the other. She decided to postpone it. She was having a good time. "Are you here on vacation?" she asked.

"No," he said, "this is not my idea of a vacation. I'd rather be in Aruba or the Bahamas. Some place with a beach. But the company I work for wanted me to meet with a couple of guys from L.A. and they wanted to meet here. One of them is into cards in a big way—poker, gin rummy, just about any game he can find."

"Do you like to gamble?"

He shook his head. "I know too much about money, where it goes, where it doesn't. I don't want to fool with any of that. Too easy to lose it all." He turned those eyes on her again. They were a little less shy now but she could see he wouldn't push, just keep his distance until she let it happen and maybe not even then. At the same time, he seemed to like what he saw, seemed to maybe like her.

"What about you?"

"Me?"

"Yeah, gambling? Vacation?"

"Work." And she told him about the shoot from the night before and then other stories of art directors and their quirks and some of the crazy places she'd stood in slinky, shiny dresses and she made him laugh and it made her like him even more.

She was still nursing that first white wine and he was on his third scotch. She needed to pee and she didn't know whether to leave or come back. She knew she needed sleep and she didn't want to do that with this guy. But she didn't feel done with him either. It was an odd complication. Most of the time, well, all of the time, it was clear to her what should happen. Yes or no. But not this one.

Dare took care of the decision. She saw him at the entrance to the bar. He nodded his head when he saw her and came over to them. She watched his walk, smooth, sure. He had such a way in his body. He wore white slacks, a pink dress shirt, a sweater tied around his neck against the air conditioning.

"Hello, darling," he said when he reached them. He leaned down and kissed her on the lips.

"Sleep well?" Callie said.

"Deliciously. But I missed you when I woke up." He looked over at the other man, smiled, and put out his hand. "Hi, I'm Darryl Delaney. Callie's husband."

The man across from her recovered quickly, she'd give him that. Faster than she did, actually. He shook Dare's hand. Said his own name. Scott Klein. Drained the scotch in his glass. Stood up to give Dare the booth. He looked at Callie with just a hint of longing, or so she imagined, and turned to leave. Then he turned back and handed her a business card. "If you're ever looking for an accountant," he said and he walked away.

For a minute, she said nothing. Then she laughed and said, "You're terrible, you know that?"

Dare grinned at her. "I meant every word."

She didn't know what that meant so she said something else. "Are you going to eat?"

"Food any good?"

"I had scrambled eggs. They were fine."

"Then yes."

She got up without another word and went out, alerting the hostess to his need for a menu. She made her way back through the casino to a corridor with restrooms. She thought about the accountant and how she'd enjoyed talking to him. She thought about what Dare had said. He loved jokes and probably thought this husband thing was a good one. It was one of the things she liked best about him. He loved laughing and joking around. She felt a twinge of pity for poor Scott. How confused he had been. Maybe she'd call him when she got back to New York. Did an accountant make enough to afford her?

When she came back, the waitress was putting a turkey sandwich down in front of Dare but she hadn't moved away. She stood looking at him. Dare had that effect on women. He was a feast for the eyes. Callie came up to the table and the waitress came out of the trance. "Anything else for you?" she asked Callie.

"No thanks." She moved around the waitress and slid back into the booth.

Dare was not a dainty eater. He didn't eat often, not when he was with Callie anyway, but when he did, he took enormous bites and relished his food. In about four minutes, the sandwich was gone, the coleslaw too, and he was looking at the dessert menu.

"It's unfair how much you can eat."

"I know," he said. "I've got the perfect metabolism."

The waitress came back by and he ordered pie, then he settled back into the booth and stretched his long legs out on the seat. He yawned and smiled at her.

She smiled back, liking the way he looked at her. It was a look of friendliness, of candor. That was the word she wanted. Then she just came out with what she was thinking. "Why don't you want to have sex with me?"

He looked at her and then away. "I do," he said. "Or I might if things were different."

"What does that mean?" She felt a tangle in her chest. There was the sexual humming that she often felt when she was around him. But something else as well. An ache she never wanted to listen to, something deep and old and unsure.

The waitress brought the pie, filled her tea, his coffee. He waited until the woman moved away.

"I want to tell you a story," he said, and she knew she wasn't going to like what she was about to hear.

"Once upon a time in a St. Louis suburb, there lived a boy. We'll call him Darryl. He was sixteen and a swimmer and passionate about drama. He was also a half-assed student and his father told him he'd never amount to anything. But his mother called him her golden boy and somewhere she found money for acting lessons and then modeling lessons. And his father called him a fairy and a faggot, but the boy knew it wasn't true for he was in love with Mindy Shelton, who kissed him in the wings at the Community Theater before they went on stage in *Romeo and Juliet*. He and Mindy were really just friends because she had the hots for Roger Newsome, a senior who played baseball like a pro. But Roger didn't have the time of day for Mindy and so she let Darryl kiss her sometimes and one afternoon in her basement when her mother went to get her hair done, Darryl got Mindy's clothes off and she got his clothes off and they fooled around and touched each other and it was all going really well until she touched his balls and they hurt. And he tried to think that that was normal but it wasn't and it really hurt."

Callie watched his face but there was nothing there, no feeling, no expression. He had turned his palm up on top of the table and she put her hand in his.

"And it was cancer and he had surgery and radiation and now walks around with an empty sac and patches on his arm or his thigh or his butt so he can be a man. And the patches don't always work very well and sex is not often very satisfying, but the good news is that I don't really care and the other good news is that I don't have to shave every day."

"So you can't . . . you don't . . . you . . ."

He still didn't turn her way. "It wouldn't be much fun for either of us."

"So you just don't have sex."

"Not with women." And now he did look at her and there was a smile on his lips but it wasn't in his eyes. And something squeezed her heart but she was afraid it was pity and that wouldn't do. So she let emptiness back in and put a smile on her own lips and squeezed his hand.

"Your turn," he said after a moment.

"What is this? Confession time?"

"Truth and Dare. Remember when we met?" And now the smile was in his eyes and she felt relieved somehow that she knew this though she still didn't want it to be so. So she told him some of her truth. About life in Portland with Lola and Frankie. About cheerleading and getting kicked off and running away to Seattle with Bill. She didn't talk about Jonathan or G. or how she made her money. There was no need for any of that.

When she pushed the door to her room open an hour later, the sunlight was blinding and she hurried to pull the drapes. Housekeeping had done their best with her mess and the bed looked fresh and inviting. She took a Xanax to counteract the last vestiges of the speed, then another half. Then she stripped off all her clothes and got into the clean sheets.

She didn't like this time before sleep. Usually she watched TV or did crossword puzzles until the drug made her loose and sleepy. She didn't believe much in thinking. Planning was okay. Planning was smart. But mulling, even though that was a really good-sounding word, mulling just got you into trouble. She'd seen it make Frankie unhappy. That's why she tried to be more like Lola, who just lived her life and didn't think about it.

She felt terribly alone, more alone than she had in a long time, like when Lola left them or when she first arrived in New York and knew no one. She felt like some precious possibility had just been snatched from her hand and there wasn't going to be a happily ever after, not that she was dumb enough to believe in that. Then the Xanax kicked in and the tangle in her chest eased and her mind grew cloudy, but the loneliness hung on. She turned the pillow over looking for a cool spot. She wanted somebody to know how she felt. Somebody safe. She picked up the phone and got through to an outside line, gave her phone card number, then the phone number. What were the chances that it was still the same? It rang four times and then there was her sister's voice.

"Hey, Frankie, it's me," she said after the "hello" but the voice went on talking, "35-2019. Leave me a message." Callie waited for the beep, but then she hung up and pushed away the tears that filled her throat and went to sleep.

Spring 2001

"Callie, come on in." Angela had a thick portfolio on her desk and was leafing through the photos with a woman Callie didn't know. "We were just looking at all the work you've done in the last decade. Pretty amazing."

"Actually, it's eight years, not ten."

"Even more amazing then. Some great, great work." Angela was fifty, stick-thin, still elegant from her own modeling days although the thinness had creased deep lines around her lips and eyes. She sat back from the portfolio and looked at her client. The other woman remained standing beside her. "How's that darling friend of yours?"

"Dare? In Tokyo, where he's a huge hit. Everybody wants him to model there. He's very exotic to them, he says."

"I'm so glad. The look here for men has really changed in the last few years. A move away from that kind of aristocratic, Scandinavian look that Dare does so well to something darker, more ethnic and rugged. The tastes of the public are so fickle."

Callie said nothing. She knew this last sentence wasn't about Dare. In the last three months, she'd had only one big shoot.

"Are you planning to go over and join him? I understand you two are close."

There was something gossipy in the woman's voice and Callie didn't like it. "I hadn't planned to," she said. "Why? Do you have work for me there?"

Angela looked at the other woman and waited. "Not yet," the other woman said, and she came around the desk and extended her hand. "I'm Sherri Jensen."

"I'm so sorry," Angela said. "How gauche of me. Sherri's with our international division." She paused a long moment as though she were expecting Callie to say something. Then Angela said, "Doesn't Dare have some good Tokyo contacts by now?"

"We don't usually agent for each other." She looked out the window at the river in the distance, then back at Angela. "And I thought you didn't want me to find my own work."

Angela tilted her head again. "We haven't been in this kind of drought together before." She paused. "Callie, your look is gorgeous, extraordinary, amazing. And it's been all over the magazines. And that's the problem. You're not a new look. You've had a good run. Longer than I would have guessed for a redhead. But it isn't a classic look, and the classic look has a longer shelf life. You're going to need to find something else." She looked at her and smiled. "Or somewhere else."

"Like Japan."

"Yes, or South America. Maybe Brazil or Argentina. Like Dare, you'll be exotic there. And they like older women, especially in South America. You're moving in on thirty, right?"

Callie nodded. She kept her smile small, relaxed, loose.

"So I was thinking it might be time to turn your account over to our international division to see what they can do for you."

"Are you letting me go?"

"Heavens, no. But Sherri will be your direct contact. She's got the connections abroad. That's not my market. No, I'll certainly be here to support you. But you will work with Sherri."

Angela looked at her colleague, who nodded and held out her hand to Callie again. "Give me a couple of weeks to see what I can do and then come see me," she said. "Okay?" She left without waiting for an answer.

Callie began to gather up her bag.

"Do you have another couple of minutes?" said Angela.

Callie looked at her, then settled back into her chair.

"I've had a call about you from *Playboy*. They are doing a spread on women at thirty and your name came up. Interested?"

Callie looked at her. She was interested but was unclear how much to show it.

"They want to see photos of you nude. Just simple shots but it's full frontal. There's a contract beforehand even to try out, although no money at that stage, and those nude images will be protected whether they choose you for the spread or not. If they choose you, it's terrific money. And it opens up some other possibilities for you. One of the women will be on the cover. There could be public appearances. It's a big deal. And, of course, it moves your career in a different direction. There may be some renewed interest in you for fashion work, but the big houses probably won't use you at all after *Playboy*, although who knows? And I think this would only enhance your appeal in South America and Asia."

"Do you think I ought to take it?"

"I think you ought to think about it. And if you decide, here's a photographer who can do the nudes." She handed Callie a card. "Trust me. You'll get great shots. Let me know what you decide."

Outside there was no spring sunshine, only a hard, cold rain. She hailed a cab and then didn't know what to tell the driver. She couldn't face another afternoon in the apartment. "MoMA," she said finally.

She used her membership card, a gift from Dare for her birthday, and took the stairs up to the café. She ordered cheesecake and a cup of coffee, then sat down at a smaller table and hoped no one would join her. Cheesecake had become a weakness. She wasn't in the dark about that. She wasn't in the dark about anything. Maybe that was the trouble with her life. Maybe it was better not to know things, not to be so damn aware all the time. She could see why people took drugs all the time instead of once in a while.

She had never thought about getting too old. She had thought she would become more experienced, better able to wear the clothes, to create the look the photographers wanted. And she had thought she would have enough to put money away. She thought of Lola waitressing all those years, bringing home money each month that wouldn't keep Callie in dry cleaning. She wouldn't do that. She'd die first.

After the money from G. had run out, she'd gone back into the penthouse party circuit. A dozen or so of these parties took place every week all over the city. She learned which ones were about simple, old-fashioned sex and got on that invitation list. She only did those twice a month. It was enough, and her career went well for a good long time. She and Dare were often on shoots together and they palled around in the social scene enough to get free drinks and free meals, and he paid for the endless cab fares and the tipping of this doorman or that waiter. And she could still borrow dresses and suits for special occasions. But since she was no longer new and happening, designers, especially the younger ones, weren't so eager to loan her things. They made excuses, couldn't "fit" her. She could see the doors closing. The card parties were drying up, too. The men wanted innocent, naïve, fresh or at least the illusion of it, the modern-day version of virgins and the *droit du seigneur* that Richard had explained to her early on.

Callie looked down at the table. The cheesecake was gone, the tea pot empty. She was still hungry. The waitress came by and she ordered a bowl of clam chowder. She could feel Angela's disapproval from twenty blocks away, but she knew she wasn't really in any danger of forsaking her thinness. The clam chowder came. It tasted more decadent than the cheesecake, and she ate it very slowly.

Two thin blonde women came and sat down at the next table. They had smart clothes, the right accents, the rich life. But she didn't want that life, the wife-of-G. life. And she wasn't sure how much longer she could make the life she had work for her. She needed a plan and she needed a smart person to help her make one.

There was surprise and then maybe delight in his voice when she called. Yes, he could meet her for a drink after work. What had once been 36 was now a wine bar; 5:30 there would work well.

Callie wore her hair up but soft, her makeup subtle. The gray suit he used to like so much. She had bought it from the designer after a half-dozen other models had worn it. Naked underneath for old times' sake although she had no expectations. He was the same and yet not, a bit thinner, a bit fitter-looking. "Alicia makes me work out," he said. "She wants me around to see the girls grow up."

He showed her pictures of his daughters, plain like their mother, heavy like their father. The love in his eyes made her wince.

They small-talked a bit. He and Alicia were remodeling a house in the Hamptons. He thought he might retire there. The schools were great and he had a connection that would pave the way for his girls. She listened and asked questions and it felt for a moment like old times. Then she talked about her work, about how her run at the big magazines was winding down and what Angela was suggesting. "I'm not sure what direction to take, G. I'm not ready to retire. I'm not even thirty. Do you think the *Playboy* shoot's a good idea?"

He thought a moment. "That would certainly take you in a different direction. Are you thinking about porn films?"

"No. Do you think *Playboy* is porn?"

He tilted his head in the way she remembered. "Tasteful porn maybe." After a few seconds, he said, "What are the pros and cons for South America? It's great to travel and if somebody else is paying for it . . . well, why not? Anything or anybody to keep you in New York?"

She shook her head. Dare was a good friend to her, the best, but she had hidden away in her heart the desire for more with him. He was gone all the time now anyway.

"Will Europe or South America advance your career?" He signaled the waiter for another round.

She shook her head again. "No, just prolong it a year or two."

"Is there good money?"

"I don't know. And I don't know if it will even happen."

"Callie, have you thought about going to college?"

Callie looked at him. "I don't have money for that."

"If you did, would you go?"

"And do what? Be a teacher?"

"Maybe. Or a fashion coach. Or a designer. Or an agent. Or a writer. Or an accountant. You're a smart woman, and it's a handy thing to have, a college degree."

"I never thought about it." She never had. She didn't have a high school diploma. Was it possible to go to college without one? That wasn't something she could ask G.

He looked at his watch. "I've got to go. I have dinner plans. It was lovely to see you. You look great." He smiled and there was sadness in his eyes. "I miss you, Callie. We had some good times, didn't we?"

"We did, G."

The waiter brought his coat, helped him into it. He leaned down and kissed her brow. "Think about college. If you want to go, I will help you make it happen." And then he was gone.

The maître d' came over with a menu. "The gentleman left instructions to buy you dinner. May I get you something?"

She ordered a big dinner, then feigned a headache and had the waiter box it up. It would be food for a week.

On Friday morning, two days after the dinner with G., Callie walked the few blocks up and over. The address was easy enough to find, but which floor to buzz less so. At last she puzzled out the name and rang. The door clicked and she pushed it open. The entryway was dark after the bright sun of the street and she took a moment to let her eyes adjust. A scrawled sign on the elevator said BROCKEN and an arrow pointed to a door to the left. She pushed it open and climbed three flights. There the sign on the service door said, PEARLMAN. POUND HERE. and so she pounded. She heard a voice on the other side and in a minute, the door opened. A woman stood there, phone to her ear. She smiled, held the door open.

"Wait, don't . . ." she said into the phone, then gave a deep sigh. "I'm on hold with my fucking agent." She moved back into the loft and Callie followed her into the big space. Screens and cameras and tripods were set up in a corner. Around a wall of books, she glimpsed an unmade bed where an enormous orange cat was asleep in the heap of covers. The kitchen, such as it was, was against the wall. The woman went over to the counter and held up the coffee pot. Callie shook her head, then watched her as she talked.

She was about Callie's height but lean and compact. Her dark hair was cropped close to her small head. Her dark eyes were bright and lively. She wore black jeans, a tight t-shirt. Callie could see the muscles in her arms and shoulders underneath the black cotton. Callie couldn't tell her age, not young, not old, forty maybe.

"Arnie," the woman said into the phone. "The client's here. When will you know for sure about Prague? This can't be last-minute like the last time. I don't want to be scrambling the night before to find somebody to take care of Mr. Rogers. I need a yes or no by Friday. Promise? . . . You promise?"

She got off the phone and smiled again and held out her hand. "Angela said you were something special but I had no idea. This is going to be fun."

"You're Leo Pearlman?"

"Leonora. That Angela. She let you think I was a guy, didn't she? For some archaic reason, she thinks women aren't going to want a woman to photograph them. How stupid is that? I hope

Angela is paying for this at least." She grinned and Callie grinned back.

"She's paying for the first three hours."

"That's all we'll need. Call me Josie. My friends all do." She lit a joint that had been sitting in an ashtray on the big work table. "Want some?"

Callie shook her head.

"Okay, then. Bathroom behind the photo screens. Take everything off including any jewelry. I'd suggest you put on the purple robe to start and we'll get going."

And for the next several hours, Callie did what she was told, shifting her body this way and that, revealing herself in small ways, then showing everything. Posing nude turned out to be not much different from fashion modeling. Simpler, actually, as there was nothing to worry about wrinkling. Josie had her stand, sit, lie on a sofa that was draped in the same shade of purple as the robe. It was a much more elaborate shoot than Callie had expected and she said so when they took a short break.

"I like to give Angela her money's worth and you never know how you might be able to use some of these shots."

"Will you touch them up?"

"No. *Playboy* wants the real you to see what they've got to work with. It's not just the breasts, you know. It's skin tone, tilt of the head, a whole bunch of things. Your hair is a real plus. That alone may make the deal for you."

"Have you worked for *Playboy* long?" She didn't care about the answer. She just liked watching Josie's eyes when she talked, the low voice with something in it that wasn't New York.

"Oh, I don't work for them. I'm freelance. But I do shoot a fair number of women wanting to get into the nude mags and into films. So you could say I have a special niche."

The last part of the shoot was the most tiring, and Callie appreciated that Josie did the harder poses last. Most photographers wanted to get those poses over with while they were fresh. They didn't seem to think about how tired the model would be for the rest of the shoot.

As the third hour wound down, Josie put her camera away. "I've got some great shots," she said, "so we'll stop. I've got an appointment uptown and need to hustle out of here. Can you let yourself out?" She didn't wait for Callie's reply. "And come back Friday about one to see the shots. If you like them, I'll let you buy me lunch. Bye, hon!" she called.

The photos, when Callie saw them on Friday, were beyond great. They were lovely. She was lovely. She saw herself in a whole different way. And she could see that Josie had taken two kinds of photos. There were the shots for *Playboy*; they looked like great *Playboy* photos. And then there was a whole other series that she had stacked off to one side. Callie was still nude in these but they weren't about her nakedness, not her body's anyway. They were about herself.

"The first stack is for Angela," Josie said, coming to stand beside her in front of the table. "With your permission, I won't send the second group to her. They're just for you."

Callie looked over at her. "I don't know what to say. These are amazing, and they're way too important to just give me. They're yours, they're your art. I should buy them from you."

"I don't want your money, Callie. I enjoyed doing them. You are a wonderful subject."

Josie turned toward her and ran her thumb gently over Callie's cheek bone and jaw and ended at her mouth, tracing her lips and slipping her thumb between them. It was the most electrifying thing Callie had ever experienced. The humming started and when Josie's tongue followed her thumb, Callie opened up and let her body roar.

She didn't leave the loft until Monday morning. It wasn't just the cinnamon on Josie's skin or the tenderness of her tongue or the deftness of her fingers at helping Callie lose herself in the heat and softness. It was the talk, for Josie asked and listened and commented and exclaimed and sympathized. She honored the stories Callie told her, and she told Callie her own stories of loss and loneliness. By the end of the weekend, Callie had given herself away completely and, for the next two weeks, Callie abandoned her appointments, her fitness classes, her promises, her obligations, and welded herself to this woman until Josie left for Prague in the very wee hours of another Monday morning.

Callie cried when Josie left, hugged the big orange cat, who hissed and moved away, slept fitfully until the morning sun filled the loft. When she woke, the ache in her chest was enormous, the missing so sharp and ragged that she could barely put her clothes on, barely walk down the stairs and find her way home. Her apartment felt cold, barren. It wasn't just that it had been empty for two weeks; the place held nothing of Josie, no scent, no memory. She couldn't bear it. So she took a shower and packed a bag and went back to the loft and wept and waited.

Josie called at six that night, midnight in Prague. She had arrived and the city was wonderful. They talked for two hours, Callie afraid every other minute that Josie was going to hang up, that she would want to go to sleep.

"What did *Playboy* say? Wasn't today the notification?" Josie said.

"I don't know. I didn't check my messages."

"What? Callie, honey, don't tell me you spent the day moping. I miss you, too, but you've got to get back into the world while I'm gone."

"I know, I know," she said. "I just miss you so much and nothing else seems important."

"Well, call your machine and find out and call me back. I want to know what happened."

She had to wade through fourteen messages to get to Angela's voice. It wasn't good news. "*Playboy* passed, Callie," she said. "They liked you, but they had another redhead they liked better. Probably all for the best. I really do think your future lies abroad. Have you talked to Sherri?"

She moved back through the messages. Four were from Sherri, who had "exciting news about Rio." Callie didn't feel excited. She didn't want to leave New York now, not unless Josie could come with her. She called Josie back.

Josie had fallen asleep and seemed unconcerned about the rejection. "No problem," she said, and Callie could hear her yawning. "We'll use the photos in another way. I've got lots of ideas. I've got to go to sleep now. Get back into your life. I'll be home on Sunday morning."

Callie hung up. She wandered around the loft, pawed through Josie's things, anything to connect her with her lover. She coaxed Mr. Rogers back onto the bed and lay awake petting him. Then she took two Xanax and slept.

The next day, she tried to pull herself together. She found the loft too lonely without Josie so she took Mr. Rogers and his food and litter box in a cab to her apartment.

Sherri did have big news. A spring photo shoot and runway work at the end of August in Rio. She had a lead on a couple of additional shoots, one in Montevideo and one in Lima. The same German company owned the magazines in all three cities and they had really liked her portfolio. And if everything fell into place, Callie could come back via San Francisco and do two weeks of work in Hong Kong. In all, she'd be gone about six weeks. She'd make good money and get a foot in the international market. Callie pretended to be as excited as Sherri was, but all the time, she was thinking about Josie and being in the big bed in the loft with her and how she might die before Josie came home. And she didn't like that one bit and couldn't seem to stop it from happening. She called Dare.

"Sounds like you've got it bad, sweetheart," he said. "Can you trust her?"

"I don't know. How would I know? I have no idea what I'm doing."

"Ah, sweet mystery of love."

"But I'm not in love."

"Oh, but you are, Callie. This is love."

"You mean this addiction? This suffering?"

"Yes, ma'am."

"How do I get out of this?"

"You don't. You enjoy the ride, and when it's over, you pick yourself up, dust yourself off, and start all over again." Dare sang this last bit but Callie didn't laugh. She felt doomed.

Spring 2003

The last of the slush on the sidewalk was several inches deep and Callie felt the cold creep up her stockings. She didn't wait for Richard, who was paying the cabbie. She hurried on into the restaurant, handed her greatcoat to the maître d', and went straight to the restroom. Mud and wet had soaked into her new shoes. There was mud on her legs as well. "Fuck!" was all she could say. She used the paper towels to clean herself up, but she still felt dirty. She wanted to cry. She gave herself to the count of ten to feel that way. Then she went into the stall, did a half-line of coke, and went out to dinner.

The three men were business associates. Armani suits, manicured hands, plump, clean-shaven faces except for Richard, who was lean from the torture inflicted by his personal trainer, an ex-boxer who rousted him out of bed weekday mornings at four.

Two of the men had come with girls much younger than Callie, the third man had come alone. The men talked business, their disdain for the women as palpable as their power. For a while, Callie tried to listen. It gave her something to do. But the discussion was convoluted and she wondered if it was coded, so after the appetizers, she put on a mask and went inward to ride the buzz.

The coke was one of two gifts from her months with Josie. Not the powder itself, Callie got that on her own. But the craving, the increasing need to shift out of her present and into some other space.

They had had an amazing summer together, she and Josie, complicated only by Josie's travel assignments. Lovers, companions, best friends. Callie had never felt so alive, so connected. They mostly lived in the loft, Josie not wanting to leave Mr. Rogers alone too much. That was fine with Callie. Her own apartment had memories of men, ghosts she didn't want clouding her new life.

Josie encouraged her to investigate college and she enrolled in an accelerated GED course populated by aging punks and cab drivers and housewives. It was boring and tedious, just like high school, but she stuck it out and in mid-August, she passed the exam and they celebrated with a weekend on Long Island.

In all this bliss, there was only one sticking point. The same old sticking point. Money. Callie had had only two small shoots since she met Josie. There was big money ahead in the Rio trip, and especially if Hong Kong worked out, but in her business, there was no advance on trips to come. Josie seemed to be doing okay. She paid for their dinners and kept food in her refrigerator. But Callie had to find the money for her hair and nails and cabs and clothes. And she didn't want to have sex with anyone but her lover. She began to use her credit cards, something she had sworn she would never do. She figured she would pay it back with the Rio trip.

Leaving Josie on September 3 for Brazil had felt like amputation. Callie begged her to come to the airport to see her off, to spend one more hour together, but Josie had a job and wouldn't cancel it and Callie felt sick all the way to JFK. Once she arrived, the work started immediately and that saved her, during the day at least. And for the first time, she got to know some of the other models, missing the company of women now. But the nights were filled with a loneliness she couldn't bear and she dreaded the end of the day and the empty bed. Then Ingrid, the makeup girl, gave her a small bottle of pills, the information all in German. "Take one a night," she said. "You need to sleep. Whatever heartbreak you've got going on, *liebchen*, it's not doing your looks any good." The pills worked like magic and she began to crave the oblivion as much as she did the nightly phone call with Josie.

The news of the Twin Towers came as they broke for lunch. They crowded into a small bar and watched the images over and over, one of the local girls translating the newsman's words. Finally, the art director herded them back into the street with apologies, asking them please to set aside their grief and let the local crew earn their much-needed money. Callie was the only New Yorker on the team, and the others besieged her with questions at every break, but all she wanted to do was make sure Josie was okay, but there was no getting through the jammed circuits. The panic made her ill. Waves of nausea, her heart pounding in her chest, sweat rolling down her back. The pressure in her body was unbearable, and she wondered if she was having a stroke.

Back in her room that night she turned on the TV and then dialed Josie's number every five minutes by the clock. At midnight, she took the sleeping pill, grateful to know nothing for a few hours. She dragged herself up finally about ten, checked for messages, dialed the number. Then dialed it again. Nothing. There was more news on TV but she had only the pictures to go on. The Pentagon, the passengers dead in a field in Pennsylvania, the efforts to find survivors in the rubble of the Towers. Finally, at two, she heard Josie's voice on her answering machine. The familiar sound made her weep. "Call me, call me, call me," she said until the beep and the disconnect.

Josie left a message while she was at the sunset shoot that evening and then called back at eleven. Callie wept again to hear her voice, wept with relief and reconnection. Josie had been uptown, the city was chaos, some of the streets around the loft had been used by emergency vehicles and there was no easy way to come and go, so she and Mr. Rogers stayed uptown with a friend. She quickly grew impatient with Callie's fears. "I always land on my feet," she said.

Something in her tone reminded Callie of Lola and she felt dismissed. She pushed it away. "Why don't you get on a plane and come to Rio? It's beautiful here and I need you, Josie. I just need you."

"There's no way. Even if I didn't have a full work calendar and the gallery show to negotiate, there isn't any flying going on here. The whole country is in a panic. Nothing is leaving the airports."

They talked a few minutes more. Then Josie begged off and was gone. Callie sat in the dark for a few minutes, the phone in her hand. *Josie is okay*, she kept telling herself. And she was glad. But somehow it wasn't enough.

She was in Rio two full weeks, then Lima for two more, then Montevideo. She was a hit, a big success, and Sherri, the new agent, did her job and there was Hong Kong for nearly a month and then Thailand and Bali for another two weeks. The phone calls with Josie went on every night for a while, but they got shorter and shorter. And in the background, from time to time, there was another woman's voice, and Callie knew it was the same woman, the next woman, and the green-eyed monster unpacked his bags and settled in to stay.

Ingrid, the hair girl, came along on the Asian shoots and got her more of the sleeping pills and then a higher grade of speed. Callie grew thin and the art directors loved the new look. Her sculpted cheek bones, the eyes grown huge, the waist whittled down again. In Hong Kong, there were men, very wealthy men, only too eager to pay handsomely for a night with this exotic red-haired creature. And her money problems disappeared and the revenge was bitter and even she knew it was meaningless.

There was no reunion with Josie when she returned. The breakup in its final form came in an email when she was in Bangkok. "I'm just going to come straight out with it," Josie wrote. "I'm in love and she's moving into the loft with me. I'm so glad to have known you, Callie, but we just weren't right for each other. Best of all things to you. J."

When she got back to New York, she found two shopping bags of her things from the loft sitting on the bed in her apartment.

She had seen Josie one last time, at the opening of Josie's first big one-woman show in February. She'd gotten an invitation and torn it to shreds, but Dare encouraged her to go, to put Josie to rest in her head. And he volunteered to keep her company, pick up the pieces if she fell apart. "But you won't fall apart, Callie, you're too strong for that," he said.

The gallery was in Midtown. There was a small crowd of the hip and the rich. She paid little attention to the photos themselves, acutely conscious that Josie was at the end of the room, talking to Arnie, her agent.

"Callie?" Dare touched her shoulder. "Did you know these photos were of you?"

"What?" She turned to him.

"These photos. They are all of you."

She looked at him, then at the photos. And there was herself. Her shoulders. The back of her neck. Her breasts. The photos were in black and white except for the purple silk robe and her hair, in all its glory, sometimes just a glimpse, sometimes the whole mane. There was only one photo of her whole body and only one that included her face, partially hidden by her hair. But they were all of her.

And she could feel that people were looking at her and whispering but she didn't care. She watched Josie and the little blonde with her arm around Josie's waist in full possession and Callie knew it was over. It had been over for months, but now it was really over.

Josie came over to them. Callie introduced Dare, but there was no triumph in being on the arm of such a handsome man. Emptiness laid its cold hand on her heart. And then across the room, she saw G. and she escaped, leaving Dare to talk to Josie.

G. put his arm loosely around her in a half-hug and she kissed his cheek. Then he introduced her to his wife and her sister and the sister's husband, who turned out to be Richard from the card parties. And they made small talk about the photos and the two women asked questions about the modeling life and it was all she could do just to stand there and be polite and feel Dare and Josie behind her.

Then Dare came to rescue her and she introduced him. The look on the men's faces—and especially on the women's faces—when Dare turned on his gorgeousness and his charm was something. Not revenge, but something.

In the cab, Dare handed her a long white envelope. "From Josie," he said.

"What is it?"

"I didn't look." He turned on the cab light.

She pulled out the sheet of paper. It was a legal document, lawyer's letterhead, and it assigned a percentage from the sale of the photos to Callie. She could also have a print of any one of them she liked. On a sticky note, Josie had written "No hard feelings?"

She handed the paper to Dare, who read it and handed it back. "How are your feelings, Cal?" he said.

"Hard," she said. "Very hard."

Richard waited two weeks and then called. Or rather, he sent flowers, tulips and lilacs and freesia, impossible blossoms for the end of winter. There was never a note, just his name on the card. Then in mid-February his voice on voice mail, asking her to meet him for a drink.

They met at the Algonquin. She wore a dress of teal wool that clung to her too-slim body and a matching half-cape. All of it soft, fluid, seductive. She knew what Richard wanted and she had decided to give it to him, depending on the terms.

They made small talk until the drinks came. She asked after G. and the two sisters. It was strange to think that all the time she was with G., Richard had known. It was more than strange; it was creepy. She pushed that aside, asked about his work, how he stayed fit in a world of portly older men. He told her about his trainer, how he'd finally found someone who would push him as hard as he needed.

The waiter came with a tray. Double scotch for him, a Cosmo for her. "Here's to us," he said, and she clinked her glass with his but didn't put it to her lips.

Instead she put it down and said, "What is it that you are offering, Richard?"

He laughed, though there was no humor in it. "That's what I like about you, Callie. You're nothing if not direct. Some men don't like that, you know."

"I haven't met any," she said. "Not when it comes to sex and money."

He smiled. "You're right." He went on smiling, and she could see the meanness just below the surface. "I now own the apartment where you live. I bought it from Geoffrey, whose finances aren't what they used to be."

Disappointment washed over her. She'd had a fantasy that G. would give it to her one of these birthdays.

"It's a prime piece of real estate," he went on. "It should be making good money." He took a sip of his drink.

"How much do you want?"

"You know what I want, Callie. I want to use the apartment and you in it. You both belong to me now." He let that sink in. There was a coldness in his voice and it moved through her like an arctic wind. She hadn't seen any of this coming.

He spoke again. "In exchange, I'll let you live there rent-free and I'll put a generous amount in your checking account every month for as long as we both agree."

"And if I say no?"

"You won't. It's too good a deal. And you're all about the deal, aren't you? Besides, I think you're ready for somebody like me."

Callie was silent a moment. Then she said, "I want to think about this."

"If you must," Richard said, though his face hardened and something tightened in Callie's chest when she saw that. "I'll come by Friday after work for your answer."

When Friday came, she gave him her conditions. No group sex. No rough trade. She would sleep with his friends, his business associates, but she had to agree and he or the other man would pay her extra. She wanted $10,000 a month direct deposit and free rent. Each of them could give sixty days' notice and the agreement was over.

"What makes you think I'll say yes?" he said.

"Because you want me."

He laughed. "What makes you think I'll keep my part of the bargain?"

"Because I'll tell your wife if you don't and I'll tell G. and his wife. Besides, whatever other kind of shit you are, you are a man of your word. I wouldn't agree if you weren't."

"Fair enough."

And so it had begun, this next man in her life. Of course there was still Dare. They were friends, good friends. They talked on the phone often, had Saturday afternoon dates when they were both in the city, and if she loved anybody now, it was Dare. But with Dare, there wasn't any future and, more importantly, there wasn't any money.

The dinner party was breaking up. The men had eaten well, the women's plates barely touched. The other two couples said their goodbyes and left. Callie made another trip to the restroom to coke herself up for whatever was coming. In the bathroom, she thought about the two young girls who'd been at dinner, saw herself all those years before when she'd been with Jonathan, then with G. Something moved up from her chest that might have been a sob, but she took a deep breath and it passed.

When she came back, a last round of drinks had arrived. The fact that they weren't leaving yet sent a jangle through her system, tweaking the cocaine into high alert. Richard waited until the waiter had cleared the table, brushed the crumbs into his little silver dustpan, filled the water glasses. The man who had come alone eyed her, looked away. He was nervous. That was a good sign. What was his name? Tom? Todd? Tony?

Richard was speaking to her. "Ted is looking for real estate downtown. I told him about your apartment. That it might be a good investment. He's wondering if you'd want to stay on after he buys it. I told him I didn't know, that that was up to you."

Callie looked at Ted and forced herself to smile. She might have been surprised that Richard would drop her this way but she wasn't. She knew him too well. She wished she hadn't done that last line in the bathroom. "Would you want me to stay?" Her voice wasn't coy. She didn't do coy anymore. But she did charming and inviting very well. She pushed the smile up into her eyes.

"Absolutely," he said. "I'm sure we can arrange something that would work for us both."

"Well then," said Richard. "I need to be getting home. My wife is in town."

Ted reached for the bill, but Richard picked it up. "You and I can settle up later." And Callie wasn't sure if he was talking to Ted or to her.

Winter 2003

He picked up on the third ring. She recognized his voice and wondered if he would recognize hers. "Is this Scott Klein?"

"Yes, it is."

"My name is Callie Ashby. Do you remember me?"

"I don't think so. Have we met?"

"Yes, in Las Vegas. Five years ago in a bar at the Grand. You had a bet with two guys about who could buy me a drink."

There was a pause and then he said, "The gorgeous redhead. You're that gorgeous redhead."

"Yes, that's me. You gave me your card and told me to call if I ever needed an accountant."

"I remember. Wow! I had no idea you'd remember me."

"Are you still an accountant?"

"Yes, I . . . yes."

"Still in New Jersey?"

"Yes, that too."

"Can you come into the city and meet with me? That would be easiest for me."

"Of course. When?"

They met two days later in the Starbucks near her apartment. It was late in the afternoon and not too busy. The staff were putting up Christmas decorations.

He looked much the same, just a little older. *Men didn't change the way women did*, she thought as she watched him come in. *Maybe that's why they want us to be different all the time.* She stood up when he came to the table. He held out his hand. She took it and leaned in and kissed him lightly, briefly on the lips. "That's for leading you on last time."

He blushed, then smiled, and the smile lit up his whole face—something she rarely saw in the men who came in and out of her life. She liked him for it.

She ordered green tea. He got a peppermint latte. She could smell it when he brought the white cups to the table. It smelled like the holidays.

"Are you still modeling?" he asked.

"Yes, but almost all of it is abroad, mostly Asia. I'm headed to South Africa and then on to Morocco right after the New Year." She paused, then said, "Actually, Mr. Klein . . ."

"Scott."

"Scott. The truth is my career is winding down. I'm thirty-two and I'm not on the way up. I have a very particular look . . ."

"And it's a fabulous look."

"Thank you, but it's not, well, working for me much anymore." She laughed at the look on his face. "I can see this doesn't mean much to you."

"No, I mean, you're still gorgeous. Who wouldn't want to look at you in a magazine?"

She laughed again. "You're thinking of a different kind of magazine. Women buy the kind of magazines that will pay me a lot of money to model clothes and I'm done there. They've seen me and seen me. And well, it isn't the women who buy my look anyway. It's the art directors and they've seen me and seen me. That's why I've been working out of the country."

He nodded. "So how can I help you?"

"I've been putting money away for a few years."

"Smart woman. Every woman ought to have her own money."

"Well, it's…it's not my pay check. It's another kind of money." She looked at him. "It's money I haven't been paying taxes on."

He shrugged. "Okay. Have you kept it separate from your regular income?"

"Yes, an accountant through the agency helps us with our taxes for the money we make there, and of course, the agency gets a cut. The other money is in a safe deposit box."

"And your husband? Are you still married to that blond guy?"

"No. We were never married. That was his little joke and at your expense. I'm sorry about that."

He sat back in his chair and was silent for a moment. "Is the money drug-related?"

"What? No," Callie said. "No, it's all been, uh, gifts."

"I'm assuming you don't want to pay taxes on this money."

She nodded.

"And you want to start using the money."

"Before too long."

"Why did you call me?"

"Well, you were working that time I met you in Vegas. A guy from New Jersey. His company sends him to Vegas to meet with another couple of guys . . ."

"And you've been watching *The Sopranos.*"

"Well, that too."

He laughed and drank the latte, which had sat untouched all this time. They were silent then a moment.

"Are you married?" she asked.

"Divorced. Two years now."

"Kids?"

He shook his head. "No. She wanted to but it wasn't a good idea at the time. She's got kids now."

She nodded again. "Scott, I'm ready for a change. In fact, I want to find a new sort of life. And I'm thinking maybe you can help me with that."

He smiled and it lit up his beautiful eyes again. She smiled back, and this time she didn't figure out in advance what kind of smile to give him.

Summer 2008

The sun was bright, the humidity high, and her head ached. Booze, dope, the family—you name it. The umbrella over the sidewalk table didn't help much. And Marilyn was going on and on about Eduardo, the decorator, and the plans for the remodel. Callie knew she was sleeping with the guy; she could tell by the way Marilyn was talking about him. Callie closed her eyes behind the sunglasses, took a sip of the Long Island iced tea, prayed for a miracle. That the earth would split open and swallow up Marilyn and Patsy and Maria Victoria and there would be quiet.

The salads came, big platters of food that the women would pick at, eating all the meat and cheese and olives and bread and leaving the lettuce and complaining about how little they ate and still gained weight. Callie felt too jittery to eat but forced herself to take a few bites, hoping the headache would go, that lunch would be over, and she could slip away.

She hadn't known she was marrying *this*. Scott had offered a way out of New York, out of the modeling life. He had offered kindness and security. He had good money, a good job. He adored her and wanted her happiness. Go to college? *We'll find the money.* Open a boutique? *We'll make it happen. Whatever you want, Callie, it's yours.* And while she hadn't fallen in love with Scott, she had fallen in love with how he loved her.

But marrying Scott had meant marrying the family. Not the in-laws. Scott's parents were long gone, and his sister lived in Florida somewhere. No, the "family" was his two business partners and their wives and their sisters and their cousins. The family was a string of interminable lunches and shopping trips and backyard barbecues and trips to Atlantic City and the shore in Rhode Island. It was how they did business, Scott explained, the long meetings after dinner, when she got stuck with the wives. And she'd promised him to be a wife, to go with him to dinner, to go on these trips. That was the deal.

Her phone rang and she excused herself and moved down the sidewalk as she answered. "Had enough of the wife life?" the voice said.

She laughed. "You can't know. They're insufferable, these women. And I thought *I* was shallow."

"You were never shallow, Cal. We just lived shallow lives."

"Are you calling to beg me to marry you instead?"

Dare laughed. "No. I've no more to offer than I ever did. But I'm sitting in the airport in Athens and my flight is delayed yet again and I'm bored, and I thought to myself, *I'll bet Callie is also bored, wherever she is, and maybe we can just be bored together.*"

"Newport, that's where I am."

"California?"

"Rhode Island. Where old rich meets new rich or illegal rich or under-the-table rich."

Dare laughed again. She'd forgotten how fun it was to make him laugh. They'd always been great at snide together.

"Still going to school?"

"No, I didn't like it anymore than I did high school. That's not for me."

"Just living the wife life then?"

"Yeah, for now. I could lie and tell you about my good works with the elderly or the pet shelter but you wouldn't believe me." She'd reached the end of the block and sat down on a wooden bench in front of a souvenir shop.

"You're right. I wouldn't."

"You're still working," she said.

"Yes, though it's tougher. I'm doing a few more commercials for TV. Underwear, shaving cream. Hunky guy stuff."

"Women love those ads."

"I think these are aimed at gay guys actually." He paused. "Me too."

"What do you mean?"

"I decided to bat for the other team for a while."

"For real?"

"Oh, it's just something to do, something to try. That's kind of who we are, isn't it, Callie? People who try on lives?"

"Yeah, I suppose so." She slipped her shoes off and realized just how too tight they were. Angry red marks crisscrossed her feet. "Anybody special?"

"I've got my eye on a guy. He's not too serious and you know that suits me."

"I do know that."

"How about you? Got your eye on the next guy?"

"No, I'm going to stick with Scott. He's a good man." She paused a few seconds. "You know, Dare? Married, I have more freedom. It's funny but it's true."

"Is freedom what you want?"

"Well, I always think so." She looked down the sidewalk. "I've got to go. The three stooges are on my trail. I love you, Dare. Still do."

"Always will," he said.

The four women spent the afternoon shopping. It wasn't what Callie enjoyed. She had a very different relationship with clothes than these women. It felt odd to buy off the rack, to buy something that wasn't tailored to her. She'd discovered that in the real world, she wasn't an easy fit. Waist too small, breasts too large. So she let the others try on things and she stuck to scarves and hats and bags, of which she already had enough for a lifetime.

The hotel room was blessedly dark and cool when she got back and she kicked off her shoes with relief, padded down the hall for ice, fixed a large vodka tonic. Then she turned on her laptop. It had been a birthday gift from Scott, who teased her about living in the last century. There was an email from Frankie. Since the wedding, they had stayed in touch although it was pretty one-sided. Lots of news of Frankie's little life in Portland—her work, her cats, the books she was reading. She wondered sometimes if Frankie had a boyfriend—or a girlfriend for that matter, although she couldn't imagine good-girl Frankie being that daring. Callie didn't write back. What would be the point? Frankie was also in touch with Dewey and Snow and sometimes she wrote about them. She had sent Callie Dewey's email and phone number but it seemed too complicated to connect after all this time. Just as it did with Lola. It had been an odd sort of relief to know that Frankie had no contact with Lola either. If Frankie didn't feel guilty about it, she certainly wasn't going to. None of the emails were urgent. Nothing that couldn't wait.

She went onto Josie's website. There were some new photos on the gallery page but she skimmed over them and went to the About Me page where the pictures of Josie were. Josie laughing. Josie at work. Josie on location. Callie's heart ached, just a little.

She turned the computer off, fixed another drink, took a Xanax, and sat in the cool dark. Maybe she slept a little. She was still sitting there an hour later when Scott came in.

He was his usual cheerful self. He kissed her, asked after her day, told her about his.

"Can we stay in tonight?" Callie said. "Order room service. Just you and me. I'm craving some you-and-me time." She got up and put her arms around him. She'd quickly realized that complaining about the other wives wasn't the way to go, no more than complaining about art directors or gossiping about other models would ever have gotten her anywhere. You keep it about you, what you need, what you want.

"I've got to meet Anthony for a drink, but it's just the two of us and then I'll come back and we'll order in. Maybe take a walk later when it cools off."

"Heaven," she said and she kissed him in the way he liked best.

While he was gone, she took a shower, put on a sleeveless cotton dress of pale green stripes that he liked her in. Did her hair loose and free. She looked good and she felt better.

But when Scott came back, something was off. The cheerfulness seemed strained, and underneath it was something she didn't recognize at first. It wasn't worry. She had seen him worried, although rarely. Business was good, work and money steady. The vagaries of the stock market didn't seem all that problematic to whatever it was he did. No, this was something stronger, deeper.

"What is it, honey? Is Anthony ill?" It was all she could think of.

"What? No. I'll tell you later. Let's just get some dinner. Why don't you order and I'll go shower? I need a shower."

She fixed him a drink, fixed herself another. He disappeared into the bathroom and was gone a long time. She heard the shower running but no singing. He usually sang in the shower. She set her concerns aside, turned on the TV. *Jeopardy* wasn't much but it gave her mind something to do.

They ate the seafood salads at the table. She tried to amuse him with stories from her day, and he laughed but that other something was still there. When she asked about it again, he just said, "Later."

At about ten, he clicked off the TV and suggested a walk down by the beach. The high heat of the day was gone although the air was still heavy and damp. Callie had brought a pashmina and now wished she hadn't. It was just a burden. They walked a ways on the boardwalk, then down on to the sand.

"Want to walk or sit?" Scott said.

"Whatever you want." She could feel him gearing up to say something and it made her uneasy.

"Let's walk," he said, and he offered to carry her shoes.

She slipped them off and the sand felt cool and delicious on her feet. For a long time, she would remember that feeling when she thought about this night.

"Anthony is stealing from the company," Scott's voice was low. "He's been doing it for months, maybe years."

He was silent a minute and she waited, holding back her concern. Then he shook his head and said, "I'm such a dope. I've suspected something was going on for a while. He just had too much money, too much more than me or Christopher. But when I'd kid him about it, he'd say it was from an investment or from Maria Victoria's folks, and who was I to question that?"

"So he's been spending your money, our money?" Callie put her hand on his arm and he stopped and turned to her.

"It's not our money that's gone. That's the trouble. It's money that belongs to investors. We're due to make a big payment to them and the money isn't there to make it. That's why he told me. We can't make that payment. And all hell is going to break loose."

There was just enough light from the boardwalk behind them for Callie to see his eyes, to see that the something lurking there was fear. She waited but he said nothing, just kept walking. She hurried to catch up with him. "These investors," she said.

He stopped and turned to her, tilted his head and said, "Why do you think we're out here talking about this?"

After a second, she nodded. "I get that," she said quietly. "But I don't get how this happened. How he could fool you. You always seem to have everything under control." She didn't add that this was one of the reasons she was with him.

"It's the way we have things set up. Always have. Christopher and I handle the accounts for the clients, and Anthony handles the books for our company. When we started, Chris and I had our own money to invest, but Anthony had to borrow it. We didn't ask where he got it. It wasn't any of my business. I figured he put his house up for it. Now it turns out that the money came from some minor wise guy in New Jersey, and all along Anthony's been cleaning their money through our books. And I might never have known." He stood looking out at the ocean.

She could see the weight on him, feel his heart racing though she wasn't touching him. "What's he spent it on?"

"Bad investments. Junk bonds. The crap we learned in school never to touch with our own money. He thought he could make a killing and pay the money back. How old is that story?" He shook his head.

"What's going to happen?"

"I don't know. They'll take everything he has but it won't be enough, not nearly enough."

"How much is enough?"

"Four-and-a-half million."

Callie looked at him. "You've got to be kidding."

"Believe me. I wish I were."

"That kind of money has been going through the company?"

"Apparently."

"Will they take what we have too?"

"Probably. If this were the government, I could put everything in your name. But these guys aren't going to respect that. But you know what, Callie? I don't care about the stuff. The house is just a house. But these guys are going to own us. Own the business. Own all our hard work."

She could hear the tears in his voice even though his eyes were dry. She suspected she should feel sad as well, sad for him, sad for herself. But she couldn't find it. What she did feel was cold and alone. Again.

Summer 2009

Callie looked at her watch: 4:10. She couldn't possibly go back to the apartment before 6:30. She got up and ordered another iced decaf Americano. The barista was twenty-five at best, and while he made eye contact in that corporate way and seemed friendly, she knew he hadn't seen her. Couldn't have picked her out of a lineup, as Lola used to say. Callie didn't like that. She didn't know how to live invisible.

She went back to her table, watched her reflection in the window. It seemed barely her. Her signature hair was gone, cropped chin length. Her grief at its amputation surprised her—how one part of her could feel like the whole of her. She wore jeans and a t-shirt, but she still looked elegant. She'd been trained too long not to carry her body well, but she looked like anyone, any nice-looking woman pushing forty. That was the point. "We have to keep a low profile," Scott had said.

The Americano tasted bitter. Her life tasted bitter. The wise guys had taken everything Scott said they would—the house, the timeshares, the jewelry—everything that had made them rich. Some homely New Jersey daughter was now wearing most of Callie's designer clothes and sitting in the furniture Callie had selected.

Anthony and his wife had disappeared early on. Scott figured his partner had money hidden, had gone to Guatemala or someplace in the Pacific. That had left Scott and Christopher to settle up with the wise guys. They'd kept Christopher in the Baltimore office but Scott had bargained to get out, to be allowed to leave town. The wise guys hadn't been happy about it, and Callie wondered if he'd had to beg.

Scott had not insisted she come with him. "I'll divorce you now if you want," he said. "This isn't your mistake. It was mine in trusting Anthony. But I'll have nothing to give you, no support. There isn't anything." Scott had been too afraid to try to hide money, afraid the wise guys would hurt him, hurt them both.

Callie did have money hidden. She hadn't given everything to Scott to manage when she hired him as her accountant. She hadn't mentioned it when they got married, didn't mention it now. It sat—all $75,000 of it—in a safe deposit box. In the grand scheme of things, it wasn't a lot of money to build a new life on, but it was enough to escape on. But escape to where? She didn't even have good ideas of where to go when she left the apartment each day, let alone where to go to start over.

So she had come with Scott to Pittsburgh and had helped him set up a life. They weren't poor. A woman came in to clean every week, and there was plenty of money for groceries and liquor. But Scott's joy and pride were gone, and Callie was learning that bitterness and boredom were a lethal combination in a marriage.

"Mind if I share your table?" The man was fifty or so, nice jaw, nice cheekbones, though the eyes were pale and too small. The coffee shop was mostly empty at this late hour and Callie thought about it before answering. Then she shrugged and said, "Sure."

Two hours later, she let the water in the hotel shower run over her for a long time. She was already so late that a few more minutes wouldn't make a difference. Once the guy had left, and she made him leave right after, she didn't give him another thought. The money sat on the nightstand, money to add to the safe deposit box. She wondered again how much would be enough, how many more guys she'd need to run into at Starbucks.

She dried her hair, redid her makeup, got dressed. She hadn't let the guy touch her in her clothes. She didn't want his scent on her. Scott probably wouldn't notice but there was no reason to complicate things. She gathered up the thousand bucks and headed home. It was just past eight.

She could hear the TV, the news on low, but Scott didn't call out when she turned the keys in the locks. The smell of cinnamon hung in the air. Scott liked a slice of raisin toast when he came home from work. But the flat felt empty, and something more than that. She grew uneasy.

She turned the corner into the living room. The room was dark except for the glow of the TV, the thick curtains pulled against the late summer light. She turned on a lamp. Everything was normal. The sofa, the glass coffee table, the Queen Anne armchair with Scott's foam cushion for his back. She moved on. The small dining room was also undisturbed. The table, the red placemats, fresh gladiola in a deep orange. Scott knew how she loved them. She went through the swinging door into the kitchen. It was empty and clean except for the butter dish sitting next to the toaster and crumbs on the cutting board. She called his name again but there was no answer.

She passed the second bedroom. Scott's laptop was on. She could see the golf courses of the world screen saver he used. In their bedroom, his clothes were on the bed. Shirt, slacks, as if he'd just taken them off. Puzzled and more than a little uneasy now, she moved toward the bathroom. The door was ajar, the light on, but there was no sound, not a splash, not his tuneless whistle.

"Scott?" She knocked on the door before pushing it open.

He lay in the water, his knees bent, his eyes closed. He could have been sleeping. But somehow she knew he wasn't. A half-gallon of vodka stood mostly empty on the floor, her home Xanax bottle empty on the counter. She touched his shoulder. The skin was cold, his arms and forehead bruised. A half-smoked cigarette floated in the water. She began to tremble, then knew she'd be sick. She backed away and stumbled into the kitchen where she retched for long moments into the sink. Then she slipped down onto the cool floor and went somewhere else for a while.

She woke with a start. A voice saying *get up, get up*. But there was no one there. Only the hum of the refrigerator and the water dripping in the sink above her. Her mind began to race. The wise guys. The police. *Save yourself*, the voice said. *Save yourself*.

Her body felt leaden but she pulled herself up off the floor and went to find her phone. There were three messages. Two were from Scott. One at five: "I'm on my way. Call me back if you want Thai for dinner. Love you." Then one at six: "Where are you, babe? I don't remember you saying you'd be out. Call me." She felt a wave of guilt, then of sorrow for what she'd been doing when he was calling her.

The third message was not from Scott. There was heavy breathing, then a male voice said, "She's not picking up," and then some clicks and some static and the disconnect. The nausea swept over her again and she gagged but nothing came up.

She took her purse and went into the kitchen, opened the window against the faint smell of vomit. She rinsed her mouth at the sink, then shook a Xanax from the bottle and took them. She resisted the urge to run. She knew a great deal would depend on what she did now.

She pushed away her feelings. There was no time for that. And she began to sort through who could help, really help. Dare? Hardly. G.? Forget it. Richard? Richard.

She went online on her phone, found his law office web site, dialed the number. A woman answered, a real person, even though it was after nine. Callie asked for Richard. The woman asked if it was an emergency, asked for her phone number. She didn't have to wait long for a response. Richard showed no surprise at her call. He listened, asking nothing. Then he gave her a phone number, told her to call with a credit card and charge five dollars on account. "Just do it," he said, "then call me back," and he gave her his cell number.

When she called him back, he said, "Okay, now you're my client. What do you want to do?"

"What do you mean what do I want to do?"

"Do you want to call the police? You can report it as a suicide."

"But it wasn't a suicide. There's a cigarette butt in the water. Scott didn't smoke. Not ever. Somebody else . . . I don't know."

Richard was silent a moment. "I can make this all disappear. Is that what you want?"

She hesitated, but only for a second, then said yes.

"Okay, how much money can you get your hands on?"

"Right now?"

"Yes, in the next hour."

"Not much."

"All right." He laughed, a laugh she had hoped not to hear ever again. "You're going to owe me, Callie."

She took a deep breath. "I already do."

By the time she hung up, the Xanax had kicked in. Or maybe it was having a plan. No matter. She felt calmer, clearer. She called the local number that Richard gave her. The voice on the phone was older, the accent Italian. "Pack your things," he said. "Anything you want or need. You will not be going back there."

"Okay." It surprised her how easy it suddenly seemed with someone else in charge.

"Is the apartment furnished?" he asked.

"Yes."

"Does the owner live on the premises?"

"No."

"Is there an over-friendly neighbor?"

"Yes."

"Call her from the hotel in the morning and tell her your husband has left you and you are going home to your mother."

He gave her the name of a hotel downtown, told her to take a cab. "The room's paid for," he said. "It's in your name. No need to pretend."

"Won't the police . . .?"

He stopped her. "Is anyone going to come looking for your husband?"

She thought a moment. Not Anthony. Not Christopher. They had their own troubles. Maybe Scott's sister, maybe she'd wonder. That could take years. "No," she said.

"Then consider this done. Finito. In the morning, you can give notice to the landlord. He'll find the place spotless. Any other questions?"

"I don't know," she said.

"A cab will be there in thirty minutes. He'll honk. Don't go down right away. Wait until he honks the second time so that the neighbor sees you. Understand?"

"Yes."

"One last thing. Have you showered since you got home?"

"No . . . my . . . my husband's in the tub."

"Okay. Don't. But take off all the clothes and shoes you have on. Everything you are wearing. Including the purse. Leave them all. Stay barefoot until you're ready to leave, then put on shoes from the closet but put them on at the doorway. Take a shower when you get to the hotel and send your shoes and clothes to the valet to clean. Got it?"

"Yes."

"Your car will be at the hotel when you check out tomorrow. You will not need a ticket for the valet. Give him the color and model. Leave town in the morning, no later than ten. Do you have questions? When we hang up, this phone number will no longer work."

"No, I . . ."

The phone disconnected.

She gave herself a moment to sit there. It was almost as though she were waiting. But nothing happened. She got up and went through her clothes. There was just enough adrenalin to make her efficient. She filled two big roller bags with the best of her things. Scooped all the jewelry into a velvet travel bag and then into her biggest purse. Emptied the purse she'd had that day into the big one. Found the money from the afternoon. How had she known she'd need it?

The taxi driver said little. Helped her with her bags. It was just after nine and she saw Irene Tuttle at the window in the apartment above them. She lifted her hand and Irene waved back.

The cabbie dropped her at the Omni downtown. She didn't offer him payment and he didn't ask for any.

The hotel room was chilled against the August heat and the feverishness that had carried her through the leaving began to evaporate. She turned the air-conditioning down, stripped off her clothes, and stood for a long time under the hot water. She realized this was the third shower she'd had that day. The man in the hotel room crossed her mind but she didn't let him linger. He was nothing, a distraction. But if Scott had taken the pills on his own, if it was suicide, then if she hadn't gone to the hotel, if she had gotten home on time . . . She felt sick again. But that wasn't it. It wasn't suicide. Scott wouldn't do that, wouldn't leave her. And the cigarette butt was proof. It was her good fortune that she had gone with the man or they might have killed her, too. That felt right to her, felt true.

The room was more comfortable afterward. She dried off and rummaged through the suitcase for Scott's striped cotton pajamas. They were too big on her but they were old and soft and the faint smell of his aftershave was comforting. She pulled two vodkas from the mini-bar, added tonic. The curtains were open onto the city lights and she sat in the armchair and thought about nothing.

The knock on the door brought her back into the room: 11:15. The police crossed her mind but she dismissed it. Richard would take care of her. She had to trust in that. A young woman in a maid's uniform stood at the door. "Dry cleaning service, madam?" she said.

Callie had forgotten. She turned back into the room, gathered up her slacks and blouse, and handed them to the girl.

"Shoes?" the girl said.

Callie picked up the trainers and handed them over as well.

"Call the front desk in the morning when you are ready for them," the girl said, taking the twenty that Callie handed her.

Her cell phone rang as she closed the door. She looked at the caller ID, figured it was Richard checking on her. Instead, it was a number she didn't know. She let it ring, click through to voice mail.

Callie went down the long silent hall for ice. Fixed another drink. She could see car lights going by down in the street but the windows were double-paned against the world.

Scott crowded into her mind. Scrambled eggs and toast. That's what he'd had for breakfast. He hadn't been worried, hadn't been frightened. Not that she saw anyway.

She couldn't find any tears for Scott and she didn't wonder why. What was the point? She had to do again what she did best—take care of herself. She sat down at the desk and went online. There was four thousand in the bank account, another three in savings. She had the thousand from the afternoon plus the money in the safe deposit box. She could earn her way across the country and keep all this to get started somewhere else. She just needed to know what she owed Richard. Or maybe she didn't need to know. Maybe if she stayed out of New York, she'd never have to deal with him again. She felt a surge of anger at Scott, at the unfairness of all this. She hadn't wanted Richard's hands on her or her life ever again and now look.

Maybe she could change her name, move to California. She emailed Frankie to see if she could stay in Portland a night on her way. Frankie was online. Said yes. That was settled. It gave her someplace to go.

She got offline, moved back to the easy chair in front of the window. She thought about another vodka tonic. She thought about another Xanax. She thought about Scott and how she got to this chair in this hotel on this night. None of it was comforting and so she pushed it away.

At midnight, the phone rang. She thought it might be Dare but it was Frankie instead. She listened to her sister talk, then said, "You've got to be kidding. Visiting Lola is not part of my plan."

"Why? When do you need to be in L.A.?"

"Well, I don't have a date to arrive, if that's what you mean."

"Exactly, you could come through Idaho on your way to Portland. It's not that much out of your way."

"But Dewey asked you to do this, Frankie. It's your favor for him, not mine." Callie went to the mini-bar and pulled out another vodka.

"What if I meet you there? What if we do this together?"

"I don't know, Frankie. I don't want to see her."

"Well, I don't either. But it would be a lot easier if you were there. Please, Callie."

Callie heaved a sigh. "Oh all right." Lola's nowhere town in Idaho would be safe. No one, not even Dare, knew where Lola was. Hell, she hadn't known herself until ten minutes ago.

"Great, thanks. You don't have to stay there long."

"Oh, believe me, I won't." For a fleeting second, she thought about telling Frankie what was going on. But how was that going to help anything? So they talked logistics for a moment, made a plan, disconnected. Then she made her drink, pulled out some hotel stationary, and made a list for the next day. Bank. Irene Tuttle. The landlord. Idaho.

The Reunion
Part III

When the three of them got to Lola's the next morning, there was a dirty white pickup parked in the driveway behind the old convertible. Frankie was glad they had waited until late.

Callie put her hand on the sliding door but Frankie stopped her. "Let's knock," she said.

It wasn't her mother who came to the door, but a tall lanky man with weather-worn skin and a huge belt buckle between his jeans and the open blue work shirt. His feet were bare. He pulled open the slider and said over his shoulder, "Lolie, I think your girls are here." He stood aside to let them in. The house smelled of bacon and pancakes and cigarettes and bad coffee.

Her mother sat smoking at the far end of the table in the middle of the big room. The table was still piled high with papers and coats and all manner of life, but a spot had been cleared for two plates and two coffee mugs and a jug of syrup and a glass ashtray big enough to do real harm. She wore a silky robe of blues and greens that fell open over her thin tanned chest. Her hair was long and loose, just as Frankie had remembered, but a different blonde, something bottled. She was thin, way too thin, her dark eyes huge in her face. The only signs of aging were the deep squint lines that creased her brow and marked her eyes and the loose skin of her throat.

Callie went over and put her arm around her mother in a kind of hug, but Lola didn't take her eyes off Frankie. And Frankie refused to speak first. The rage she'd expected had been too brief and she felt a messy snarl of things that she couldn't sort out. Something in her pulled toward the woman at the table, some kind of yearning, but it was weak and very old. Mostly she just didn't want to be there.

Finally, her mother spoke. "Jackson, thanks for the ride home. You should head on out now. You don't want to listen to our girl talk." She gave him a loving smile, one that Frankie had seen men get from her mother a thousand times.

The man went in the back and came out with his boots on, his jacket in hand. He gave Lola a long kiss on the mouth, nodded to the daughters, and disappeared out the slider. They heard the pickup start up and rumble away. Callie poured herself some coffee and sat down at the table. Frankie felt frozen to the linoleum. The only thing holding her up was the boy, whose warm, shy weight leaned into her side.

"You look good, Frances. Too heavy and too plain, but you look good." Lola crushed out the cigarette and lit another and the spell was broken. *This is my mother*, Frankie thought, as the hurt slid down her throat and wrapped itself around her heart. *This is what I had before.*

Lola seemed to notice T. Roy for the first time. "Is this my grandson? I never took you for the maternal type, Frances."

"I'm not," said Frankie. "This is a friend of mine, T. Roy. I'm taking him to Montana to his family."

"Still got a soft heart for strays, don't you, Frances? All those puppies and kittens you used to drag home. Some things don't change." Lola looked amused and that offended Frankie even more.

Callie laughed. "I already told her that."

"A trait I picked up from you, Lola," said Frankie, and she looked her mother straight in the eyes.

Lola frowned and then laughed. "Ah, you mean Jackson. Well yes, I still do collect those. They come in handy for all sorts of things." She pushed herself back from the table and stood up, tightening her robe around her. "I'm going to take a shower. There's batter left if you girls want pancakes. I suspect we ate all the meat." And she turned and left.

It took most of a minute for the adrenalin to ease in Frankie's body, for her to find her breath again. She eased away from the boy and looked down into his eyes. "You okay?" she said, as much to herself as to him.

He nodded.

"Do you want pancakes?"

He shook his head.

"Me neither." She looked at her sister, who only looked back. "I need a walk."

Callie made a move to get up and Frankie shook her head. "By myself. Perhaps you can find T. Roy some pens and paper. He likes to draw, don't you, T. Roy?"

"I don't want to stay here," the boy said. "I don't like it here."

Frankie leaned down so she was face to face with him. "It will be all right. I just need to be angry by myself. Does that make sense?"

The boy nodded, silent in the field of tension.

"I'm going to leave my car right outside and I'm going to give you the keys so you know I won't leave without you. Okay?" She handed them to him.

He bit his lip but she saw some of the anxiety ease away.

It wasn't until she closed the slider behind her that Frankie could take a full breath. She looked over at her car and was tempted, so tempted. She could run in and snatch the keys from the boy. She could leave her mother to Callie. She could leave the T. Roy puzzle to her sister, too. She had her laptop, she had credit cards. She could just move on. If Callie could leave her life behind, so could she.

She walked past the Civic and headed toward the pool. The little streets and cul de sacs were empty. She missed Portland and her neighborhood where people walked their dogs and strolled to the Whole Foods up a few blocks and rode their bikes to work. This was some kind of ghost town. The only noises she heard were TV voices leaking out the open windows. No wonder her mother had a Jackson.

The night before, Frankie had written out a plan. A list of things they could inquire about their mother's finances and health. They would sort out what she lived on and what she might need, and then she and Callie could see if there was any way to help. But now that all seemed impossible. Oh, Lola might take their money, she probably would, but there wasn't going to be any plan or organization or structure. She should have seen that yesterday when she first walked into the place.

Frankie went into the pool enclosure. It was deserted as before although the air was warm enough for swimming. A thin layer of dust covered the too-blue water, and the breeze ruffled it at the deeper end. The sky too was blue, a different blue from Portland. She sat down in a white plastic chair at a white plastic table, wiping the grit from both with her sleeve. She pulled out her journal and a pen and wrote SEPTEMBER 1, KELLOGG under the last entry. But her mother's words came back to her like a cuff on the head, "too heavy and too plain," and the words moved down from the old scars in her heart to her belly and sat there like cold pancakes. She tilted her head and stared into that blue sky, hoping to clear her mind and open her heart. *Accept what is.* That was the mantra she tried to live by.

But her mind stayed a jumble. Her mother was sixty. She was forty-two. And she still wanted something from Lola that she wasn't going to get. Callie seemed happy enough with whatever she got from their mother, or, more likely, she just didn't care. But Frankie had gone another way, withdrawing her trust and her affection, wary of rejection and disappointment. By the time she was ten or eleven, this was a conscious effort, pulling into herself and treating her mother with a kind of weary tolerance. Now she could see she no longer had the stomach for even that.

The wind came up for a moment and ruffled the pages of the journal on the table. The past week Frankie had written very little. That wasn't like her. The journal was a companion, a confessor, a keeper of the secrets, but she'd been unable to write about her mother, in fear perhaps of committing to some hope of reunion.

Now she saw that it would not happen, and she felt relieved that she hadn't committed such a stupid idea to paper.

She pulled the yellow legal pad from her purse and looked at the list. Tasks to get her mother organized, to save her. She read through it and was comforted by the tidiness of the plan even if it was unrealistic. She turned the page and began to write another list.

She looked up when she heard the squeak of the gate to the pool. It was Callie.

"You all right, Frankie?" Her sister sat down at the table.

"We can't help her, Callie."

"What do you mean? Without money, you mean?"

"No. Yes, that, too. But that's not the center of it." Frankie looked down at the list she was writing. "You were right. She is still the same."

"I'm sorry she hurt your feelings."

Frankie looked at her sister. This was so unlike her. But what did she know about Callie now and what she'd been through? "You don't need to be sorry," she said. "You didn't say it. She did."

"She didn't mean anything by it."

Frankie felt the fury come back. "Of course she did. Twenty-eight years that we haven't seen each other. Twenty-eight years! And the first thing she says to me is a jab meant to hurt me. The same old shit between us." She brushed the tears away with her fingers.

"Or maybe she felt uncomfortable. Or was nervous."

"Don't defend her. Please. I can't bear it." She found a tissue in a bag and wiped her eyes and blew her nose. "Was she happy to see you when you arrived?" She looked at her sister.

Callie looked away. "In her way. She's never really been affectionate with me either."

"That doesn't make it any . . ." She stopped. There was no point.

"You expected her to be different, didn't you?" said Callie. "To be some other mother."

"Yeah, I guess I did. Foolish me." She turned back to the yellow pad as if that was all settled.

Callie looked at the list. "I thought you made a list last night for us. Aren't there already enough things on it?"

Frankie looked over at her. "I had this fantasy that we could get her organized. Figure things out for her finances, her health. But that was a fantasy. The jumble of stuff she lives in, that isn't accidental. She prefers it. Sure, we could go in and clean it up but it isn't going to last. We could leave her a sparkling clean place, but in two weeks or four weeks, she'll be living in a mess again. That's just too discouraging for me. I can't do it. I won't."

"Then what do we do about the fact that's she's sick? Just ignore it?"

Another wave of anger, this time of self-righteousness, swept over her, but she held her tongue. What point was there in saying that it was her mother's own damn fault, still smoking, still drinking, living in a house so dirty that Frankie couldn't bring herself to sit down in it?

Callie started to speak but Frankie held up her hand. "Give me a minute, okay? I'm having trouble getting used to you as the good girl. That's my job in this family." She closed her eyes and found her breath, tried to sink into the calm that she wanted to believe was underneath the turmoil. When she opened her eyes again, Callie was cleaning out her purse, carefully separating the keepers (cell phone, wallet, lip gloss, body butter) from the discards (tissues, scraps of paper with gum stuck in them). Her sister looked so serious, so diligent, that Frankie had to laugh.

"What?" Callie said.

"Nothing. Just funny to see you being so tidy." Frankie looked at the legal pad. "I'm making a new list, one for me. I'll stay today and tomorrow. Then T. Roy and I leave. What do you think we should do before I go? Go grocery shopping? Balance her checkbook? Clean her house even though it will be a sty again before we reach the city limits?"

"Shit, Frankie, I don't know. I don't know what to do for her. This wasn't my idea either. Why don't you call Dewey and see what he had in mind."

"I know what he had in mind. He wants us to forgive her."

Callie gave a snorting laugh, a sound Frankie hadn't heard in decades. It made her laugh too.

After a minute, Frankie said, "Do you love her?"

"Lola? Not if love is a warm, fuzzy feeling."

Frankie thought a moment. "Do you ever feel that? Have you ever loved somebody like that?"

Callie looked over at her. There was an odd look on her sister's face. She couldn't read it. "No, that kind of love is for suckers. It just gets you into trouble. You?"

Frankie shook her head. "I don't think so. Maybe once. There was a guy for a while. We were happy for a while. So maybe once. But it doesn't seem to come natural to me. Although I do love my cats. I love them with my heart."

"Lola taught us well, didn't she?" said Callie.

Something Frankie couldn't read crossed her sister's eyes, her lips. And then the tears were suddenly just there. Frankie felt her own eyes well up too. She pushed it all away. "I guess," she said. "We didn't exactly have the most normal childhood."

"You're such a romantic, Frankie. You think anybody gets a normal childhood?"

She could hear the familiar sarcasm in Callie's voice now. It was comforting somehow. "Maybe not," she said after a minute. "But sometimes I wish things had been different."

"Don't we all?"The sarcasm in Callie's voice now sounded bitter. "You and Scott . . ."

"I don't want to talk about it. It's over. Drop it."

"Okay," Frankie said. "So what do you think we should do?"

"Let's see your list."

When they got back to the house, they found T. Roy in front of the TV watching an old Western, the kind with ridiculously clean cowboys and impossibly white Indians.

"Where is she?" Frankie asked, and T. Roy pointed to the back of the house. Callie went to find her and Frankie began clearing the breakfast dishes.

They spent the rest of the day cleaning the house. Callie had presented it as a gift they wanted to give Lola and she'd accepted although she didn't feel up to helping them. Once the Western was over, Frankie turned off the TV and gave T. Roy a choice to help them or draw in his notebook. He did a little of both. As the sisters had arranged, Callie asked Lola to sit at the dining table and sort papers—stuff to toss went in a big black plastic bag, stuff to keep in an old moving carton they found in the carport. And for the next several hours, she did that, smoking cigarette after cigarette, making trips to the freezer for vodka, and singing along to the oldies station. And a kind of peace settled over the house and the energy of order and freshly washed surfaces seemed to do them all some good.

About two, they got pizza and sodas delivered and afterward T. Roy begged for some time in the pool. "I've got my trunks on already," he proclaimed, pulling up his T-shirt and showing the chili-pepper-patterned cotton to the three women.

"Callie, you take him. I want some time to talk to Frankie." Lola had been quiet all day with only occasional comments to Callie, and Frankie had been grateful. She wanted as little to do with her mother as possible. Now she felt afraid, afraid and guilty—old, old feelings.

Callie looked at her and Frankie shrugged. "That okay with you, T. Roy?"

"Yeah!" he shouted. "Pool, pool, pool!" He went over to Callie. "You got trunks, too?"

Callie made a little grimace, then smiled. "Not exactly, but I've got a bathing suit. I'll go put it on."

Frankie was too nervous to sit still. She gathered up the napkins and pizza boxes and soda bottles and stuffed them into one of the black bags they'd filled. Then she took a sponge and began washing down the refrigerator door.

Callie came out in a black hooded terrycloth robe and jeweled sandals. Frankie gave a laugh in spite of herself. "This isn't Las Vegas, Callie."

"Hey," her sister said, frowning. "It's what I have with me."

"And you look great," Frankie conceded. "Way too good for Kellogg."

The sisters looked at each other in recognition. "But not too good for me," they said in unison and laughed. And chanting "But not too good for me," Callie and T. Roy passed through the slider, leaving mother and daughter with only each other.

"I appreciate you girls cleaning the house for me. I just haven't had the energy to keep things up."

Frankie recognized it for what it was, a peace offering, and she saw this might be as good as it was going to get. She put down the sponge and went over to the table and sat down across from her mother.

"How sick are you?" Frankie hoped there was real concern on her face.

"I don't know exactly."

"What does that mean?"

Lola lit a cigarette and took a long drag. "I saw a doctor in Coeur d'Alene. He wanted to do some tests. But when he found out I didn't have insurance or money to pay for them, he prescribed some pills. Told me to eat better and exercise."

"Did the doctor tell you what he thought it was?"

Lola shrugged. "High blood pressure, heart disease maybe, something called COPD, whatever that is."

"Did he tell you to stop smoking?"

"Of course." She rolled the cigarette tip in the ashes in the ceramic dish. Sparky's in Spokane, the dish read.

"Did you take the pills?"

"Of course, but they didn't make me feel better. I wasn't going to spend money on something that wasn't working."

Frankie nodded. She was out of questions and she wasn't going to offer her mother advice. That had never worked before and it wasn't going to work now. She looked at her hands and then at her mother's.

"What's your life like, Frances?"

Frankie looked up, surprised. She could see a vague curiosity in her mother's eyes. And she could also feel some kind of trap right around the corner. A handful of responses bubbled up from somewhere, including the one she knew would hurt her mother the most. She pressed it back.

"I live pretty simply," she said finally. "I have a little house in southeast Portland. Not all that far from where we used to live."

Her mother nodded, played with the cigarette.

"It's a quiet neighborhood. Lots of stuff you can walk to. Restaurants, an old movie theater, coffee shops. I work at home. I'm an editor, freelance."

"Last I heard from Beth Ann you were working for the State."

"That was years ago. I was a social worker."

"Good pay and benefits, I imagine."

"Good enough but the work was too sad, too painful."

"Couldn't save all those strays, huh, Frances?"

Frankie looked at her. "No. No, I couldn't." After a moment she said, "You still see Beth Ann?"

"Yeah, when I get to Coeur d'Alene. And we talk on the phone some. She wants me to get a computer so we can email but I can't seem to care about any of that."

"You don't have to have your own computer. Most libraries have them that you can use." Frankie heard herself go into fix-it.

Her mother didn't say anything in return. And as the minute stretched out, Frankie wondered if Lola was waiting for something. For a few years after her mother's disappearance, Frankie had imagined how proud her mother would be of her for having gone to college, gotten a good job, taken care of herself. Then in other daydreams, she had unleashed her anger on Lola, spewed all the hurt and pain, the loneliness and fear, and her mother had been prostrate with guilt and there had been a tender and loving reconciliation. But now that she had the chance, neither of those things seemed likely to happen.

She said the first thing that came to her mind. "I thought you'd be living in the house you grew up in, that you moved back here to do that."

"That house of misery? Hardly."

"Did you sell it?"

"I never owned it."

Frankie tried again. "Do you . . . do we have any family here?"

"I have a brother, but you don't want to know him. I don't want to know him."

"Do you have friends? Have a hobby? Have a job?"

Her mother pulled her gaze from the ashtray and looked at Frankie with a question in her eyes. Frankie still couldn't tell what Lola was after. She tried hard to look kind and interested.

Her mother shrugged again. "I get by okay. Beth Ann helped me get disability so I get a check each month. Is this what you want to know?"

Frankie nodded.

"I run errands for a few of the folks in the park, who are old. Older than me anyway. They pay me or buy me groceries. Sometimes I clean for them as well. Sometimes I clean at the Jug. Which is why I never clean here. I don't want to spend my whole life cleaning."

"Makes sense," said Frankie.

Lola picked up her glass, saw that it was empty, and headed for the fridge. "You want one?"

"No, I don't drink."

Her mother raised an eyebrow in question.

"I drank for a while but it never did me any good," Frankie said.

"You didn't drink long enough then. Drink long enough and it does a world of good." She poured the glass half-full.

"Got any friends here in the park?"

"They're not my type. I like a livelier crowd."

"Well, I was just hoping there was someone around who could look out for you. If you got sick or sicker or needed anything. We all need that."

"You got someone like that in Portland?"

Frankie nodded. "My back-door neighbor, Melanie. We don't hang out together all that much but I know I could call on her in a flash if I needed anything."

"That's good," her mother said. "You been married, Frances?"

"No." She wasn't going to talk about George or Dimitri or Tom. "You ever hear from John Blalock?" she said instead.

"Actually, yes. He sends me money from time to time. Not alimony. Nothing like that. Just, I don't know, memory money."

"I thought you didn't believe in marriage. That's what you always told us. The way of the past. For sissies and idiots. Am I remembering right?"

Her mother gave a laugh. Frankie couldn't tell if it was bitter or not.

"Yeah, I used to say that. Not smart enough to follow my own advice. He was a romantic. And I was in the mood for romance,

I guess. And well, what the hell! It was something different. The great frontier and all that."

"You and Jackson, are you . . .?"

"Just friends. Friends with benefits, isn't that the term? You got a Jackson in your life?"

Frankie didn't say anything.

"Well, you should," her mother said. "They come in handy."

"I do all right on my own."

"Of course, you do. You always did." She shook a cigarette out of the pack and lit it. The loving attention she gave to the stick of tobacco stirred up something in Frankie's gut that she recognized as jealousy.

"I met Jimmy McPhee," Frankie said.

Her mother looked over at her with real interest for the first time. "When?" she said.

"In 2000. In Vancouver, BC."

"Jimmy McPhee. Haven't thought of him in years, decades," said Lola. "How did you find him?"

"It wasn't all that hard. He's still in love with you."

"No, Frances." She shook her head and laughed, a strange kind of chortle. "He's in love with a girl he met in San Francisco. He's not in love with me."

There was a long moment of silence. Lola smoked, Frances waited.

"What did he tell you?" her mother asked finally.

"Not much. That he wasn't my father."

Lola nodded.

"That somebody named Tony was."

Lola nodded again.

"Will you tell me about him?"

"Jimmy?"

"No, Tony."

Lola shook her head.

"Why not?" Frankie tried to keep her voice calm, neutral.

"There's nothing to tell. We had sex a few times. He left."

"That can't be the whole story. I want the whole story."

Her mother shook her head again, then lit another cigarette. The ritual was slow, agonizing. Then she looked her daughter in the eye. "I have no regrets, Frances."

Something old and deep in Frankie came rushing through her. Then it sputtered and went out.

"I'm imagining you want me to." Lola turned her attention back to the cigarette and the ashtray. "To have regrets."

Frankie sank back into herself and, for a few beats, she watched her mother's hand play with the cigarette. Then she spoke. "I gave up on that when I was sixteen."

Lola shrugged. "Good. Although I don't believe you." She took a long drag and stubbed out the cigarette. "I don't believe in much, Frances. Not the whiny God of those TV guys, not the Beatles' 'let it be' bullshit. And I won't give you any of that New Age crap that I did the best I could. It's a lot simpler than that." She looked back at her daughter. "I did what I did. End of story."

Frankie said nothing, just sat looking at her mother, willing this to somehow be different.

Lola took a sip of her drink and pulled another stack of papers over in front of her.

"Wait," said Frankie. "We're not done here."

Lola looked up.

"You got to say what you wanted. I want that same chance. It's been twenty-eight years."

Lola put down the paper in her hand. She looked at her glass, then made another trip to the fridge, lit another cigarette. She settled back in her chair. Frankie searched her mother's face for an opening but there wasn't one. She was on her own.

"All those years on the farms, when Callie and I were kids, how you were, it didn't matter. We didn't know any different. It was normal to us. There were women who loved us, who mothered us. There was Cassie." She looked at her mother and saw the wound open, and she was both sorry and glad at the same time. "We didn't need you. I didn't miss you when you weren't there." Frankie had to work to keep her voice steady, neutral. The pain was so big, so old. "But when we moved to Portland, it was different. We no longer had the Family. We just had you."

"There was no 'Family,' Frances. They were a bunch of horny men and loser women who didn't want to pay taxes or work regular jobs."

"They were our family, the mothers and fathers you chose for us." Frankie felt a door open inside herself and something clicked into place. "But in Portland, we had no one, no one but you. And then we didn't have that."

"There was Dewey and Snow."

"Not after they moved to Montana." She paused. "You never told us they wanted us to come with them."

Lola shrugged. "I didn't want to move again."

Frankie went on as if she hadn't heard. "I don't know what fantasy, what delusion you've been living under these past twenty-eight years. That it was okay to uproot two kids from their life, drop them in a house in a town, give them a few months, and then take off for someplace that suited you better. You should have left us at the Landing."

"You don't know the whole story." Her mother's voice was matter of fact.

"Okay, I'll grant you that. But whose fault is that? Who's never told the whole story?" Frankie gripped the table edge with both hands. "Well, I'm listening," she said after a moment.

"The family, as you call it, wasn't safe anymore. You girls were too old."

"What are you talking about? Too old? No one would have hurt us at the farm. They loved us."

"You're being naïve, Frances. Get me another drink, will you?" And her mother pushed the empty glass over to her.

Frankie took the glass and went to the fridge. She watched her hands pull out the bottle and twist the cap and pour the thick liquid into the glass. The fumes wafted up toward her and it was so familiar, too familiar. She put the bottle back and closed the freezer door and handed the glass to her mother. She couldn't bring herself to sit back down.

"I'm listening," she said again.

"There's nothing more to tell. I made a decision to leave and I went to Portland and I took you two with me. I was not going to leave you there."

"Yeah, and look what happened to us."

Lola scowled and shook her head. "I'm not responsible for what you've made of your life, Frances. Or Callie, for that matter."

A black river of anger surged up Frankie's throat. "And you don't care," she said.

A dark cloud passed through Lola's eyes. Then her face went blank. "You're right," she said. "I don't."

"And you never did." Frankie was close to tears.

The dark cloud moved over Lola's body this time, or so it seemed to Frankie. A strange energy, a vibration. And then the blankness again. "No, I never did," said her mother. "Just get over it, Frankie. Let it go and move on. I have."

Frankie stood in her sorrow there across the table from Lola. To hold herself together, she counted to sixty with Mississippi's like Cassie had taught her. And then she asked what she really wanted to know, although she already knew the answer.

The afternoon was mostly gone when Frankie went out the slider. Callie's car in the street next to hers was a jolt. She'd forgotten all about her sister and the boy. The desire to leave, to just get in the car and go, rose up again even stronger. She saw herself driving to the motel, packing her stuff, leaving Callie money for the boy, heading home to Portland. She let the idea play out a moment, and then she headed down to the pool.

"You owe me big for this," said Callie. She was sitting in a plastic lounge chair painting her toenails. T. Roy was asleep on the lounge chair next to her, wrapped in a towel.

"Geez, lighten up," her sister said when she saw Frankie's face. "I'm just teasing. You get things sorted out with Mom about the money?"

Frankie sat down next to the boy. She watched him sleep.

"Earth to Frankie."

"Sorry." Frankie shook her head. "What did you ask?"

"Mom, money, sorted out?"

Frankie tried to focus. "I guess. She gets disability. Some kind of government payment, I think. And maybe insurance.

She works some." She decided not to mention the money from Blalock. What was the point?

"So we're off the hook?"

"I think so. For now, anyway."

"Well, good. Mission accomplished." Callie screwed the top on the cherry red polish.

"Yes, mission accomplished."

Callie handed her sister the polish. "Put it in my purse, will you? I don't want to move until these are dry."

It was a relief to do the practical. Wake the boy up, drive to the motel, order takeout, teach T. Roy canasta. She needed to take her computer down to the lobby again, to work on the client projects, but she couldn't do it. By nine, she was stupid with fatigue.

Callie went back to their mother's for the night. Frankie insisted. If she could have justified sending T. Roy with her, she would have. She desperately needed to be alone, to have some sort of a chance at soothing her heartache. But the boy slept like a log and that would have to do. She crawled into the other bed and thought she'd lie awake all night but she didn't.

The night was very dark and the sidewalk was rough and cracked, tree roots pushing up into it. Frankie felt the flashlight in her hand, but its beam was small and of little help. The rain seemed to have stopped but the tree branches hung down and big drops hit her head and face. In the distance, she could hear children laughing and shouting, sometimes close, sometimes farther away. She walked slowly, watching her feet so she didn't trip, all the while holding tightly to the flashlight and to the small plastic bucket in her other hand. From time to time, she shone the small beam into the bucket to be sure the candy was still there. Once, up to the right, she could see a big porch, the lights in the house shining, the carved pumpkins glowing. The porch was crowded with children, pushing and shoving, and two women smiled and handed them something she couldn't see. The children shouted "Thank you!" and then flew off like so many blackbirds. The porch disappeared and she was left in the dark on the sidewalk with her flashlight and her bucket. She walked on.

Then ahead of her was a streetlamp, an old-fashioned kind of wrought iron with a golden glass ball at the top. Leaning against it was a man. He was smoking and singing to himself. Even from a distance, she could see the blue jeans, the denim jacket open to reveal his bare chest, the gleam and texture of his boots, the knuckles of his fingers, the smoothness of the nails. And she knew the feel of those fingers on the back of her neck. And she knew what his low voice sounded like in her ear and what his mouth felt like on hers. And a wave of heat coursed through her body.

The sidewalk became a path in the woods, the very last light of the afternoon glowing through the trees. In her hand, a piece of paper now put off a small beam of light onto the path, the bucket still dangling from the other hand. The woods ended abruptly, the path leading down a steep slope to the beach below. Her heart beat faster, the anticipation of what she longed for. She began to run though the sand was soft and her legs clumsy. She called out "Mom!" but the woman didn't turn. She called out again and reached the water's edge and the woman was gone. Loss and grief descended upon her and she stood laden with their weight, the sand cold and wet beneath her feet. The paper had gone dark, the bucket empty. Then she smelled something metallic, like ozone after lightening, and she felt the man behind her and he spoke her name.

LOLA

Winter 1967

She stood in the half-open door of the restroom. She'd been watching truckers get gas and tighten their loads for the last ninety minutes. It wasn't courage she was waiting for but some invisible sign, some unseen nudge that this guy was the right one. She'd let a couple of handsome guys go by. She already knew that handsome guys were trouble. Finally, she saw the right one. Short. Thinning hair. Older but not too old. A belly pushing over the belt that said two pieces of pie every night with extra ice cream.

She reached down and picked up the battered leather suitcase that Beth Ann had loaned her and stepped out into the sleet of late February.

"Are you going west?" She smiled her best smile.

The driver turned to look at her, then stepped down from the running board. "Spokane, then Seattle," he said.

"I'd really like to ride along. I'm trying to get to my mom in Seattle."

"We're not supposed to pick up hitchhikers."

She opened her eyes a little wider and looked at him with as sad a look as she could muster.

He blushed and she knew she had picked the right one. "What's your name, honey?"

"Linda Jean. I don't have enough money for the bus and I need to go now, right away. My mom is sick." She wasn't quite sure how thick to lay it on.

The trucker looked away for a minute, then said. "Okay. Climb in. We'll sort something out."

In Spokane, he made her wait at a diner while he did his delivery. Then they drove all night to Seattle. She learned he was from Fargo, had a wife and two little boys, grew up on a farm. She made up a story about divorce and cancer. He seemed to buy it all, to feel sorry for her, and that's all she wanted. He didn't try to touch her. She knew that might be a possibility and she didn't know how she would handle it. That's why she had picked a soft-looking guy.

The last two hours she slept, and when she woke up, she found a gray morning of rain.

"Where's your mom live?"

"On Tenth Ave West in Queen Anne." Her mother had a cousin who'd lived there once. "Do you know how to get there?"

He shook his head. "But I've got a city map somewhere in the back. Why don't you get it and find it for us?"

They got lost only once. On Tenth Avenue, she guided him to a big white house in the 1900 block. "This it?" he said.

She nodded. "Thanks, Mr. Carlson. You've been really kind to me."

He pulled out his wallet and handed her forty dollars.

"I can't take this," she said, holding her breath.

"No, I want you to have it. You may need it."

"Thank you." And she leaned over and kissed his cheek, then climbed down. She stood on the sidewalk and waved up at him, willing him to go. But he waited. So she walked up the steps to the porch and waved once more. Still he waited. So she opened the screen door and made knocking motions although her knuckles never touched paint. And at last she heard the gears engage and the motor go off down the street. She left the porch and walked away from the house.

It took her ninety minutes to get back to the highway. The next ride took her to Portland, then to Medford, then to Sacramento. By the time she got to San Francisco, she'd gotten six free meals, another eighty dollars, and a new name.

Early Fall 1968

Some of the candles were still burning when she woke up. The air was stuffy with old incense and slow-burning wax, and she was sweating from the sleeping bag and the heat coming off the naked boy. Her head ached and her mouth was dusty from smoke and drink. She picked her way through the clothes and record albums and books that had taken up residence on the floor and pulled up the window. Cool air and the wet of the November rain came rushing in. It was still deep in the night. The street was quiet, the coffee shop across the street still dark. She heard the cable car rumble by a block over, heard the boy behind her moan in his sleep. She stood there five minutes as the sweat dried from her breasts and belly. Then she pulled on jeans and a t-shirt and opened the door.

The long hallway was lit by a single sconce in the wall. She stepped over two more boys stretched out in bags on the old Persian runner that padded the corridor. She glanced down at the second one. Mike. The one she had wanted last night. She felt a small twinge of desire.

The john was empty and it was cool in there, too. Someone had cracked the window open. But next door there was someone asleep in the tub and so she went to the kitchen to wash her hands and splash water on her face.

The street lamp from the corner lit up half of the big table with its still life of wine bottles and dirty dishes. There was orange juice in the refrigerator and she poured a big glass and sat down. The flat was seldom this quiet. Four others shared it with her—and their friends and lovers and sometimes kids just passing through or coming in to settle. None of them had much money but there always seemed to be enough for wine and spaghetti and dope. Three of her housemates had regular jobs and they paid most of the rent and the bills and got to say what went on and who spent the night.

Lola had met Cassie, one of the three "owners" of the flat, on the bus on the way to her job. She had found part-time work at a magazine called *California Farmer* on Lower Market. It sounded glamorous, sort of, when she told people, but the magazine was really a sideline for a company selling life insurance to farmers and she was the file clerk. She didn't care. She worked mornings and got a check each week, and that paid for her share of the groceries and rent with enough left over for bus fare and a trip to See's Candy a couple of times a week. The spring passed that way, the summer and early fall, too, and it had been enough.

It had served her well to have no expectations. Many of the kids she'd met when she first arrived had migrated to the City the summer before, during the Summer of Love. They'd expected peace and romance and some kind of vague brotherhood that would somehow meet all their needs so they could get high and listen to music in Golden Gate Park and not have to worry about things like where to sleep and where to get a shower.

Even at seventeen, Lola knew better than that. You had to pay your own way. But if you were smart, you could choose your way. You could escape the hand you were dealt and make something else happen.

She glanced at the clock over the refrigerator: 3:45. She thought about home, 4:45 in Idaho. Her mother would be getting up about now. Making breakfast for her dad and Bobby and Danny. The smell of bacon and stale beer and cigarettes came back to her. Her father gruff, the boys sullen. She couldn't remember a kind word or a kind touch from any of the three of them.

She heard the strike of the match and the smell of sulfur before she saw Mike in the doorway. His voice was deep. "What are you doing sitting alone in the dark? You could be curled up with me."

She kept her reply to herself, and he stood there for a moment and then came into the kitchen. She was glad he didn't turn on the light. He went over to the sink and in the slanting street light, she saw him bend his head to the faucet and drink, the cigarette held out at an odd angle, the light glancing off the muscles of his bare back. After a long moment, he straightened and came around behind her. He touched her shoulder and then sat down in the chair at the end of the table, a ways from her and out of the light. The touch was brief, almost like a whisper, she thought, and she was sorry it didn't go on.

"I've been watching you, Lola. I don't think you're all that happy here. And maybe you'd like to try someplace else."

The kitchen had been cool before he came in. Now the heat was back in her body. There was something in the pull of his voice, in his smell, something that made her afraid, that made her want to be afraid.

He waited a while before he spoke again. "I'm heading south for the winter. Baja. Maybe into Mexico. Someplace where there's sun. We'd have good times, Lola, you and me." He stubbed out the cigarette in a dinner plate.

"I know you feel it. That kind of feeling is always mutual." He got up and stretched and she saw the light again upon his body. She wanted to touch it, have him touch her. But he turned and went out into the dark of the hallway.

When she went back down the hall to her room, his sleeping bag was empty and she wondered where he had gone. The boy was still sleeping in her bed. His tenderness of the night before now seemed like an embarrassment. She lay down beside him on top of the covers. She knew she wouldn't sleep, but then she did.

She heard the alarm clock from some deep, muffled place. The boy groaned and rolled over but she sat up and swung her legs to the floor. The two windows were still dark, the rain steady out the small opening. She needed a bath and hoped the tub was empty. In the dimly lit hallway, there was only one sleeping body and it wasn't Mike. She felt disappointment, disappointment and relief.

Late Fall 1968

The rain that late fall and early winter was a constant companion in the City. Winters in Kellogg had been cold and white and often sunny. She didn't miss the cold, but she missed the sun. She daydreamed of Mike, fantasies of beach walks and sunsets, of fancy drinks with little paper umbrellas in them, of lying on a hot beach or sleeping in a hammock. And of sex. The desire she'd felt that night in the kitchen stayed somewhere in her blood, erupting from time to time in a fierceness that shocked and intrigued the boys who passed through her bed.

Thanksgiving came. At her house, the holiday had been a grim affair. Her mother worked all day in the kitchen. Her father and brothers watched football and slowly got drunker than usual. The turkey was never right. Her father would complain it was undercooked or overcooked or tough or too salty. Her brothers would stuff themselves and go off to play pool. She would help her mother clean the kitchen, aching to get away and meet her friends, to be anywhere but there.

But this San Francisco Thanksgiving was going to be different. They'd each invited friends to dinner. Cassie said she knew how to fix a turkey and she pressed Lola into service. They cooked all morning: potatoes, green beans, a raspberry gelatin salad. They smoked a joint after lunch and lit candles against the gloom. Jackson cranked up his stereo and they danced around to "Lay Lady Lay" and "Tuesday Afternoon." Then they all pitched in to clean the flat and by early afternoon, it smelled of clean and of roasting meat. Lola took a bath and curled her hair and put on a new soft white peasant blouse with colorful stitching and her best jeans.

About five, people started arriving. Only it wasn't just the ten they'd invited, but friends of theirs and friends of friends and people they'd met on the street. The few women among them brought food, mostly store-bought pies. The boys brought beer or wine or dope. Things went all right for a while. They ate in shifts as they didn't have plates or forks for that many. By seven, the dinner was long gone. What's more, their flat wasn't set up well for such a big party. The only communal space was the kitchen and while it had a large table, it only had six chairs and a bit of walking space. The other four rooms, including the former dining room and parlor, were bedrooms, and people sat on the floors or on the beds.

The mellow hung on through the end of the afternoon and the early part of the evening. Then an argument started in the kitchen between two guys nobody seemed to know and somebody put on the Rolling Stones to cover up their shouting, and the mood grew dark. Lola felt uneasy and she went to her room where a small group was talking about the draft and whether Canada was really an option. One of her roommates, Jimmy, had already put out feelers for a place to stay in Vancouver. "I'm not going to the fucking war," he said.

The shouting from the kitchen got louder, a sound Lola recognized all too well. She felt an old, familiar fear in her chest, and it crowded out what Jimmy was saying. Alcohol and anger and men hurting women. She got up to close the door, to keep it out, but Cassie and one of the roommates stood in the doorway.

"Things are getting out of hand," Cassie said. "These older guys have crashed the party. Two of them are really drunk and they're picking fights with everybody. I asked them to please stop and they ignored me."

"I don't know what you want me to do about it," said Lola. She tried to sound belligerent so they wouldn't hear her fear. Something crashed and broke down the hall.

"Well, you have those brothers and we were hoping maybe you knew how to deal with big guys who are out of control," said Cassie.

Lola just looked at her and shook her head.

"What's going on?" Jimmy said.

Lola ignored him. "How many of these guys are there?"

"Three," said Clark, the roommate. "Three that came together." He ran his hands through his hair and pulled at his shirt collar. "I don't like this. They're ruining everything."

"We could call the police," Jimmy said.

"Don't be stupid," said Cassie. "We aren't calling the police, not with dope in the house."

Lola didn't want this to be her problem, but for some reason the others were waiting for her to do something about it. There was a strange feeling of power in that. "Are the guys in the kitchen?"

"Last I saw," said Cassie.

She thought for another moment. "Jimmy, go turn off the music. Unplug the stereo if you have to. Tell everybody the party's over."

"Then what?" said Cassie.

"You and I are going to get those guys to leave."

"And just how are we going to do that?" Cassie looked scared, too.

"I don't know," said Lola.

In a couple of minutes, the music had stopped and they could hear voices in the hall. When they opened the bedroom door, people were complaining and putting on their coats and heading down the stairs. Lola and Cassie moved past them to the kitchen. Lola felt sick and the old break in her jaw throbbed.

But it wasn't as bad as all that. The fight seemed to be over. One of the men stood at the sink. He was wetting a dishcloth and then he pressed it against his bleeding nose. The other two men sat at the table, passing a whiskey bottle between them. They were all dressed alike, black t-shirts, jeans, work boots. Their hair was long, but their faces clean-shaven and tan.

"Hello, ladies," said the man with the bottle. He smiled and it was a sweet, friendly smile. "Just in time." He held out the whiskey to Lola, who took it and handed it to Cassie with a tilt of her head. Cassie left the kitchen. The guy frowned and started to protest, but Lola held up her hand to stop him.

"What happened to the music?" This from the third man—thin, wiry, tough-looking. His eyes were dark, hard to see into, and his lips were narrow and tight.

Lola recognized the meanness in him. *This is the problem*, she thought, *not the other two*. She felt her courage waver, but she shrugged and said, "Party's over." She moved to the counter and began stacking dishes in the sink. The man with the bleeding nose stepped aside.

"It's early yet," the third man said, and he got up and came over and stood right behind her. She could smell the whiskey on him and that animal smell of power. Her jaw throbbed again. Then she turned abruptly and looked him straight in the eye. They were inches apart and he was only a little taller than she. A few seconds went by, a few very long seconds, and Lola waited for the blow or the chokehold, and then he stepped back with a grin and his hands up in mock surrender.

"Okay, okay," he said. "Let's go, boys." He pulled his jean jacket off the back of the chair and shouldered it on. He grinned again and she saw the grin transform his face into something less threatening. "You're one tough cookie. I like that," he said and he winked at her and left, trailing the other two behind him who muttered in protest.

The weeks between Thanksgiving and Christmas were busy at the office, and Lola got on full-time. While she was glad for the extra money, the work was mind-numbing and she hated going home in the dark. Most of the bus trips home, she thought about Mike and wondered if he was lying on the beach or drinking a margarita with some other girl. A part of her wished she had said yes.

Then one night in early December, as she came out of the low brick building that housed the *Farmer*, a long-haired man crossed the street toward her. Her heart sped up and her mind raced. But as he drew closer, she saw that it wasn't Mike. It was the third man from the party instead. He was dressed the same way as before, except that the jean jacket now had a sheepskin lining against the cold.

She hesitated, wanting him not to have seen her, but it was too late. The grin was there. So she stood on the sidewalk and waited for him.

"Miss Lola." He had grown a mustache since the party, and it softened the cruelness of his mouth. He took his hand from his pocket and extended it to her. She shook it and he tightened his grip just a little so he could hang on to it.

"How did you know where I worked?"

"You can find anybody if you really want to." He grinned again. "I'd like to buy you a beer."

"They won't serve me."

His eyebrows went up. "How old are you?"

"Eighteen." She pulled her hand free.

"Well, I could get some beer and we could drink it at your place."

She shook her head. "I'm meeting somebody."

He turned his head and looked down the street. "I don't think I believe you, Lola. But that's okay. I am a patient man. I'll see you tomorrow." He reached out his hand toward her breast. She was sure he was going to touch her there and everything in her tightened and tingled and heated up, but he touched one of her long blond curls instead. Then he leaned in and said, "This is going to happen." And he turned and walked off.

He was true to his word. He was there the next night. She had hoped to leave early, to be long gone if he came, but her boss kept finding little things that needed doing and it was 5:10 when she came out to the street. He was leaning up against a beat-up station wagon, and he smiled at her when she came out. She didn't stop, she didn't speak to him. She just turned left and started walking. He fell into step with her. She smelled incense on his coat and wondered where he'd been. After a couple of blocks, he put his hand on the small of her back and guided her through the crowded rush hour sidewalks. She hesitated briefly at the bus stop

but he urged her forward with his hand. They still hadn't said anything to each other. They turned and headed away from Union
Square and when they got to a brightly lit deli, he stopped and
smiled and said, "Safe enough?"

She looked over at him and nodded.

The place was busy and they had to wait while the waitress
cleared the table at a booth in the back. They ordered turkey
sandwiches and Dr. Brown's cream sodas and Lola asked for extra
dill pickles.

"Where do you come from?" he asked.

"Nowhere, Idaho," she replied. "You?"

"Nowhere at all." Then, as if he thought better of his clever-
ness, he said, "Michigan. Near Detroit. But it's still nowhere." He
said nothing for a moment.

"Are you going home for Christmas?" Lola asked. He wasn't
handsome but there was something in his face that she couldn't
escape.

He shook his head. "You?"

"No reason to," she said, although she felt a stab of sadness at
the thought of her mother alone with her brothers and her dad.

"You were brave to stand up to us that night."

"I know about thugs."

"Whoa," he said with a kind of laugh. "Is that what you think?
That I'm a thug?"

She shrugged. "Okay, drunk and disorderly."

He smiled and shook his head. "That I buy."

"So you're not a thug."

"No, I'm a sweet guy when you get to know me." His eyes
were intense and she could feel him watching her when she
looked away.

The food arrived and he joked with the waitress and she joked back, and somehow that made Lola feel better. The silence while they ate, too, seemed calm and she began to relax.

"Are you living in the City?" she said.

"Not exactly."

"Working?"

"I get by." He smiled and touched her hand where it lay on the table.

She pulled it back but not right away. "So you're a drifter."

"That's probably fair," he said. "For now anyway. I like adventure. My dad works the line and I don't want that life."

"What's the line?"

"The assembly line. General Motors. He puts the wheels on. It's death."

"What do you want to do?"

"I'd be a cowboy if they still had them."

"Maverick or a lawman?"

"Maverick, for sure. Cards, whiskey, dance hall girls. That's the life for me."

She couldn't help but laugh.

"You're beautiful, Lola," he said. "Especially when you laugh."

She blushed and looked away. The waitress came for their plates.

"Do you like cheesecake?" he said.

"I don't know. I've never had it," Lola said.

He ordered a piece with strawberries and two forks, and she could feel that something had been settled between them although she wasn't sure what.

It took a week of dinners for Tony to get into her bed. That seemed a respectable wait to Lola. She liked the feel of his hot hands on her ribs under her sweater, liked the way he kissed her both gentle and hard. When they went places together, when they were with his friends, she felt respected and safe. After that week, he spent most nights with her. But he didn't move in. That would have taken a vote of the housemates and she wasn't ready to ask for that. So he kept a toothbrush and a few clothes in her closet and left each morning when she got up, returning after dinner and sometimes fairly late into the night. His buddies from the party, Turk and Miguel, often arrived with Tony when he came late, spreading their sleeping bags in the hall outside her room. Lola wondered if Tony had some kind of gang or if they all just had no place to stay. She didn't ask.

Lola felt herself sinking deeper into the relationship. They made love several times each night and each melding was like another link in a chain. She had not known this kind of physical hunger before, this kind of need, and she wondered if this was love. Those words had not passed between them.

The flat had another potluck on Christmas Day, but Tony and his buddies stayed away. He gave Lola a soft silk shawl of greens and blues on Christmas Eve, then told her he was headed to San Diego for a job. She pouted and tried to seduce him into staying but he stood his ground. "I'll be back before the end of the year," he said. "We'll have New Year's Eve." She had no choice but to let him go.

The housemates were relieved. They hadn't been looking forward to a repeat of Thanksgiving, and they had let Lola know that.

"To be honest, Lola, we don't like having Tony here," Jimmy said at breakfast the day after Christmas.

Lola put the spoon down in her bowl of oatmeal. Some part of her had known this was coming. "Are you wanting me to move out?" She kept her anger on simmer, her voice cool.

"No," Jimmy said quickly. "It isn't that at all."

Lola knew that Jimmy had a crush on her. He had given her an expensive pair of pearl earrings for Christmas, a boyfriend gift. She liked him, he was a gentle boy, and she hadn't had the heart to refuse the present. He looked at her now with his big sad eyes.

"Actually," said Cassie, "Tony isn't the problem. What's really true is that we don't like having his friends here. They scare me. It's almost like he has bodyguards, that he's some kind of mobster."

Lola gave a little laugh. "That's ridiculous. They aren't bodyguards and he isn't a mobster. Mobsters are Italian or maybe Jewish. But they aren't white and they aren't from Michigan. And why is it any different if they sleep on the floor than some friend of yours?"

"Well," said Clark, "first, they aren't friends of ours or yours. They're friends of Tony's and he doesn't live here. Second, it's the vibe. There's something, I don't know, dark about them, something dangerous."

Lola said nothing. She knew they were right but she needed Tony.

"What does Tony do?" Cassie asked.

"I don't know," said Lola after a minute, shaking her head.

"There, see," Clark said. "It could be something dangerous or illegal. Maybe drugs."

"Tony doesn't do drugs," Lola said. "He doesn't even smoke dope."

"That doesn't mean he doesn't sell them, or, I don't know, import them from wherever they come from," Clark said.

"We want you to be safe. And we want the flat to be a safe place," said Jimmy.

"Well, if they are bodyguards, wouldn't that make it safer?" Lola searched her mind for a way to get what she wanted.

"No," said Cassie. "That would just bring trouble to us." She reached over and touched Lola's shoulder. "Maybe you could stay with Tony at his place when you want to see him."

"So you do want me to move out."

"No," Cassie said. "We just don't want them here."

"We all talked it over," Jimmy said. "We're in agreement on this."

Lola got up, no longer hungry. She scraped her breakfast into the garbage and left without washing the bowl and oatmeal pan, a clear violation of the flat's rules and the only act of defiance she could think of in the moment.

She got her things together and left for work. She felt sick. She didn't know how she could approach Tony about this. The others weren't always with him, but now that she thought about it, they were there most of the time. It had made sense. It was Turk who owned the car they drove around in, and Miguel was Tony's best friend. They all shared a house in Oakland so when they came to the City, they needed a place to stay. She didn't want to go to Oakland at night. It would be a long commute to work. She would have to find a job there. And she didn't want to live with those men. It would be too much like home. She just wanted things to go on as they were. When she got home, she would ask the others to give her a month to sort this out. Maybe she could find a way.

Tony came back as he'd said he would, and miraculously, he didn't have Turk and Miguel or anyone else with him. It was as if he had overheard their conversation. He convinced her to take the next day as a sick day and, after the others went to work, they spent the day making love and sleeping. New Year's Eve dawned cold and clear and they went to the Zoo and walked in the sunshine in Golden Gate Park and hurried home to make love in her bed.

Voices in the hall woke her, and she heard her roommates heading down the stairs. She listened for the sound of the outer door closing. Before Tony, they had all been good friends. A little family of sorts. They didn't have a TV so they'd played cards and board games after work and gone to the Fillmore or to the movies on the weekends.

And they'd talked. No one had talked about anything in Lola's family. Her father barked orders, shouted when he was angry. The brothers picked that up. And her mother said nothing. Lola could barely remember the sound of her voice. But the housemates talked. They talked about the war, they talked about the economy, they talked about civil rights and the Black Panthers and homosexuality. Things Lola had never thought about as being a part of her world. She didn't buy all the stuff they talked about. Cassie was full of ideas about women's equality and a lot of that Lola wasn't sure she agreed with. And she didn't want to think about black people as needing anything from her. But she liked being part of these conversations. She liked being part of the group. And now she felt like an outsider again.

The flat had settled into a quiet emptiness. Tony slept on, turned away from her toward the wall, his breathing deep and rhythmic. She switched on the lamp so she could read the clock radio: 7:20. She switched it off again and got up and ran a bath.

Tony wanted to go to a party. His boys, that's what he had called them, were all going to be there and he wanted to celebrate with her and with them. When he'd said "my boys," she'd thought about her conversation with Cassie and Jimmy. Were they a gang of some kind? He hadn't said "my friends" as she would have. But it seemed silly to freak out over one word or another. Who didn't want to be with their friends at the holidays?

He had given her money to buy something new for the party, and she had bought a long red velvet skirt and a low-cut red top. She put on the pearl earrings from Jimmy and if Tony asked, she'd tell him they were a gift from her folks. She was brushing her hair when she heard him come down the hall. He stood there in his jeans and bare feet, leaning against the jamb. He smiled at her.

"You look good enough to eat, Lola."

She smiled back at him. "Up or down?" She pulled her hair back into a twist.

He came in and stood behind her, his hands on her breasts and his lips on the nape of her neck.

She leaned back into him, laughing. "Up or down?"

The party was in an empty storefront on a back street at the edge of the Haight. The place was crowded and noisy when they arrived. Tony slipped the guy at the door something Lola couldn't see and they went in. Against one wall was a makeshift bar and Tony got a beer for himself and a sweet drink for her. Then he took her hand and they wandered around until they found the big table with Miguel and Turk and four other men she didn't know. There were women with them, women much older than she. They were all dressed in jeans, men and women alike, the men with t-shirts and jean jackets, the women in low-cut leotard tops. She felt out of place in her velvet finery. The women also wore their hair up and she was sorry she had worn hers down. It made her look even younger.

Tony sat her down at the big table, but then he moved away with Miguel and Turk and the other men. The women talked to each other and ignored her, and she felt anxious and thought about Cassie and Jimmy and wondered where they had gone and if they were having a good time. A ways further down the room there was a dance floor and a stage. Musicians were setting up and on the screen behind the stage, lights swirled and shifted. She took a sip of her drink but the liquor was strong and she didn't like it much. She wished he'd gotten her a glass of wine. She'd gotten used to wine.

"You must be Lola, the Wonder Child." A tall woman with an impossibly small waist and big breasts sat down in the empty chair next to her. Her hair was a mass of dark curls and although she wasn't pretty, Lola liked the way she looked.

Lola watched her open a silver cigarette case and take a long moment to choose one, although they were all the same. Then she lit it from a silver lighter and blew the smoke up toward the ceiling. She slid the case, still open, over to Lola, who shook her head.

"What do you mean 'wonder child'?" It had never occurred to Lola that Tony's friends might talk about her.

"Rumors have been going around that he had a new girl-friend, some teenybopper from the sticks. That you?"

"I guess," Lola said. "I'm Tony's girlfriend."

"One of them, anyway," said a bottled blonde across the table and she snickered.

"Don't be mean, Ally," said the woman sitting next to Lola. "Don't listen to her," she said to Lola. "She's just jealous. She's had a thing for Tony for months and he won't give her the time of day. She's had to settle for Carlos."

Ally glared at her and turned her back.

"I'm Angie," the dark-haired woman said. "I'm Turk's wife."

"I didn't know Turk was married," Lola said.

"Well, we are."

"Do you live at the house in Oakland?"

"Tony's house, you mean? No, we lived there a while, but when the kids came, we got our own place near the Oakland/ Berkeley line."

"Wow, you have kids."

The woman smiled. "Two, a boy and a girl. Twins. They're about to turn five."

"Wow," Lola said again. She didn't know what else to say. She couldn't imagine having kids. Her mother had married her dad because she was pregnant with Bobby. She'd told Lola this when Lola had her first period. "Don't get pregnant," she'd said, "whatever you do. It's a trap you can't get out of."

"You haven't touched your drink," Angie said.

"I don't like it much."

"Let's go get something else then. There's food, too. Do you want something to eat?" And the two women moved to the bar and then to the buffet next to it. Lola felt less alone and she began to relax.

Tony and his boys were gone a long time. The band began to play and Angie convinced her to get out on the floor and dance with her. There were lots of men and they got asked to dance a lot. Lola wasn't sure Tony would approve but since Angie danced with other guys, she figured it was okay. She passed on all the slow dances, though. Yet in spite of the dancing and in spite of

Angie's kindness, she felt sad and lonely. This wasn't how she'd wanted to spend New Year's Eve.

Tony came back about 11:30, all apologies, smelling of rain and the street. He kissed her in front of everyone and she felt again like his girl. The men got food from the buffet and were eating and drinking beer. They were in high spirits, lots of talk and laughter. Not much of it included the women. Tony didn't eat much. He took a few bites and pushed the plate away.

"Are you okay?" she said.

"Fine and dandy. Fine and dandy." He drained the bottle of beer and then looked away from her and Lola saw someone across the room signal to him. "I'll be back," he said and touched her shoulder and headed off.

In the women's bathroom, two girls her age were crowded into one stall with the door open. One of the girls was throwing up. The other women seemed to pay no attention. They brushed their hair, checked their teeth for lipstick.

A girl with shaggy brown hair and ratty jeans came up to Lola. She was sure the girl was going to ask for spare change, but instead she held out her hand. In the palm were three white pills. "Five bucks?" the girl whispered. Lola shook her head. The girl took a hold of Lola's arm, but she pulled it away and went into the empty stall on the end and locked the door. She was close to tears. She'd had several glasses of wine and she had a headache and she wanted to go home. She looked at her watch. It was 11:50. She washed her hands and brushed her hair and went back out to the party.

The music was deafening. The band was playing "Louie, Louie" for the third or fourth time and the crowd was shouting out the incomprehensible lyrics. As she headed back, she saw

Tony standing with Ally a little ways from the table. Ally was trying to put her arms around his neck and he was laughing and pushing her away. Lola stopped moving and held her breath and watched Ally keep trying and Tony keep laughing until suddenly something ugly crossed his face and he grabbed the woman's long blonde hair and pulled her head back and put his hand around her throat. Lola could see his lips moving but she couldn't hear what he was saying.

The people around them backed away and then Miguel was there next to Tony, and Tony released his hold on the woman and walked back to the table. Lola saw Miguel beckon to Carlos, who brought over Ally's purse and coat, and the two of them disappeared into the crowd. Lola felt bolted to the floor, her legs impossibly heavy, her heart barely beating. She wondered how much money she had in her purse and how she would get home. She didn't want to go back to the table but she had to get her coat. And then the band struck up "In the Midnight Hour" and Tony came to find her. He wrapped his arms around her and kissed her and wished her a Happy New Year, as if nothing had happened. And in turn, she shut out what she had seen and returned his kiss. She pushed the old familiar fear deep into its cave and remembered how much she needed him.

Tony left on January 2 for Southern California, where he and the boys were working demolition for a new freeway section. They talked on the phone most nights and he came back on Saturday afternoon every couple of weeks and spent two nights with her. It was the same and yet it wasn't. He wanted her just as much and she wanted him more. The two weeks seemed a long time to go without his body and the way he satisfied hers. But when he wasn't there, life settled into a rhythm that was comforting, and Cassie and Jimmy welcomed her back into their circle and that made her happy.

In early March, Lola got the flu. She took several days off work, unable to keep much of anything down. Thursday, she still felt lousy but went back to work. It was a Tony weekend and she wanted to take Monday off to be with him. Friday morning she was in the john retching when Cassie knocked on the door and came in. She held Lola's hair back and gave her a wet washcloth to wipe her face.

When she stood, Cassie took her hand. "Lola, is there a chance you're pregnant?"

Fear shot through Lola. "No, I'm on the pill."

"Have you missed any? Forgotten a few?"

Lola shook her head. "I don't think so. I'd remember, wouldn't I?"

"Are you having your periods?"

"Not really." With the pill, her periods had shrunk to not much at all.

"Have you gained any weight?" Cassie's face was kind, concerned, and Lola nodded and started to cry.

"Hey, it's not the end of the world," Cassie said, pulling her into a hug.

"Oh, but it is," said Lola. "This just can't happen."

"Look," said Cassie, "how about you pull yourself together and go to work. This afternoon I'll take off early and go with you to Planned Parenthood and you can get a test. Then we'll know and we can figure out what to do. Okay?"

So Lola went on to work. It was a busy morning and that helped but not much. She didn't want to think about this, but she knew what the test would say. She felt stupid. How had she not figured this out? Over the last couple of months, her jeans and skirts had gotten tighter, her breasts fuller, much to Tony's delight. But sometimes it hurt when they made love and there were moments when she had felt odd in her body. The truth was she hadn't wanted to know.

She felt trapped. She was eighteen. She didn't want a baby. She didn't want a house in Kellogg even with Tony. She didn't know exactly what she wanted, but she didn't want that. She wanted to be free to go places, maybe India like the Beatles, or Paris like her French teacher in high school, who went to Europe every summer, or Mexico if Mike came back for her. What if she wanted to be a stewardess or a singer? She couldn't do that with a baby.

At 2:30, she met Cassie at Planned Parenthood. The exam was quick.

"Ten or eleven weeks," the doctor said.

"Do you know what you want to do?" the counselor said. She was a woman about the age of Lola's mother. "Do you know all your options?" And without waiting for a reply, she talked to the girls about prenatal care and adoption services and about abortion. "We refer to a small hospital in Los Angeles for terminations, unless you have insurance and your parents' consent."

"Why has this happened?" Lola was close to tears. "I'm on the pill."

The woman gave her a kind, sad smile. "We don't really know. It isn't 100 percent effective. Some women ovulate during their periods. Do you know what 'ovulate' is?"

Lola didn't but she nodded.

"Or you can forget one day or take that day's pill at a different time or start the new package of pills a day late. We just don't know."

"How much does it cost in L.A.?" Cassie asked.

"Five hundred dollars plus your expenses. And you'd have to go soon. They only do up to twelve weeks. Do you know anyone there you could stay with?"

Lola had stopped listening at the five hundred dollars and gone deep within herself. She had no money like that. She had no way to get to L.A. She brought herself back into the room only when Cassie stood and touched her shoulder.

"I've got all the information, Lola. Let's go."

Lola followed Cassie to the bus stop four blocks away. The sun was out but the wind was cold and Cassie buttoned Lola's coat for her as they waited. She gave her a hug. The bus came and on the ride back to the flat, Cassie put her arm around her and pulled her close. Cassie was plump and soft and motherly and it made Lola want to cry.

The flat was quiet, all the boys at work until late. Cassie offered to fix some soup and toast for them but Lola wanted to lie down. She went into her room and closed the door. She did her best to keep her mind blank as she took off her work clothes and pulled on her pajamas and got into bed. She wished she had curtains so the room would be dark, but all she could do was pull the covers over her head. She fell into a deep black hole.

She woke out of a jumble of dreams and faces. Her brothers knocking on the bedroom door she'd kept bolted all through high school. John, the first boy she slept with in his basement rec room one night when his parents were at a tavern. He never spoke to her again, but in the dream he was phoning her over and over. He kept insisting he had something crucial to tell her. Mike was in the dream and Mr. Owens, the old man who was her boss at the *Farmer*. She found it weird that she would dream of him. But Tony was not in the dream. Tony was nowhere.

She felt sluggish and still tired, but she threw back the covers and got up. When she opened the door, she could hear voices coming from the kitchen radio, Judy Collins and Cassie singing "Both Sides Now." She used the john and went on down the hall. Cassie was ironing on the kitchen table. Lola saw that it was one of her own blouses. "Hey, you don't need to do that," she said.

"Oh, you know me, domestic goddess," Cassie said with a smile. "Rather than listen to you snore, I took our clothes to the laundromat. Late Friday afternoons are a great time to go. You can always get three washers and two dryers."

"I meant the ironing."

"I know, but I like doing this. I find it relaxing."

"You're crazy, you know that?"

"You hungry? There's tuna mixed up in the fridge and I can put on some soup. You should eat something."

Lola got one of the no-name colas out of the fridge and put two pieces of sourdough bread in the toaster. She sat down on the spare chair up against the wall. "What am I going to do? I can't have this."

Cassie nodded. "I have ninety-five dollars in savings. You can have that. And maybe the guys have a little they could each give you. Do you have anything saved?"

"About fifty dollars. That's nowhere near five hundred. And we'd have to find a car or bus fare and how would I get from the bus to the hospital and back to the bus and where would I stay down there? I don't know anybody in L.A."

"What about Tony? Would he give you some money? He's the father, isn't he?"

"Of course, he's the father. But . . ." Lola went over to the toaster and smeared butter and peanut butter and jelly on the toast.

"But what?"

Lola's mother suddenly stood right in front of her and then evaporated like smoke. "If I give him a say in this, he'll own me. He'll own my life. That probably doesn't make any sense."

"Oh, it does," Cassie said. "It does." She sighed. "Maybe he would give you money for something else you needed."

"You mean lie to him."

"Well, yes, I guess so. I know. You could tell him you cashed a big check and you lost the cash on the way home from the bank. And," she thought for a moment, "and you need the money to send to your mother." Cassie looked so pleased with her idea that Lola had to laugh.

"Okay. Let's say I could do that. I still won't have enough money. I can't ask him for three hundred dollars and I still have to get to L.A."

"Maybe you don't."

"Don't what?"

"Have to get to L.A."

"What do you mean?" Lola said. She leaned over and put the empty plate and glass on the counter.

"I called a woman I know and she told me there are places in Oakland that do it. They run ads in the *Berkeley Barb*."

"Has she done it herself?"

"No, but she knows someone who did. And it turned out okay and it cost three hundred dollars. We might be able to get that much, don't you think?"

Lola nodded. "Do you have a *Berkeley Barb*?"

"No, but Clark usually does. Why don't you go look? I'll call if you like."

She headed out, then turned from the doorway "Cassie?"

"What?"

"Thank you."

Cassie smiled. "You'd do this for me."

There were six ads in the classifieds for pregnancy services. Two arranged trips to Mexico City. They were about a thousand bucks a piece. Two more were for L.A. It sounded like the same hospital that the woman at Planned Parenthood had suggested. The fifth one was answered by a man. He would only take a number and said someone would call back later. The sixth number was disconnected.

Lola sat at the table with pen and paper while Cassie used the phone on the wall. But there was nothing to write down. After the last call, Cassie came over and sat down too. "Guess we wait," she said.

"Guess so," said Lola.

They looked at each other for a long moment. "Something will work out," said Cassie.

"It has to," said Lola. "It just has to."

The phone rang just after midnight. Lola was lying awake and she jumped up and went to answer it. A woman's voice. "How far along?"

"What?"

"How far along are you?" The woman sounded impatient, angry almost.

"Oh. Ten or eleven weeks."

"Too far. We can't help you."

"Please, you have to help me. I can't do this." Lola swallowed her tears. "You have to help me."

The woman's voice softened a little. "Look, we just can't. We don't do past eight weeks."

"Please, do you know anybody else? Anybody here?"

The woman was silent.

"Hello? Are you there?"

"You might try this number," she said finally and she rattled off seven numbers. And then she was gone.

At breakfast the next day, the guys seemed to already know. They had pooled together about seventy dollars. With Cassie's ninety-five and her own fifty, she still didn't have enough. She would have to ask Tony for the rest.

Once everyone cleared out of the kitchen, she called the number the woman had given her. Cassie offered to stay and be there but Lola shook her head. She had to do this now. A woman answered and gave her another number to another woman who gave her a third number. She hadn't used it, she said. Just knew that it was a doctor. At the last one, a man answered. He had a heavy accent, but Lola understood his questions for they were the same ones she'd been asked before. A week from Tuesday, he said, 9:30 in the night. $325, cash only. He gave her an address in Oakland. "Don't eat any dinner," he said. "And tell whoever brings you to stay in the car. You understand?" He didn't wait for an answer.

Tuesday night was rainy and cold. Jimmy borrowed a car and he and Cassie drove her to Oakland. Jimmy had insisted on coming. It was sweet of him to want to do this, and she told him so. Jimmy had said he knew Oakland a little, but they had to stop several times to look at the map and still they got lost. The streets got poorer and meaner, and the few faces on the street were black.

Lola sat in the back, holding the cash in her hand. It had been surprisingly easy to get the rest of the money from Tony. She had used Cassie's story about the lost cash, and he'd nodded and pulled out bills from his pocket and handed them to her. When she offered to pay them back, he'd kissed her and told her not to worry about it. It was no big thing.

"This is the street," Cassie said from the front seat. 'What's the number again?"

"Uhm . . . 246," said Lola.

"It's across the street there." Cassie pointed to a door between two boarded-up store fronts. The only lights on the block were at a corner store a ways down and from a window two floors above that door.

"What time is it?" said Lola.

"It's 9:25," said Jimmy.

They sat in a silence for a long moment. Then Lola said, "Okay," and she slid over behind Cassie, who opened her door and moved the seat back so Lola could get out. The two girls hugged and then Lola went across the street.

The door was unlocked and the steep stairs dimly lit. She pushed the terror down and thought of her mother and her mother's life and how she didn't want that, and those thoughts moved her up the stairs. On the second floor, one door was ajar with light spilling onto the landing. She knocked softly on the door and the voice from the phone said, "In here."

The outer room was empty. No furniture, nothing. To the left was a doorway and in it stood a short fat man. He was older but not old, his hair short and dark, a small beard on his chin. He wore a white coat over a raggedy sweater, and although the room was icy, Lola could see beads of sweat on his forehead.

"You have the money?"

Lola thrust the bills out to him. He took them, licked his index finger, counted them. Then he stepped out of the doorway and into the empty room and said, "In there. Take all your clothes off and get on the table with the sheet over you. Call me when you're ready."

In the center of the second room was a long narrow table covered with towels. A bright light hung down from the ceiling over the table. Paper shades were pulled down on the windows. There was a wooden chair at one end of the table and a small stand with a tray of metal instruments next to it. Lola didn't look at them. There was no place to put her clothes so she folded them up and put them in the corner on the floor. Her fear mixed with the miserable cold of the unheated room and her teeth chattered. She thought she might faint, but that passed and she climbed onto the table and opened the neatly folded sheet and put it over herself. "Ready," she said as loud as she could and she closed her eyes to make it all go away.

She heard the man come into the room, heard a lid on a bottle being turned. She thought she smelled whiskey. She heard his footsteps come and then a cloth was over her nose and mouth and it wasn't whiskey but something chemical and sweet. She panicked and she fought to get her arms out from under the sheet and then . . . nothing.

She awoke in the cold. At first, she wasn't sure where she was. There had been dreams and they still tugged at her. Then she could feel the bare wood of the table beneath her and the satin lining of her coat on her bare breasts and belly. Something heavy covered her legs and her feet were wrapped up tight. The light over the table was dark but the door to the outer room was ajar and the light was on there. And she looked down and saw that her jeans were lying on her legs and her sweater was wrapped around her feet.

Her head ached, her stomach was queasy. More than that, her breasts burned and her vagina felt raw and sore and sticky. It took all her determination to get up off the table, to pull on her underpants and her jeans over the pad he had put between her legs. She stuffed her bra into her coat pocket, pulled on the sweater and her boots, put on the coat. Except for the table, the room was bare: no chair, no tray of instruments. The towels and the sheet were gone too.

She moved out into the other room. The door to the landing stood open, the stairs still dimly lit. As she reached the top step, a wave of nausea rushed up her throat and she vomited out what little was in her stomach onto the landing. The acid burned her mouth and she realized she was terribly thirsty. It seemed to take forever to get down the stairs. She stopped every few steps though she was desperate to get outside, to get away. Finally she reached the door to the street and when she opened it, she saw Jimmy and Cassie get out of the car and hurry over.

She slept then. In the car, then in her own bed. Once she heard the door to her room open, smelled Jimmy's aftershave, but the dream pulled her back down. In the dream she went up and down the steep stairs, sometimes in bright light, sometimes in dim, sometimes in the dark. Her legs ached from the effort. The voice with its heavy accent kept saying, "In there, in there, in there," and she felt a heavy weight settle on her.

Late on Wednesday morning, she woke up enough to pee. The house was silent except for the clicking of Clark's typewriter as she passed his room. She went first to the kitchen for water, then to the john. She was surprised to see that the pad was stained but not with blood. The smell coming off it was unmistakable and Lola knew awake what she had known in her dream. Her only solace was that the baby was gone and she was free.

Tony came at the end of the next week. She'd gone back to work on Thursday and Friday. It felt good to go back to normal. She was still a little queasy in the morning, but the Planned Parenthood counselor had said that would go on a while as her hormones settled back down. And the physical effects of the night in Oakland faded in the face of her relief. However, she hadn't thought about Tony and what to do with him. Sex was the last thing she wanted. And the counselor had said she should abstain for a month, to prevent infection. How was she going to explain all that? Why did it have to be so complicated?

Tony arrived late, just before midnight. Everyone was still up playing cards and drinking beer. Jimmy buzzed him in and Lola got up to greet him. His kiss was warm and eager and he tried to pull her out of the room. "Hang on," she said. "Our game's not over." And she went back and sat down and tried to concentrate on the cards. Tony watched for a minute and then left the kitchen.

When the game broke up, she found him in her bed, waiting. The soft light from the lamp glowed on his bare skin, glinted off the St. Anthony medal around his neck. "Come on over here, Miss Lola," he said, running his hand over his lap. "I've got something special for you." She hesitated, then sat down on the edge of the bed. "No, baby, over here." And he reached for her. She tried to find in herself the old feelings, the desire and need, but it wasn't there. She pulled away.

He frowned. "What's the matter?"

She bit her lip and said, "I've got an infection." She looked over at him to gauge his reaction.

He frowned again and then his face lightened and he said, "Oh, one of those. Too bad. But we can work around that. Come on to bed. I've missed you."

She took off her clothes and got in beside him. His body was warm and familiar, and she snuggled in to the comfort. But then he began to kiss her and fondle her breasts and when he moved her hand down to his cock, she couldn't. She just couldn't.

"What is it, baby?" he said, frowning. "What's wrong?"

Lola turned onto her back and looked at the ceiling. "I've just been pretty blue lately."

"Well, then let me make you feel better."

She shook her head and felt the tears start. She closed her eyes against them. "I don't want to. Can you just hold me?" She felt him relax beside her.

"Sure, baby," he said. "You'll feel better in the morning." And he wrapped her in his arms and within minutes, he was asleep. And she let the guilt and shame come in wave after wave.

In the morning, she got up early and went out for bagels and Tony's favorite jam and the newspaper. When she came back, Jimmy was making coffee in the kitchen. He smiled when she came in and his affection for her felt good now, not the embarrassing burden it had been. Since the night in Oakland, he had been a steady kindness and she wanted to lean into it.

She toasted him a bagel, buttered it, and set out the jam. He poured coffee for her, adding milk and sugar just the way she liked. Then they sat down to read the paper. From time to time, she glanced over at him. He was a nice-looking boy, sandy hair, smooth skin, regular features. His eyes were blue like hers, although not the same shade. When they were out together, people sometimes took them for brother and sister. The assumption pleased Lola. Jimmy was nothing like Bobby and Danny, who were big, dark, and cruel, and she was glad to have this new brother.

She got up and poured them more coffee, made herself a bagel.

"Well, isn't this the quaint scene? A portrait of domestic bliss." Tony stood in the doorway.

Jimmy smiled but Lola heard the meanness in his voice.

"Come back to bed, Lola."

It wasn't a request and Lola knew it. She didn't move. Jimmy looked over at her. The air grew thick.

"Tony, would you like some coffee? Or a bagel?" Jimmy made a move to get up.

Tony ignored him. His voice was low, almost a growl. "Lola."

She knew that voice. She'd been hearing that voice all her life. She took a sip of her coffee and looked at Tony and shook her head.

In less than an instant, he was behind her, his hand wrapped in her hair. He forced her to stand. Jimmy sat there in shocked silence for a second, maybe five, then he too was on his feet.

"Stop that, Tony. She's been through enough. She doesn't need your bullying."

"What do you mean? What has Lola been through?" Tony loosened his grip on her hair and moved his arm around and placed it across her chest. It could have been a gesture of affection but Lola knew it wasn't. It was possession, pure and simple.

"What do you mean?" Tony repeated. "What has Lola been through?"

Lola looked at Jimmy, her eyes wide, and Jimmy sat back down. "Let's go back to bed, Tony," she said. She heard her mother's voice, the familiar beseeching. She turned as best she could within his embrace and put her arms around his waist. "Come on."

The room smelled of sleep. It faced north and the thick fog that would burn into a clear Sunday afternoon covered the bed, the small table, and Lola's few belongings with a pale gray light. She felt hot with what was coming and the not-knowing of how it would turn out. She pushed the window up a few inches and the cool air rushed in like salvation.

Tony closed the door to the hall behind him and leaned against it. "Out with it, Lola. What is it that I'm the last to know?"

She had another vague sense of her mother and then she knew again that she had already chosen. She looked him in the eye. "I had an abortion."

"You what?"

She heard disbelief in his voice and something else. She said nothing, just watched his face and waited for the anger. But it was disbelief, disbelief and then tears rolling down his cheeks. She moved to hold him, he looked like a little boy, but he held up one hand in front of him and with the other wiped the tears on his sleeve. She backed away a little and then he squared his shoulders and the cruel Tony she had seen at New Year's with that blonde girl Ally was there in the room with her.

"You cunt," he said, "you miserable cunt. You have killed my child. I don't believe this." He moved past her and around the bed. Picked up his wallet from the apple crate next to the mattress. Pulled on his boots, took his jacket, and without another word, he was out the door. She heard his boots on the stairs, the front door slam. And the house was quiet.

Three weeks later, when her period didn't come, Lola went back to Planned Parenthood. She was nearly four months pregnant. She told the same counselor about the abortion. The woman was kind and sympathetic, but there was nothing more to be done. Lola didn't tell her about the fat man raping her or Tony leaving her. It all seemed some price she had to pay.

Fall 1971

Lola heard Frances cry and then Cassie's soothing voice. The old stairs creaked as the woman and the child descended and the attic was quiet again. She lay on her back, Jimmy's arm across her belly, his hand firm on her hip even in sleep. The late September sun slanted in across the wood floor and played with the colors in the hooked rug. She could see the dust motes dancing. The window was open and she heard Reggie the Rooster crowing and the bell on the Billy goat ringing and ringing. The goat had some kind of ear mites and she would need to get salve from Dr. Cody when her shift was over.

She left Jimmy sleeping. He'd be cross that she didn't wake him, but she wanted a quiet bath and he needed the rest. So she pulled on her robe and went down to the second floor. There was hot water for a bath, and she poured in a capful of Dr. Bonner's. The peppermint vapors filled the high-ceilinged room. There was a mirror on the back of the bathroom door and when she saw her reflection, she sighed. In the year since the birth, she had lost all the weight but her body had changed, the breasts larger, the hips too. She'd been slender, willowy before, but no matter how little she ate or how hard she worked, she couldn't seem to get that back. Her long hair had darkened as well, blond still but not light. Lola didn't know this new body and she didn't like it.

But Jimmy liked it, although he didn't know what to do with it. Lola was his first and she found she had to teach him about sex and pleasure. He was a willing student but he lacked imagination or drive or perhaps it was his endless sweetness that got in the way. Sometimes in their bed, she missed Tony with an ache so deep in her sex that she could hardly bear it. But Jimmy adored her and told her so every chance he got. And he was in love with the baby, claiming her with a fierceness that surprised Lola each time she saw it. That all had to count for something, didn't it?

She eased herself into the water, relishing the heat and the little cool draft from the window where it didn't quite close. The old stained glass in the top half of the window streaked her body with red and blue. The baby had been born in this tub with Cassie and a midwife from Olympia to help her. It had not taken all that long, none of the horror stories of hours of agony and exhaustion. Lola assumed the baby was as eager to be free of her as she was of it.

She heard voices from the yard as she soaped her hair. John and Trevor and Andy. Then Kerry's laugh. Then the sound of a car starting. Kerry and Andy on their way to classes at the college in town. Footsteps in the gravel. John and Trevor on their way to the barn to start the day's work. She leaned back into the water, giving herself ten minutes to daydream.

She saw herself back in San Francisco. Some mornings she was a singer for a rock band, on stage at the Fillmore. There were always men in the crowd who wanted her, who would come up and ask her out when the band took a break. Sometimes she would imagine Tony in that crowd, watching her, giving her that grin. Other days she was a movie star, going to work where she would have to kiss Paul Newman all day long. Or a stewardess who flew to Rio or Istanbul, meeting rich men who would want to marry her.

She came back into the day. The water had grown cold.

"Ma-ma!" she heard Frances say as she came down the stairs. "Ma-ma." She turned the corner into the kitchen, and her daughter was banging a spoon on the high chair and singing out the word to Cassie, who stood at the stove, stirring applesauce. The sweet cinnamon smell hung in the air.

Cassie smiled at her when she came into the kitchen. "Morning, Lola."

"Wo-wa," said the toddler girl and banged the wooden spoon again.

"Mama," Cassie corrected, but Frances looked at her and beamed and said, "Mama."

Cassie picked up a small bowl and spoon and handed them to Lola, but she shook her head and busied herself with making tea, so Cassie sat down on the end of the bench to feed the little girl. "What time are you working today?"

"Lunch shift till three and then at the vet's until seven when he closes."

"Jimmy's driving you in, right?"

"No, why?"

"We need the car to do the shopping."

"Shit, I forgot," said Lola. "I'll go wake him up."

"No," Cassie said, getting up and untangling the child's fist from her long red hair. "You spend a little time with Frances. I'll go make sure he's up." And before Lola could protest, she had gone.

Lola sat down next to her daughter, who smiled and waved the spoon. Frances was a healthy, happy child and that happiness was more than Lola could bear. If she'd been fussy and difficult, Lola might have bonded with her as a kindred spirit. Or she would have had an excuse not to love her. Instead, guilt mingled with the heartbreak and disappointment, and she was only too eager to give the child over to Cassie and Jimmy.

The baby frowned. Tony's frown. Tony's dark eyes. Tony's dark hair.

After that Sunday morning, Tony had never come back. It was as though he had never existed. Except for the baby moving in her, making her life impossible. She had fallen into a dark place in the later months of the pregnancy, and Jimmy and Cassie had kept her from harm.

Then in early June, Jimmy's cousin John had come to visit. He was moving to a farm, a commune up in Washington. He was full of back-to-the-land talk and ideas of a better future and Lola only half-listened. But Cassie and Jimmy were quickly caught up in his enthusiasm. San Francisco had grown weary of the hippies, and there was a bitterness now as the war dragged on and the protests in Berkeley drew tear gas and riot squads. Jimmy no longer talked of going to Canada, but Lola knew he stayed behind for her although he never touched her, never tried to come into her bed. He talked now of how he would be out of sight on a farm in rural Washington.

In mid-July, John came back and they all moved to Calliope, two adjoining farms about fifteen miles from Olympia. There the baby had been born in late September, there Jimmy had become Lola's lover. Twelve months later, the community was still finding its way. Among the twelve of them, only one fellow had had any experience with farming. So they studied and started slow with a big vegetable garden and goats and chickens, and the men learned to plant and build and the women learned to can and cook.

Lola had little interest in the "new life" as they called it. But she knew she couldn't care for the baby on her own, and the farm was beautiful and the life was simple, and at night she was tired and slept well, and Jimmy was sweet and kind to her and seemed to need so little in return.

"Wo-wa!" The baby's mouth opened and closed, the little bird hungry. Lola spooned the applesauce into it, avoiding Tony's eyes.

Jimmy dropped her at the café on Highway 99 about 10:30. She wore her white uniform and nametag and carried the clothes for her second job. The 99 catered mostly to working men. She would have preferred something nearer the college where she might have met some kids her age, but this was closer to the farm and the men tipped well. A few of them flirted with her but when she said the magic word *husband*, as Lou Ann, the senior waitress, had suggested, they backed off. She didn't mind the work. It was busy for three solid hours and the place rang with talk and laughter and it was an antidote to the serious quiet of the farm.

And she was good at the work. Good at keeping the orders straight and communicating with R. J., the lunch cook. Good at anticipating who needed more coffee or another napkin. Good at backing up Lou Ann. It made her happy to be good at something. On the farm, she knew nothing about anything. She'd never worked with animals, never cooked much, never been in a garden. In Kellogg, she'd lived in a small house on a small street of other small houses. She'd babysat for pocket money, hating every minute of it. She'd worked the summer before her escape at a soda fountain at the Rexall, but scooping ice cream wasn't a valued skill on the farm.

When they'd arrived at Calliope, she was in the last months of carrying Frances and no one in the group had expected her to do too much so they'd divided up the big responsibilities among themselves. But she knew the community needed cash, there never seemed to be enough, and so a month after the baby came, she took the car into town and got the job at the 99. The others applauded her initiative and her willingness to sacrifice time on the land for work in the evil city. She didn't explain what a relief it was to get away five days a week.

The lunch rush went late and it was 2:30 before they had filled the salt shakers and ketchup bottles and cleaned the tables and divided their tips. Lola went into the restroom and came out in her jeans, plaid shirt, and the white coat she wore at the vet's and headed across the road to the bus stop.

She was counting out change when the pickup pulled up. The passenger window was down in the warm afternoon and the driver called out to her. "Need a ride?"

She squinted into the sun and when she saw who it was, she stepped over to the truck. "I do," she said, smiling at him. "I'm late to work."

"You just got off work." His eyes were dark and mysterious but his smile pulled her in.

"Second job."

"Hop in."

His truck smelled the way he did. Machine oil and fresh-cut wood. She'd noticed that the first time she waited on him. Most of the lunch crowd smelled of sweat and aftershave, of metal and dirt. They smelled of construction, or metal shops, or farming. But Ben smelled like trees.

"Where are we going?" He looked over at her and smiled again.

She smiled back. "About four miles. It's on 99. Olympia Veterinary. On the left."

"Not nearly far enough." That smile, those eyes.

She looked out the window. She could feel it. That jolt that went up and down the core of her body. Something she never felt with Jimmy.

"How come you're off in the middle of the afternoon?" She tried to move away from the feelings.

"We work early, 6:00 to 2:00."

"And you just happened to be driving by the 99?"

He laughed. "You caught me. I've been wanting to talk to you." He had both hands on the wheel. His fingers were long and slender. His shirt sleeves were rolled up and his forearms were strong and tan.

She felt the jolt again. "Talk fast," she said with a laugh. "You've only got a mile left to say it."

"Guess I better drive slower then." He caught her eye and held it.

"Hey," she said after a few seconds, breaking the spell. "There's the vet's."

He slowed and waited for the oncoming traffic, then pulled into the gravel lot next to the one-story building.

"Lola," he said, and she heard something in his voice that sounded like music.

"I've got to go. I'm late." She opened the door and stepped down.

"What time do you get off?" he called.

"Seven o'clock," she called back and hurried inside.

They were busy and she was glad. Folders to file, forms to fill out, the phone to answer. She made appointments, took money. She and Michael, the vet's son, fed the animals in the cages in the back. And all the while her body spoke to her.

"Lola, your friend's here," Michael called from the front desk. She went into the bathroom and checked her hair, tidied her clothes. She tried not to think of what might happen. But when she came around the corner, she saw that it was Jimmy.

"I thought I'd surprise you," he said with that same eager look she could have drawn in her sleep.

"You have," she said, pushing the disappointment to the back of her mind, moving her face to neutral. "You didn't need to use the gas. Dr. Cody and Michael would have dropped me off."

"Well, I'm here now. Are you ready? Cassie said they'd wait dinner for us."

"Okay, good," she lied. "I'll get my things." She took her time, gathering her waitress clothes, her purse. The weight of Jimmy—the weight of the farm and what she had agreed to there—clutched at her, and her feet felt leaden, impossible to lift.

When she came back out to the front, Jimmy was chatting and laughing with Michael and Dr. Cody. He was so friendly, so cheerful. Everyone loved Jimmy, and she felt mean and small because she didn't. He took her bag of clothes, opened the door for her, put his arm around her, asked about her day.

On the side of the parking lot, she saw the pickup, Ben leaning against the door, waiting. And then they were at the car and getting in the car and she tried not to watch him watch her as Jimmy went around and got in the driver's seat. She heard her name and turned to look at Ben, but it was Michael hurrying over with something in his hand, the salve for the goat's ears, and then they were on their way back to the farm.

Winter 1971

Lola opened the refrigerator in the dark little kitchen. White bread, baloney, mustard, beer. Milk, orange juice, doughnuts. So different from the farm where white flour and white sugar were forbidden. By consensus, the community was vegetarian, eating as best they could from what they grew and canned and the eggs and milk of their animals although there was a running joke that anybody who drove to town solo was headed straight to Elmo's Burgers. Lola didn't think much about food. She ate whatever she wanted during her shift at the 99, and now she ate whatever she wanted when she was here.

She thought about a beer but pulled out the orange juice instead and poured half a glass. She took the juice and a doughnut across the room to the scratchy, unfriendly sofa Ben had gotten at a thrift store. She wrapped herself up in the afghan Cassie had made for her last Christmas. The curtains were open and the streetlight cast shadows into the little apartment on the second floor.

She glanced at her watch: 9:50. She'd have to wake him soon if she wanted him again before the witching hour. But it was so delicious to be alone, to not talk to anyone. She had realized she was only alone when others were sleeping. In San Francisco, she'd had her own room, but at the farm she shared her bedroom with

Jimmy. And Cassie was always there, doing whatever it was she did. And the baby, calling her Wowa and looking more like Tony every day. It was no wonder that she couldn't stand to be there, that she worked two jobs, that she had a lover in town.

After that first drive to the veterinary clinic, Ben had become her afternoon chauffeur. He'd wait outside the 99 for her to get finished. If there was time before her shift at the vet's, they'd stop at a drive-in for a milkshake or a cone. It was like a date. Lola hadn't had many of those and she found it romantic.

Ben didn't seem to need to talk much. Eventually, she learned he'd grown up in Tacoma, enlisted out of high school, did his stint in infantry in Vietnam, hated every minute of it. He'd come back in 1967, worked odd jobs until a buddy told him the mill was hiring. It was good money and he was putting most of it away. Maybe for college, maybe for a house. He'd been once to a town on the Oregon coast called Manzanita. Thought he might like to live there.

He was curious about the farm. "Hell," he said one afternoon, "we're all curious. Lots of rumors flying about that place."

"We're pretty harmless," said Lola. "Just a bunch of kids wanting to live on the land. Honest."

"No radical politics? No orgies?" he asked.

"Is that what you think? That I'm an orgy girl?"

He blushed, and she laughed and began to sing, "Hey there, orgy girl."

He frowned, so she explained, "It was a movie. *Georgy Girl* . . . Never mind."

"I'm serious. What goes on out there?"

"You really want to know?"

He nodded.

"We have goats. We milk the goats. We're learning to make cheese. We have chickens. We get eggs from the chickens. We don't eat the chickens or the goats. We have a huge vegetable garden but not much is going on there now. We have some fruit trees and are planting more. Want more?"

He smiled and shook his head. "That's it? It's just a farm?"

"Yeah. I mean, it's different I guess because we are a made-up family. In my house, there are seven of us. A couple are students at Evergreen. They pay rent and mostly do house chores. Then there's Cassie, she's my best friend. We were roommates in San Francisco. And she's now with John, who's Jimmy's cousin. And then there's Trevor, who is John's best friend. In the other house, there are six more, but I don't know them very well."

"There are two houses?"

"There are two farms, next to each other. Calliope is the community of the two farms."

"Calliope," he said, shaking his head.

"What?" She laughed and touched his arm.

"Nothing." He was quiet a moment. "Who's in charge?"

"Uh, nobody. Everybody. We make decisions together."

He shook his head again. "That doesn't work. Somebody has to be in charge, somebody has to give the orders."

"No, we decide together."

"Who owns the land?"

"Trevor does."

"There. He's the one in charge. The owner is always in charge."

"It's not like that." She didn't know why she felt a need to defend the farm.

"If you say so," he said. "Any of these guys vets?"

"No, we use Dr. Cody."

"No, I mean army vets. Any of them been to 'Nam?"

She shook her head.

"Lucky them." He finished his milkshake and put the glass on the tray on the window.

"Are you with Jimmy or Trevor?" He didn't look at her as he said this.

"Neither," Lola lied. "I'm with you."

From the bedroom, Ben shouted something but she didn't answer. He had dreams, nightmares of the jungle. After they made love, he would fall into a deep place and lie leaden for a time, then jerk and tremble, sometimes shouting out names, other times groaning as if in pain. The first time she had tried to wake him and he had come to with a start and flailed out and hit her and fallen back asleep. When she told him about it, he had no memory of it. On one of the drives out to the farm, she asked him if he wanted to talk about Vietnam, but he said no. "You don't want to know about that place."

And he was right. She didn't want to know. They had no TV at the farm, no newspaper came to the mailbox at the end of the road. They had voted to keep the poison of the world out of their lives. At the 99, she'd hear snatches of conversation about it as she served the plates of food or picked up the dirty dishes, but she didn't try to string them together into knowing.

So she didn't wake him. He had an alarm clock and it would go off in time to get her home. Most nights she didn't sleep after they made love. She got up, like now. Sometimes she read. Ben had a lot of books, more than she'd ever seen in a home before. She told him that.

"I like books," he said. "I like knowing what other people are thinking. And I like stories. I like imagining the places and people in them."

"We never had books when I was little."

"No library in your town?"

Lola shrugged. "I don't know. We never went there."

"It's never too late to start reading," he said, and he recommended a few titles for her: *Catcher in the Rye, Franny and Zooey, Native Son, Run Rabbit Run.* It was hard at first but it got easier, and she began to look forward to the hour or so between sex and the drive home.

It was 10:15. John and Cassie had teased her about wearing a watch. Time pieces were not part of the new life, where the community had vowed to live by the rhythms of nature. But she'd defended her need to be on time at her jobs and they'd allowed it. When she'd told Ben about this conversation, he'd shaken his head. "Sounds like mind control to me," he'd said. "I wouldn't want anyone telling me what to do like that."

"You mean your boss at the mill doesn't tell you what to do?"

"Okay," he'd laughed. "You got me. But not the folks I live with. That's different."

At the farm, only Cassie knew about Ben. Lola had told Jimmy that Dr. Cody needed her to work much later on Tuesdays and Thursdays and that he or Michael would drive her home. Jimmy believed her. He always believed her. But Cassie was the earth mother, the mother hen who waited up for her chick to come home.

One strangely warm night in January, she and Ben sat in the truck after they got to the farm. Ben was laughing and teasing her and they got to kissing and touching and it was too hard to stop. Half an hour went by before she climbed down from the truck and went inside.

"Hey Lola." It was Cassie.

Lola closed the front door softly and followed the light into the living room. Cassie sat in the big armchair, knitting. Her long hair was loose, her robe a patchwork of greens. Lola had never given much thought to how Cassie looked but tonight she was beautiful and soft.

"How was work?"

Lola thought back to the day so she could give an honest answer. "Slow actually. We ended up cleaning out the files of old patients."

Cassie nodded and the light gleamed on her hair. "Is it Dr. Cody or the son?"

"What?"

"That you're sleeping with."

Lola bit her lip. "Neither." She sat down on the old sofa a ways from Cassie but close enough to be in her warmth. If it had been one of the others, she'd have lied, but not to Cassie. "His name is Ben. He works in a sawmill to the north of town. I met him at the 99."

"Are you in love?" Cassie's smile was sad somehow and that made Lola sad, too.

"I don't know. I like him. I like being with him. We have fun together. It isn't all seriousness and ideals, you know?"

Cassie gave a little laugh. "I know the farm isn't exactly your thing. We all know that. And it doesn't matter." She looked at Lola and Lola couldn't read her face. "Does Ben know about Jimmy?"

"No."

"About Frances?"

Lola shook her head.

"Are you going to leave us?"

"No! I . . . no." Lola thought a moment. "No, I just want to come home late."

Cassie nodded. "Don't break Jimmy's heart, okay? He loves you."

"I didn't ask him to. And I've tried to love him. But I just don't."

"I know. But he's a good guy. And he's good to Frances. So don't hurt him."

Cassie was only half right. It wasn't the farm Lola didn't like so much as the community setup. She'd liked the company and the friendship of the flat in San Francisco and she'd expected the farm to be the same. But rather than people living together with coming and going and a seriousness to some conversations and a lightheartedness to the rest, here it was serious all the time. Trevor, and John to an extent, were determined to make a go of the community. Cassie had taken on the same kind of commit-ment now that she and John were lovers. But Lola had grown up with more than enough of that grim determination in her mother to last a lifetime. She'd learned it turned you cold and bitter. And however her own life turned out, she didn't want that.

What she did love, more and more, was the land. They'd come in midsummer when things were green and gold and the sun shone. She spent the last weeks of her pregnancy going for long walks and sitting on the porch in an old rocker. She watched the shift into fall, the fog and rain of the winter, the new greens of the spring, the bright colors of the summer. For Trevor and John,

Jimmy and Cassie, these were agricultural events that required planning and strategy and assigning of responsibility. For Lola, this was about something else, something deep inside her that opened up and responded. Before Calliope, Lola had only known bounded landscapes, though she wouldn't have known to call them that. Kellogg was in the mountains. No matter how high up you went, there were always mountains in the way. And San Francisco, except for the occasional trip out to the beach, was really no different. Buildings and streets and hills and every so often a view out. But from every window of the house at Calliope, there was a view of the fields, and the mountains were a long way into the distance. There was space, space and beauty. She loved that.

The alarm went off in the bedroom and the light went on: 10:30. Time to shower and go home. Ben was good about not asking her to stay. He'd tried once or twice early on, but she'd told him she had commitments in the morning, things she'd agreed to be responsible for, and he seemed to understand that. Still, she wondered if he suspected about Jimmy, if he could tell that she was sleeping with someone else, too. *She* would have wondered.

In late February, Jimmy and John were gone for three weeks. The farm work was in winter slowdown and the two men hitch-hiked east together to visit their families. They planned to come back through Canada so Jimmy could check things out. He believed it was only a matter of time before the draft board caught up with him. Lola wanted to stay in town during those weeks. She had all kinds of reasons—the roads were slippery that time of year, she could save gas, she could work some extra hours—but Trevor and Cassie put up a fuss.

"We need you here," said Trevor, tugging on the rubber band that held his long brown hair. "What you do with your evenings is up to you but in the mornings, we need your help with the animals and the house and your child."

Lola opened her mouth for a smart remark, but Cassie gave her a warning look and she closed it again.

Trevor didn't wait for an answer, just turned and left the kitchen. Lola and Cassie both watched him go, his narrow shoulders and long legs strong inside the old gray sweater and corduroy slacks he wore when he wasn't working.

"He's not my boss," said Lola, crossing her arms.

"No, he's not," said Cassie. "But he's right. With John and Jimmy gone, there's too much to do. And Kerry and Andy aren't going to fill in much. That's not the arrangement. It's our community and our farm."

"Trevor doesn't like me."

Cassie looked at her and gave a little laugh. "Quite the opposite. He likes you too much. But he doesn't understand about you and Frances. And I don't know what he thinks about the late nights you keep. But he thinks things should be a certain way. And when they aren't, he gets nervous and angry."

Lola thought about that.

"Don't you get tired of this double life, Lola? It would wear me out."

"I guess, maybe. I don't know. But I need to be with Ben." She looked at Cassie. "I need him. And Jimmy needs me. It's just how it is."

"But love, Lola. Where's love in all this?"

Lola pushed her tea cup around on the tablecloth. Then she shrugged. "I don't know, Cass. I don't think I know what that is.

You and John, you're lucky. I can see that you have something. But I can't seem to find it."

"You could find it with Jimmy."

"No. Not Jimmy. I hoped maybe with Ben, but now I don't think so."

"And Frances?"

"What about Frances?"

"Don't you love her?"

Lola shook her head. "I know I'm supposed to. Isn't something magical supposed to happen when you have a baby? But it didn't. I didn't want her then and I don't want her now." She looked at her friend.

"But she's so easy to love, Lola."

"Not for me. Maybe there's something wrong with me, that I can't love anybody."

"I know you love me."

Lola smiled. "You're right. I do. That's good. At least I love somebody."

The days of Jimmy's absence flew by. Lola spent a couple of nights in town with Ben but coming home at five in the morning was worse than coming back late in the evening. It was easier to be at the farm where she had the room to herself. And she was there for chores, which appeased Trevor. Appeasement was another valuable lesson Lola had learned from her mother.

The days lengthened, and the first greens appeared in the fields and on the trees. After work one night, she asked Ben just to drive her someplace pretty, someplace open. And they went up into the coast range a little ways to a lookout he knew, and they sat and talked and made love in the cold truck. And when she got home, everyone was up and in the kitchen and there were the travelers, returned.

Jimmy's face lit up when he saw her and for just a moment she felt guilty. But she smiled at him and let him kiss her and hold her for a moment. Then she made tea and sat down next to him at the big table. For the next hour, John and Jimmy told of their adventures on the road, the people who gave them rides, taking the train over the mountains in Canada and how beautiful it was. Then the talk turned to the farm and Lola went up to bed.

She brushed her hair, brushed her teeth, washed Ben off herself as best she could, and put on her long, warm nightgown against the chill of the attic. And all the while, she was trying to figure out how to handle Jimmy. She had not missed him and she didn't want to have sex with him, not tonight, not anymore.

Jimmy had never asked very much of her. He seemed content with sex every couple of weeks as long as she was affectionate with him during the day. And usually if she was asleep when he came in, he would let her sleep. But she knew that tonight would be different. He was different somehow—stronger, leaner, less of a boy. She could feel it.

He came in a few minutes later. "I don't think I've ever seen you reading before," he said. He put his pack down on the chair.

She put the book down. "Seemed a good idea to start."

"A very good idea. What are you reading?"

"It's a novel. *The French Lieutenant's Woman.*"

He rummaged in his pack, then turned to her. "I found us a great place to live in Vancouver."

"You what?"

"I found us a great place to live up there. It's a little house with a yard for Frances. It's right on the bus line into the city. And there are a lot of jobs up there. I'll get something with no problem. And there are a lot of Americans. We met tons of them."

"I'm not leaving the farm."

"Oh, I know it will be hard. But Cassie and John can come visit us. John says they will. And I won't have to worry about the Feds anymore."

"Jimmy, you're not listening. I'm not leaving the farm."

"Don't say that. Please. I have to go and I don't want to go without you, without the baby. We're a family. I want us to get married and be together always." The little boy was back in his eyes, in his voice.

There was a long silence. Then he said, "Say something."

She looked at him. "Jimmy, I'm not in love with you. I came to the farm because Cassie was coming to the farm and I wanted to be with her and have her help with Frances. And you came too and that was fine with me. And it was fine with me that we started sharing a room. I didn't mind. I don't mind now. You're my friend. But I wasn't in love with you then and I am not in love with you now. I am not going to marry you and I am not going to Vancouver."

"But that was our plan."

"No, that was your plan. You never asked me."

"I'm asking you now."

"And the answer is no."

"Have you got somebody else?" There was a desperation in his voice that made Lola sad and angry. "Have you hooked up with Trevor while I was gone? He's always had the hots for you."

"Trevor? You've got to be kidding. Look, there's no use in talking about this anymore."

"But please, Lola!"

She shook her head. "No, Jimmy." She watched his face crumple and the tears come to his eyes and again she felt sad and angry. Then he turned his back and picked up his pack. "Do you want me to sleep somewhere else?" He didn't turn to face her as he spoke.

Lola hesitated, then lied. "No, you're welcome here."

"Okay. I'm going to take a bath."

She nodded and went back to the book.

She woke when he got into bed. It seemed a long time later, and it must have been, for the moon had moved a good ways across the sky. He had turned his back to her but she could hear him crying. She put her arms around him and held him to her, for even though she refused to feel guilty, she knew she had hurt him and she hadn't wanted that. And when he wanted to make love to her, she let him, as she wanted to be kind. And afterward, as they settled into sleep, she said softly, "The answer is still no."

Within a week, Jimmy was gone. Lola was relieved, but she hadn't thought about what this would mean for the others. Trevor was angry. Spring planting was coming fast and he was short a man to work the fields. This meant extra work for him and John or hiring someone with their precious cash. John was more stoical. He'd been 4-F all along and he knew the risks that Jimmy had taken to stay with them as long as he did. But Frances was inconsolable, crying and calling for Papa. Lola had stopped noticing the time Jimmy spent with her daughter and how much he had loved her. It took several weeks for the toddler to settle down and turn her affection to John.

One night in late April when she came back from Ben's, Lola was surprised to see Trevor on the porch when they drove in. He got up and came out to the truck. Ben looked at Lola, then rolled down his window. Trevor stuck his hand in for Ben to shake.

"Hey," he said. "Can I talk to you guys?"

"Sure," said Ben and he sat back.

"Uh, how about in the kitchen?"

"Okay," said Ben and he and Lola followed Trevor inside.

The downstairs was dark except for the soft light coming from the kitchen. Lola heard John's guitar upstairs, then his low voice singing. The kitchen was clean, neat. Cassie's work.

Trevor sat down across from them, his hands gripping the edge of the table. Lola had never seen him so nervous.

"I'll get right to the point," he said. "I'm sure you know that Lola's man Jimmy has gone to Canada. We all know he did the right thing but that leaves us in a bind here at the farm. We need another man for the team, and I was wondering if you wanted to come and live here with us and join us."

It was as though Trevor had hit her in the gut. She felt Ben's eyes on her, but she didn't turn to look at him. Instead she stared at Trevor. "Jimmy was not my man," she said.

Trevor looked at her and she saw that something in his eyes, the look she'd seen too often in her father—and in Tony. "Okay," Trevor said. "Your lover, your roommate. It doesn't matter." He looked back at Ben. "What do you say?"

"When was this decided?" Lola said.

"Oh, I haven't talked to the others about it, but Kerry and Andy won't care and Cassie and John will be happy if you're happy. Everybody wins." He smiled but Lola could see that look still there in his eyes. "What do you say, Ben? You and Lola could spend more time together and you could get a chance to spend time with her daughter. You have met her daughter, haven't you?"

At that, anger and fear threatened to undo her, and Lola pushed back her chair and stood up, but Ben stood up too, fast as anything. He gripped her arm and held her there beside him and his body was rigid and she didn't know what was going to happen.

Then his body relaxed some and his grip on her arm softened but held firm and he spoke for the first time since they'd come inside. "You just blew it, kid. You know that, don't you?"

Trevor frowned.

"I knew guys like you in 'Nam," said Ben. "Guys with small minds and a meanness in them. 'Roosters' we called them. Guys with something missing. The other men didn't respect them, the women wouldn't touch them. But rather than try to sort anything out, they just threw their weight around even more. Did cruel and ugly things. Most of them didn't last long. Nobody would help them. And over there, you needed every buddy you could get." He lowered his voice. "You have that meanness in you and it will taint everything you touch." He let go of Lola's arm and pulled her to him and kissed her hair. Then he looked back at Trevor. "If you ever touch Lola with that meanness again, if you hurt her again, I'll kill you."

Lola watched Trevor's eyes grow wide and then narrow, his jaw twitch and then stiffen. Then that tiny moment of pleasure was swallowed up in the misery she could feel was coming, and she followed Ben out to the truck.

The air was cold and fresh, a relief from the heat of the kitchen, and Ben leaned against the pickup. The yard light was on, high above them, but she couldn't read his eyes, couldn't tell if he was wanting her to explain, but there was too much to say. So she just waited.

"How old is your daughter?"

"Two and a half."

"Is she Jimmy's?"

"No."

"You've had a complicated life, Lola."

"Yes, I have."

"You cold?" His voice was kind.

"Yes."

"Do you want to go in?"

She shook her head. "Not yet."

They got in the truck then, facing each other with their backs to the doors. Ben spoke first. "I knew you had secrets, Lola. We all do. And you and me, we aren't the kind to talk about the past. I don't care much about what's back there. I don't want what lies behind me. It's the future that interests me."

Lola felt some of the tension leave her shoulders. Maybe this wasn't the end after all.

"But this community farm setup is not in my future and Trevor is definitely not in my future. I'm not a group decision kind of guy, although I can see that that's bullshit here anyway." He looked out at the house and then back at her. "You ever watch that Route 66 show with those two guys who drove around the country in a Corvette? They were vets. Did you know that? From the Korean war. I loved that show. Those guys were free. Free to start over every week. They worked, they paid their way, but they didn't get attached."

"I'm not asking you to get attached."

"I know. That's why it works between us. No 'I love you's.' No plans. Just the nights for as long as we want them."

He smiled at her and in the silence that came next, Lola heard some possibility she hadn't known she wanted fade into nothing and her heart shrank a little more, but she pushed that all aside and smiled back at him. "It's late," she said. "I need to go in."

He nodded, leaned across the cab, touched her hair, and kissed her. And as she walked toward the house, he called after her, "I'll see you after work." She turned and waved at him and then turned back, and she knew it was all going to change.

Spring 1973

The children rushed out to greet her. They pounded on the car door with their little fists, shouted her name, and then ran off toward the barn, their rubber boots sloshing in the winter puddles. Frances and Timmy and Gerald, the "wild Indians." She parked the old yellow Dodge in her usual spot next to the battered pickup and the VW bus they had painted for a lark the summer before. She picked up her purse, stuffed the mail into the bag that held her uniform, hoisted up the two bags of groceries, and headed round the house, up the porch stairs, and down the long hallway to the kitchen.

The lower house was quiet, the kitchen Cassie-tidy like always. A big pot of soup simmered on the back of the wood stove. She gave it a stir and then put away the things from the list Cassie had given her that morning. She left the mail unsorted on the table and went up stairs.

"Lola?" The voice was low and soft. Lola pushed open the door of the bedroom Cassie shared with John. Cassie sat in the rocker, near the window, Callie at her breast. She smiled at Lola, a smile of peace and happiness.

"You look perfect," Lola said, "like a mother in a painting."

"And you look beautiful, like a fashion model."

"What, in these old things?" And Lola struck a pose in her jeans and second-hand sweater and made Cassie laugh. "Do you need anything?"

"A glass of water, if you don't mind."

"Course not." Lola went back to the bathroom and let the water run cold before filling the glass pitcher from Cassie's nightstand.

"How was your class?" Cassie said. She shifted the little girl to her shoulder and rubbed her back.

"Interesting enough," Lola lied. "But he gave us another huge assignment."

The two women looked at each other for a moment. Then Lola smiled and bent down and kissed her friend on the top of her head. "I'd better go. I've got the Indians for lunch."

"I made up some tuna salad and the soup should be ready." Cassie glanced at the clock. "The second round will be at 1:00 if you want to join us."

"I'll eat with the little ones," Lola said.

"Okay. I'll be down after she's asleep."

The kitchen was still quiet although the big bear with the improbable name of Dewey sat at the table, reading the paper, oblivious to the shrieks and laughter of the children from the porch. He nodded at Lola when she greeted him and went back to reading. Lola checked the food schedule and pulled things out of the refrigerator before setting the other end of the big table with five places. She made tuna sandwiches, wrapping one to go and putting some of the vegetable soup in a thermos. Then she went to the porch and rang the bell. The kids trooped in, noisy, happy. She sent the two older kids to the bathroom to wash their hands and helped the three Indians use the stool in the kitchen to do the same. Once at the table, they sang grace: "We thank the earth, we thank the farmers, we thank the animals, we thank the vegetables." Sometimes the kids would go on and on, thanking everything they could name, but today they were hungry and soon settled down. Lola kept an eye on them while she tidied up.

"Lola?"

"What, Frances?

"When I was a baby, was I in Mama's stomach like Callie was?"

This was not a new question, but it always made Lola uneasy. John and Cassie and Lola and Frances had all arrived at Eiderdown together when Trevor had decided to "cleanse" Calliope and rebuild his community with "people of like minds." Frances had gone on calling Cassie Mama and her Lola and, in the unspoken acceptance of all the adults to parent all the children of the farm, no other explanation seemed necessary. Besides, people on the farm never asked about the past. The past was done. It was the future that mattered, just as Ben had said.

Lola gave her daughter the same answer as she had before. "Everybody is in their mama's stomach before they are born. Even me!"

"But Rollie says I wasn't in Mama's stomach."

Rollie was eight, a thin whippish boy with a streak of malice that reminded Lola of Trevor. Lola looked over at him but he was studying his soup. She looked down the table at Dewey, who was watching this play out.

Lola sighed. "Rollie is right, Frances. You were in my stomach."

"Oh, okay," Frances said and went back to her sandwich.

Dewey's low voice came from the end of the table. "You are a lucky girl, Frances. You have two mamas. Most of us only get one."

Frances looked at him, then at Lola, then at Rollie. "Yeah, I got two mamas and Rollie only has one," she crowed.

Lola looked down at Dewey but he had returned to his paper, a small smile playing on his lips. The kids began to chatter about a game they'd made up and Lola relaxed.

Frances was a sweet and solemn child. Her dark curly hair and eyes were from Tony but as she grew older, Lola could see her own mother's face in the girl: the Ashby nose and jaw, the strong eyebrows. Frances also had a way of tilting her head that reminded Lola of her mother, and that tiny gesture somehow endeared the girl a little to Lola. Or maybe it was her age. Babies were, well, just babies. But the little kids were cute and funny. She especially liked reading to them. Reading kept her in touch with Ben. She was surprised how much she missed him. Maybe that had been love after all.

After the showdown with Trevor, life had gone back to the way it was. Work at the 99, at the vet's, late evenings with Ben. He came to dinner at the farm twice, met the others, but Trevor refused to come to the table while he was there and the others let her know that Ben wasn't really welcome. Then at the end of the summer, Ben got laid off at the mill. Perfect timing, he said, for he was ready to move south to the Oregon Coast. Did Lola want to come? She'd thought about it for two days, then said no. She told him she couldn't leave Cassie or her commitment to the farm, but in truth, she didn't want to play house, to be married in any fashion. And so he had gone and when the harvest was in,

Trevor sent them packing. John had written to a friend on a farm near Sonoma, who had suggested the Eiderdown community in Humboldt County north of San Francisco. The community there had written back that the four of them were welcome.

Eiderdown had been in operation for more than two years when they got there in November. The founding members, twelve of them, were students of the Maharishi and advocates of Transcendental Meditation. Now grown to twenty-two with the new foursome, this group too had cobbled together several large pieces of property on Hammond Truck Road into the hills east of Moonstone Beach and to the north of the little town of Arcata. There was valuable timber on the land, which they were determined to husband wisely. There were two farms, mostly in large vegetable gardens as before, and goats and chickens.

Eiderdown was a peace community, opposed to the war, to the military, and to everything Nixon stood for. Farming was not at the center of their ideas but rather a support for their lives. Instead, meditation and peaceful protest was the common link. They meditated as a group morning and evening. Those working in town, like Lola, were expected to use their coffee breaks as meditation time if they missed the group sessions.

The four from Calliope had settled in well. The community was willing to rearrange a little so that they could live in the same house. Frances was two by then and Cassie and John were her anchors. John worked on the farm and in the woods. Cassie asked to work in the kitchens and soon became indispensable. Lola found a job first as a waitress in Arcata and then eventually a better-paying job at St. Joseph's in Eureka, where she worked the front desk of the emergency room on the night shift. At

New Year's that winter, Cassie and John were married, and their daughter was born the next fall.

At Eiderdown, there were nearly twice as many men as women and Lola quickly realized that the group hoped she would "mate" with one of the single men. Over the first year, each of the seven men courted her in turn, on work projects, in the evenings, on the Sunday afternoons. She felt like she was in an old-time movie. A couple of the men sparked something in her, but something else held her back. She knew she only wanted sex, the thrill of it, the oblivion of it. She didn't want the responsibility of holding someone else's life together, she didn't want to be owned, and she didn't want to be tied to the farm any more than she already was. At the same time, she was envious of the love between Cassie and John, of what appeared to be a perfect understanding. What's more, they were happy with each other, something she had felt very little of.

"Lola?"

She came back to the half-eaten sandwiches, the empty soup bowls, and Dewey's voice. She looked over at him and he nodded toward the big clock over the refrigerator. She scrambled up and started to clear the table.

"Go on," he said. "I'll do it."

Lola smiled her thanks. Dewey was a gentle man. He worked hard, said little. He and two of his best friends had enlisted, gone to Vietnam for adventure. One of the friends had been killed the first day on patrol. The other had lasted four months. Dewey had come back with a head wound, spent months in a VA hospital in San Diego, then found his way to Eiderdown. Of all the singles, Dewey had been the best candidate. Not because she was attracted to him, but because she would have felt safe with him.

But she also knew she would cheat on him eventually and with Dewey that didn't seem right, not if *she* chose him.

Lola packed up her lunch and went up and pretended to shower. She'd already showered at the motel but again she hadn't shared her double life with anyone but Cassie and so she kept up the pretenses. She spent the time instead cleaning the bathroom, a chore she had asked for, then went back to her room to get dressed. She was brushing her hair when Cassie came and stood in the doorway, an envelope in her hand. "You didn't go through the mail," she said.

Lola shook her head.

Cassie handed her the envelope and Lola saw that it was the card she had sent her mother for her birthday. She sent one every year. She never got a response but she sent them anyway.

"Turn it over," Cassie said.

On the back in a big scrawl were four letters: D-E-A-D. Lola turned it back over. On the front was a post office stamp with a hand pointing to the address. Return to sender. She turned it over once more and then looked up at Cassie.

"I'm so sorry. What can I do for you?"

Lola shook her head. Then she opened the envelope but there was nothing inside she hadn't put there. A silly card from the drugstore, a couple of green leaves from the farm, a photo of her with Cassie and John and Frances and Baby Callie taken at the beach on a sunny afternoon. On the back she had written "Me and my friends."

"Can you call someone? Call one of your brothers?"

"Yeah, I guess." Lola stuffed the card in her purse. "Look, I've got to go. I . . ."

"That's all right. You go ahead. I'll tell the others."

Lola looked up. "No, don't . . . it's not their business."

"But they'll want to know that you've, that you're grieving."

"No. Don't say anything, okay?"

Cassie looked at her, her eyes so full of love that Lola couldn't bear it. "Okay." She moved toward Lola to touch her, to hug her, but Lola picked up her purse and the paper bag with her lunch and brushed past her friend. In less than a minute, she was down the stairs and out the door and into the car and on the road where she could breathe again. Thank god for the car.

She and John and Cassie had acquired the Dodge before they left Calliope and this freedom was a precious thing. As long as she did the shopping for the house, she could come and go as she pleased. To her, this was the American dream. Not back to the land, or an end to the war, or sitting cross-legged for hours on end. It was solitude and speed.

The morning fog was burning away as she wound through the woods and the farmlands on her way to 101. She still missed the openness of the Washington farm. This land was more secretive, the forests old and deep, the farms carved out somehow in the flatter places. It was beautiful, too, but different. What she did love here was the closeness of the ocean and she went to the beach every chance she got.

It took her nearly twenty-five minutes to get to Arcata, twenty-five minutes in which she tried very hard not to think about anything at all. She parked on the square and went into the bank and got five dollars worth of change. Then she went over to the drugstore. It was quiet. Nobody at the soda fountain. A couple of women down by the pharmacist. She slipped into one of the two wooden booths, put her purse on the little wooden ledge, and gave the operator the number she knew by heart.

She answered on the second ring.

"Beth Ann, it's me."

"Who is this?"

"It's me. Linda Jean. With the dog bite scar on my lip." She heard a sharp intake of breath.

"Oh my gosh! Your dad said you were dead."

"Well, I'm not."

"Where are you?"

"California. North of San Francisco."

"Oh my gosh! I can't believe this. When you didn't come to the funeral, I . . ."

"I didn't know there was a funeral. I didn't know anything until today."

"Oh my gosh! Wow! How are you?"

"What happened to my mom, Beth Ann?"

"We don't really know. The Highway Patrol found her in the lake."

"In Coeur d'Alene?"

"Yeah."

"Was she at your folks' place?"

"No, about five miles further on."

"How'd she get there?"

"We don't know. Your dad and brothers had the cars. They swore she'd been fine and at home when they last saw her."

Lola was silent for a few seconds. "How'd she die?"

"They said she drowned. There was an autopsy and everything. For a while they called it a 'suspicious death.' I didn't see her but

I heard she was pretty beat up. But they decided that was from the rocks on the shore. She'd been in the water a couple of days."

"And my dad didn't report her missing?"

Beth Ann paused too long. "No."

"I hope he rots in hell."

"Oh, Linda Jean. Don't say that. He's your dad."

"Not anymore he's not."

The operator came on and Lola put more money into the phone.

"There was a lovely funeral. The whole town turned out. You would have been proud."

Lola said nothing and the seconds ticked away.

Beth Ann filled the silence. "I got married, Linda Jean. To Tommy Dietz. He was a year ahead of us in school. Do you remember him? We have a little boy, Dennis John. I wish you'd been here to be my maid of honor. I had to have Tommy's sister instead."

"My mom knew where I was." Lola could hear the bitterness in her own voice and she shook it off. "I'm happy for you, Beth Ann." She paused and almost mentioned her own child, but it was all too complicated.

"Are you coming home, Linda Jean? I miss you. I want you to meet Tommy and Denny." She sounded sincere, lonely.

"No, I'm not. I'm . . . I have to go. Happy trails!" Their old sign-off. And without waiting to hear her cousin's response, she hung up.

The phone rang almost immediately and she thought it would be Beth Ann, but it was the operator asking for another fifteen cents and she put in the coins and then went out to the car.

The fog was gone and the sun was bright and the air clear and blue, and it felt unfair that it was so beautiful and she would never see her mother again. She sat behind the wheel for a long time without moving. She thought she would cry but there was nothing, nothing except a hard, stiff place in her chest.

She walked on the beach at Moonstone for a long time, up and down, back and forth. It was a weekday afternoon and she saw no one except an old man and two dogs, one a black lab, the other a small, furry mutt. For a moment, she wished she had a dog. She'd take him and just drive some place. Maybe to Baja to find Mike. Maybe up to Oregon to find Ben. Or she could go to Canada or even Alaska.

Images of her mother in the water swept across her mind and she pushed them away. Tried to find another memory, one of her mother happy, but there was nothing. She could see her mother sad, worn-out, resigned. But not happy. What had her mother dreamed of when she was twenty-three? Maybe nothing. She already had Danny and Bobby, worked at the hardware store when she could for a little extra money. Waited for her husband to come home drunk from the tavern. Hoped he wouldn't be angry, wouldn't hurt her. Lola would not have that life. She wouldn't.

When she got back to the parking lot, the red T-Bird was parked next to the Dodge and her lover stood waiting, his solid body in jeans and a Stanford sweatshirt, so different from the way he looked in his scrubs. He was blond like her, his hair as long as the hospital would allow, his eyes a pale blue. He wasn't handsome exactly, but he had a way about him that made the nurses turn their heads when he passed by.

She stopped a small distance from him even though he would have held her, comforted her. This one was good at that. "How did you know I'd be here?"

"Just a hunch. Beautiful afternoon. I know how much you love this beach. As much as you love me."

"More."

He frowned. "More what?"

"I love this beach more."

He laughed, that low chuckle that always did something up and down her spine.

"My mother died."

"Oh, Lola. I'm so sorry." He took a step toward her but she shook her head and he leaned back against his car. "Was she ill?"

Lola looked at him. "No." She looked back at the ocean. "She never got to see this. She spent her whole life in that damn little town."

"Do you want to walk some more?"

She shook her head and opened the door to the Dodge.

"Don't go yet. I haven't even had a chance to kiss you."

At that she smiled and got into the car, and he came around and got in beside her. He asked more questions but she wouldn't talk about it and so the conversation turned to the hospital and its politics and gossip and he made her laugh—he was good at that, too—and he kissed her. Several times.

By the time he let her go, she had to hurry. The farm's weekly meeting was at five. The community had moved it earlier just for her so she could attend the first hour before she headed to the hospital. She hadn't asked them to and didn't want them to, but there was no way out of it. She didn't mind the discussion and decisions about the farm, but the updates on the war and whether it had really ended and what the government was up to now bored her. Their efforts to change things seemed more puny and worthless than ever now. Who cared about Watergate and Nixon's lies when no one could save her mother?

She drove down the long familiar road, past stands of trees and the occasional farm house. For the first time today, Bill had said "I love you." Tony had never said it. Ben either. Jimmy had said it all the time but she hadn't wanted him to. It always carried a pleading to it that chafed. Bill didn't plead. He was as straightforward as Ben, and maybe that's why she liked him. Lola had been warned by the men at the farm that the doctors would hit on her. She laughed, said she could take care of herself. And she had. But she had been unprepared for the false flattery of the nurses, the games of favorites, the gossip and back-biting. Somehow Bill stayed above that and he had everyone's respect. He was sincere and asked for what he wanted. Including her. And that had charmed her and she said yes, yes to mornings at a motel on the north side of town, yes to walks on the beach and making love in the cramped back seat of the Dodge.

Lola had seen him with his wife only once. She was at the grocery store after work filling the list for Cassie. He and his wife had come around the end of the aisle, laughing and talking. He was pushing the cart and clowning for her. She was pretty, had long dark hair and green eyes that seemed to sparkle. Lola knew they had met at Stanford, that she taught math at the high school in Eureka. Bill nodded and smiled at Lola as they went on down the aisle. He wasn't flustered; he wasn't nervous. That would have seemed somehow more real to Lola, less devious. She went through the check-out line before they did and sat in the Dodge waiting for them to come out. They looked happy as Bill put the bags in the tiny trunk of the sports car, a real couple, like Cassie and John. Lola felt a deep longing for that.

She hadn't responded today to Bill's "I love you." He'd murmured it into her neck and that had saved her from having to look in his eyes and let him see that she didn't love him back. *How could he not know that?* she wondered. She knew what love in the eyes looked like. Cassie and John had it in theirs. Cassie had it when she looked at her baby, when she looked at Frances. Lola didn't think that look had ever been in her own eyes. Maybe when she was little. She had loved her mother fiercely when she was little. And maybe for the land at Calliope and maybe now for the ocean. But it all disappeared. Her mother had. The land at Calliope. The ocean would stay, but would she?

She pulled up at the farm house just as the last peal of the bell went off. Dewey smiled at her from the porch and she hurried in to sit in silence with the others.

Summer 1976

The sun was full in the sky and the breakfast chaos in full swing when Lola came down the stairs. The children's voices were a tangle of high pitches and the only two she could pick out easily were those of Frances and Callie. Cassie was herding the six kids to put their oatmeal bowls in the sink before they went out to play. At the end of the table, Dewey sat reading the paper. Next to him his wife, Snowdrop, was nursing their baby, Bliss.

"Lola!" shrieked Callie, who rushed over and wrapped her arms around Lola's legs. She picked up the four-year-old and hugged her and smoothed the wild red hair that Callie wouldn't let anyone brush. All the while, Lola was conscious of Frances, who hung back, watching. Finally, she put Callie down and went over to the other girl.

"Good morning, Frances." She reached out to touch her daughter's face, but the six-year-old pulled back and then turned and left the room. Callie ran after her and Lola heard the screen door slam.

Lola pushed the hurt down and moved to annoyance. "What's she on about now?" she said to Cassie.

"Oh, she says she doesn't want to have two mothers anymore. Says she feels like a freak. I suspect Rollie put her up to this. "

"That little shit." She poured herself a cup of tea from the huge ceramic pot on the counter and laced it with milk and honey.

"He's just a child."

"No, he's twelve and he's evil. You grew up with decent males and I grew up with evil. I know evil when I see it."

"Frances will get over it. You know how she is." Cassie smiled at her friend.

Lola smiled back and the two women chanted, "Dramatic, dramatic, dramatic."

"Did you remember I need the car today?" Cassie asked over her shoulder as she washed the dishes in the sink.

"Yes. Are you taking me in?"

"Yes and we'll come get you. Does that work?"

"Sure. I do find it amazing that you want to spend your one free day going door to door."

"It seems a small thing to do. I want Carter to win. Ford is an idiot and Reagan is scary."

Lola shrugged. "It's your time. I'd rather be at the beach." She finished drying the dishes and putting the last bowls in the open cupboards. Then she dished a bowl of oatmeal for herself.

"When do we need to leave here?"

Lola looked at the clock. "Hm, 10:15 should do it."

"I'll be down before then."

Dewey had gone out to the animals and Snow got up as Lola sat down. The new mother smiled her shy smile and scurried out.

Lola liked the kitchen best when she was in it alone. It reminded her of San Francisco, of the others asleep in their rooms down the hall, and her on her own in the quiet. Truth was she liked living communally, liked having the others around, but she didn't want them with her very much. She wondered if that meant that something was wrong with her. The others seemed to thrive on lots of together time, but she needed the beach, she needed a room alone, she needed the quiet.

That was why she clung to her job, even after Philip had come to the farm the year before. Philip with his money and his big ideas. Philip with his prep school clothes and white-blond good looks. At twenty-five, he had inherited more money from his grandfather than any of them had ever imagined. He had heard about the farm from a friend of a friend of a friend and he wanted to join them and support them. So he bought his way into the community, paying off the land and building himself a small cabin close to the edge of the woods.

John thought Philip felt guilty about all that money, that that was why he was funding them. Mark, one of the original group from 1970 and now their leader, didn't care. They had become desperate for money in the last months before Philip arrived, and now they could go on with their experiment and get even more involved in politics. Philip was their savior.

Lola was still at the hospital, working the main desk from 11:00 to 7:00 now. Bill, too, was still there in the emergency department, but they didn't see each other. He had broken it off six months after her mother died, saying he felt too torn about loving her and loving his wife. But Lola heard through the hospital rumor mill that the green-eyed wife had caught him in their same motel with a surgical nurse and had threatened to leave him if he didn't stop.

Lola and Philip had had a brief thing the summer before. A few nights of talk and unsatisfying sex in the little cabin. Lola

liked listening to Philip. He had ideas and he had read a lot, like
Ben. He took to tutoring her, gave a list of books to read, and
said to come back and discuss them with him. Then he went back
to writing all night and she returned to her room on the second
floor of the big house. And neither of them made a move to try it
again. Just as well. She dumped the oatmeal in the compost and
was making a peanut butter sandwich for her lunch when Cassie
came back down, ready to go.

The September sun had been out early in this land of morning fog, but now storm clouds were rolling in as they got to 101.
Cassie was talking about a new cookbook her mother had sent
her and how she was learning to adapt recipes for them. Lola
always felt happiest when she was with Cassie. She was so solid,
so real, so content.

"Are you seeing anybody, Lolie?" Cassie looked over and
smiled.

"No, but Don, that student at the college? The one with the
broken leg? He's coming back this week when school starts."

"Have you heard from him?"

"Yes, several letters of undying passion that always include
the things he's doing with his girlfriend back home."

"Men can be so stupid." And the two women grinned at each
other.

"And you, Cassie, are you seeing anyone?"

"Oh, only that old husband of mine. You know the one."

"You're really lucky," Lola said. "You know that, don't you?"

"I do. And you'll find somebody. You will. Mark says some
new people are coming to the community in late October. They
want to buy a farm down the road and join us. Maybe there'll be
a great single guy."

"Maybe. But I'm not holding my breath."

"What time are you through tonight? Philip and I are canvassing together and then we'll come pick you up."

"Six ought to do it."

It was minutes before her shift when they got to the hospital. Lola jumped out and hurried to the locker room to put on her uniform. She found it ridiculous that the receptionist had to dress like a nurse and she hated having to iron the damn dresses. There were also weird white tights and old-lady shoes that went with it. She agreed to the tights—it was often cold at the desk—but she wouldn't buy the shoes, insisting they didn't fit her feet. She and the administrator had compromised on a pair of loafers.

It was an ordinary day. She answered the phone. She looked patients up in the room directory and sent family and friends to visit them. She accepted flowers from the florist and gave them to Vicki, her favorite candy-striper, to deliver. She flirted with old Dr. Howard and kept an eye out for the intern in pediatrics. She'd bumped into him, literally, the day before, and he'd hung on a little too long before saying "Excuse me." He had dark eyes with mile-long lashes and a goofy grin. She hoped he'd show up in the cafeteria during her lunch break at three but he didn't. So she spent the time thinking about Don and about making love in his narrow bed and maneuvering around the cast on his leg and listening to "Good Vibrations" over and over.

The second part of the shift usually went faster. People got off work and came to visit patients. New patients checked in; others checked out. The last of the day's flowers arrived. She handed them off to Margie, the next candy-striper. Lola filed paperwork, answered questions, and didn't think about anything much until it was 6:00 and then it was not an ordinary day any longer and Bill stood in front of her.

She wasn't pleased to see him. They had agreed to respect each other's jobs and keep their distance. "What do you want?" she said and went back to the file on the desk.

"Lola, the ambulance just brought two people to the ER. I think they may be friends of yours. A blond guy named Philip Van something and a red-haired woman about your age. Will you come and see if you know them?"

Lola looked up at him and though she'd spent a year looking into those eyes from pillow to pillow, she couldn't make out his features. Something had descended between them. Not a curtain exactly, not a fog or a mist, but something cold, something hard, something sharp.

Somehow she got to her feet. She felt him take her hand, lead her along the corridor and through the big doors to the ER. The light, the sounds, the smells were familiar, and she found some small comfort in that. Her vision cleared, her hearing sharpened.

"Lola," Bill said and he stopped moving and turned her to face him. "You need to prepare yourself. They were badly hurt."

She found her voice. "You don't even know yet if I know them."

He looked at her and the sadness on his face was unbearable. "But you recognize this guy's name, don't you?"

She nodded.

"And the woman?"

"It'd better not be her. It'd better be somebody else." Lola looked down at his hands and their tight grip on her arms and then she took a deep breath and looked up at him and nodded.

Philip lay on a table in the trauma center. His face was a maze of cuts and scrapes. There was a bustle of activity around him and the familiar beeping of the machines.

"Is it him?"

"Yes."

"They're getting him ready for surgery. His legs are not good." He put his hand on the small of Lola's back and moved her down the long room.

In the next cubicle, Cassie lay as though asleep. There was a dark smudge on her cheek, as if from cocoa, Lola thought. She looked all right, unharmed, and Lola took a full breath for the first time since Bill had appeared at her desk. And then she saw that there were no machines going, no nurses, nobody helping her best friend, her only friend in the world. She looked at Bill and he shook his head and that hard, cold, sharp something seized her by the back of the neck, shook her twice, and then settled into her heart.

She heard his words as if they floated on the wafts of rubbing alcohol and anxious sweat that filled her nose. The words swirled around her. *Curve* and *swerve* and *ditch*. They washed over her, receded. At one point, Bill pulled her to him, held her tightly against him. She felt trapped, choking on the emptiness that stretched before her, and she pushed him away.

He left. She stood next to Cassie, holding the cold hand that didn't hold back. He came back, held out a paper cup, and she drank the two swallows of whiskey and then let go of Cassie's hand. The room came back into focus.

"Is there a phone at your farm, Lola?" Bill's voice was steady now, doctor not lover.

She shook her head.

"We'll send the police. Is it John? The husband?"

"Yes, John."

"Okay. I have to go back to work. But Margie is going to come and sit with you."

"I don't need anybody. I don't . . ."

"Yeah, you do. I'll come and check on you when I can." And he stood to go.

"Bill, why is she dead if she isn't hurt?"

He looked at her for a moment. "Her neck is broken, Lola. The hurt is all on the inside."

She woke from a dream of San Francisco, of Cassie and Jimmy at the kitchen table playing hearts and laughing so hard they could barely talk. Toasted bagel hung in the air, the smell so vivid she woke hungry. For a moment, she lay in the happiness of the dream. Then she saw where she was and the truth crept on like nausea and the despair was right behind it. She rolled over and looked out at the fog.

"Lola? Are you awake? May I come in?"

She rolled back over and sat up against the pillows. Her mouth was dry and there was a bad taste in it.

Dewey came over to the bed in his big, quiet way and handed her a cup of tea.

"May I sit down?"

She just looked at him, then nodded.

They sat together in silence for a minute or two. Lola sipped at the tea and Dewey watched her.

"There's, well, no easy way to ask this."

"That's why they picked you."

He smiled. "Yeah, I guess. We need you to get up, Lola."

"I'm not going back to the hospital. I can't."

"No, we know that. We need your help here. With Frances and Callie. John is . . . he's taking this very hard. He's locked himself in Philip's cabin and is drunk. Snow and I can only do so much and . . . the little girls need somebody. They need you."

"I can't help them." She closed her eyes.

"Yes, you can. Lola, look at me."

Dewey's face was so kind, so loving, that she could hardly bear it. "We have a choice when the worst happens. We can stand or we can fall. We can grow up or remain kids. My time came in Vietnam. Many of the guys I knew didn't grow up. I did. Now it's your turn. You can grow up and you can be a mother to your daughter and to Cassie's daughter or . . ." His voice stopped abruptly.

"Or remain a kid."

"Or remain a kid." He reached over and took the tea cup from her. "We'll help you. We'll all help you." He stood. "How about getting a shower? There's stew on the stove and fresh bread. You can help me feed the kids." He smiled at her. She wondered if this was what good dads were like. Then he was out the door. She hesitated just one more moment and then she closed the steel door that had come to stand in front of her heart and she stood up and got on with things.

Summer 1982

Lola pulled the sheets out of the washer and fed them into the wringer bolted onto the old sink. It was hard work but she didn't mind it, for it was clean work. She liked best the chores that involved soap and water. Dishes, bathing the children. She'd never been fastidious but grubbing in the dirt wasn't her thing. So she left the kitchen garden and the bread baking to some of the other women and did laundry most days before she went to work.

She picked up the big wicker basket and carried the sheets up the three stone steps to the yard and out across the grass to the clotheslines. In the winter, they used the dryer, but in the summer and fall, the weather dried all the clothes. Lola's arms were bare, brown, muscled. She admired them as she wrangled the big sheets straight and hung them up by herself. She'd grown lean since they'd come north into Oregon and joined the community at the Landing.

She heard shrieking and laughter and kids came tearing around the corner of the house. Callie's red hair streaked past. She was ten and the ringleader of the smaller kids. She was going to be tall, like John, but her looks were pure Cassie. A blessing and a curse for Lola, whose heart still ached for her friend.

Eiderdown had struggled on for eighteen months after the accident. There had been a quiet ceremony for Cassie and they had buried her on the land in defiance of her parents, who threatened to sue and who then let the matter go. John stayed drunk nearly a month before coming back to them. When he did, he had changed and aged, his hair graying, his soul shrunken somehow. Lola knew how he felt.

They did their best to go back to normal. Snow took over the cooking. Lola shared the chores on the land and cared for the two little girls in her own way. Their grief and heartache was so real that she could empathize and that endeared them to her. After a month or so, Callie had adopted her as Mama, and for several months, she slept in Lola's bed. Lola thought of her as Little Cassie and pretended her friend had come back as a child and it was up to Lola to raise her.

Frances was another story. After the funeral on the land, she had stopped crying, stopped calling for her Mama, mostly stopped talking to anyone but Dewey. She'd already become a serious child, but now that took a darker turn. She spent most of her time alone in the woods no matter the weather. She followed the rules and she did her school lessons with Marcus as before. She also stayed within the loosely marked perimeter of the land but she kept everything to herself. Lola made an effort, a real effort she thought, to get through to her daughter. She tried to hold her, tried to comfort her, but Frances would have none of it, going to Dewey instead and then to John when he resurfaced.

As that first winter moved through its fog and rain, John sought solace for his loss with Lola. He talked to her endlessly about Cassie until she was sick of it. One night he came to her room, crying, wanting Lola to hold him. She knew what he wanted, but she said no as kindly as she could, though she would have welcomed the tenderness and the oblivion herself.

Then came the anniversary of the accident and a visit from a San Francisco lawyer. Philip had never returned to the farm. He had been flown to San Francisco for additional surgery, then home to Boston for rehabilitation. The lawyer told them that Philip wanted nothing more to do with the community. His family intended to sell off the timber and then sell the land. Did the community want to buy it? They asked for time to consider this and the lawyer told them they could have six months. Philip's family was in no hurry. As the man was leaving, Marcus asked after Philip. He's doing as well as can be expected, said the lawyer. His left leg was too damaged to save but he's learning to walk again.

In the end, though, there had been no money to buy the land. No one wanted to stay and rent the house if the timber was going. One by one, the more recent arrivals to the community departed. Dewey and Snow and their two kids found space at a large community in Oregon east of Eugene called the Landing, and Lola and the girls went north with them. John promised to follow. He never did.

As Lola hung the last sheet, the wind picked up a little. It was going to be another hot day, and by evening, everyone would be cranky. She thought about taking the girls to the beach at Florence. It was such heaven having her own car. However, it would take an hour and a half and being in the car that long with Frankie—as Frances now wanted to be called—might be pure torture. She could be such a shit these days. On the other hand, both girls loved the beach and the coolness would be welcome. She'd make it happen.

They pulled up in front of the big house on Fairmount in Eugene at ten. Lola left the girls in the car and rang the bell. Charlie answered the door, the phone to his ear, cigarette dangling from the corner of his mouth. He smiled at her and beckoned her in, then went to the kitchen to finish the call. She sat down in her favorite chair, one ear listening for trouble from the car. The big living room was in its usual disarray of cameras and photographs and newspapers and mail. It was curious to her that this public room was the workspace and all the other private rooms of the house were tidy. It was as though two people lived here instead of just Charlie and his cats.

"What's up?" he said as he came back in.

"The girls and I are going to the beach to escape the heat. We're wondering if you'd like to come."

"Is this a request for my charm and good looks or to serve as mediator between you and Frankie?"

She pretended to think for a few seconds and said, "How about good-looking, charming mediator?"

He grinned and went to get his things.

Charlie was a regular customer at the Glenwood and when Lola started waitressing there, they'd become friends. They were lovers off and on, when Lola made the moves, but mostly they were friends. Charlie didn't seem to want or need anything more serious, even anything more physical. Lola wondered if he had another girlfriend somewhere or if maybe he was just one of those guys less in his body than most. Whatever it was, it was less complicated than her life at the Landing and she appreciated that.

Charlie got along well with the girls and that was a bonus. Frankie told her that Charlie was like Dewey and Lola could see the resemblance. Not physically. Charlie was thin, wiry, more like Tony in his looks. But there was the same softness in their voices, the same gentleness in their ways. And like Dewey, Charlie had the amazing knack of listening without an agenda.

Lola drove the winding road along the river and through the forests, and the coolness came upon them as soon as they left the valley. Charlie had brought his ukulele. He was terrible at it but the girls loved it and sang old songs with him. Everybody laughed and it was a good day.

It was foggy in Florence, almost cold, and they drove north beyond the giant dunes and found a beach access. She gave the girls the jackets she'd insisted they bring and they raced off down the beach like wild dogs. Charlie gave her a look and she nodded and he went after them. She was glad. She needed time alone. She didn't get much of that at the Landing. It was a very different place, full of men trying to be roosters, as Ben had called them, and women trying to still be girls.

It hadn't seemed that way when they'd arrived in 1978. The Outlanders had welcomed them. It was a big group, nearly thirty people, and a big property with three large houses a bit of distance from each other and A-frame cabins in the woods on the way to the river. There were still idealists among the group, both peace and justice types and some back-to-the-land'ers. But the two philosophies weren't always compatible, and the community couldn't seem to find a common belief to unite them. Or rather the belief that united them—a desire to escape the confines of the "real" world—wasn't enough to create a stable community. A cynicism and resignation settled in that changed everything. Slowly, people left. Some, like Lola, had lived communally for more than a decade. Others had put in a year or two. The sixties' ideals seemed long-gone, dead even. The binding element of the war was behind them, and the couples in the group wanted real schools for their kids or graduate degrees for themselves. Those with ideals now wanted to save the world rather than ignore it.

Lola and the girls had moved into Star House. Frankie and Callie shared one room on the second floor. Lola had a second to herself. Dewey and his family were in Winston, the next house over. Lola missed the quiet times with Dewey at the kitchen table. The girls sought him out but somehow that didn't work for her.

The efforts at gender equality of Calliope and especially at Eiderdown were also long gone from the Landing. The women cooked and cleaned and cared for the children. The men worked in the woods and built new cabins and did home repair. Some of the men worked at a nearby saw mill and made good money. The only mutual workplace was the big kitchen garden.

In the first years, there were more women than men in the group. Because there were plenty of women to do the household work and teach the kids, Lola was able to work in town at the Glenwood. She gave some of her money to the community, but she also held back some to keep up the Dodge and put a little money aside each month. She wasn't sure this life would work out for them for the long term.

Lola shook off her thoughts. She could see the trio a ways down the beach, walking along the water line, Frankie a short distance ahead of the other two. She knew Callie would be filling her pockets with stones and bits of shell, talking a mile a minute. Frankie would be dreamy or sulky, daydreaming probably. She would be twelve in a few weeks, her woman's body coming on.

For the first time, Lola saw herself in her daughter. The sullenness, the secretiveness that her own mother had complained about was right there in front of her. But where Lola had been angry, defiant, rebellious, Frankie was anything but. She was smart, really smart, a top student. She was obedient, doing her chores without complaint, staying out of the way. But there was something else that Frankie carried like a scar. And whatever it was, it made Lola feel guilty.

They had lunch in Florence at a little café. Charlie was always generous about picking up the check. She'd protested the first couple of times, but he'd shrugged and said he had plenty and she didn't and that was the end of it. There was more joking around over chowder and cheeseburgers and even Frankie seemed lighter. Lola was glad they had come.

The girls fell asleep before they even got out of Florence. Charlie was behind the wheel and, for just a moment, Lola saw them as a family. A mom and dad who got along pretty well, two sisters who cared for each other. She rested there a little, then shook that off too.

"How are things at Flanders Field?" The first time Charlie had called the community that, Lola had had to ask him to explain. He told her of the poem, the battlefield. Charlie read a lot, like Ben. He'd been to a fancy art school in Chicago. He read the paper, read a lot of big books. Lola felt ashamed of her ignorance but Charlie said it was never too late and loaned her books, just like Ben.

"Things are changing," she said. "There's a lot of coming and going. I don't much like it."

"Isn't that just part of the deal? People coming and going?"

"I guess. Maybe it's who's coming and who's going." She looked over at him. "There's something going on, a bad vibe. Robert's hiring more guys to work in the woods. And they're not . . . I don't know how to explain it. Yes, I do. They're thugs."

Charlie looked over at her with a grin. "What do you know about thugs, Lola the Hippie?"

"I grew up with them. My dad, my brothers. The men they knew. When you grow up poor, there can be a lot of meanness."

His grin was gone and there was sympathy in his eyes. "You could move into town."

She waited to see if he would say "move in with me," but he didn't. Then she shook her head. "I can't. I can't make it alone. Rent, food for the girls, their clothes, the dentist, all that stuff. I don't make that kind of money. Besides, I couldn't live with just the girls. Frankie would drive me crazy in no time." She looked out at the passing trees, the sun dappling the highway in front of them, felt the air still fresh on her arm. "Don't you get lonely on your own?"

He thought for a moment about her question the way he always did. "Sometimes. But I like being on my own."

"I'm sure I'd like it, too," said Lola. "But that's not going to happen anytime soon." She looked back at the sleeping girls.

"Is Robert the problem?" Robert ran the Landing. He was an original member and was the oldest among them, nearly fifty. He wasn't handsome, but he was powerfully built and charming. That combination made him a natural leader with both men and women. The Outlanders had their own version of the farm meeting each week, and everyone had an equal vote, even the children in their teens, but Lola had quickly seen that not everything came up for a vote and that Robert made a lot of decisions without them, mostly concerning the work in the woods. Because there was plenty of money, no one argued with that.

"No, it's not him. He's a good leader. He listens and he thinks about things like you do. But most of the believers are gone now and the new ones coming in . . . well, like I said, some of them are thugs."

"Are you a believer?" He smiled at her and she couldn't tell if he was mocking her.

"No. Well, maybe. Living in community suits me. It's, I don't know, safer than living in a family. In a family, husbands can do what they damn well please to their wives, to their kids. Nobody stops them."

"The police stop them."

She laughed. "You're so naïve sometimes, Charlie. The police don't stop them. A man's home is his castle, or his prison, and he's the warden. In a community, there are other people watching, caring about you and what happens. They share the chores, they share the problems. Like when Cassie died." She heard something different come into her voice. "There wasn't just me or John. There were others to help pick up the pieces."

"You miss her, don't you?"

"Every day. All day. She was just the best."

The heat assailed them as the country road turned into farm equipment stores and car lots and the newest multiplex cinema, and they shed their jackets and then their conversation. When they got to Charlie's, the girls woke cranky and slow and Charlie plied them with lemonade and brownies. Callie sang made-up songs the rest of the way home and Frankie sang with her. Lola kept to herself.

The sun was descending and the heat abating a little as they drove along the pastures up the lane to the Landing. Ahead, Lola could see a gathering of cars and trucks. She'd checked the schedule before she left. There was no celebration planned and no community meeting. She felt uneasy. There was no room for her car, so she let the girls off and parked back down the lane.

As she walked past the barn, she saw the men in circle in the yard, the familiar faces and a dozen or so strangers. There wasn't a woman among them. Robert stood, talking, but his voice didn't carry. Her uneasiness grew although she couldn't have said why.

She went into Star House. It was cooler there, cool and quiet. There was no one in the kitchen, no sounds from the upper rooms. She went up to her own room and lay down on the bed. She heard the kitchen door slam, Callie's chatter, the girls' footsteps on the wooden stairs.

"Where is everybody, Mom?" Callie stood by the bed, Frankie in the doorway.

"I don't know. Maybe they all went to the river. It's a pretty hot day."

"When are they coming back?"

"I don't know, Callie. I don't know where they went."

"Can we have brownies for dinner?"

"No."

"What are we having?"

She looked at them and waited.

"Whatever shows up on the plate," said both girls at once.

"Right," said Lola. "Why don't you go and take your baths now? No one will bug you." She looked at Frankie. "Will you help Callie?"

Frankie nodded and the girls went out. Lola turned the pillow over for its coolness and went to sleep.

The engines woke her, so many of them, it seemed. She'd been dreaming of Ben and his apartment and his shouting in the night. Maybe the men down by the barn had been shouting. Or maybe it was in the dream. Then the engine noises faded as the trucks and cars went down the lane and she could hear Robert's voice wafting up from the side of the house and another voice, deep, low, threatening. She couldn't hear the words, just the tone. But she knew that tone. It came with slaps and shaking and overturned furniture and broken dishes. The uneasiness she'd felt before turned darker, heavier, and she could feel Tony's hand in her hair and him pulling her out of her chair in the kitchen in the San Francisco flat. And then the voices were gone.

Summer 1983

Lola was six cars back when the school bus stopped at their lane. The lunch crowd at the Glenwood had been thin and her boss had let her go early. She could see her girls and the two oldest boys, Carson and Todd, getting off the bus, and then there was another tall boy getting off that she didn't know. He and Frankie took off across the fields and Callie and the boys headed up the lane.

She passed the younger kids in the lane and she headed on up to the houses and parked in her usual spot and waited for them. After weeks of rain, the sun had finally made an appearance. Everything was lush and green, and the air was cool and fresh on her skin. Callie's red hair shone in the sun and she was laughing with the boys. Her child's body was lengthening, shaping itself, not quite adolescent but moving fast in that direction. She had Cassie's ease with herself and it drew people to her. For just a moment, Lola let herself be fond of the girl.

Callie split off from the boys and came and gave Lola a hug. "How was your day, Mom?"

"Good. And yours?"

"Really good. I got an A in math and there's going to be a play and I am going to try out and in science we saw a film about frogs and their innards and it was gross and during PE I fell and cut my knee. Want to see it?"

"Did the nurse look at it?"

"Yeah."

"Then no thanks." Lola hesitated just a moment and then said. "Where did Frankie go?"

Cassie frowned. "I promised not to tell."

"Okay, promises are important. Can you tell me his name?"

"Yeah, I didn't promise that. It's Joshua and he works at the drugstore and he's a sophomore and he lives a couple of miles further down the road and they're in love."

"And what did you promise not to tell me?"

"That they're going down to the river—oh, Mom, I guess I just broke my promise." Callie looked stricken and Lola wanted to laugh.

"Not to worry. I won't say anything." She smiled at Callie. "Are you hungry? I'm sure that Snow has snacks for you kids."

They went into the house, Callie heading for the kitchen and Lola to the bathroom to shower off the restaurant. A few minutes later, she stood at the window, toweling off. The bathroom looked out over the half-acre of garden and most of the women were at work out there, getting ready for the new plantings. She saw Dewey come out of the barn with a big tray of seedlings. Typically, he was the only man on the farm in the afternoons, the rest working on the property in the woods ten miles further on. Lola didn't know what kind of an understanding Dewey and Robert had, but she knew Dewey had refused to work in the woods when he found out that it was marijuana they were growing, not Christmas trees. He and Robert had argued at the

Meeting one week, Dewey firm in his belief that cannabis was addictive, Robert equally firm in his stand that it was harmless, everybody did it, and why shouldn't they profit from that? Lola had been afraid Dewey and Snow would take Bliss and Tim and leave, but so far that hadn't happened. They were her only connection to Cassie, the only people who seemed to love her, and she couldn't lose that.

She glanced at the clock: 3:15. She had thirty minutes before study hall. The children did homework from 3:45 to 5:15 each school day and, to stay out of the garden, Lola had volunteered to oversee and help them. She got dressed and then poured herself two fingers of vodka from the bottle in one of her rain boots and sat down in the rocker near the bedroom window.

The Meeting had been scheduled early, before dinner, so they could meet outside in the warm remains of the afternoon. After being crammed together all winter in the living room of Winston House, it was lovely to bring their chairs and cushions and yoga mats out to the lawn behind Star House. There was more laughter than usual, a good feeling of community, and Lola felt glad to be where she was.

It was business as usual. Fitz, the garden supervisor, reported on the plantings and plans and asked for more volunteers. Everybody hooted at that. He was always trying to get more help although he never lifted a finger himself. A born administrator, somebody called out. Everybody laughed again. The treasurer spoke up about April 15, offering to help all those working in town with their taxes. This had been a major political discussion the year before, with the land-workers wanting the town-workers to refuse to pay, to refuse to support what was surely going to be

Reagan's government. Robert had convinced them all that having the IRS come out to the farm was the last thing they needed. In the end, they had agreed with him. They always did.

The Meeting was winding down when the trucks and cars drove up. A dozen or so men climbed out. Lola looked over at Robert, whose face went hard, the jaw tight, the eyes small. Then he found his smile, his charm, and went out to greet them.

Robert had hired them the summer before to clear more land, grow the plants, and guard them. The plan was to double production and Robert promised improvements to the Landing— better plumbing, a new generator for the three houses, a big new barn, and perhaps even a dairy like Ken Kesey's. This had all been announced at the weekly Meeting after Lola had seen the men in the barn. There was a lot of opposition. These men would be outsiders. Would they respect the vision, the community? Would they respect the women and children and care for the land and the animals the way the community did? Robert had assured them the men would be handpicked and only those with the right beliefs would be selected. And they'd live on the land up there and not be part of the community. In fact, it would be a separate company that hired them, so the Landing wouldn't be implicated in any legal actions. Robert put it up to a vote, but Lola knew from Dewey that it was a done deal. The men had been hired and were already living on the land in the woods.

The laughter and good spirits slowly leaked away as Robert stood talking to the dozen men who had climbed out of the vehicles. Lola felt the waning sunlight darken, got a scent of something on the wind. It was like they were all suddenly in a western and the bad guys had just ridden into town and the sheriff had walked out to meet them.

Five minutes went by and then the group came over to the Meeting and Robert introduced them all by name, as though somehow that would make everything all right. Lola saw that they all had tough-boy names like Chip and Lazarus and Gonzo and Bear, names less of who they were than how they were, and she thought of her brothers, who'd been Bobby and Danny at home but Jacket and 45 to their friends.

Lola steeled herself for something unpleasant but nothing bad happened. The men joined the circle, sat on the ground, stayed quiet. After the Meeting, they stayed and talked a while, mostly to the women. They were polite and well-mannered. There was some joking, some flirting, but it was harmless. Lola watched the others relax into it, but she stayed wary. And she saw that Dewey had taken his family into Winston as soon as the Meeting was over.

Two weeks later at the Meeting, Robert announced that some of the men from the woods were going to move to the Landing. There were two empty A-frames at the far end of the woods and they would use those. Dewey argued with Robert, but no one else got involved. Lola sided with Dewey but didn't see how saying anything would make a difference. It was another done deal, so much so that there was no more discussion and no vote. And so the men came. And they were there at the Meeting and at meals after that. They did their shifts in the woods, but they didn't help out on the land. They just hung around in the late afternoons and evenings, flirting and watching.

Then, as the spring went on, there were parties out at the far cabins. Loud music, drunken shouting, once or twice guns going off. Motorcycles chewed up the dirt road into the woods. And there were girls from town, young girls. Their high-pitched laughter carried across the long garden into the open windows of the three houses.

One morning in mid-May, Lola came into the kitchen at Winston, looking for cereal for the kids. Dewey and Robert were squared off, both glaring. Robert's fists were clenched. Lola thought to back away, then changed her mind. "What's going on?"

The men eased up at the sound of her voice.

"I was asking Robert to get rid of the men in the cabins. Either to confine them to the property in the woods, or better yet, replace them all with kinder folk," said Dewey. "We've worked so hard to have a good relationship with the people in town and now it is all going to hell."

"I'd vote for that," said Lola.

"It's not that simple." Robert's voice was tense, almost pleading. "They know where the dope is. They can take it, sell it, or call the sheriff and shut us down in a minute."

"Let them take it," said Dewey. "We don't need that money that badly." He looked at Lola for agreement and she nodded.

Robert shook his head, and Lola saw a kind of sorrow in his eyes that surprised her.

"You have no idea what it takes to support this place, either of you," Robert said. "You think we can live on Lola's contributions from the Glenwood? Or Annie's work at Safeway? Even if two or three more of you men were willing to do sawmill jobs, which pay a hell of a lot better than waitressing, we still couldn't pay the taxes or the land payments or the medical bills or the groceries." He gave a deep sigh and went over and sat down at the end of the kitchen table. All the tension was suddenly gone from the room.

"We need that dope," he said. "It'll mean enough money to carry us through next winter."

"But Robert, I don't think my family is safe here now." Dewey's voice carried the same sadness Lola had seen in Robert's eyes.

Robert looked Dewey in the eye. "I have their word that they will leave the community alone. They're just waiting for the plants to fully ripen and get their pay. If I had the money, I could pay them now, but I don't. And even if I did, who would harvest the plants?"

"We would," Dewey said. "Right, Lola?"

She nodded again.

"It would be a community project. We would do it, Robert. Can you borrow the money to pay them?"

"Against what? I can't borrow money against the dope crop."

"Against the land," said Dewey. "Some kind of mortgage."

"There isn't enough equity to borrow."

"Why doesn't the community know any of this?" Dewey was angry again.

"Because they don't want to know. They want to go on with their fantasy of the simple life. But life isn't simple and money is always a part of it." There was deep bitterness in Robert's voice now. He got up from the table and went to the back door and opened it. "I'll think about this some more—see if there's a solution I haven't thought of. Please don't talk about this with the others. Not right now." And he was gone.

"Are you going to leave the farm, Dewey?" Deep anxiety washed over Lola.

"I can't stay if those men do," said Dewey. "My family isn't safe and I can't have that."

"Where will you go?"

"To Portland. Snow has a sister there. We'll find work, schools for the kids. It's time, Lola. This just isn't working anymore."

"I don't want you to go." She realized she was holding her breath.

He smiled at her, his big bearded smile. "You can come with us."

She shook her head. "I don't know, Dewey. Living in a big city? The girls . . . it's all they've ever known."

"They'll adapt, Lola. You know they will." He smiled at her again. Then his face grew serious and touched her arm. "We're leaving soon. This weekend probably."

Panic rose up in her and she took a big breath to steady herself. "I can't do it that quickly. I . . . the girls should finish the school year."

"That's fine. Just join us when you can. We'll stay in touch." But he didn't look her in the eye when he said it, and she didn't trust it was true.

She could feel the tears start and she choked them back. "Okay," she said and she turned and hurried back to Star House.

Eight weeks later, the worst happened. The morning after, the girls went off to school and she left a note for Robert. She went by the Glenwood, picked up her pay, and she went by Charlie's and left him a note. Then she picked up the girls from school and drove north to find Dewey and Snow.

The Reunion
Part IV

Frankie woke with a jolt, the voice of the dream man still ringing in her ears. The clock said 3:30. T. Roy murmured in his sleep, then was quiet again. Frankie listened to him breathe and felt her heart slow to normal. She got up and stood by the window. She'd left the curtains open and the dark sat heavy on the silver mining hills in the distance. Sleep and dreams had not made her feel any better. Her mother didn't love her. Never had. She'd said so, loud and clear. The parting gift of their conversation the day before. All these years, Frankie had felt badly loved by Lola. Now she knew she hadn't been loved at all.

She'd thought she'd come to Kellogg with low expectations. Help her mother sort out finances. Give Dewey a good report. She'd wanted to please him, not Lola. But of course that wasn't all. Of course not. She'd wanted to reconcile with Lola, forgive her for leaving them, start over maybe with some sort of love and understanding between them. But Lola had now made that impossible. And Frankie felt burned once again.

The boy murmured again in his sleep. He'd begun to relax with them, with her and Callie. Sat closer to them. Took an occasional hug without stiffening his body. Frankie knew about disordered attachment. You couldn't work in the child welfare system and not become an expert. She'd seen mothers indifferent to their children. One woman at Flora T. had told her, "I wish those kids had never been born. I didn't want them. Not a one of them. My husband wanted them, so he could feel like a man." At the same time, she'd seen kids desperate to return to mothers who beat them, burned them, starved them.

She'd gone the other way with Lola. For as long as she could remember, she didn't trust her mother. No matter what she did, she couldn't get Lola's affection or attention, and so, at eight or maybe nine, she'd given up trying. While Cassie was there, it hadn't mattered much. Then when Cassie died, Frankie had no mother. Now she had no mother. Or maybe it was "still." She still had no mother.

At least she was free to leave now, take the boy on to find his family, leave him there. She could visit Dewey and Snow or maybe just go on home. The visit with Dewey had seemed a reward for all this. Now she didn't have the heart for it. She didn't have the heart for anything.

She got back into bed. She knew she wouldn't sleep, but she could rest. Then after breakfast, they'd head out.

"Are you leaving without me?"

Frankie looked up from the trunk where she was stowing her computer. Callie stood a few feet away, both hurt and fury in her eyes.

"I need to do this alone. I don't know why, Callie, but I just do."

"So you're going to leave me with her."

Frankie sighed and then laughed. "What is it you say, 'Earth to Callie'? You're a grown woman. I know Lola makes us feel like kids again but we aren't. You've got a car. You're not stuck here. Do you want the key to my house? You can go to Portland and wait for me there. Or go on to L.A. Or go back to Scott."

"Scott's dead."

"What?" Frankie turned from the car to face her sister.

"He was murdered. By some mobsters."

"You're kidding, right? Scott was an accountant."

"Turns out he was an accountant for the mob, only he didn't know it."

"Jesus, Callie. You aren't kidding, are you?"

Callie shook her head.

"That's awful. Why didn't you say something earlier? Are you in danger? Are you on the run?" In spite of herself, Frankie felt a little thrill. She thought of Roxie, of *General Hospital.*

Callie shook her head again.

"Who's in danger? Are we in danger? Is it my mom?" T. Roy stood next to Frankie, as close to her as he could, his face solemn in anxiety.

"No, honey, we're safe," Frankie said. "Callie's husband . . . uh . . . had a problem but he is safe now, too."

"That's right, T. Roy. We're all okay," said Callie.

The boy nodded but the solemn look didn't go from his face.

"Okay," Frankie said to break the spell. "How about breakfast before we hit the road?"

In the end, she took Callie with them to Montana. Contrary to her sister's belief about her habits, she hadn't made a plan—just knew she needed to get out of Kellogg, to get moving. It was Callie who came up with the idea to stop at Dewey's, to leave T. Roy there, while Frankie went on to Victor and looked for his mother.

"And you know he's not going to want to hang out with strangers. But if I'm there, he'll be okay," she said. They were waiting for T. Roy to come out of the men's room in the restaurant. "He likes me."

Frankie hesitated. This was not what she wanted. She wanted to be free of her family, free of the past. Except for Dewey, and if she was going to Dewey's, she wanted him all to herself. She didn't want to share him with Callie. She wanted something good and kind and safe that was just hers.

But Callie was right. She couldn't leave T. Roy with strangers, even kind strangers like Dewey and Snow. And she knew she needed to find out what she could about his mother without him around. So she left Callie waiting for T. Roy and went outside to call Dewey.

Victor was only 162 miles from Kellogg, southeast to Missoula on I-90, then south on some state road. Three hours or so. Callie had produced an iPod and headphones from her purse and she gave them to T. Roy, who sat in the back seat with a big grin on his face, his head moving to the music.

Callie grinned as well. "I do know how to entertain men."

Frankie couldn't help but laugh. She looked over at her sister and then said in a low voice. "Tell me what happened to Scott."

"There's not much to tell. A couple of years ago, he discovered that one of his partners was laundering money for some small-time gangsters and that his partner had spent their money."

"The mob's money?"

"Yeah."

"Even I know that's stupid."

"Yeah, well, so the guys they owed took everything we had as payment. Scott and I moved to Pittsburgh to start over but something must have happened because I came home and found him drowned in the bathtub."

"Jesus, Callie. That's awful. What did the police say?"

"I never talked to the police. I . . . I had some connections in New York and they took care of everything."

"You mean, like getting rid of his . . . getting rid of him?" Frankie glanced in the rearview mirror, but T. Roy seemed absorbed in his drawing and the music.

"I don't know. I just followed instructions and got out of there."

"Jesus! This is like something from a movie. This doesn't happen to ordinary people."

"Where do you think the movies get their ideas?" Callie said, looking over at her sister.

"You're right, I guess. Are you safe? Are they going to come after you?"

Callie shrugged again. "Yes, I'm safe. I don't know them, I don't know who they are. I don't know anything. And if they'd wanted to kill me, too, I wouldn't be here now. But it didn't seem smart to hang around the East Coast anymore."

Frankie shuddered. It all made her queasy. She was sorry she'd asked.

"You know, Frankie, it's such a huge irony. When I married Scott, I thought I was marrying Mr. Ordinary, Mr. Safe. Of all the men in my life, he was the least exciting, the least likely to . . ." She looked out the window.

They rode in silence for a few miles.

"Did you love him?" Frankie broke the quiet.

"Scott?"

Frankie nodded.

"I don't know. I guess. I liked him well enough." She hesitated. "I loved a woman once."

Frankie looked over at her.

"Don't look so shocked. Lots of people are bisexual."

"I know that. I just never imagined you . . ."

"Josie. That was her name. I really loved her."

"What happened?"

"The old story. She left me for somebody else." After a moment, she looked over at Frankie, "You ever love anybody?"

"Yes."

"What happened?"

"Another old story. He went back to his wife and kids."

Frankie waited for a sarcastic remark, but Callie only nodded. They rode on a bit, the freeway rushing by.

Frankie let enough time pass so she could change the subject. "Did Lola ever tell you why we left the Landing?"

"She said some guy was after us, some older guy."

"When did she tell you this?"

"Back in high school."

"She just came out and said this?"

"No, we were having a fight about something."

"Do you know who she meant?"

"No." Callie looked at her sister. "Were you fooling around with one of the old guys on the farm?"

"No," Frankie said quickly. "I was in love with Josh. You remember him?"

"No."

"He worked at the drug store in town. He served us ice cream."

"That guy? Eeeooo!"

"I thought he was really cute."

Callie shuddered. "Were you dating him?"

"No, how would I? We lived out in the middle of nowhere."

"Well," said Callie, "I can't imagine he was the big threat. Maybe Lola just made it up."

"I don't think so. When I asked her why we left, you know, when you and T. Roy were at the pool and we had our big heart-to-heart?"

Callie nodded.

"She wouldn't tell me."

"Maybe there's nothing to tell."

"No, there's something. I mean, come on, the night before we go to bed like always, we get up, we go to school, and then we never go back? Something happened."

"Yeah, it does seem weird."

"Do you remember anything about that last night?" Frankie said.

Callie was silent for a long moment. "No," she said finally. "Do you want me to ask Lola? Maybe she'd tell me."

"No," Frankie said and tried to mean it. "It doesn't matter anymore."

They saw a first sign for Missoula. "Do you think you'll find his mother?" Callie said, her voice low.

"I don't know. Probably not. My hope is that this Henry Lee is his grandfather and that he's a kindly old gentleman eager to raise his grandson in a sober home."

Callie gave a low chuckle. "How likely is that to happen?"

"It's not. More likely he is dead or a drunk or a deadbeat. Molested his daughter, couldn't care less."

"Geez, Frankie."

"I worked in the system for years, remember. I didn't develop a great opinion of fathers. Or mothers for that matter."

"Why'd you give it up? Seems perfect for a rescuer like you."

"Burned out. Too sad. Ran out of idealism. Came to my senses. Take your pick."

"I'll bet you were good at it."

Frankie looked over at her sister to see if she was being sarcastic. But Callie looked sincere, nothing hiding behind her eyes. She couldn't remember a compliment from Callie, ever. She didn't quite know what to do with it.

Finally she said, "Thank you, I was. For a while anyway." After a moment, she said, "What are you going to do in L.A.? Is there modeling there for you?"

"No." Callie looked out the window. "I'm done with that. And I'm not sure I'll go to L.A. Maybe San Francisco. Any big city with old rich men will do."

"Is that what you want? To hook up with some rich guy?"

"It's what I do best."

"I don't believe that, Callie," Frankie said. But who was she to say? And hadn't she done that herself with George and Dimitri? "Isn't there something else more, I don't know, interesting, more challenging that you'd like to do?"

"Looking good is a big challenge."

"You know what I mean. Besides, time-consuming and challenging are not the same thing."

Callie seemed to think for a minute. "I don't know. I tried college but it was too dull. I thought about running a boutique—Scott would have paid for it—but all that business stuff is just too boring. I'm easily bored, Frankie. That hasn't changed. I don't think you can fix me."

"I wasn't trying to fix you."

"Yes, you were."

Frankie looked over at her sister. Then she laughed. "Okay, I was."

Callie smiled. The smile was real. It lay there in her eyes, and Frankie wondered how often her sister smiled like that.

They got to Dewey's about 1:30. The property looked much the same. Maybe the trees were a little bigger, a little older, the cabin a little more weathered. But the gravel road that wound through the trees, the big clearing, the half-acre of garden, that was all the same.

"It looks like the farm," said Callie.

"A little bit. For me, it's more that it feels like it," Frankie said. "I always feel like I'm coming home when I come here."

Dewey and Snow came down from the porch to greet them. Dewey had aged, his hair gone white, his beard mostly gray. He was still lean through the middle although Snow had gone soft and stout. *They look like grandparents*, Frankie thought.

Frankie was out of the car right away. She wanted the first hug from Dewey. He held her for a long moment and she thought she might cry. But then he released her and moved over to hug Callie and to shake T. Roy's hand and she pulled her feelings in.

There was lunch and warm blackberry pie and coffee waiting in the kitchen. Dewey and Snow made T. Roy the center of attention in a kind, gentle way, and the boy relaxed and showed them some of his drawings. Jenny came in with Tyler, their grandson. And the two boys and Jenny went into the big living room to play with Tyler's trucks.

"Tell us about the boy," Dewey said, and Frankie told the story of the rest stop, the woman, and the boy with the new clothes and the gun in his duffel bag. She pulled out the money, the locket, and the paper with Henry Lee's name and the number.

"I don't think this is a Social Security number, Frankie," Dewey said. "And if it is, it probably isn't Henry Lee's. Assuming he's the grandfather and assuming he's from Montana, he'd have a number starting with a five, which is the West Coast numbering for my generation. More importantly, the first three digits here are our area code. I think it's a phone number with a number missing. Maybe we can figure it out." And he went out into the living room and up the stairs.

"Computer," Snow said. She stood and cleared the dishes and Frankie got up to help. "No, Frankie, head up and see what Dewey finds. Callie will help me."

Frankie looked at her sister, who still sat at the table. Callie frowned and Frankie laughed and went through to the stairs. The boys had spread out a plastic cloth with markings.

"Look, Frankie," said T. Roy, "it's a parking lot." He and Tyler were backing up toy trucks into parallel spaces.

"Very cool," said Frankie. She went up the familiar stairs to the landing. Dewey's office was down to the right in Bliss's old room. As she went into the room, she opened her bag and took the gun and its clip out and put them on the desk. "Can you get rid of this?" she asked Dewey.

"Of course," he said and put it into a drawer and locked it. Then he held up the paper she had given him. "I'm pretty sure this is a phone number. The prefix for Victor is 534 and we've got the 34. Do you want to call it?"

Frankie felt a moment of panic. She hadn't really thought about finding Henry Lee, just about looking for him. Her imagination, her planning had only brought her here, to Dewey's.

"Do you want me to call it?" His voice was quiet, the long-familiar kindness there.

She nodded and he reached for his phone and dialed. Then he hit the speaker button.

"Mr. Lee? My name is Dewey Ridgefield and I'm looking for the mother of a young boy named T. Roy Thompson. Our search has led us to you. Are you his grandfather?"

There was no response, but Frankie heard the strike of a match, the familiar inhale, then the exhale. She could almost smell the smoke.

"Mr. Lee, are you there?" Dewey said.

"China Diner." The voice scratched into Frankie's hearing.

"I beg your pardon?" said Dewey.

"China Diner." And then there was a dial tone.

Frankie and Dewey had no trouble finding the China Diner. It sat at the far end of Victor on the corner of a block that was mostly strip mall. Two of the mall storefronts held FOR LEASE signs. Only the pawnshop and a used bookstore were in business. A parking lot separated the red, white, and blue diner from the mall. Two dirty pickups and a green Pinto beater filled half the lot. In an earlier incarnation, the diner had been a Skipper's.

Wooden booths lined two walls. Plastic floats and sea shells filled a couple of fish nets near the entrance. There was a large murky fish tank with two lethargic lobsters but no customers.

"Sit anywhere," the waitress said. She too was middle-age stout, with graying red hair in a French twist. Her uniform had MOLLY in blue script above her left breast. She smiled at them, friendly, open.

They took a booth mid-way into the place. Molly swept in, deposited two glasses of ice water and two menus, and was gone before they could say a word. Frankie took the photo out of the manila envelope. Back at the farm, she had taken it out of the locket and Dewey had scanned and enlarged it and then printed it. It was grainy but still clear, the girl grinning, her arms around the dog.

Molly came back. "What'll it be?"

"We aren't here to eat, I'm afraid," Dewey said. "We're looking for the mother of a young boy. Do you recognize this girl?"

Frankie handed her the photo and watched the woman's eyes.

"Are you cops?" Molly's face was closing down.

"No, ma'am, I'm Dewey Ridgefield. I teach biology at Big Sky in Missoula. This is my friend, Frankie Ashby, from Portland."

Frankie reached into her purse, took out a worn business card, and handed it to the woman. Her face closed down even more. "You're wanting to take the boy from his mother." It wasn't a question.

"No," said Frankie. "Just the opposite. We want to reunite the boy with his mother."

"Where's the boy?" The woman looked only a little less suspicious.

"He's with my wife," Dewey said. "We have a place on Enders Road, been there more than twenty years."

The waitress nodded.

"How'd you come by the kid?"

"I met his grandmother," Frankie said, "who asked me to help find his mother. The last the grandmother knew was that she might be here in Victor."

"So why are you asking me?"

"Because Henry Lee told us to try here," said Dewey. "You know her, don't you?"

The waitress looked at Frankie, then at Dewey. "Yes, it's Christy, Henry's daughter."

"Does she work here?" Frankie said.

"Not any more. She was here off and on for a couple of months."

"Is she still in town?"

The waitress tilted her head and bit her lip. "I don't know. I haven't seen her."

"Do you know where we might find her?" said Dewey.

The woman hesitated. It seemed a long moment to Frankie, who broke the silence. "We just want to see if she wants the . . . is ready to have her son back."

"And if not?" The waitress frowned.

"Perhaps Henry Lee?" said Dewey.

The waitress gave a snort. "I wouldn't give a dead dog to Henry Lee."

"Are there other relatives that you know of?" Frankie heard herself come fully into her old social worker mode.

"Not here," the woman said. "Christy had a brother, Jerry. He was friends with my boy, Paul. But he took off a long time ago."

"Do you know where we can find Christy?" Dewey asked again.

The waitress looked at each of them again and then turned and went to the cash register. She returned with a piece of receipt paper. On the back was an address. "Crummy little white house. Yard hasn't been touched in forever. You can't miss it. If she's here, she's probably there."

"Thank you," said Frankie.

The woman shrugged. "Just take care of the boy. He deserves better than any of them." She paused. "You going to order something and make my boss happy?"

Big clouds were starting to move across the sky and a breeze kicked up the dust in the alleyway. They said nothing to each other at first, just sipped at their iced teas, the deep-fry of egg rolls wafting around them and out the car windows into the late afternoon.

"You don't have to do this, you know, little lamb. You can find another solution."

Dewey's voice washed over her, a cool shower of temptation. She looked at him and shook her head, then looked over at the little white house and its yard of thistles and dead grass and a shabby fence with half the pickets missing.

"Shall I come with you?"

She took a deep breath and sighed it away. "No, chances are she'll be more receptive if it's just me, another woman." She opened the car door and got out.

"I'll be right here if you need me."

She leaned in the window and smiled at him and then turned and went up the walkway and knocked on the screen door.

"Who the fuck are you?" The kid standing there was twenty at best, shirtless and drug-thin, stringy brown hair past his shoulders. A cloud of dope and old pizza and unwashed bodies rushed out at her when he opened the door.

"I'm looking for Christy," Frankie said.

"Well, I can't imagine she's looking for you." Another man, an older version of the kid, came into view. He too was shirtless but his body was muscled, his hair pulled back in a ponytail.

Frankie could feel the temper on him and it felt familiar, although she'd never met him before. "I have news about her boy, about T. Roy," she said.

"You social services?" the man asked.

It was his voice that was familiar, she realized, like the voice in the dream, the man from the Landing.

"No," she said, coming back to the moment. "Is Christy here?"

"She might be," the older man said.

"I just want to talk to her for a few minutes."

"Who's the dude? He the police?" He gestured toward the car.

Frankie turned and saw that Dewey had gotten out and was leaning up against the car, watching. "No, that's my . . . dad. He's a high school teacher in Missoula."

The man chewed on the inside of his cheek for a few seconds, then turned and went inside. Frankie didn't know whether to follow or wait, so she stepped out of the glare of the sun and stood just inside the room. There wasn't much to it. A brown-and-orange plaid sofa, an old recliner with the stuffing coming out of the arms. Shag carpeting in olive green housed pizza boxes and beer cans. And a big flat screen TV was turned to the shopping channel, the sound on low.

The man came back to the doorway to the kitchen and motioned once for her to join him. Frankie was glad the front door was still open, glad that Dewey was at her back. She moved toward the man.

Christy sat at the kitchen table. A worn wraith of a woman, thirty going on fifty. There were traces of the girl from the locket—the fine arch of the eyebrows, the delicate nose, the line of the jaw, but they'd gone gaunt. And T. Roy was there, too. In the eyes and in the mouth. She looked up at Frankie, then at the man, who bit his cheek again.

Frankie went over to the table. "Mind if I sit down?"

Christy shrugged. "Suit yourself," she said. She lit a cigarette from the pack on the table and blew the smoke out the side of her mouth. The gesture was one that Frankie had seen Lola do a thousand times.

"What do you want from me? Did that bitch send you?"

"You mean your mother?" Frankie said.

Christy gave a snort and smoke billowed out. "Louise is *not* my mother."

"Who is she?"

"My dad's sister. Married rich. Got out of this hell hole. She dump the boy on you?"

Frankie didn't say anything.

"Figured as much. Empty promises. 'Anything you need, Christy, just ask.'" Her voice became mincing, the sarcasm dripping onto the table like acid. "'Just ask, Christy. I'm always here for you.' I hadn't figured in that she was just like my father. Good for nothing."

Behind them, Frankie heard noises: the refrigerator opening, the pop of beer can tabs. The man put two cans down on the table and went back to leaning in the doorway. She saw that he had positioned himself square in the middle where he could see both them and the front door.

Christy picked up one of the beers and drank down a good part of it. She nodded toward the second beer but Frankie shook her head.

"You got a name?" Christy said, licking the beer off her lips.

"Frankie Ashby."

"And you've got my boy."

"Yes, he's with me."

The woman looked over at the man, then back at her. "What do you want from me? I haven't got any money. You can see that. We wouldn't be living like this if there were any money."

Frankie gave a deep sigh. She'd known to expect this—the house, the man, the look of the mother. But it still saddened her. "It isn't about money, Christy. I don't want any money from you. I want a good home for T. Roy." She resisted her impulse to look at the man. "He's a great kid. He's loving and kind and smart. He deserves a chance to stay that way. With somebody who loves him and takes care of him. He wants that to be you."

Something crossed over the younger woman's face then. Guilt or sorrow, Frankie couldn't tell. It wasn't anger, although she probably had good cause for anger, a ton of it.

"I took good care of him for a long time." Christy's voice was softer now, almost wistful.

"I know you did. I can see it in him. He's a good kid, and good kids have good moms. It's not too late to be a good mom to him again." Frankie heard herself go into agency speak again but she meant every word.

For a moment, something lighter crossed the mother's face, a glimpse of something new or some earlier time with her boy maybe. Frankie felt a flicker of hope. Then the man shifted his weight forward and Christy looked at him. Frankie could see the decision happening right then, right there.

Dewey honored her silence on the way back to the farm and she was grateful. She watched the unfamiliar land pass by out the window and tried not to think, tried not to expect. All her years at the agency had taught her to hold her hopes for others very loosely. Finally she pulled her gaze inside the car and looked at Dewey.

"Any possibility?" he said.

"I don't know. No. Maybe. She said she'd call tomorrow. I gave her my number and yours. Told her I'd meet her at the diner anytime in the afternoon. Told her I could bring T. Roy." Frankie looked out the window again and then back at him. "She loves her son, Dewey. I saw it in her eyes, but the man she's with, he holds all the power. There's no room for the boy in that. She'd have to break free. And that's . . ." She took a deep breath and shook her head. "That's probably not going to happen. Not now anyway."

"What will you tell T. Roy?"

She sighed. "Some part of the truth. That his mother is ill, that she is trying to figure out a way to have him live with her, that she will call us if she can do that."

They were silent a moment.

"I wish you were angry about this, Frankie."

"Why? What good would that do? What would it change? It won't make Christy love him enough." She looked over at him.

He looked back and she saw what was in his eyes. "I see the parallel with Lola, Dewey. The irony's been in my face the whole damn trip." Tears came then and she wiped them away with her fingers. "Why can't I get free of her?"

"Depends on what *free* means."

"My question was rhetorical."

"I don't think so," said Dewey. "There's no undoing the past, Frankie. We take what we've chosen and figure out how to live with it, how to make something good of it."

"I didn't choose Lola. I just can't believe that I would pick her."

"Maybe not. Maybe it was chance or destiny. That part really doesn't matter. What matters is what you do with it."

"I'm tired of 'doing' with it."

"You're tired of reacting against it. That isn't the same."

She could feel herself shutting down. She didn't want to talk about this or have to fix this. She hadn't asked for T. Roy, she hadn't asked for Lola. She didn't want to be responsible for any of this.

"Just trust yourself," he said. "You will know what's best to do." They pulled into the driveway and up to the porch of the cabin.

Frankie put her hand on his arm to keep him from getting out. "Dewey, did you know Tony, my father? Do you know his last name?"

He shook his head. "Lola never talked about him. Cassie talked about their San Francisco days a couple of times with me, but she didn't mention his last name or if she did, I don't remember."

"One last thing," said Frankie. "Why did we leave the Landing?"

"Snow and I just felt it wasn't safe for our kids. And, to be honest, I'd lost all respect for the leader. It was time for us to find our own way."

"Yes, but why did *we* leave the Landing?"

"You'll have to ask Lola that."

"I did and she won't tell me."

"Then let it be, Frankie. She must have a good reason to want to keep it to herself."

That wasn't the answer she wanted.

Christy called late that evening. She would meet them at 2:30 the next afternoon at the diner.

"Are you going to be there for sure?" said Frankie. "I don't want to bring T. Roy if there's a chance you won't show up."

The voice on the line was silent for a few seconds. "I'll be there," she said finally. "But I can't promise more than that." And she hung up.

The tension in Frankie's gut tightened. None of this sounded like a good idea. She'd expected a barrage of questions from T. Roy about his mother when she came back from the initial meeting, but the boy had had only looked up briefly from the plastic parking lot and then gone back to pushing the toy trucks around. Frankie had sat near him on the floor and waited but he said nothing. And when she got up to leave, she reached over to give him a hug but his body went rigid at her touch. She could feel the misery radiating off him and she realized he'd expected his mother to come back with her. And then he was quiet all evening.

The boy who'd been coming out of his shell around her, around Callie, had retreated. At bedtime, Frankie went in to say goodnight. He was turned toward the wall. She saw that he hadn't put on his pajamas but instead had gotten into bed in his clothes.

"I met your mother," she said, sitting down on the edge of the bed. She didn't touch him though she wanted to. "I told her you were a great kid and she'd been a good mom to bring up such a great kid."

The boy sucked in a shaky breath and she knew he'd been crying.

"She wants you to be happy, T. Roy," she said. "But she's still sick. That's why she left you with Mrs. Louise. She knew she couldn't take care of you."

"Is she getting better?" His voice was very small. "I can take care of her."

"I know you can. But that's not the way it's supposed to work. Moms—and dads—are supposed to take care of their kids, not the other way around. So when a mom can't, we have to find another mom."

"I don't have another mom."

"Well, we'll find one, a good one to take care of you until your mom can."

"Do you think that will be soon? That my mom can?"

"I don't know, honey. I don't know."

The next morning after breakfast, they all trooped over to the second cabin where Tim and Jenny were packing for the move to Denver. It was the first time Frankie had been in their cabin, which was about four hundred yards further along the little creek in a pretty spot. It had two bedrooms and a sleeping loft over them. The rest was a great room: living, dining, kitchen with a picture window out onto the meadow behind. Frankie thought of Dimitri and their conversation about their dreams, hers of living here with her cats. Suddenly she missed him fiercely, wanted him to divorce his wife and kids and come back to her, live here with her. It was only a few seconds, that fantasy, but it left her grieving for what would never be.

"What will you do with this space now?" Callie asked Dewey.

"I don't know," he said. "We may move our office down here. Snow's been wanting a much bigger space for her quilting. Why, you interested?"

Callie laughed. "Noooo, sir! I'm a city girl. It's going be San Francisco or L.A. for me."

Dewey laughed, too, that low familiar chuckle that Frankie loved.

The boys found a place to spread out the vinyl parking lot and Dewey had given his grandson a miniature U-Haul truck, which opened in the back so they could put little things in it. They ran around collecting small objects and loading and unloading the truck. Callie half-heartedly agreed to help Jenny and Snow with packing the dishes. Frankie and Dewey worked on the wall of books.

"I haven't told T. Roy that his mother has agreed to meet us." Frankie kept her voice low. "Do you think I should tell him? I think there's a good chance she won't show up."

"Tell him the truth. That his mom might join you. It's always best to tell as much of the truth as you can."

"I know, but I don't want him hurt again."

Dewey looked at her then with such a look of affection that she had to turn away. "We can't protect each other from heartache, little lamb. We can only support the healing." He waited a moment, then said, "You've let him in, haven't you?"

"What do you mean?" she said, although she knew full well.

"I've watched you try to stay out of it, try to be the social worker, keep your distance. But the walls are crumbling. It's a good thing, Frankie, let it happen."

"He needs to be with his mother."

"Yes, he does. Whoever she is."

T. Roy asked Frankie to drive by his school on the way to the diner. Dewey had told them there'd been a school in Victor since the pioneer days and she expected a log cabin or old peaked roof house but it was a long low building from the 1950s.

"Do you like school?" Frankie asked him.

"Some of it's okay," he said. "But some of the teachers don't let you draw on your papers. I like to draw."

"I know you do," said Frankie. "Maybe we can figure something out about that. There are schools where you get to draw a lot."

"There are?"

She nodded and gestured at the playground. "Do you want to get out and play a little?"

He shook his head. "I don't want to keep my mom waiting."

China Diner was empty just as before. Molly, the waitress, gave T. Roy a hug, greeted him like an old friend. The look she gave Frankie was a shade more cordial than the time before. Frankie ordered cokes and spring rolls for them, then a big to-go order for the packing troops back at the cabin. That helped improve Molly's mood.

Two-thirty came and went. Then 2:45. Sick with anxiety, Frankie distracted them both with paper and pens and something called speed art that she'd read about on the Internet, drawing objects as weirdly as possible in one minute. They were both laughing when T. Roy slid out of the booth and ran across the room. Christy stood by the cash register. She pulled the boy close to her but she didn't look at him. Instead she looked at Frankie.

Frankie smiled at her, tried to keep the wariness out of her eyes. But she quickly saw that his mother was unsteady on her feet and as the pair moved toward the booth, she could see the skitter and glint of the high in Christy's eyes and the dark shadow of a fresh bruise along her jaw. The conflict in Frankie bubbled up again.

The mother and son sat down across from her. At first the boy pulled on her arm, talked at her, his voice wild and excited. Callie's sports car, the pool in Kellogg, the cabin, the toy parking lot. All of his adventures. But it didn't take him long to see that she wasn't listening. Just as it didn't take Frankie long to see that Christy was using everything she had just to keep it together, just to be there. T. Roy fell silent and whatever was bottled up in Frankie pushed harder at her throat.

"Can I order you something?" Frankie said. "How about a coke?"

The younger woman nodded. "And a couple of candy bars. Hershey's."

Frankie got up and went over to Molly, who stood at the cash register pretending not to watch. Frankie waited while the waitress filled a large red plastic glass with ice and coke. Then she spoke to her for a moment and came back to the table with three chocolate bars and the coke. Christy devoured the first chocolate bar and shared the second with her son. Molly came by with a refill for the coke, iced tea for Frankie, and a hot chocolate for T. Roy.

"How you been, Christy?" she said.

"Oh, you know." Christy didn't look up at her for more than a second. Then she went back to breaking up the chocolate into smaller and smaller pieces.

"T. Roy, Frankie here tells me you're quite the artist. Will you come and show me some of your drawings?"

The boy looked at his mother, then at Frankie. Frankie smiled and the boy picked up his notebook. Then when he saw his mother wasn't going to move, he slid down and under the table and crawled out. Frankie and Molly both laughed but Christy didn't seem to notice.

The boy and the waitress settled into a table a few feet away.

Frankie waited for Christy to speak but she seemed stuck in her fascination with the candy bar.

"He's not going to let you have T. Roy, is he?"

Christy didn't look up, just shrugged.

"Is this the way you want it, Christy? Some guy calling the shots, keeping you from your child?" Frankie tried to keep her voice low, even, but it was a struggle.

"I love him," the younger woman said.

"More than your boy." It wasn't a question. "And you love the drugs more than your boy." Frankie knew this was unfair, knew that addiction wasn't about love, but about need, about physiology, not about emotion. But she couldn't keep herself from saying those things.

Something crossed the mother's face. Shame maybe, guilt. But it lasted only a second or two and Frankie couldn't read it.

"Rehab doesn't work for me. I've been twice. It's just a lot of talk and sitting around. Then they let you out and tell you go to meetings. They don't tell you how to sit next to somebody in your living room who's got the spoon and the lighter and the needle."

"You'd have to leave him."

"I know that. I'm not stupid. But I can't. I just can't."

"Not even for T. Roy."

Christy shook her head.

As if on cue, as if this were some kind of movie, the man came in through the front door. He didn't come far, didn't approach them. He just leaned against the wall near the cash register counter. Frankie looked at the boy. He had shrunk back against Molly, making himself small. And Frankie knew what she'd already known.

T. Roy was quiet in the car. He got in the back seat again, huddled himself against the side, stared out the window.

Frankie thought about the last few minutes in the diner. Christy hastily asking her for money. Frankie knew this was the man's idea, not hers. At first she refused, then she slipped her a hundred dollars. "Keep it for yourself," she said. "To leave with."

Christy nodded but there was a look of relief in her eyes that didn't have to do with leaving. And then the man left and Molly released the boy from the booth. T. Roy came over and stood by their table. He looked at his mother and she looked at him and something passed between them that Frankie couldn't get. Then Christy got up, hugged her son, and went out.

Frankie looked in the rearview mirror. "You okay?" she said.

The boy looked at her. "Are you taking me back to Mrs. Louise?"

"Is that what you'd like?"

"No."

"Okay then. We'll figure out something else."

There was a long pause and Frankie turned her eyes back to the road.

"I hate her," said a small voice. And Frankie didn't ask who he meant.

At eleven the next morning, Frankie dropped Callie off at Lola's to get her car and the rest of her things. She refused to go in, which did not endear her to Callie.

"Lola and I don't have anything else to say to each other. She made that very clear before we went to Dewey's. I'm not setting myself up for more insults or more cold shoulders."

"Well, I don't want to go in there by myself." Callie crossed her arms and pouted.

Frankie had to laugh. "You look twelve."

"I do not."

"Do too." Frankie felt suddenly tender toward her sister and she reached over and touched her arm. "I'll wait out here if you want to just go in and get your stuff and leave. We can drive tandem to Portland. That's fine with me."

"Okay," Callie said finally and she got out of the car.

Frankie got out of the car, too, and stretched. Then she pulled out her pen and notebook and began making a list of all she needed to do when she got home. It was a good distraction from the long, lonely drive ahead of her and the butterflies that filled her gut and threatened to spill out her throat. She was moving into the second page when Callie came back out. Frankie looked over at her.

"I'm going to stay a bit, maybe overnight. She's not doing so well today. She seems, I don't know, lonely."

"Now who's the soft touch?"

Callie shrugged. "I can leave tomorrow. No big deal."

"Did she ask about me—or T. Roy?"

Callie hesitated one beat too many.

"Never mind. It doesn't matter," said Frankie. "She is who she is."

"She did ask me to give you this. She said you'd know what it meant." Callie handed her sister an old grocery receipt.

Frankie frowned, then turned it over. On the back in Lola's hand were two words. Tony O'Donnell. She stared at them and waited, but the knowing didn't make anything different. She smiled and shook her head.

"What is it?" Callie said.

"It's the name of my father."

"Jeez, just what you need. Somebody else to find."

"Maybe, maybe not." Frankie looked at her sister. "I've got to go. I want all the daylight I can get. Are you still coming to Portland?"

"Sure. At least overnight. I'll call you."

Frankie went around the car and the two women hugged. Her sister seemed a little less stiff, a little less distant. That pleased her.

She got in the car and started the engine. When she looked up, Callie was gone.

It took her about ten minutes to get onto I-90, ten minutes in which she didn't think about much at all. The freeway was busy with trucks and cars with roof carriers and kayaks and bikes. The last vacations of summer coming up over Labor Day.

She looked down at the grocery receipt on the seat beside her. Tony O'Donnell. She wondered if he were still alive, if she could find him on the web. It didn't seem so urgent anymore. Maybe all she'd wanted was for Lola to tell her. And she had.

Next to the receipt was her notebook of lists. Find a renter, pack, move. She thought of herself waking up in Tim and Jenny's cabin, having tea in front of the big window out onto the creek, working at her desk in the big room. Walking over to have supper with Dewey and Snow. Fixing breakfast on snowy mornings. Helping T. Roy to get ready for school. And something like peace washed over her and she drove a little faster.

LOLA

Fall 1983

Lola sat in the halo of the floor lamp in the big green velvet chair. The rest of the room was dark, the hall was dark. Only a faint light shone from the kitchen, the lamp over the stove that was always left burning. It was just past nine, and the laughter and shouting from the rooms upstairs had fallen away as the kids loosened their hold on the hot summer day and the excitement of a sleepover from one house to another. She was deep in *A Tale of Two Cities* when she heard boot steps on the porch. It was too early for the others to be back from the movies in town and she hadn't heard a car. She waited and there was a long silence and she wasn't sure of what she'd heard. She went back to reading but then she heard the screen door close quietly, and the boot steps crossed the floor and went silent until they hit the top step onto the landing on the second floor, which groaned. Then that too went silent.

Her mind raced and she tried to pull herself together. She set the book down and finished the vodka in the glass on the side table. Then she crept into the kitchen, took up a large knife, and followed up the stairs, stepping to the side on the top step to keep it from groaning again. The door to the attic ahead of her was closed. It had a notorious squeak that no one had been able to fix and she hadn't heard it. She stood a moment and then saw down the hall that moonlight was streaming out of the door to the girls' room. She crept on down the hall.

Frankie and Callie lay asleep in the twin beds. Miracle, who was ten and new to the farm, slept in the trundle up against the wall. Her daughters had thrown off their covers in the August warmth, although the two windows were wide open and a fresh breeze came rolling in off the river. They wore baby doll pajamas and their arms and legs gleamed like marble in the moonlight. Other than the three girls, the room appeared empty. She stood just outside the doorway, listening, but there was nothing but the breathing of the girls and the normal noises of the night. She stepped into the room.

In a flash, he had pulled her back against him, one long arm around her waist, the other gripping her right wrist so tightly she thought it would break. "Let it go," he whispered into her ear and she let the knife fall onto the carpet. There was a faint smell of marijuana on his clothes, the hot sour smell of whiskey, and the metallic odor of male power.

"Beautiful, aren't they?" he whispered. He'd let go of her wrist and wrapped his other arm around her. Lola realized they were standing like two proud parents. His arms were bare in the heat and so were hers, and she was sickened by the touch of his skin.

"So ripe. So ready." He smacked his lips next to her ear. And then she knew who he was. The dope men called him Roger Dodger. He always sat next to one of the younger girls at the Meeting, flirting, mesmerizing. But she'd never seen him touch one of them and she had asked Frankie if he'd tried anything with her.

"Are you kidding? That's gross!" was all her daughter had said, but Lola wondered now if that were the whole story. Had Frankie flirted back? The woman in Frankie was coming on—the breasts, the waist, the hips. And there was that something passive and desperate in Frankie that Lola recognized from her own mother. She hadn't thought about preventing that in Frankie, only about avoiding it in herself.

All of this tumbled through her in an instant, fueled by deep fear, as much for herself as for the girls. For her and for her girls. Then she caught a thought and went with it.

"I judged you wrong, I guess," she said. "I would have thought you man enough to take on a real woman, not some teenybopper who hasn't a clue what a man likes." She turned slowly in his arms, pressing her breasts against him, putting her mouth close to his. And they looked at each other for a few seconds in the dim light of the moon and then he stuck his tongue in her mouth. It was hot and rancid and she knew it was a test. She steeled herself and responded, and he took the pins out of her long hair and wrapped his hands in it like a bridle and she led him downstairs to the spare room off the kitchen.

She let him ride her three times until he was exhausted and he stumbled out into the night. Then she got up and showered until the water ran cold. After that, she packed all their things into the car and waited for the dawn and the end of this time.

Acknowledgments

Writing doesn't happen in a vacuum. My thanks to the women of Writing Fridays and to the supportive friends at Aldermarsh (thanks, Joy and Dana) and Netarts writing retreats. Thanks also to my agent, Andrea Somberg, and the folks at Skyhorse. And special thanks to all the friends and family who go on believing in me. You know who you are.

About the Author

Jill Kelly is a writer, painter, editor, and coach. She is finishing her fifth novel and has just created an online program for those struggling with sugar and food. She lives in Portland, Oregon, with her three cats, who listen thoughtfully to every word she writes. She loves to hear from readers and other writers.